The Chronicles of Ara

CREATION

Joel Eisenberg

Stephen Hillard

TB
TOPOS BOOKS

The Chronicles of Ara

CREATION

THE CHRONICLES OF ARA: CREATION

For more information, to inquire about rights to this or other works, or to purchase copies for special educational, business, or sales promotional uses please write to:

Incorgnito Publishing Press
Division of Market Management
Group, LLC
Pasadena, CA 91106

FIRST EDITION

Printed in the United States of America

Incorgnito Publishing Press and logo are trademarks of Market Management Group, LLC

ISBN: 978-0-9861953-3-4

10 9 8 7 6 5 4 3 2 1

DEDICATION

I almost didn't make it to junior high.

Mrs. *Smitty* (name changed to protect the guilty) informed my parents that she could not, "in good conscience," advance me to the next grade. "Joel's reading comprehension levels are severely behind those of the other students," she said. "I just don't see how I can pass him." I was present for that meeting and remember being embarrassed for everyone sitting around me: Mom, Dad, *Smitty*, the principal...

But Dad knew best. As he suspected I was a voracious reader under the right circumstances, due to a three thousand-strong comic book collection and a hyperactive imagination, he proffered a deal: I would choose a book I wanted to read, and write a final report. This effort would determine a reconsideration of my academic future.

Smitty agreed, reluctantly, repackaging his words as her own. "Any help or cheating would be a disservice to your son's further scholastic endeavors...We are all in agreement?"

We were all in agreement.

As a horror buff, I chose Shirley Jackson's *The Haunting of Hill House*. Smitty approved the choice and I devoured the book. I excitedly ran to my parents and reiterated the novel scene-by-scene. My dad was so proud. "Why am I not surprised?" he asked. "Do I know my son, or do I know my son?"

I subsequently wrote a five-page critique and received an A for my passion.

I entered junior high three months later, the culmination of a one-month period many years ago that has since been permanently (one hopes) etched in memory.

He always knew what to say and how to encourage. Based solely on that report, he suggested, "Maybe one day you'll be inspired again and write a novel."

So, some forty years later...

"The Chronicles of Ara" holds great emotional resonance for me. As the words that follow in this ambitious eight-volume series explore the concept of artistic inspiration, for myself that awakening and this book is respectfully, and tearfully, dedicated to Dad.

Richard Eisenberg passed away on January 10, 2011. Not a day goes by when I don't feel his presence.

Perhaps it is no coincidence that the titular character of this work is a muse...

As this is my first novel, Dad's dedication is shared with my beautiful and ever-supportive mother, Nettie, my brothers Mike and Neil and their families...and my extraordinary wife, Lorie.

A spouse puts up with a horrific amount of *tsuris* when married to a writer. I love and appreciate you all.

Joel Eisenberg
January 29, 2014

***

True inspiration tends to come quickly and from the most unexpected source. Sometimes, as in my case, an innocuous life-event can have far-reaching repercussions.

Many years ago, my children, then young, sat abed as we all took turns reading *The Hobbit* and *The Lord of the Rings*. This endeavor spanned several years. When we had finished the last page and closed the cover of the last book, there was a collective sigh followed by a long silence—a feeling of completion, of loss, and of wanting more.

One of my daughters furrowed her brows and asked, "So, where are the heroines?" Caught completely off-guard, I fumbled and then fashioned an explanation:

"There were many heroines in that world. Professor Tolkien just didn't get around to them yet." Neither one believed me.

Unsatisfied, and being children of an attorney, they both pressed at once: "Tell us about one."

"Is that a challenge?"

They looked at me, smirking, waiting for me to bury myself. I had no choice, so I responded:

"Well...there was once a halfling lass, a *hobbitess* if you will, named...*Ara*. Her name was famous. Her name was lost. She would change the world by the most powerful of tools: inspiration."

I wasn't so sure they believed me there either, but nonetheless so began a tall-tale that inspired my prior novel, "Mirkwood," which in turn begat a new epic vision with my partner, Joel, and finally came into full realization in the work you are about to read and, hopefully, enjoy...

Stephen Hillard
January 29, 2014

ACKNOWLEDGEMENTS

The fairy tale of *the writing process* holds little bearing on its reality. Many of us do not hole ourselves away from humanity for months at a time, sipping coffee in front of a fireplace as snow falls. Or, staring outside a window at a marvelous beach, swilling beer, writing, sleeping, swilling more beer, surfing, back to writing...

Bills still need to be paid. Money needs to come in from somewhere. Some of us work other jobs, some ply our art for our living...but in the end what do all writers have in common, aside from the physical act?

We're not one-man (or woman) bands. Inspiration must come from somewhere. And then, during the *process*, order must be maintained in life's *other* areas. And then, after...

Ditto.

As to the *gratitude*, for Joel Eisenberg's part: Parents Richard and Nettie—as cliché as it may read—a more special pair I've sincerely never known; brother Michael, his wife Jennifer and their wonderful children Ethan and Eliana; brother Neil, his wife Randi and their champs Justin and Matthew; and...my patience, my pleasure, and my smile, my wife Lorie Girsh Eisenberg.

A good wife is tough enough to find. A supportive, thick-skinned, beautiful wife is something else entirely.

Koko. Our rescue. Quite literally. A boxer-pit mix. Calling her a *dog* is almost disrespectful. She's a *K-10*. Trust me, you come home after a long day of staring at a computer monitor only to be smothered in kisses by a four-legged bundle of love who could have been euthanized if she wasn't *saved*—you can't help but become addicted to the animal adoption process.

My co-writer, Stephen Hillard, thank you for pitching me your

"Mirkwood" project all those years ago. It has been a pleasure further exploring that universe.

James Crewe is a super editor. Seriously. He *got* the intent of this series immediately. (And he's pretty damn smart.) Michael Conant and Alicia Love. Marketing superheroes. Travis Grundy, Janice Bini and the rest of the team at The Zharmae Publishing Press' fantasy imprint Luthando Coeur are a great bunch of people. And daring, let me tell you.

Paul Levine, agent extraordinaire.

Eric Shaw. *Best friendships* are difficult to maintain. When you're in business together and one goes off to attain their dream...and the other dude's still there, rooting you on despite a sudden *gap* in that business...twenty-five years and we still haven't killed one another.

Steven Levine, ditto the previous *best friendships* line, it's been a pleasure helping you with that damn lottery ticket!

Ricardo Costigliolo, write that book! You have a unique voice that must be shared. Greg Tanner, I learn a great deal from our conversations.

To JL, for giving the time of day to "the most optimistic person in Hollywood." You've been a mentor from Day One, like it or not.

J.R.R. Tolkien, Lewis Carroll, Mary Shelley and Joseph Campbell, in memoriam.

And to every creative artist who has come before and paved the way, several of whom will appear in this ongoing series. Indeed, your collective influence lives on.

Thanks one and all.

***

As for Stephen Hillard: First and foremost, to all those who Joel just acknowledged, because they are part of Joel and he is one great partner.

Second, the core of who we always are—family. To my wonderful children, Jessica, Scott, and Stephanie, and their families; to my wife Sharmaine and my step-daughter, Aliah; along with my parents, brother, sister, aunts, uncles, primos and primas.

Third, to the mentors who have given me guidance and lucky breaks time after time. Bernie Rollin and Justice William H. Erickson are hallmarks of that help.

Thank you for inspiring our universe.

Table of Contents

PROLOGUE

She has always existed. Always. She was never born, conventionally or otherwise, and, to date, she has never died. She just always...*was*. And *is*.

She has also, however, *faded*, having been cursed and ostracized by the other goddesses for not sharing their aesthetic. Cursed, as in over the course of eons she will become mortal. Her shame is that, unlike her immortal sisters for whom time and space are one, she has to wait, endlessly, because she can only see to the Infinity Pass.

She is imperfect, a halfling when personified as a living equivalent—*living* being the immortals' favored form for mostly peculiar reasons—sentenced to be alone as she could never be sublime like her sisters nor have power over all things like they do. Amused by the advent of written tongue for which she alone motivated, they call her *Ara*, Sumerian for *outcast*.

Day and night offer little differentiation for Ara and still less comfort. She will one day witness both the Big Bang and the events as written in *Genesis*, yet her personal accounting of both will be in stark contrast to what would gradually devolve into simplistic, uninformed debates over science and religion. As with the beginnings of earth. *They will know of the shifting plates and the ice but man must never know about the fires*, she thinks. *The truth would destroy them.*

Ara is a muse and her gift is singular: through time immemorial, she influences creation. Creation of majestic art and invention, which in turn inspires beliefs and cultures that shape worlds. Holy books and fine poetry, paintings by great masters. Tools. Weapons. And so on. She can influence, yet interference is strictly forbidden.

The other gods have ensured that Ara remains obeisant to *the natural order of things* and ignorant as to the extent of her abilities. She has never been told that she is anything greater than an embarrassment because they all know that her imperfect nature is, in truth...an enhancement.

What the others do not know, however, is that Ara has embraced her stigma. They are unaware that she has been exploring her impending mortality by bathing her long, flowing blonde hair in the blood of human spirit. They have accepted only that her rebellion has been confined to her neck to ankle covering when in human form, dress that blends with the starkest shade of dark...as opposed to the godly shade of light of which she has no right to assume anyway.

The natural order of things. No more than an ideal, a fiction even, as Ara's condition implies that the universe maintains its own set of rules outside of the gods' dominance. Why the flaw amidst the gods is a taboo query, of which they have agreed amongst themselves to never again address as the sole sensible answer very nearly caused a terminal rift in the ranks having been once delivered. That their control extends to the existence of the elements and the mortals and all the other living things and yet the universe is not only its own master but also theirs...has become, at best, a blasphemous consideration and a treasonous ideology.

~~~

To each star in the cosmos an immortal. An overseer.

Surely, inarguable proof of their existence.

Each immortal is possessed of a particular gift. Each gift is responsible for a particular miracle.

Earliest man developed a system of governance based on abject subservience to their gods. When a proud but foolish new father innocently questioned, during a hunt, why the lights in the sky appeared to outnumber the souls below, he would be driven by a sudden madness and fall upon his sword. Before the new nightfall, he would be cannibalized by his fellow hunters so as to rid the world of his poison.

The doomed hunter dared question those responsible for his miracle, his young child, and the gods did not take kindly to what they perceived as his doubt.

Hence, the *first* version of the story, shared by his surviving companions as reports of the incident spread.

Amongst themselves, the immortals represent a collective, self-governing lot. Prior to Ara's exile, no god had broken from the collective.

Immediately upon her sentence, Ara's star lost its light. Then resumed. But now the muse's star is red. This star is dying. No god has ever died.

The unlawful considerations among the gods begin anew, silently, and then become whispers. Those who whisper agree that the muse's first breath as a human child will initiate a new natural order. They will debate amongst themselves the proper course from there.

The dissidents are destined to break further. But, regardless of belief, one secret must remain constant: Neither those who whisper, nor those who deny nor those who are silent can breach the Infinity Pass.

The muse has been deliberately misled. What she knows is only what she has been told. What she does not know is that she is the most dangerous god of them all.

Ara has been warned that ignoring or disobeying her boundaries, regardless of accident or intention, will result in her absolute corruption and a universal firestorm that will threaten to destroy all semblance of both god and man—and introduce an unimaginable new paradigm. This is but a fraction of Ara's terrible burden, and the immortals' reciprocal responsibility to contain her from afar.

That she has been experiencing temptation of late compounds her misfortune. She is awakening, stunned and shattered by a very latent *human* emotion, taboo for a muse, that is threatening to overtake the very core of her existence.

Long has she watched the mortals fall in love. And now it is happening to her. This much she understands. As she sits, alone and frightened atop a mountain looking down at the raging flames below, she finally, privately, acknowledges the crux of her turmoil. The conflagration has little to do with her fear. The greater concern is this: Despite her lot, Ara recognizes that the universe is not entirely without its riches.

~~~

The dragons are returning, she senses. *I can smell them.*

Hundreds of thousands of years before the Triassic dinosaurs, cavemen and the primitive apes, long prior to Adam and Eve, were the *scorchings*. Life's first footprint. In the far future, fantasists such as J.R.R. Tolkien, Anne McCaffrey, and the Brothers Grimm will subconsciously refer back to this *Age of the Dragons* and engage a compulsion to create stories and mythologies that will subsequently influence and inspire generations.

But truth has always been stranger and richer than myth.

In reality, the first dragons provoked The Great War as a matter of territoriality. They were *thinkers*, instinctively strategic, though not especially intelligent. Their plan was simple. Original man, woefully-armed and unable to survive a dry, seared earth, would vanish by way of dragonflame. Once the dragons claimed the earth as their own, they would next hunt down and destroy their remaining pre-reptilian brethren—the lazy, sloth-like *thrawn*—the precursor of the prehistoric dinosaur, gelatinous blobs fought off by the humans whose mass would grow exponentially in the course of ingesting everything in their path, mass that would also break away and disperse in response to physical force and eventually, following this cycle, form new multiplicities.

If a thrawn were to attain its natural maturity, the blob would be exposed as a birth-sack, bursting and giving way to a new state. The size and shape of the sack would determine the dinosaur genera that followed.

The dragons understood that the thrawn must never again be allowed to mature—this had occurred once before and the dragons lost too many of their own during first combat. And so the thrawn were extinguished during this era. Or so thought their hunters.

The dragons, in summation of their strategy, would hibernate until the gods brought forth a new race, then awake and the battles would start anew. They would again survive, claim their land and propagate. And they would always outnumber any being in their stead.

That was the intent. What the first dragons could neither foresee nor comprehend was that man as a species was never reborn, as they were not annihilated. There were indeed survivors, bands of them, predominantly dragon slayers and their families, who fled from their huts and tents to find shelter in the caves and build subterranean kingdoms. They would draw symbols on the cave walls to communicate—later to be misunderstood as early alien contact—they too would propagate, and they would come out of hiding only when necessary.

(Communication symbols would also, later, be utilized for the *tales*, morality tales, most frequently, as previously only orated by the scops; the then-most current version of the hunter's story—he who fell upon his sword after questioning the gods—would become the first ever etched for posterity.)

Thrawn, meanwhile, scattered as their numbers lessened. Away from the humans, away from the dragons. They will return many years hence, but for now, dragon and man were to remain fated adversaries. As fires raged, much of the new planet became little more than a murky wood—*Mirkwood*—and this battle for earth and toil appeared to have no end. But end it did. In the most unexpected, tragic way imaginable.

~~~

Mirkwood. The planet Earth in *Earliest Days*. A scorched, volatile landscape, open for the claiming.

The dragons have finally arrived, swarming the base of the mountaintop from where Ara continues to observe. Down deep in her core their presence has caused excitement, even—daresay—arousal. Not fear. Because where there are dragons, there is Eron. A dragonslayer, a mortal. Her beloved. Eron has always protected her, she believes...though he has never seen her. He cannot. He protects her by representing something she strives for but can never find on her own.

Hope.

The single-minded, purposeful Eron, however, is entirely unaware of Ara. Though he has never grasped the forces that motivate him, he stubbornly refuses to be bothered or paused with introspection. In moments of such *unnatural* consideration, he simply tasks through the impulse until it loses its power.

So unlike the others.

The dragon army slowly surrounds him. Ara is wistful, as is her wont.

'Time immemorial' ...and yet how shall I remain a muse for his scion

once I too am mortal?

Her next thought tenders for the first time the possibility that she has been manipulated. But she quickly brushes the intrusive query aside and goes about her business.

~~~

As the fires rage and threaten to overtake him, Eron draws his implement. He's been here before, sans the advantage of this quite singular weapon—considerably larger and more impressive in every way than any dagger he or others have previously utilized—forged of arsenic-copper and gold. Once unsheathed, the sheen reflects a slight hint of engraving. The dragonslayer's hand fits inside a metallic glove attached to the bronze hold, a robo-claw tightened or loosened by impulse. Though as a whole, weighty and cumbersome—the blade is just over one thousand millimeters long as opposed to the usual one hundred to two hundred millimeters—the hold itself is position-adjustable and pelleted for maximum control.

Eron wields a shield with his free hand. He is further shielded on his back, the bronze plate hidden under a body-length gray cape. His gear— both face and body—is fully armored.

Ara watches excitedly from above.

The dragons maintain a fixed, mid-air position. The first group of eight is circled around the warrior, wings touching wings for support, in standoff.

Eron awaits his moment.

What happens next will change an immortal, and a universe, forever...

CREATION

BOOK ONE

ON THE FIRST MEASURE OF CREATION

J.R.R. TOLKIEN

"BEOWULF"

THE FIRES OF MIRKWOOD

"There is geometry in the humming of the strings,
there is music in the spacing of the spheres."

- Pythagoras

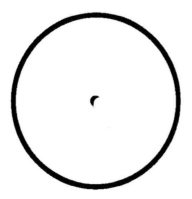

SPARK

BIRMINGHAM, ENGLAND, SPRING, 1901

He was always braver in his dreams. *If only they could talk.*

The trees, that is. Always the trees. A momentary lapse from slumber to semi-consciousness as he shifts in bed from his side to his stomach and yet again ponders...

The trees. His friends, when he sleeps.

In tonight's reverie they are mostly old and hallowed yet overpowering, majestic, very nearly touching the clouds. Identical to the obsessive etchings that hang on his bedroom wall like nurturing giants, images of objects he fears yet has no qualms drawing, that will protect him in slumber. That's the boy's perspective anyway. Surrounding the child in this *taboo forest*, for whom the trees approach the heavens, dried leaves crack and break into panoramas of red and green snow, swirling down and embracing him in response to quick, staccato gusts of wind. He stands still, hands in pockets, steeling himself as he waits for the air to return to normal. He's not all that scared but, he figures, if he moves prematurely he may be blinded. After all, he fully comprehends that he has wandered to a path, far from his home, that his parents and all the other of the town's elders deem forbidden and a loss of sight, temporary or otherwise, may be considered a kid's version of capital punishment. Or *karma*, or whatever his mother called it, Indian for *even-Steven*.

At the moment, though, he could not care less. Back in the mundane world, Mum is sewing a new nothing, Dad is with her too though he died over four years ago—she says they will never be apart as his spirit looks over her—and yours truly is here now, striving to fall back asleep.

Success. The path beckons.

~~~

The path is not really forbidden in any lawful sense; it's just that parents are so over-protective. Their kids run the risk of getting lost, in this case lost in a maze of brush. So what? They worry and fret that their children may be stolen—what are the chances of being kidnapped hopping a fenced pathway to a desolate, distant forest?—or catch a death of cold or malaria or something else you can come down with apparently just by breathing.

But, what about the creatures and those other sneaky pests? He'll take care of them too if need be. Like always. This time, though they cannot reassure him, he has to believe the trees will be his cover. His nocturnal adventures have always been more thrilling than his wakeful world and if this was to be their final encounter, well, both South Africa and also all of Europe will realize once and for all that good is a much stronger force than evil.

And the trees will surely be impressed by his spirit.

The importance of his confidence cannot be overstated. What the boy discovered earlier today was that he, like his friends, had been misled. Now, as he dreams, he is quite afraid he will never dream again.

That means this *must* be the final battle! Winner takes all.

~~~

A tenuous grasp of a very brief rearing in Bloemfontein, South Africa, served to exaggerate the claims of this precocious yet exceedingly well-intended child, who earlier today celebrated his ninth birthday. As the most vivid of his early remembrances were clouded by his dreams—precious narratives of a small boy overcoming the most abject terrors, despite his size—his storytelling already showcased a flair for the heroic. What he had dreamt and what he had lived were, to now, indistinguishable. Until today, he was unsure as to whether his recall was accurate at all. Then, when he saw the headline on an old newspaper that his mom brought home with his cake...things changed.

EVENING NEWS

Friday 16 March 1900

THE BOER WAR!
LORD ROBERTS
AT BLOEMFONTEIN!
SURRENDER OF THE CITY!

"But Mum?" he asked. "Today is January 3, 1901."

"Of course it is," his mother, Mabel, responded quizzically. "Would Hilary and I be sharing your birthday cake if..."

He stared at her purse. His younger brother, occupying the seat directly

3

across from him at the opposite side of the slight, oval dining table, noticed nothing as he ravaged his dessert. Mum, still standing with knife in hand, followed the birthday boy's gaze. The newspaper rested inside the purse's open top pocket, which hung, by the straps, off the back of his late dad's empty chair. The headline was clearly visible.

"Oh...I see." Under her breath, she asked for a blessing from God. "Finish up," she gently requested. "Meet me out front, on the stoop."

~~~

Hilary washed the dishes as Mum sat on the top of the stoop's four cobblestone steps waiting for her older son, nervously observing the passers-by. Finally, he joined her. He didn't say a word; he just looked at her with his soulful eyes and let her speak the truth. In actuality, she told him, she had the paper mailed to her last year; she would use it when the time was right to introduce her eldest to the harsher realities of the world, when it was time to assume the role of man of the family and he would appreciate the necessity of taking on more responsibilities. Today's events were deliberate and she had been well-prepared. Still, she privately acknowledged her risk. She informed him his dad thought Bloemfontein was becoming too dangerous for the family. A good home was a stable home and Father was convinced Bloemfontein was on the cusp of irreversible political instability. They had been exploring a move back to the parents' native England when Father unexpectedly passed of rheumatic fever. Their oldest boy was barely three when Mum carried out her beloved husband's wishes. She moved the boys to England after Father's death and they stayed with her own mother and father as she was left with a pittance.

She further talked with her son about the senselessness of war and the occasional senselessness of the world in general. She went on about the virtues of the father he would never know—a decent, hardworking man—

4

and how he must now contribute and help pick up the slack. Though her wording was careful and her intent good, he didn't care. All he was curious about was one thing, so he asked her one question.

He asked about the forbidden forest.

She admitted she lied to him. And so did his father. And then she told him why.

As he listened to her explanations, he realized that he was growing up. As he slept that night, he realized that growing up hurts.

~~~

The fancy of the taboo forest, and the fears of all the moms and dads, was based on something quite real: October 11 of last year had wrought the Second Boer War in Bloemfontein, the place of his birth. At the time, parents dared not tell their children about the town's increasing dangers and the heightening presence of the British forces that would soon conquer their land; they didn't want to scare them so they conspired and perpetuated a cock and bull tale about a dangerous forest inhabited by dragons and other prehistoric monsters. A small, close-knit community, mum was the word back then.

The children would be none-the-wiser until they grew up a bit and either their parents filled them in or, as the boy had thought, the truth was discovered accidentally. As both scenarios tended to coincide with the advent of common sense, the question was always the same: *They wouldn't tell us about the real war as they didn't want to scare us...so they created a fable about dragons and monsters?*

Regardless, curiosity grabbed him, as always, and his thirst for knowledge was unquenchable.

Why would they make up such a thing? So, in his dream, the boy prodded on. *Parents never make any sense.*

5

~~~

As he traversed his nighttime fantasy, he asked himself what possessed him to undertake this journey in the first place. He had been dreaming about this forest for as long as he could remember and now it was coming to its natural end. *Why here? Why now?* His father planted a grove in this forest well before the boy was born, when visiting Bloemfontein with *his* father during an important business trip. He must have snuck away also. The boy heard how the grove had grown over the years and he had to see it for himself and plant his own grove to prepare for when he had his own family one day.

He just had to. As his father before him. And, maybe, *his* father too.

John Ronald Reuel Tolkien was a grown up nine-year-old when he took advantage of this golden opportunity. It would be the end of one adventure...and the stark beginning of another: a lifetime of mythic adventure, through personal creation well beyond the drawing of his trees.

House Of Usher, Brooklyn Heights, November, 2014

I shoulda been a writer, he figures. *I coulda been a writer.* But he's not. *Shoulda coulda. Fair with the pen, not great, but the stories and knowledge only I have—*

The bolt cracks.

What is it that Anaïs Nin said? "The role of a writer is not to say what we all can say, but what we are unable to say ..." Think that's it, right? That was why she was who she was. My head's always too busy though. Woulda been nice—

Once more—*SMASH!*

He stands still. No one has heard; he's safe. *Guess I am who I am. Whatever that is.* He pushes the door. "Open, sez me," he mutters. He peeks around and enters the formerly locked hallway leading to the single room upstairs.

Not a man of words. Stop fooling yourself.

He managed to get into the brownstone in a matter of seconds; that was relatively easy with a quick jimmy of a stolen credit card and a re-wire of the security system he jacked during his last visit. He brought the hammer for the inside; what he can't figure is why she would additionally padlock this one particular room and its adjoining corridor entrance. It doesn't make a hell of a lot of sense; she's not so hard-up like he is that she needs to rent the space, to some eccentric artist-type or otherwise. She's one of New York's most successful publishers and has more money than God. The rest of the two-story dwelling is—was—scrupulously secured.

Unless it's a set-up and she was expecting a genius burglar who couldn't pick a lock?

He cleared long ago that she lives alone. And there are no padlocks anywhere else in the house, as far as he could tell.

Wait! Maybe she's reserving it for his baby or somethin', he speculates. *The next bastard—or bitch?—in the McFee family tree.*

The very idea brings him renewed determination. He stands in front of the destination door—

SMASH!

He turns his hammer and inserts the top of the claw into the lock's u-shaped shackle.

Brooklyn Heights has become the 'heights' of arrogance is what I think. She owns half the damn brownstones on the block, is a miserable landlord from what I hear...Poe would turn over in his grave. House of Usher, shit...

The lock falls off the knob fixture with little effort. He catches the lock with his free hand as it drops.

The boy, an African-American teen wearing a hoodie and *Mets* cap on this unseasonably mild day, slowly opens the door to as few creaks as possible. He's struck by the reveal. The room, not a stitch of furnishing and in pristine condition—two windows showcasing a spectacular view of Manhattan, and a spotless hardwood floor—is definitely larger than the main area downstairs and is rife with the scent of fresh paint.

So...where do I look first? He shakes his head at the irony. Irony because, surely, he's a better person than she and he deserves spoils such as this brownstone far more that she does. Being misunderstood isn't his fault. He should own *this*, he considers...as opposed to his own common thuggery.

What does she know about suffering?

Self-pity happens, and he wonders if he should leave and finish up another time.

I did promise myself I'd take advantage of that 'other' opportunity too...For sure I'd be read today, at the very least. What more could a writer ask for, right?

He makes his decision as he walks in and carefully closes the door behind him.

Shoulda coulda. Shoulda coulda.

SCARP PUBLISHING, INC., NEW YORK, NEW YORK

"What the hell is going on down there?" Denise Watkins walks to the open office window in response to blaring sirens. Outside, police cars race to surround the perimeter. "My God," she exclaims, stunned. "They forgot..."

Denise's prized client, a reluctant though regular TED contributor lauded as one of New York's literati, Thomas McFee steps to her side. "Looks like you're right," he says. He turns to her, smirking. "For a change."

She spitefully pulls the drawstring and shuts the blinds, nearly trapping his hand.

"Christ, Denise!"

"Christ has nothing to do with it." She sashays, seductively, across the office, passing potted trees and two framed, poster-sized book covers hanging side by side on the wall to the left of her desk.

The book covers on display represent tomes written by Thomas. The first is his study of *Beowulf* and the epic poem's influence on J.R.R. Tolkien, entitled, *The Midgard Codex.* The second, a titular bio of C.S. Lewis, author of *The Chronicles of Narnia.*

"My publisher, an assassination attempt on the very hands that built her company..."

Thomas watches as Denise sits atop her desk, facing him. Her skirt is short, seductive. Prada high-heeled shoes, a Rolex and white clingy blouse unbuttoned to barely-professional complete the image. "They've announced these safe-gas terror drills for—how long? Two months? Three?" He acknowledges her with the slightest nod. "And mass hysteria ensues. People can be such idiots. Don't they watch the news? Or, better yet, read?"

He tries not to stare as she swings her top leg to cross over the other, and slips off her shoes with her feet.

"Cliché, don't you think?" he asks.

"You don't think I'm hot?"

"You're too old to be hot."

"We're the same age, Gandalf."

"Exactly."

"Speaking of which—"

"Done."

For the briefest of moments, Denise is at a loss for words. "Done what?"

"Done," Thomas reiterates.

She considers the response. "Please tell me you're not bluffing because I'm so turned on right now—"

"Your Board will be validated; I promise. And Tolkien, he'd be proud. I'm fact-checking before I submit. The index is done, and yes, I figured a way to incorporate the spider." He pauses for dramatic effect. "Did I answer everything?"

Denise nods, flabbergasted. "I feel threatened. Like I *owe* you or something." She stares at him, curious as ever, testing whether he will take the bait. He doesn't react. The leg stops swinging. "Well, one of us is 40 and still fab," she sighs.

"Remind me to tell you there's nothing less sexy than an older woman trying too hard."

She ignores him. "So, your Tolkien bio is, apparently, finally completed nearly six months past deadline. Mazel tov. I guess then I just have one more question."

"Madame General? I never said anything about a Tolkien *bio...*"

Denise draws a breath, as if preparing for an outburst. Hastily changing the subject so as not to engage him: "Have you spoken to your daughter, wiseguy?" *Touché.* Not what he was expecting, and he does what he can to contain *his* mounting anger. "She called *me*, you know."

"How about we keep it professional from here, huh?"

She took the chance and received what she anticipated; lucky for him any remaining give and take is overcome before it continues by still-more incoming sirens. What neither the publisher nor author are aware of is that the unfolding drama twenty-two stories below is not part of the city's latest planned terror drill at all.

For now, all Denise can conceive over the din is that her client's book is finished, in whatever fashion, and she cannot abide any more noise.

Indeed, four bodies have been discovered on the ascent of the Chambers Street subway steps, burnt beyond recognition as smoke escapes from the tunnels.

They almost made it out.

In the midst of chaos, a filthy, scruffily-bearded vagrant blocks and grabs the shoulders of a panicked young woman holding her baby.

"The trees are scorched by their root. The dragons have returned!" The woman wriggles free and runs off, looking back in horror. He yells after her, "MATTHEW WAS WRONG!! THEY HAVE RETURNED!!"

BIRMINGHAM, ENGLAND, SPRING, 1901

He has passed the first blockade of trees.

Leaves crunch under young Tolkien's feet as he takes slow, methodical steps. As is his wont, particularly when nervous, he talks to himself in an imaginary language so as to be as discreet as possible.

"Byut...forvar...inchone...metado..."

Translation: *One foot in front of the other. You can do this. One, two...*

"Salendee...salondah...byut...by—"

Almost there. One, t—

He sees a hole. Not just any hole, but a hole in the dirt about a foot in circumference and almost as deep as he is tall. He stands on his toes to be sure. To about his upper ribs, best he can tell.

"Stonata..."

Wow...

He walks closer. Though not positive, he's as confident as he's going to get that this hole is what he's been looking for. "That's pretty damn deep," he blurts to himself, in English.

Translation: *If I'm old enough now to be the man of the family, certainly*

11

I'm old enough to swear.

Nonetheless, he regrets his momentary loss of control. He stops for a second when he steps on a twig. He bends down and retrieves it, just in case. A gift, from a tree. The twig is a bit over two feet long, and skinny. It'll do just fine. He will use it as a wand.

He resumes walking, waving the twig in a circular motion—"Sonady...silumi...profisael!"—and then points and *shoots* it directly at the trees around him. "Isoca Pfum! Pfum! Pfum! Pfum!"

Thank you for guiding and protecting me. In turn I will protect you! And you! And you! And you!

He has reached the hole. He looks down. It appears empty. This is where he will place the seeds from his pocket, and grow a tree as big as the others.

But first, he must mark his territory. He utilizes the twig as a *writer*, composing a *top-secret code* in the dirt:

ΣΗΘμαθΙσθισξ

"A word," he says quietly. He adds two more—

ΣΗΘμαθΙσθισξ θ[αιθδησωοα ζφξ εξλαμδγωε

"Then three to watch over me..."

Satisfied, he kneels, holding the twig to its bottom to get a better measurement. He then looks back up to the skies to capture the skyscraper-like heights of the nearest trees. He does not notice the mound of dirt that suddenly pulsates on the bottom of the hole, just alongside the twig. Neither does he see the dirt *break*, giving way to a sharp, hairy leg, no larger than his own index finger.

The leg is followed by another. And another. And...

Young Tolkien blocks the sun's penetrating rays with his free hand, then slowly looks down in dread as he feels something unnatural begin to scratch the hand that holds the twig.

He sees It. He's horrified by It. He freezes in terror as the monstrous, hairy king baboon spider methodically makes its way up his arm, prick by prick, one agonizing creep after another. His heart pounds; he struggles to breathe.

But, ultimately, he is able to scream—"STONADO!!"

HELP ME!!

PARK SLOPE, BROOKLYN, NEW YORK

Thomas couldn't wait to get home. The office visit inspired him, as always. He couldn't wait to get home to write; he couldn't wait to get away from her to do so. She's got him pegged. Bug the shit out of him until he delivers.

No matter. He's been working hard on this one and he's thrilled with the results. Still, what he is really looking forward to is a vacation. Destination: anywhere else, because once she sees it she just may poison his coffee.

He sighs and pulls away from his computer, admiring his handiwork. He reads some of the lines, smiling broadly. "McFee, she's gonna kill you," he whispers to no one in particular.

As he scrolls the pages, he considers what brought him to this point. Denise had wanted a full-length bio of J.R.R. Tolkien. Nothing unusual there, save for a) it's been done before and more than once, b) the rights to anything official are owned by another publishing company and c) he was loathe to compromise the work by repeating the usual factoids that had been printed for decades.

He has money and is well-vested. His last two books have each sold over three million copies internationally. He believes he's earned the right to be arrogant occasionally.

Though Thomas on his own elected to compose a work of fiction, the ambitious intent was to present a portrait of the revered author that would, in the context of story, debate widely accepted Tolkien mythology—as opposed to *Tolkien's* mythology—to encourage a re-assessment of his place in history. McFee lauded Tolkien as a writer, yet he did not believe him to be beyond reproach.

Case in point. When she was a small child, Thomas's daughter, Samantha, was fascinated by *The Hobbit*. He would read it to her out loud; they would bond over it. For her tenth birthday he bought her the *Lord of the Rings* trilogy, all three books which she read voraciously in just over a month. She couldn't get enough of Tolkien. Neither could he, especially as he considered the scribe's works as, if not directly responsible for his daughter's substantial intellectual gifts, then at the very least enhancing of them.

Samantha—*Sam* to friends and relatives—was named after Tolkien's Samwise Gamgee, a key character, a hobbit, in his *Rings* books. Father was an aficionado; mother preferred Mary Shelley, whom she credited the most important feminist writer in all of literature.

Which, to her mind, was all that mattered.

Sam was always closer with her father. An A-student throughout her school career, valedictorian of her high school class, presently working a high-level overseas government job at the tender age of twenty-one...she was labeled a prodigy at eleven when she tested with a 175 IQ. On that difficult day at the school psychologist's office, she had her father swear he would never tell anyone else, including her mother.

She didn't want to be "different," which was something that upset her well out of proportion to her condition. Thomas McFee promised he would keep their secret, "no questions asked." He went for a pinky swear; she instead reached into her pocket for her "good luck charm": a rabbit's foot. He would keep it for all his life...unless he broke the sacred secret, which would be represented by its return.

The rabbit's foot used to be affixed to his keychain until they stopped talking. Now, though, it is still on his person. Always. He keeps it in his pants pocket.

Though presently estranged, he looks back on their old relationship with fondness and, secretly, he could not be any more proud of her.

It's been nearly two years since they've spoken. He had always encouraged her to be the very best Sam she could be, yet he could not forgive her for getting on with her life following her mother's death. Specifically, she is engaged to be married. A nice young man from a good family. Solid. Military. Thomas thinks about this constantly; he knows he's foolish, yet he has been unwilling to stand up to his pride. That would be Denise's job, pushing the matter until he comes to his senses. To this point, he's allowed it. *It's the safest way*, he rationalizes. *On the off chance I impulsively change my mind.*

There's more. She lived with her father for over a year after Elizabeth's death. This new guy, Daniel Baxter, she met several months ago at a local coffee shop. He had concluded his Army service in Iraq and was visiting his brother in the Heights. He convinced her to move to London for an opportunity; he followed.

He took her away from him.

By standing on principle Thomas broke a promise to his beloved Elizabeth. He was supposed to watch over their daughter. She would remind him, in her final days, of the time Sam completed the *Rings* novels for the first time, when she turned innocently to her dad and asked, "Why doesn't Tolkien have more heroines in his books?"

The query always touched Elizabeth, as did her husband's flummoxed, stuttering response which she found charming. "Be-because...um, maybe only elvin women existed during that time?" Sam vehemently disagreed as if she had somehow received confidential information. She precociously insisted there were other worlds in Middle-earth that hadn't yet been explored, and it was "a father's responsibility" to help find them. Thomas simply did not know the answer to the provocative question and he has lived with that challenge since.

He's acted upon it for the past year.

He would title his new book *Mirkwood*, which would in itself work appropriately regarding Tolkien mythology. The name, widely credited as of his invention, was not. As J.R.R. himself said, "*Mirkwood* is not an invention of mine, but a very ancient name, weighted by legendary associations."

Chances are, despite the vastness of his own intellect, his research and creativity, the brilliant J.R.R. Tolkien had no idea of the extraordinary power of those associations.

Or, just maybe, for those same reasons, he did.

HOUSE OF USHER, BROOKLYN HEIGHTS

Maybe a writer, still. Maybe the new Sherlock Holmes. The urban version.

The boy suspects that if anything is to be found *here*, he would come across a loosened floorboard. As he traipses over the flooring, he realizes he was correct when a section shifts under his foot.

Right there. Now, let's test the theory.

He ducks under the height of the window sills, inadvertently kicking a digital alarm clock that rests on the floor. He stills for a moment.

Safe.

Taking the hammer claw, he pries open the board, feeling every bit the badass.

The first law of physics...is there are no laws in *physics. Despite what everyone else thinks.*

The section is removed with little effort. He places the wood to the side, grabs a tiny flashlight from inside his sock and lights it in his mouth as he gets on his knees. He holds onto the sides of the hole and sticks in his head.

"Yep."

He quickly pushes up and stands, and wipes his hands on his pants. He was right all along.

Now, ain't I brilliant? Actually, he is, which has always been his biggest problem. *Don't get too full of yourself, boy. Can't afford to get careless.*

THE HEIGHTS COFFEEHOUSE, BROOKLYN HEIGHTS

Denise has been waiting twenty minutes and is about to leave. Soy Chai lattes don't stay warm forever and she's tired of nursing hers. The timesuck of forwarding pithy rejection letters attached to curt email responses to last month's slush stack loses its allure within seconds. Smartphones were built to play *Angry Birds*, not to communicate with hacks.

Right now, she resents the very thought of him.

So, here's the plan. If he arrives in the next ten minutes—if not, she'll be gone—she'll go to great lengths to embarrass him. She'll cause a scene by publicly blowing her stack and loudly taking sole credit for his career. She will remind him yet again that she paid for his success by sacrificing having a child. "There was no time!" she'll say. She'll further remind him that if it wasn't for her devotion, he likely would have remained just another undiscovered, starving *artiste*, a line she'll deliver with all the pretension and fake-venom she could muster.

But, then again...

Though she so wants him to feel a sense of obligation toward her, to cut him down to size, she also feels sorry for him. Still, she only needs to stay on his good side most of the time.

The perpetual conflict is a major pain in the ass for them both, but she is right in one sense. They need each other. A symbiotic relationship if there ever was. They sell an awful lot of books and make an awful lot of money. Together.

Self-righteous son of a—

The door opens and its chimes ring. She thinks it's him; it's not. Some mohawked punk kid. *So thirty years ago. Just not cool anymore.* This time, she's really going to give him a piece of her mind. *This is seriously unacceptable—*

"Sorry I'm late. Woulda bought your drink." He sits, tossing the manuscript on the table. "Here's your book." Sloppily wrapped in brown wax paper with a red bow. "Lost my blasted credit card."

She stares at the display. "You're kidding, right?"

"The store was out of bows—"

"No...*blasted?* When were you born, seriously?"

He ignores the question. "You have no idea what I had to go through." She stares at him. "It's not what you're expecting but it's so much better. You're going to want to kill me so I needed to find you a nice bow to distract you—"

"I hate bows."

"Really?"

"And I want to kill you anyway. But why do I want to kill you according to you?"

Now and again they both enjoyed the give and take nature of their partnership. Intentionally or not, she pays him the attention he otherwise sorely lacks. As a man, as a human being. She knows him better than anyone. Anyone, platonically, despite the frequent urges to knock the other off and, sometimes, otherwise.

As such, Denise comprehends the true nature of his wife's passing more so than even Thomas's daughter. And she knows more about him. And...the only person Thomas consistently trusts with the truth is Denise.

Stalemate. She would never, though she may raise hell, be so careless as to completely alienate him. And vice-versa.

"The book is fiction," he says, "but—"

"I know." Stunned doesn't describe Thomas's reaction. He motions falling backwards off his chair.

"I saw your notes, flyboy. Sloppy, sloppy—"

"What notes? Everything is in my computer and backed into my tablet...You didn't?"

"Yeah, Charmin called. They want their cloud back."

"You hacked into my—"

"Correction. *You* work for *me*, remember?"

"Bitch."

"Thanks. I try. Gotta protect my investment." She removes a manila envelope from her purse, and hands it to him.

"What's this?" he asks.

"It's called an envelope." Thomas grimaces. She watches him open it. "As much as I hate to admit it, I love watching you squirm."

As he reads—"Where did you get this?"

"Keep reading..."

He does. "Who is Donovan Bradley...The U.K.?"

Denise smirks. "This is where it all wraps up in a neat little bow—no pun intended—and we haven't even started yet." Thomas is intrigued. "This life-long fascination of yours with Tolkien has made us all a few shekels throughout the years," she continues, "and for that we're...eternally grateful." She dramatically places her hand on her heart.

He looks at her blankly. "You're a *sarcastic* bitch."

"And you're still old. And, cocky and disrespectful as all get-out and that's why I love you dearly...and also represent only two books of yours on my office wall, as opposed to all six. Reserving space for that ego has been a bear, you know—"

"I have no eg—"

"What if?"

He hasn't a clue. "Excuse me?"

"Tom, what if...*Adam* bit the apple? What then?"

He's really not in the mood. "Okay. I don't respond to coy—"

"What if *man* didn't walk on the moon—"

"What are you talking about? Denise? You're doing that thing again where you switch the subject, and I thought we had an agreement after the last time—"

"What if there were no Bible, or no Koran?" His attention wavers. Denise notices. "What if Fred Flintstone had never invented the wheel?"

"He didn't invent the wheel..."

"Mr. Slate, whoever." She smirks then moves in closer to him. In response he, reluctantly, moves in as well. "What if your daughter Samantha—"

"Careful, there—"

"What if your daughter Samantha proved to be right all along?"

Now she has his attention. "Meaning?"

"Why hadn't Tolkien featured more heroines in his greatest works? Because, if what I am about to share with you is true—my friend—his inspiration, his literary inspiration for the entirety of his creation, his canon..." Yet another pause, purely for impact.

"So, my translator has the day off and—"

"...was indeed a one-legged muse?" Thomas is becoming increasingly impatient and angry. He delivered his work, as promised, and now she's playing games.

Thomas loathes games; usually the very thought of being toyed with compels him to storm off like a child, just like he used to do before he met the woman who would one day become his wife, when he was picked on by school bullies for being too smart for his own good. He had a reputation for being very fast back then. He had always escaped physical harm, except for once. Now he's older and, he fears, stupider. He continues to engage his publisher, day after day. He believes that there is either something seriously wrong with him, or he enjoys her patented brand of abuse...or both.

Right now, he wishes he was anywhere but in her presence.

Who has time for this? He contemplates.

Denise notices his shaky demeanor, and distracts him. "Before we go any further, why don't you go to the counter and get me another chai, hotshot. This one's cold. I deserve it after waiting an hour for your ass."

"It was barely twenty minutes."

She looks at her watch, and is genuinely surprised. "Look at that." She taps the face with her finger to re-start the piece. "Huh. They don't make Rolexes like they used to—"

Thomas stands. "Soy?"

"Yes, please," she responds, in as phony and demure a tone as she could muster.

As Thomas approaches the counter, he notices neither his watch nor the clock above the register. Both of them have also stopped.

HOUSE OF USHER, BROOKLYN HEIGHTS

Esme Chaconte hauls her conspicuous ass up the stairwell, broom in hand, grabbing her key from a latch on the wall.

Tougher every week. She stops, gasps and resumes. *Clothes are still big enough, nobody knows...Need the job. Need the job...Need the job.*

She's *curvy*, not overweight and eminently proud of her backside, which she believes enhances her Botticelli-like charms.

Do people realize housekeepers are not dumb and appreciate culture too? Sometimes I wonder.

She always self-talks when she's bored.

I may speak with an accent but it doesn't mean I think with one.

She's in a foul mood. Hormones are a bitch though she's never been the calmest sort. Her husband had to stay home from work today to handle PTA affairs, which led to a huge argument. Denise is her biggest client and pays better than the rest. He could skip today; she can't take the risk.

I want to strangle that man, I swear to God...but I love him. I think.

Esme dreads *D-Day*, defined as those two Fridays a month when Denise returns from her Manhattan apartment to the Heights for her favorite latte and a weekend of grounding.

We should all have the luxury.

She always deals with a downward spiral on D-Day. Today, *Murphy's Law* continued when she was called a "Spic" by a bike messenger on the way to the brownstone.

"I''m fucking French!" she returned.

Such a long story...

Not to mention the building trauma she was supposed to have slept off, that she instead has been suppressing since last evening's final coffee and email check. She reaches the room and attempts to unlock the door as usual. The lock is stubborn this afternoon, as if its key is new and has not yet been used, or the lock has been replaced. Maybe both.

Can nothing go right today? Lord, I'm a good Christian...

Finally. After some fidgeting, she pockets the lock.

Merry Christmas.

As she grasps the knob, she nearly doubles over in response to a sudden, sharp abdominal pain. May as well be a knife, twisting inside. She remembers what the doctor told her. "Stay in position until the pain passes. It's just a kick."

She stands still, hunched, and the moment passes...

One more month. Baby three and I'm out...Praise Jesus.

Esme opens the door. She takes one step inside and immediately covers her mouth in horror.

Tagged, by red marker, scrawled along the expanse of each of the four walls in large and small lettering, is the following:

She is unable to look away. She drops her arm and takes it all in. *May as well be written in blood*, is her knee-jerk conclusion. She shakes her head, not in disgust but...frustration?

"Damn!" She turns her head to all four walls. "Goddamn him!"

In her angst, Esme recalls last night's one-sided communication. As to precisely why her name and address has remained on that infernal mass email list, when these days she is but a simple housekeeper and incapable of *spreading the word*, she has her suspicions. As with most anything she wished to revisit or analyze later, however, she printed his email because this one was longer than his usual one or two-sentence ejaculates and her curiosity was immediately ignited. There was a second part attached too but she ran out of toner and has not, as of yet, bothered.

The first, though, she read last night, before bed. His words struck her as being as high-minded, highfalutin and obsessive, as always. His style was as over the top as ever. He had previously insisted he was close, so close, to solving the greatest mystery and now a conclusion has been reached—a culmination!—and at first glance last night she thought the outcome really was something. Something dark and, catastrophic if correct, nothing short of expected because she did, indeed, trust him.

She expected he'd pull something like this today. Of all days. She assumed he'd get back at her, whether she deserved it or not, no matter the effort.

Esme reluctantly removes last night's email from her purse, unfolds the two pages—*Once more, with passion! Ugh*—and she revisits *its* sensational contents.

An Open Letter to the Media

11/6/14

WARNING

We have identified the catalyst of human inspiration. You are not supposed to know this.

Nor this: Its essence is corrupted.

What, then, of our creators?

Unbeknownst to them—and the rest of us—an endgame of their collective entertainments and innovations was engineered from the outset.

But what unspeakable tragedy occurred along the way!

I would have presented these findings to you sooner but I needed to be sure. I had reserved my most intense scrutiny for those driven, frequently unsettled artists and inventors who have attained significance by toiling within man's darker nature. The most perceptive—and most obsessive—among them have long understood that their influence could be dangerous; that would appear to be the crux of the matter, wouldn't it? A sort of privileged comprehension that the end of the world may well converge upon the inspiration that fires them and the imagination that enables them.

The passage of time has taught us that innovators who have so trolled and exploited their primality in search of The Truth were fated to become the vessels who would inform us of our course. They peeked into the unknown more than most, and by so doing returned from the void with a warning.

Indeed, we have—finally—been warned.

The Truth was recently decoded, not surprisingly my dear skeptics, within the literary works and lives of history's greatest fabulists. Many of these special men and women have since passed into legend; all were compelled by a singular force well beyond their ken to ply their trade in the shadows of the fantastic.

It went down like this: On a whim, I attacked the enigma of artistic inspiration as a mathematical equation. I devised a formula that I christened The Ten Measures of Creation, whereby the lives and works of a test group of prominent authors were analyzed in relation to their longevity, personal influences, links to paradigm-shifting world events and other, equivalent variables.

The day before my conclusions were to be publicly disclosed, I stumbled upon the cipher—a grave portend hidden deep in the texts of the darker tales. At first I was mildly amused by the reappearance of certain names and phrases from book to book but the deeper I peered into this portal, if you will, thoughts of possible conspiracies and coincidences dissipated and I feared a most terrible secret had been unleashed. I cursed my ambition; my tampering would prove a grim responsibility.

I temporarily withheld the fruits of my labors and continued the study for several months in silent dread. I then submitted my new findings, in-person, to a trusted associate for a second opinion. But, while away, my office was ransacked; my hard drive was compromised and my portable back-up platforms stolen.

As to my associate? Never heard from her again. However...

Tomorrow you will be leaked a re-draft of my original notes, in the form of a classified narrative, that will answer most of your pressing questions. My recovered scribblings and these seized pages had been incorporated within a much larger confidential document that I have captured, in its entirety, and will share in full soon enough.

I beg you to take me seriously; we must not allow The Truth to be suppressed. The end of time and space as we know it is imminent. If there is any chance at all to set things right, we must consider this warning and prepare for a horrific battle. A battle, however, that is not ours alone.

We will be heeding a cry for help.

(I know, I know, but please, I'm asking you to be open-minded and allow me the opportunity to earn your faith. Despite the anticipated personal repercussions, I am disclosing these pages for your benefit.)

P.S. BTW, feel free to wish me a happy 16th birthday, and I apologize if I ruined anyone's Thursday with this blanket e-blast.

Esme flicks an interfering tear. "'Never heard from her again?' Oh, I'm sure she tried ..."

She looks back up, slowly, to the walls. "Sixteen...too young and just too smart for this, has his whole life ahead..." On a whim, her eyes then dart to the clock on the floor. *4:24 AM.* She grabs her belly; the pain returns. "Damn him!" This time, Esme does double-over but remains on her feet. She manages to crumble and return the pages to her purse before retrieving and then dropping her cell phone. She is not having a good day.

On her hands and knees, slowly regaining her strength—

"What have I gotten myself into?"

THE HEIGHTS COFFEEHOUSE, BROOKLYN HEIGHTS

Thomas is too curious to fight.

Denise ignores her ringing phone and switches the mode to vibrate. "The housekeeper," she says. "New emergency of the day, probably out of soap. I'll get her later. More important fish right now." Under the calming influence of her chai, Denise—finally—is business. "Tom, for once I would like you to listen to me and not judge. That *legendary* missing book of *Beowulf?* The alleged remainder of the original saga of Middle-earth, Arda, Orcs...*Mirkwood* that Tolkien so seamlessly weaved into his *working mythology of England* and one of our only records of early Germanic history? Found."

She awaits a reaction that does not come. Tom remains stone-faced, so she tries again.

"Found, Tom. Apparently. The oldest English manuscript in existence may have a *sister* that is...not. Not in English, that is. And you cannot say a word."

"Anything else?"

"There is, actually." She mocks him. "*So, Denise, what would be the cultural repercussions of such a find?* Well, Tom, glad you asked. Just maybe the entirety of Tolkien's primary mythology might be...invalidated somehow because of the presence of a woman as the true hero of the entire *Beowulf* saga. What then?"

Thomas considers it.

"Furthermore," she continues, "you make history, *we* make history, by including this material in your next masterpiece...Regardless whether it all contradicts *this* masterpiece, of course."

Though fascinated, he does his best not to let on.

"If art...if books can change the world, Tom, you become the architect of that change—"

"Only my publisher would suddenly and conveniently accuse one of the world's most influential authors of basing an entire career writing fan fiction for *Beowulf* and somehow fooling generations of readers—"

"You are so full of it. I'm telling you nothing you haven't hoped for since your daughter was a little girl." She's right, of course, and Thomas fights himself to not get his hopes up too high. "Only your publisher would care enough for this company's reputation, credibility and bottom line to spin this piece of history to the world. First."

"If this is all as presented, why would we have to *spin* anything?"

She casually looks to the clock, immediately noticing, then nervously down to her watch. She bites her lip but does not say a word.

"Time will tell. Let's leave it at that for now." She's bought a second or two to gather her thoughts as he ponders. "In your envelope is a round-trip plane ticket. On your eminently generous publisher. London—"

Thomas boils. "I swear to you, if this is some elaborate ruse to interfere between my daughter and I—"

She ignores him. "Donovan Bradley is one of the preeminent book dealers in the world."

"*That* Donovan Bradley…"

"Ever met?"

"Not in person."

She doesn't ask as she knows she won't get a straight answer considering the banter. "He's a god to collectors, with an unmatched reputation for integrity. You are the only person he would show this to. He's asking you to validate the material. A second opinion—"

"What else?"

"What else do you want?" Denise too-casually sips her tea.

"I'm just a writer."

"There's nothing *just* about you, believe m—"

"He could've asked anyone."

"I don't know this?"

"And?"

"I don't care. Maybe something more could come of it, no?"

"Such as?"

"Time will tell."

"Profound. Are you telling me everything?"

She ignores him. "So, this entire affair is, of course, purely confidential. Bradley is known as a bit of an eccentric. Be sure you read your dossier before you meet with him."

"Who said I'm going?"

She sighs. The b.s. she has to deal with. "Can you really walk away?" When he looks askance, she again peeks at the clock. *4:24 AM.*

Oh God, please be related to the drills.

U.S. Embassy, London, England

A computer scan in progress. Forward. Back. Return to cover.

PROJECT ARA: CONFIDENTIAL

Perfectly-manicured red fingernails tapping the spacebar. *Save As. Log Off. Power Off.*

She unplugs the computer for good measure. Satisfied, Samantha McFee, impossibly beautiful and immaculately-dressed along with her other attributes, shoulder-length silken hair, no makeup save for the indulgence of the nails, grabs her purse from the back of her chair, stands and walks to the door. The room is nearly identical to a high-tech bank vault; silver metallic walls and reinforced controlled bars are the only decor.

Her retina is scanned; the door slides open and she exits.

The door closes. Immediately outside, a security guard returns her cellphone. "Have a good evening, Ms. McFee."

"Thank you, George."

Samantha's cell rings as she rushes to leave the building. Ever-hopeful, she checks the Caller ID. Her father...

Exactly whom she had been anticipating, and hoping for. She couldn't make sense of it at all, but last night she had a premonition. Or something like that, anyway. She knew he would call today.

About time, she considers. *Only took him two years.* She lets the call go to voicemail, waiting patiently, as she enters her 2015 Lexus IS.

He doesn't leave a message. She's not surprised, as much as she"d like to be. *Well, he picked up the phone*, she considers. *Can that be considered progress?* She checks her rearview and pulls out in a screech of brakes.

Not a minute after she leaves, the computer powers; the files are manipulated. There is no one present inside, and no one is warned.

The following familiar characters are the first to appear onscreen:

ΣΗΘμαθΙσθισξ θ[αιθδησωοα ζφξ εξλαμδγωε

The security guard remains outside the door as the symbols disappear and *PROJECT ARA* re-boots.

MIRKWOOD

The blade he has drawn glistens as if enflamed. It was commissioned for him by his father, a king, and gifted to Eron as a token of appreciation as guardian of the family crest.

The commission was won by an artisan and mystic called *S'n Te*, a human both feared and revered in Mirkwood for his rumored mastery of the supernatural arts. Not a crime of itself, though considered morally dubious as infringing upon the territory of the gods. This is no small matter. If discovered, he would surely be threatened and the king himself secretly criticized for the effort. As history will soon prove over and again, once a king's morality is questioned, the entirety of his living bloodline becomes a target.

Nonetheless, the blade would not be the only gift S'n Te would deliver to him that day; the fitted glove, the source of the blade's overwhelming power, can be neither removed nor worn by another mortal. S'n Te would bless the glove before attaching, forming the final piece of a most advanced weapon.

On Eron's judgment, this all-inclusive weapon—so-named by his father a *sweord*—would be unsheathed only once, on the day of his greatest challenge. That day has come. Befitting a warrior, should Eron defeat the dragon swarm, the king has ordered that the sweord be hereinafter guarded as a lasting monument to the greatest champion the world has ever seen.

He does not understand why nor does he try to, but Eron knows that this tool he now holds is considerably more powerful than anything he alone could possibly conceive.

The dragons are upon him. They maintain their positions yet withhold their flame, appearing to await Eron's first move.

The dragonslayer looks up and around. Any potential view of the sky, or any close or far distance, is obscured, completely, by dark wings. There is no break in the collective span. He is enveloped. Fully blinded, and the fight has yet to begin.

He will rely on his tactile sense. Eron detaches his cape and gingerly spreads it on the ground. This will absorb any accidental sound as he executes his plan. He removes the glove from his shield hand and places it atop the cape, as stealthily as he can, feeling first for the presence of rock or any other potential noisemaker. He reasons that as the dragons' heads are above the span, they are buying time still determining their offense. And they would likewise be unable to see him.

Eron quietly plants his front shield on the cape. He removes his armor and finally, his helmet, similarly placing both. He never lets go of the sweord. He is attack-ready; his weapon is poised, wielded to conquer.

The dragons break formation. Sun rays streak through and reflect off the weapon upon the face of a determined young man who appears much older than his twenty-one years. His dark black hair is shoulder-length, his slightly lined face closely-bearded, betraying a hint of scarring, his eyes the brightest blue. He was raised into warfare; he has been fighting most of his life.

Eron looks back upward for a scant moment, squinting under the sun's full power as the fire-breathers poise to strike. His knuckles redden as he tightens his grasp around the sweord's pelleted grip. As the dragons rear back and their mouths open...

Eron propels the sweord with all of his might, severing the neck of the breather whose head is now closest to him. The creature convulses and falls, drawing its last breaths as the others watch in awe. The sweord is reclaimed by Eron. *Now* he understands:

The power possessed by the holder of this weapon is transcendent. Even for the best, most naturally gifted slayer of them all.

The dragons set to regroup. Eron sprints up the neck of the next fire-breather; his sweord penetrates its eyes. In a panic, the dragon targets and scorches members of its own army—fire intended for Eron. The two injured dragons, instinctive creatures, respond in kind, bearing down on their sightless companion as the four remaining attempt to defend their fallen from this sudden rogue faction.

Eron takes the initiative. As the dragons fight amongst themselves, he escapes...into another horde. In the unlikely event he survived the first group, a second had been waiting behind them. This time, a bigger faction: ten.

Their strategy is similar. They will surround him, blind him, but they will eat him. Their teeth are bared; drool spills. No matter. In a near-superhuman display, Eron swathes through each and every one, leaving a bloody body count in the process. He escapes again.

Now comes a third swarm. This time the dragons are bigger. Above them, floating in a circle are dragons bigger still, ready to swoop in the event of another escape. And, above them, *another* formation.

Eron is empowered, yet to what limitation is in question. As ever, he is inspired. But for the first time, he momentarily rests his impulses and ponders, as the dragons cautiously maintain their positions:

Why?

Above the highest cascade of dragon, just below the top of the tallest mountain, Ara is now standing.

Why, when so many others before me have failed?

As before, she watches, captivated.

Perhaps it's this...sweord?

If only she was able to communicate with him, to guide his efforts.

Father would not tell me who built the sweord, who or what inspired its construction.

She didn't notice at first but...yes! He's looking her way! He may not see her; he will not hear her, but maybe he *senses* her?

Eron is confused, distracted. He knows he could win this battle alone. He knows he can take this fight to the end and emerge victorious. But he is losing his focus because he realizes this advantage simply should not be. His skills are sublime...he is still human.

I have been infected.

He maintains his gaze on the mountain, as if he indeed sees the muse. He hears the dragons slowly approaching.

Father...why?

They are nearly upon him. He looks up, and then quickly back at the mountain.

That glimpse would be Eron's last. He closes his eyes. Then, with a sudden fluidity, turns the sweord upon himself, cocking his elbow, severing his heart as the weapon penetrates his ribcage. Blood pours from his chest and mouth and he falls.

Dead. Eron, the great dragonslayer, is dead.

And, from a nearby mountain, a muse screams, a guttural, ear-piercing cry—heard by god *and* mortal—that will now, quite literally, pause the evolution of a world.

"NOOOOOOO!!"

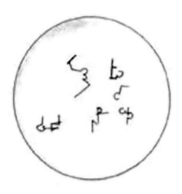

SMOKE

An Open Letter to the Media

11/6/14 (Part Two)

The clocks stop at once and to the second. Now, if that makes little or no scientific sense, consider this: The anomaly can only be noticed upon resumption from an abeyant state as, save for sundials, all manmade timing devices remain frozen.

Any mechanical entity would need to be reset by hand, while sundials naturally resume upon cessation's end.

This is your explanation as to the mass stoppage—a brown-out of time, so to speak.

Regardless, be skeptical. Continue to ask the sarcastic

questions. But then, ask yourself this:

"Do I have a better explanation?"

I doubt it.

St. Peter's Children's Hospital, Cancer Ward, Kensington, England

From the dark a sturdy male voice, emanating from a mouth covered by a disposable surgical mask, the bridge of his nose and penetrating eyes illuminated by flashlight:

"And somewhere, her sisters laugh…"

The flashlight turns to illuminate a second, much younger face, similarly covered. "Ha ha ha ha, ho—Oh!" replies the child.

"Oh," he responds in kind, as the lights in the recreation room, and the rest of the cancer ward, are turned back on.

The storyteller, Daniel Baxter, mid-twenties, Samantha's fiancé. And Marlo Sangster, 13, bald and alarmingly underweight. Chemotherapy treatments for Stage 4 head and neck cancer have left her nearly immobile.

They turn to a nurse, who stands impatiently at the light switch. "Time's up," she says. She holds a local newspaper—*Final* edition as still clearly visible—under her arm, folded to the second part of X's letter.

Twelve kids are present, all in wheelchairs, all, like Daniel and Marlo, wearing surgical masks.

"I think we can shut this off now?" Daniel flicks off the flashlight. "Making fun of me, Marle, huh? Don"t like my stories?"

"Eh."

"Thanks. Makes me feel good."

"You"re welcome. They didn't like it much either."

Some of the kids give him thumbs down. Others just watch.

"Come on. Wasn't *that* bad." He turns to one of the boys. "Hey John. Help me out here."

"Can you bring Samantha back next time? I didn't get it."

"Sam? What does she have that I don't—" The kids giggle. "Scratch that. Paige, do I get a pass?"

Another young girl, Paige, shakes her head.

"See, it really wasn't that great," Marlo ribs, smirking. "How 'bout your watch?"

Daniel looks to his wrist. "It's tickin'." Then, to the wall. The hospital clock has resumed as well.

"Okay, come on kids," the nurse says. "The clocks are back on and ghost story time is over." Other nurses enter, de-braking the patients" wheelchairs and lining them up to leave.

As the children, grudgingly, are wheeled outside to their rooms, Marlo leans her head on Daniel's arm, looking up to him with puppy dog orbs. "You"re right," she says. You weren't all *that* bad but don"t get a big head about it."

Grinning an obnoxious, playful grin, she leaves with the rest, the only one to do so under her own power.

~~~

The armed titan known only as *Brikke*, pronounced "Brick," ward security, motions for Daniel to hold as he aids the trail of chairs on the way out. Huge. 'Six foot six, just south of three hundred pounds. Not obese, all muscle, an omnipresent Norwegian powerhouse who works the early evening shift between, apparently, training for bodybuilding competitions and charm school reassignments. Apparently, as he is by nature a reticent figure who strategically intimidates to avoid unwanted confrontation. He arrived at St. Peter's, highly recommended, nearly two months ago, as a man who could handle most any emergency. There had been a series of violent episodes not too far from the hospital; his hire was, some would say, a necessary evil.

Brikke returns, rejoining Daniel. "Can we speak?" the bigger man asks.

Daniel looks around, extends his arm for Brikke to take a seat. "Please," he requests. Brikke stares him down. Daniel sits first.

"How's your woman?" Brikke asks.

"She's good," Daniel responds. "Works harder than I would like..."

"Works harder than *they* would like too. Will she be back soon?"

"They don't love me anymore, huh? I spoiled them when I brought her."

"Nah. Except for Marlo. She can't stand her." They both laugh. The ice is broken. "Besides, Sam came first."

"I won't hold it against her," Daniel replies.

"Hope not. You're fine. Don't worry about it—"

"I do my best."

"I know. Seriously, they appreciate you too. *I* appreciate you."

"I'm thrilled because you scare the hell out of me. Didn't even know you could talk."

Brikke stays on course. "My job. Walk quietly and carry a big gun. Someone's gotta guard this rowdy bunch, especially with all this outside nonsense. But come on. Anyone who takes their personal time meeting with these kids...they're okay with me."

"You also have a heart, I'm floored. I won't tell, don't want to kill your image. What can I help you with?"

"Listen," Brikke continues, suddenly as serious and no-nonsense as his reputation. "All kidding aside? I have a question for you."

"Okay..."

"Between us. I have a suspicion. When I suspect something not too good I ask questions. Also my job." Daniel is curious. He says nothing as Brikke expresses his concern. "It would probably take a security specialist to ask you this, so it may as well be me. What does your wife do for a living?"

Daniel shifts in his seat, anger mounting. "I don't know. Regardless, that's government business and, respectfully, not yours—"

"Exactly what I expected from you—"

"Why are you asking—" He is interrupted by a flashing red light and alarm from the hall, along with panicked sounds of an incoming emergency.

They stand. "Stay here," Brikke says, hand on his holster. He runs to the open doorway, getting there in just enough time to see Marlo, an oxygen mask now held to her face, wheeled down to emergency on a stretcher. "What happened?" he asks a nurse, following alongside.

"Her heart stopped."

Brikke turns to Daniel. "Go home. We"ll call you. Marlo coded." He rushes out of the room, as a bewildered Daniel stands by.

LONDON

Stopped at a red light, Samantha notices her blinking voicemail display. One message. The caller ID just below reads *Denise.* She presses *Play.* "Driving..." Samantha informs, to no one in particular.

"Sorry I"m late, hon. Don"t be upset. Brownstone was broken into."

That raises a brow.

THE HOUSE OF USHER

Sirens turn and flash from a line of police cars. Neighbors and some press are held back by hand-holding cops protecting the perimeter.

A typical high-profile New York crime scene.

Upstairs, the last investigative photo is snapped. Denise watches passively as yellow tape is struck and gathered. The remaining detectives exit the second-floor room as Denise waves her hand in front of her neck, cutting off further questions. She waits by the window until all officers have pulled away, then picks up her cell.

LONDON

"There's no real damage, and I don't think anything's missing." Samantha hears that as a piss-poor attempt at being convincing. "Regardless, I'm okay. You're okay, we're all okay."

"That the best you can do?" Samantha says to herself.

"I'm still working on his stubborn ass," the voicemail continues. "I need you to please sit tight, and—"

Another call comes through. *Daniel. Damn his timing!* The light turns green. Samantha cuts Denise's voicemail and clicks in. She can barely make out his words through the haze of sirens, and is immediately concerned. "Babe?"

SCARP PUBLISHING

Denise. Feet atop her desk; her office door locked. Her hands are clasped at her waist, her neck is relaxed at the top of her favorite black swivel chair. Her eyes are closed.

Her nose points upward as usual. She's tired, and more irritable than usual. The day has been a calamity so far. From the break-in of her brownstone, to playing interference with Thomas and his daughter.

Now is Denise time.

The cops have, for today, completed their matters at the homestead. This afternoon she is "hardcore busy." This epithet represents her usual excuse to her underlings when she wants to be alone. It is presently her excuse for evading anything domestic for a while to escape into the private confines of her office. Denise takes the time to reminisce on how she *got here.*

~~~

In the event of an occasional bout of "the shits"—a term she uses to articulate her mood, nothing more—Denise Watkins always feels better when she reflects upon her *humble beginnings.*

In her younger days, long prior to the moniker of "bitch"—a personally-coveted honorific equivalent to a distaff knighthood—it was not uncommon for Denise to be called a "snoop."

She wore the term like a gold star. She embraced it. In fact, she embraced any expression that offered her a moment's spotlight. Childhood Shotokan Karate classes ingrained in her an early discipline; later, throughout high school, her ambitious nature would trigger enmity. Budd Schulberg's *What Makes Sammy Run* became her favorite text. When Sammy Glick, the protagonist of the novel, decides early on he would escape the ghetto and succeed in the relatively new business of Hollywood via deception and backstabbing, she was thusly inspired. In her case, not because she was in any way evil, but because Glick proved that anything was possible.

The novel's abiding claim, "What man creates is inside him from the beginning," became her mantra. She believed that the capability of the mind was unlimited and that the soul contained all answers. The soul never died; it just transferred states. The body, however, was a time bomb. It was the mechanism that enabled the journey to enlightenment, but typically the body expired before attainment.

Denise also believed that most would never agree with her *New Age bullshit* and tended instead to erect unspoken limitations as safeguards.

Their loss, she thought.

At the very least, she decided to attain success well before her expiration date.

Until her junior year, Denise wanted to be Sammy Glick, who lived as though he didn't believe in limits. She cheated on her tests and blamed others when caught. She stole boyfriends. Though she never considered herself gay or bisexual, she stole girlfriends if she "needed to get somewhere," as she once confided to her school counselor.

Denise did not sleep with them, any of them, but she allowed her tarnished reputation to flourish. Image was everything.

She was a heartbreaker. Soon they all wanted to be with her. They all were terrified of her and yet allowed themselves to be used in hopes of winning her over and gaining a potentially valuable ally moving forward. But use them she did. She would befriend one to gain information on another, snoop for more, and then used the negative against them both unless, or until, she received what she wanted. Whatever it was.

She would continue to build the finest, the prettiest, the most formidable Denise Watkins. She would exert her influence and unleash her particular brand of hell on anyone who dared challenge her. Upon her passing, she would have that *New York Times* front-page obituary even if she had to kill herself to get there.

Denise's great insecurity, though, her chronic fear and the most difficult challenge of all, was her ability to hold her vulnerabilities in check.

When attacked, she would fight back. After a while, her opponents would back down in submission to her growing gift of trash-talk. She would later temper this talk as mere *banter* and learn to utilize it professionally to her best advantage.

Always a voracious reader, Denise chose publishing as her career path. She would tell anyone who asked, "it was preordained." When in college, she discovered Edgar Allen Poe and other classic authors (Tolstoy, Steinbeck, and Twain were early favorites) and converted her NYU dormitory into her first office. Her goal, arrived at by her junior year, was to own a company that would make her wealthy. And then she could breathe. At that moment, though, aside from her stacks of novels and texts, a bed and freezer-less fridge—24 inches high—were her only concessions to normalcy. She did not consume radiated foods; a microwave was out of the question. And, hence, no reason for frozen foods, so a freezer was unnecessary.

She would settle only marginally once she owned her own business, which she indeed opened on her twentieth birthday after a year of sourcing investors.

SCARP. An anagram. *Sublime Craft Augmenting Real People.* Publishing. A house of myth-building, in other words. Her personal philosophy, in truth.

"There are things you can control, and then there are things which lie beyond any sense of human interference, regardless of want or intention." A nameplate, purchased by her first author as a show of appreciation.

It's more subtle than a yellow 'Caution" sign, the author figured. We"ll do our business and I"ll be loyal; but if she thinks she's going to run me over, she's got another thing coming. He noticed the warning signs early. The desperate flirtatiousness, her bulldog manner. On the other hand, the author's new publisher was also his first publisher and he could not alienate her. He had his own career to launch but she needed to know upon signature that he was no pushover.

44

A *bird in the hand* scenario. She was the first he submitted to; pushing his luck was never his favored draw. Thomas McFee, himself a piece of work.

Over the years, he's told her, almost, everything.

Throughout his early life, McFee was shy to a fault. He was convinced he was born sensitive, to a much greater degree than his peers. If he had to cry, he did so when he was alone. Laughing was good, he believed, but also usually best in the confines of his bedroom, door shut.

His bullying in school was the engine that revved his moodiness. He was once assigned to write, and then read an original short story to his English class. The grade was based on content and presentation. He fretted all week and worked just as much. The plot of his creation: *The crew of the Starship Enterprise hires the Six Million Dollar Man to free the humans from the Planet of the Apes.* As he shared the work, his classmates made faces and laughed mercilessly. The story, that he labored over so diligently, was just so...uncool.

McFee ran out of class mid-read and didn't return for a week. His parents were informed of the unfortunate event; he convinced them that he hurt his back that morning and the injury flared up while reading. The following afternoon, Saturday, when his parents ran the flea market circuit...he stripped to his skivvies, walked to his door, turned, aligned his lower back with the knob, closed his eyes...and banged his lower spine into the protuberance of the metal.

He wouldn't let anyone see the bruise until it darkened.

~~~

McFee would return to school six days later. The ringleader was gone by then; his family had been planning to uproot to Alabama but he was asked to say nothing until Monday. Mrs. Threm, their first-year teacher, called McFee personally and promised that he would be okay if he came back. She told him that *Rance* was gone, and she threatened to suspend the others if they ever tried "this nonsense" again.

No matter. He received an *A* for content and an *F* for presentation. The final grade was in the middle: a *C.* Circled in pen, at the top of his paper—

You are a very talented writer but no one will ever know if you continue to run away.

In the future, those will become words to live by. Today...he resented the grade, and felt he was betrayed by that awful, unfair woman who certainly was much too young to be his teacher. He closed the door to his bedroom and cried.

His peace was always his bedroom, his private space. No fan of sports, his walls lined with thumbtacked fantasy art and movie posters (*Planet of the Apes* and *Star Wars* most notably), shelves displaying *Aurora* glow in the dark monster model kits (*Frankenstein, The Creature from the Black Lagoon, Dracula* and the elusive *Forgotten Prisoner of Castle Mare*) and a near-complete set of *Heavy Metal* magazine, which he hid from his parents due to the frequent nudity, assuming a special place under his bed that pre-puberty had been dedicated to his dirty drawers.

He was average; he was safe. An average student of average looks and nondescript manner, he was an avowed non-risk-taker who only left his comfort zone when forced by his parents to attend social functions. As an only child after several difficult pregnancies, they lived to show him off. To his recollection, he never had fun at any of these events.

Until he met Elizabeth. The first time. At her older sister's sweet-sixteen. His parents and hers were casual friends. The kids danced; everyone thought it was cute and applauded.

She didn't want to do it either but, after...she thought she"d get back at the adults and asked her dance partner to do her a favor.

"Meet me in the alley," she said. "I"ll go first. If anyone asks, I'm in the bathroom."

~~~

Alley. Minutes later.

"How old are you?" she asked.

"Twelve."

"I'll be thirteen next week. When will you be thirteen?"

"Next year."

"Next year ..?"

"Today's my birthday."

"For reals—"

"Don't say anything, okay?"

"No way..."

"You think your sister is the only one who has birthdays?"

"Her birthday was Wednesday. My parents waited till today so more people could come and give gifts."

"Huh."

"Why are you so quiet?"

"I'm not so quiet."

"Shy?"

"I just...stay to myself...Sometime—"

"Did you get your birthday present yet?"

"Later."

"Great! You know what?"

"What?"

"What you're getting?"

"Air Hockey, I hope."

"No way? I love Air Hockey."

"Yeah?"

"Seriously."

McFee sticks his hands in his pocket, figuring what to do next—

"You know what else?" she asks.

"What?"

"Wanna get back at them for making us look like idiots back there?"

"Would love to—"

"I'll give you your first birthday present—"

"You don't have t—"

"Look. If you were Jewish you'd almost be an adult."

"Well..."

"I'll show you mine if you show me yours."

He was fascinated by her. He had no idea whatsoever what she was talking about.

"Huh?"

"Is that all you can say, is *huh*?"

"No..."

"I'll show you mine," she repeats, "if you show me yours."

"Your what?"

She presses her index finger against his lips, to shut him up. Elizabeth steps back, hands slowly curling the bottom of her skirt before bending her legs the slightest bit and reaching under...

"What are you doing?" he asks, mortified.

"Sshhh!"

Her panties attack his face and he quickly shakes them off his head. He covers his eyes with his right hand, then spreads his index and middle finger so he could watch.

"So silly…" she says. "Ready?"

He nods his head, fingers still divided.

She grasps the skirt tightly and, before his next blink…

~~~

It was over so fast.

Too fast.

She asked him to show her *his*. McFee realized he had little choice. If he didn't do it, she may tell. If he did…she may not. He reluctantly undid his belt, grabbed the fly on his underwear…when his father found him.

"Where the hell have you been?" Franklin McFee catches Elizabeth holding a laugh. "Who are you laughing at, young lady?"

"I''m not laughing," she lies.

"Get back inside before I tell your mother."

She runs, without another word. Eyes firmly on her until she is out of sight—

"Fix your pants." Thomas fixes his pants.

He would have shown her his too, if it wasn't for his dad. Now he cannot wait to see her again. As his father grabbed him by the ear to escort him inside. "Ow!" he protested. Thomas McFee immediately realized two things. First, that though he would he not be allowed to see her again, he had found the girl he would one day marry. And second, that his father would have no choice but to accept it.

He did. Thomas always thought his father, in truth, accepted *any* possibility when it came to his boy. Even then. While most parents would define the situation as little more than a childhood indiscretion, Thomas believed Franklin was *smarter* than most because he recognized his son was different than most.

The next day, young Thomas's still-grumpy but slightly softened father said, "When you turn eighteen you can do whatever the hell you want. For now, you're under my roof. My rules."

Thomas took those words as his father's blessing, and Franklin immediately realized his egregious error. Eighteen was not all that far away.

And there was not a damn thing Franklin could do about that.

Denise has *awakened*, and she finds herself staring at her blank computer monitor. "He must have planted this. He's too smart." Denise says to her coffee mug. The mug on her desk offers a frontal portrait of a hirsute male photographed from the waist up. Muscled and bare-chested, the masculine presence leans longingly against a defenseless tree. Denise addresses him now, turning the handle to the right, to the left. "What is that man doing to me?" she asks of the eye candy. "What's his point? What do *you* think?"

The mug is empty—as is he. *As are most men*—as always. No meaningful answer there. Her typical guy. The type she tired of long ago. Though she never tires of looking. *Unfortunately,* she thinks, *the dick who writes for me is the only dick for me.*

As she tilts the mug, her other hand rests on the McFee surprise: three handwritten pages, as if from a journal. They detail his "I'll show you mine if you show me yours" exploit with Elizabeth. They have—somehow—made their way into the midst of his current hard manuscript copy. Instead of ignoring the pages or calling McFee to inform him, she devours the excerpt.

Now, she figures, *I need to know more.*

As Denise re-reads the records she reflects, with curiosity, that in all these years of their knowing one another, McFee had never once discussed his mother. She also comprehends the message:

Elizabeth was his one and *only* love. She gets his implication as well and imagines him slipping the papers into his book: *Just not interested. Sorry.*

She responds with thoughts of her own: *It ain't over till it's over. Once I lay dying, then he'll finally understand.* Impressed with her musing, she reconsiders that last point. *Once I lay dying...then we'll be together and I'll begin again. It's the spin of the world.*

She is simply unable to let him go.

DESTINATION: LONDON HEATHROW AIRPORT

The next days passed without incident.

Thomas had loved the process of landing for as long as he could remember. Not so much because he'd be that much closer to his destination, nor due to any fear of flying. It was the clouds. And, after a forty-eight hour delay—which they attributed to a "widespread computer malfunction"—he couldn't touch white sky soon enough. *White sky.* A phenomenon he coined to describe those transcendent moments during landing where the plane seemed to glide upon the clouds before going through them.

Yesterday, once his plane had begun its initial descent, he plugged in his Walkman earphones and listen to music by *The Doors*. His daughter used to tell him—like his publisher, in fact—that he was an old man before his time. In response he bought a smartphone. It took him three months to figure it out, but he used it now to prove them both wrong.

"*The Doors?*" Samantha would tease him. "Morrison's dead nearly 20 years before I was born and this is the best you can do?"

"Morrison was a genius," he would respond. "Not like that noise you all listen to. Guns and Hoses. What the hell is a Lady Gaga?"

"*She has robes and she has monkeys, lazy diamond studded flunkies. She has wisdom and knows what to do. She has me and she has you.* What the hell is *that?*" she'd needle him.

51

"It's poetry, junior."

He's always loved *The Doors*. Though he never doped like they did, he found their music Zen-like, spiritual. Whenever he was this close to clouds, or driving in an open vista, he listened to them. Their songs would relax him, prepare him, for his latest journey.

The plane descended through its first layer of cloud cover, minutes after all portable electronic devices were turned off and stashed away. Though he had vicariously taken the band's drugs for only fifteen or so minutes, he was, effectively, hypnotized.

As was the desired effect.

Maybe, he contemplates, *that's why some of the clouds suddenly seem so...red? Maybe I overdosed?* He reconsiders. *If so, may I never awake.*

Indeed, a reddish hue has appeared without warning, notably streaking within the cotton then disappearing just as quickly.

Once below this layer of scattered white, he looks above and peeks though a break at the brilliant sun.

Nothing new there.

He glimpses the passengers. No panic, no questions; business as usual. Collecting luggage from the overhead compartments in defiance of the fasten-seatbelt sign and orders of an impatient flight attendant. Last-minute sneaking into the bathroom, fingers pointed out of windows—mostly innocuous acts of anticipation as the *souls* return to terra firma and embark on life's latest chapter.

Too bad. Was looking forward to something different.

The second and, for today, final cloud layer beckons. "One Mississippi, Two Mississippi, Three..." he intones, just low enough so no one hears him.

Almost there. He smiles. It's a contest and only he understands the rules.

"Four Mississippi, Five and—"

In.

Staring at the clouds in this state was second nature to Thomas. His perpetual escape, which explains the predilection. Before he lost his beloved wife, the habit brought him calm as she would lean into his chest and they would both gaze out the window. "The view always gives me hope," she would say. She loved the same music; she shared this predilection, and she felt that first-class seating was a special sort of privilege. When she was diagnosed and he had to fly away on business, upon landing to and from, he thought of her words in the context of the calm of heaven. Now, following her passing, during this too-brief period, he simply feels physically closer to her and, once again, alive.

HEATHROW AIRPORT

"Finally," Thomas mutters to himself. "Left the plane nearly an hour ago." *Between customs and baggage, does everything have to be so needlessly complicated?* Bitching to himself, another habit, this one reserved for that snap back to reality whenever he lands.

He grabs his two suitcases, each, fortunately for him, close to the other.

A limo driver awaits. He takes the luggage and wheels both pieces outside, jacket over his arm. Thomas enters the limo. The doors close; the divider is activated and up for privacy. Seconds later, Denise speaks to the harried writer on his phone, on *FaceTime's* vidscreen, as he again peruses the dossier.

"Change of plans. Bradley's expecting you within the half-hour. We kept him abreast of your arrival. Stop there first, before you check into the hotel. And—one more thing big boy?"

"What's that?"

"I'm shocked. No argument?"

"C'mon Denise, I—" He stops. Thomas squints at her image through his glasses, noticing her eyes abruptly darting downward. Then back up at him with mouth open, seemingly about to disclose something. Down again, and settling uncomfortably on him as if in a trance.

"Oh Captain, my Captain." he prompts, in a familiar echo of Whitman.

"I'll tell you later. Enough with the squinting," she snaps.

"Okay. What's wrong?"

Denise's face remains expressionless. "Good luck, Tom."

"Denise—" Her image contracts. The phone screen goes black.

The House Of Usher

As smoke fogs the glass, Denise tosses her cell alongside the mug of steaming coffee that rests on the windowsill. A bucket of white paint rests at her bare feet. The tags on the walls are gone.

If they came upstairs, it goes to follow they probably tried finding something downstairs first. Nothing here, but the graffiti means they spent some time poking around, she deduces. *Whoever it was had time to write, so they must not have been too pressured by time.*

Denise methodically taps the floor, board by board, bending her toes at each step to test for something loose.

One hour later, and nothing. Not a loose floorboard anywhere. She leans against the door and takes one last look around. "Come on, girl," she mumbles. "Maybe it was just my lucky day. Coulda been anyone."

She glances at the walls. *Coulda been anyone but nothing was taken.*

"You're damn lucky nothing was stolen so time to get your shit together, Watkins. Back to work tomorrow. Busy, busy week." She turns and exits. "It's up to the gods now."

Meanwhile, on Denise's rooftop, the young intruder sits comfortably, leaning against the chimney. He broods as he observes the stars and fumbles with the robo-glove that once belonged to a dragonslayer. A hobo sack is untied alongside him.

She's surely trying to figure it all out, he ponders. *The name's 'X,' lady. Didn't exactly try to hide it from you.*

Denise's brownstone. One week ago.

The intruder reaches into the hole where there was once a floorboard, and slowly pulls out his treasure.

But he asks himself, confused upon a quick look at the object, a thought process which is not at all in his genetic makeup: "Where's the rest of it?"

Rooftop.

It's time.

He intuitively opens his right hand, palm to the sky, and holds the gauntlet next to his extended fingers with his left. He may have spent a week dreading as much, but he stands, stunned, as the glove takes on a life of its own, fitting and adjusting over his free fingers and clasping around his wrist.

Power courses throughout his being, a unique physicality that exceeds even the capacity of an intellect that a special teacher once told him verges precariously on the edge of what is human...and what is not. And now, this new gift. This new gift which can only be considered, for certain, *supernatural.*

His teacher, who had taken the boy in when the troubled youth ran from his parents, has been missing for nearly nine months and is presumed dead. Professor Searle left school one afternoon and never returned the next. Therefore neither did his only student, who has slept on the streets and in strange homes every day since. The student is terrified of his intuitive understanding of everyone and everything save for himself.

Only student being metaphoric for *most meaningful.* There have been sporadic others, including one in particular whom X looked up to as an older brother. This other was only there in an all-too-brief stopover. Then he went off to fight in Iraq because he didn't have a whole lot of choices as to his destiny either. But that was over a year ago.

When X awoke on that next rainy day after Professor Searle left, he instinctively knew his mentor would not be returning. X decided that he wouldn't either. He could never face the truth if something terrible had happened to the man he loved like a father. Therefore he avoided the scene entirely.

The week prior to his disappearance, Searle bequeathed to his student his prized possession: a 1923 antique Underwood No. 5 typewriter. "It's because you are honest." Searle explained. "And this is how honest men communicated in writing before technology collided with humanity. When you have a message, share it. Use this. It would mean a great deal to me if you kept it." The typewriter, in the sack, is never far from its current owner.

Only Searle understood the boy. When Searle vanished, the boy lost a soul that was only briefly awakened during this period of acceptance.

Still, the boy had no beliefs then, and neither does he presently. He knows that destiny is a natural cause and effect of creation, which only makes everything worse. He also knows that the cycle of reincarnation is its frequently unfair by-product.

So now, today. This glove would not have fit if it was not *meant to be.* "*Go with your instinct,*" *Searle would say.* "*Your first instinct is always the answer.*"

With a thought and a flip of the wrist, the glove opens and slips off.

The glove was built to attach to a weapon. A sword, judging by the design. A week to think about it, and my mind hasn't changed. He doesn't like it. He doesn't like it at all. *Now what?*

Bradley and Son Bibliotheque, London, England

The limo slowly pulls away from the largest shop on Burgess Place, a touristy block of local artisans and bars, a commune for the collective intelligentsia.

Thomas stands in the store's stead as the limo pulls into a parking space close behind him.

Inside, the lights appear to be off, yet the sun's blare helps Thomas see behind the drawn, slightly-transparent red curtains that cover the expansive front display window. In the midst of the expected antique furniture and stacks and shelves of rare and first-edition books, stands a small, rickety-looking pine table. Atop the table rests a framed 8x10 newspaper story.

As he approaches he focuses on the story—an obituary. From this distance and obstructed view, though he is able to decipher certain sentences, he can only deduce the entirety:

"Donovan Bradley, Jr., victim of a house fire. He was 24 years old. Said to be lost or irreparably damaged in the fire was a personal collection of one-of-a-kind manuscripts and scarce books. Arson is suspected.

Date of the death was sometime in 2014. Very recent.

Thomas McFee attempts to walk inside the store. The door is locked. He rings the buzzer. No response. He rings again. Nothing.

He turns back to the street, angrily.

Inside, however, a discreet, bent form—a male—parts the curtains slightly. The man spies on the author, who is now shouting on his cell. Donovan Bradley, Sr., 90, nicely-coiffed white beard, well dressed in slacks and white button-down shirt, watches and tilts his head in curiosity.

The only words he makes out: "... damn wild goose chase!" Donovan nods his head, releases the curtains and walks away. Thomas clicks off his phone and looks back to the store. No sign, no lights, nobody. He rubs his temples, then waves for his limo.

ST. PETER'S CHILDREN'S HOSPITAL

"Babe, I'm here." Samantha shoves his shoulder. "Danny, c'mon, wake up." Daniel awakens with a start, clothes rumpled after sleeping on a chair, in the busy waiting room just outside ICU. He never left. "I'm sorry it took me so long."

"I called you hours ago," he groggily responds. "What time is it? I left you three messages."

"I'm here now. Doesn't matter." She takes the seat next to him. "What happened?"

"You didn't listen to the messages."

"Please, no third degrees. I wouldn't be here if I didn't listen. How is she?"

Daniel stands and looks outside. The ICU doors are closed. Brikke is standing by. "Stay here," Daniel says. He walks into the hallway and approaches the guard. Ignoring him, she follows.

"I can't let you go in there." He notices Sam. "Oh, hello, Ms. McFee. Long time."

"You don't work this unit," Daniel answers.

"I'm off-duty. Volunteer—"

"Have you heard anything?" Samantha asks.

"I have. But you understand I'm not at liberty to discuss this."

"What have you heard?" she demands.

58

"A doctor will be with you shortly."

"Why is that an acceptable answer?" Samantha presses him.

"Ms. McFee, respectfully, I—"

"Respectfully? My fiancé loves these kids. He takes time out of his schedule every week to visit with these kids."

"They love him as well—"

"Then Christ, it's not like we're strangers."

"No." Nothing further.

"What's your badge number?"

"My badge number?"

"Yes, your badge number. You're the only reason I didn't come back before." She turns to Daniel. "I apologize," she concedes to her fiancé, but I wanted nothing to get in the way of you and them so I never said anything." Daniel is flustered. She turns back to Brikke. "Please." Brikke reluctantly opens his wallet and flips to his ID. She jots down his information.

"Thank you. You'll be hearing from me."

"Finally," Brikke cryptically responds.

Daniel intervenes. He stands in-between them. "Back off," he says to the guard.

Samantha sidesteps. Upon quick consideration—"Don't you understand? Ar—Marl is like a daughter to him—"

"Sam!" He seems upset at that last. "Enough."

Brikke notices Daniel's stern reaction. "I'm sorry, Ms. McFee. Who?"

Samantha maintains her gaze, studying Brikke's response. The guard weighs whether he has successfully manipulated her into anger, making her lose her train of thought, as is his intention.

"I said Marlo is like a daughter to him. Now, I need to speak to a doc—"

"Sam, you too. Pull back."

Brikke carefully observes them. "She's fine," he admits. "I'm not supposed to say anything. It could be my job."

Daniel confronts him, as if he's ready to fight. "You could spare us all this—"

"It's not about either of you. It's about that beautiful little girl in there." Sam and Daniel relax their guard. "Doctors expect a recovery but they haven't identified a cause. Her vitals last I heard were normal. That's all I know."

After a brief stare-down, Daniel turns away. "Come with me," he says to Sam. He escorts her down the hall to an empty enclave as Brikke resumes his watch.

"You did that intentionally," says Daniel.

"Did what?"

"You wouldn"t allow yourself to get caught like that—"

"You know me too well."

"You think he bought it?"

"No idea."

"Why did you do it?"

Samantha ponders her response. "I felt that I needed to give him something."

Daniel studies her. "This is where you drive me crazy. I never told you he doesn't trust you either...Have I?"

"You just did." She doesn't waver.

He sighs. Game lost. "I love you, God knows why. How 'bout you cut me a break?" Daniel knows the drill all too well. Anything considered remotely work related is off limits. Otherwise, she's an open book. Manipulative though she can be, they have an understanding and he *does* trust her, implicitly—except when he's angry. He appreciates that she works that much harder than most would in a relationship, by necessity, and when she gets like this he's supposed to know better and respect the position. At the moment, though, he just doesn't care. "What does he know that I don't Sam?"

"Not important."

"What is it that you *gave* him?"

"Babe, you know I can't—" Samantha looks to the ground, unwilling to hold his gaze. "You'll need to figure it out for yourself." She forces a smile, meant to be comforting. He doesn't buy a second of it. He wasn't supposed to, actually; the weak attempt was her way of commiserating. "Follow your own advice and please pull back." She allows him the slightest glimmer of optimism. "For now, huh?" She cups his cheek. Before he could respond, she drops her hand and peeks out in response to a barely audible conversation.

She sees Brikke pointing to the enclave, directing a surgeon their way. "Doctor's coming," Samantha warns.

CLARIDGE HOTEL, LONDON, ENGLAND

Room 1401.

Thomas McFee, tired and wearing his specs, researches the Bradley fire on his laptop. He would never wear the glasses in public, except infrequently in airports when he gets flustered; he figures he already assumes more than his share of weakness.

Why admit to more?

At first, there doesn't appear to be anything of note in the search engines. The stories recapitulate the general facts of the obituary from the store window, with little or nothing new. Just page after page of the same information.

Until—

He clicks on a Wikipedia link, then another from there: *Bradley Fire's Historic Parallel*

A video auto-loads. Thomas turns on his speakers.

"The Cottonian Library. A collection of ancient coins, medallions, books and manuscripts privately amassed by Sir Robert Bruce Cotton, antiquarian and bibliophile. Born 1571, died 1631. The basis of the contemporary British Library, regarded as the world's greatest resource of Old English and Middle English literature."

Still photos accompany the illustrative vid clips.

"With the dissolution of the monasteries, numerous priceless and ancient manuscripts once belonging to the monastic libraries began to disseminate among various owners, many of whom were unaware of the libraries" cultural value.

Thomas fast-forwards through some of the proceeding, familiar material.

"Following Cotton's death, the collection was maintained and supplemented first by his son, Thomas Cotton, and subsequently by John Cotton. What would become known as the Ashburnham House Fire occurred on October 23, 1731. Several manuscripts were damaged and many others destroyed. Surviving works included world classics such as 'Lindisfarne Gospels' and 'Beowulf'. As a footnote, however, a long-standing, controversial theory supporting 'Beowulf' as an incomplete work—"

He is riveted.

"—with the purported remainder of the epic poem rumored to have perished in the Ashburnham conflagration, has been recently reconsidered following the untimely death of Bradley and Son scion, Donovan Bradley, Jr., who claimed to have owned a page-by-page facsimile of the legendary lost tome."

Thomas acts on compulsion and skips still further, pausing briefly at a pencil rendering of The Library of Alexandria conflagration, before forwarding again and stopping at his desired section: a detail of the largely forgotten incident in an academic building on London's Gower Street, which once housed a particularly notable press.

"The Gower Street fire is best known to literary historians and J.R.R. Tolkien enthusiasts as the blaze that destroyed all but a few copies of one of the master of fantasy's earliest works ..."

Thomas removes his glasses for a moment and rubs his eyes. This much, he already knows. He attempts to press on, without wavering, but within seconds his peripheral vision begins to darken and he loses his latest battle to the incoming demon of slumber.

When he manages to shake himself awake barely two hours later, still at his desk, Thomas is unable to distinguish between what he's read and what he's dreamt. He backtracks to where he thinks he left off—to the 'reconsideration' of the 'remainder' of *Beowulf*—then pauses the play mode for a much-needed piss.

As he hits the loo and nature happens, he remembers what he once told his daughter. "Sleep," he said to Sam at her mother's bedside, "is the ultimate time-waster. Just think of all those additional hours we could have spent with her." Thomas rues the day he shared *that* bit of wisdom with *that ungrateful* young lady.

He flushes the toilet and returns to his computer.

BRADLEY AND SON BIBLIOTHEQUE, LONDON, ENGLAND

Inside the bookseller's shop, a light is illuminated in the premises' basement area. A shadow appears on the wall of the stairwell. It is followed by Donovan. He is wearing white surgical gloves and carries a thin, browning manuscript between an oversized folder-cover. Each of the forty or so pages is protected by a transparent, acid-free mylar polyester sleeve.

The basement is a veritable storage unit of books and related paraphernalia. In its center is a desk, littered with papers and a row of early and modern *Beowulf* editions, several opened. Donovan sits and scoots in his chair.

"Both theories, however, continue to be denounced as manufactured literary folklore by influential antique book dealer Donovan Bradley, Sr., a vocal critic of his son regarding these matters who contends, quote, "such convenient revisionist history diminishes the historical accord of my industry by engaging an air of distrust built upon outright fabrication, and is an affront to proper English gentlemen everywhere."

Donovan gingerly places the manuscript on the desk and removes four select pages from their mylar as he sorts with his fingers. The papers he removes are all brittle to the touch, some of them burnt and appearing to be damaged by fire. Miraculously, though, like the rest, these pages are still in one piece.

He spreads the four pages side-by-side.

Each contains a single etching that appears to hew closely to the known *Beowulf* legend, as based upon certain visible illustrations within the open books...with two glaring differences.

These exceptional images, for one, are underscored by *words* written in a language heretofore unknown to the poem. Donovan scrutinizes one such example:

ΣΗΘμαθΙσθισξ θ[αιθδησωοα ζφξ εξλαμδγωε

Further, the drawings in question portray a character unfamiliar to the myth. The hero and the dragon are fighting to the death in each—the penultimate act of the original epic—but there also appears a new presence. In all four images two eyes are witnessing the battle, as if they belong to the tale's *narrator.* Two eyes implied as belonging to an omnipotent entity of some sort, that have been drawn on the pages as looking down upon the action and, further implied, somehow *dictating* the outcome.

Two eyes that very much appear to belong to a *female.*

Unacceptable.

As he carefully places the documents back in their sleeves, and then into the folder, he skims the contents of some of the other, similarly-designed pages. They share the same style of writing though none of the others are thusly illustrated. He shakes his head in validation as he packs, validation of his instinct from long ago that, despite his words to the contrary, what has he has come to possess is far from a hoax. Or a facsimile.

How long ago will be made apparent to him in time. Reasons for everything ...

Donovan is horrified at the prospect of the material's authenticity and, for one, prays McFee can change his mind. But he's doubtful. Carbon-dating, a useful and necessary avocation for an antiquarian of his industry and stature, was the first order of business for this material.

His results led Donovan to conclude that this *version* pre-dates the original.

Every conclusion, everything that I have believed...what if I was wrong all along? Donovan frets. He turns and regards some of the other historical work present, a veritable collective of human history and thought. *How much more is there? Our perspectives are based on what we ingest.* Donovan regroups and wearily stares at the blank wall in his stead. *Alas I, again, seem to have allowed the poison to seep.* He clasps his hands, elbows on desk, and rests his chin atop his knuckles. *In the end, if my life's work proves to be of little consequence, whatever shall become of the world my treasures leave behind?*

Outside, a sudden hailstorm showers the street as surprised pedestrians run for cover. A bike messenger, head covered in a baseball cap, pulls in front of the store. He shoves a package into the front door mail slot, and bangs hard on the door three times with the back of his fist.

Donovan has returned upstairs. He notices the package, a clear-taped, brown paper wrap, approximately nine inches by eleven inches, and carefully bends to retrieve it. The addressee information has been written with black marker: Thomas McFee, c/o Bradley and Son Bibliotheque.

The old man stands and straightens as he regards the delivery. He looks to his mail slot and says, simply—

"What took you?"

Somme Offensive, World War One, Village of Ovillers, France, July 14, 1916

The Franco-British commitment, deep in the trenches. Barely a single tree left to protect any of them. Germans rapidly advancing.

Explosions and fires are everywhere. As J.R.R. Tolkien, age twenty-four, progresses into enemy territory, he is transfixed by the sight of the young men on the field who now lie dead or gravely wounded.

In the first weeks of the great offensive, Tolkien, a commissioned officer, had thought his battalion might be spared. This was not a selfish consideration. The battalion was ordered to remain in reserve indefinitely, in the village of Bouzincourt where he had personally come to know several of the soldiers.

Despite his superior officers' philosophies on the matter—

"Never get close to your troops as they may not be there tomorrow."

"Grief will kill a soldier."

"You are a machine for the cause so check your humanity at the door!"

Tolkien took the time to talk to his new brothers and understand their greater risk, so—considered as in most every instance prior to the battlefield his troops still possessed their idealism, of a life greater and better than this temporary circumstance. Not that they didn't fear death. They did, each and every one, when it came down to it, despite the occasional bravado. But their ideals and hopes for a future were related most frequently to their families or the women they were destined to make love to who would be deprived of their love or love-making, or the books they were certain to write that would change the world.

They all wanted to do something more that would change the world, other than fighting.

Certainly, it was not their time to die. So, Tolkien's heart opened.

To his detriment.

As he advances with his men, one with whom he had been marching falls. "SULLY!" He can be heard by no man through the *rat-tat-tat* of the machine guns; he may as well be dead too. Tears well in Tolkien's eyes and he nearly sacrifices himself in mourning. Explosions surround him, and he kneels alongside his fallen comrade.

Tolkien is harshly pulled up by an older fighter, who has placed his own life at risk in the process. "Soldier! SOLDIER!" Tolkien reluctantly stands on his own power. "You deviate from your orders, boy?! Are you soft?!" Tolkien says nothing in response. "ARE YOU A SYMPATHIZER, BOY?!" Though he can barely hear him, Tolkien studies the officer's eyes for a shred of humanity. The deceased was a friend. The officer appears not to care.

Not now.

Intellectually, Tolkien understands fully that it's not the time to give a damn. Intellectualism be damned. Tolkien is flesh and blood; he is no machine. Tolkien looks back down, closes his eyes and utters a quick prayer. Then he straightens. He is not defiant. He is, in fact, compliant; he, struggles to reconcile his orders with the human toll of a *real* nightmare. Most dangerously, Tolkien struggles to regain his focus.

He *flashes* to the trees that once so horrified him in his innocent youth. How utterly banal his childhood concerns are now...

He *flashes* to his father's death and the life-altering conversation with his mother on the cobblestone stoop in Birmingham.

He *flashes* to the spider and how he watched, frozen, as a smallish savior—he could not make out the face—approached before he tripped and banged his head. He fell unconscious but then woke up at home, in bed, with his mom at this side and the most pleasantly warm water-soaked dish towel just above his eyes...

Where is my savior now?

Tolkien is shoved by the other soldier, and they advance.

His superiors had been right all along, a fact that he would consider hereinafter both indisputable and irreconcilable. If he hadn't marched onward he too would have been killed, though the battalion's initial attack, on Ovillers, would prove to be unsuccessful.

It should not have been. No logical calculation dictated that their firepower would come up short against the barbed wire fortress of the Germans. The larger risks were elsewhere. But the Germans remained entrenched, and once the allies believed to have successfully penetrated the enemy defense and so advanced, many of their own troops were killed in a hail of machine gun fire.

His unit would be relieved within 72 hours.

PEMBROKE COLLEGE, OXFORD, ENGLAND, OCTOBER, 1935

A distinguished-looking *Professor* Tolkien, wearing a woolen-brown suit and appropriate matching loafers, stands in front of his rapt classroom. In his hand is a pointer, which he is using to direct a slideshow.

He lectures over images of happier times. "Allow me to advise you of the T.C.B.S., the *Tea Club and Bavarian Society*. It's all relevant to the War, trust me." Scattered sighs of relief and excited, apprehensive glances. Tolkien is fortunate; the students love him.

Click.

A new slide of the teacher in his younger college days elicits chuckles, applause and a few wolf-whistles. The image is of four classmates, Tolkien being one, holding a meeting under a T.C.B.S. banner.

"Settle, settle..." he smiles.

"You were better looking than me back then!" shouts the class jock.

"What's changed?" he deadpans. "May I continue?" The student nods, smirking. Tolkien resumes. "A group of young boys, students of the King Edward's School in Birmingham, once shared an unquenchable interest in ancient languages, natural sciences and the arts." Dramatic pause. "Much like each of you, of course."

"Well, the last ..."

"Not to fret, you'll get there. So, this band of merry men formed a *fellowship*, a bond we would carry until death."

The next slide: The men, same location, hands raised and clasped. "Remember this image of these four hopeful young lads, among my most cherished of memories." Tolkien regards the picture, pausing for a moment.

Click.

"And then, five years later..." Gasps and some tears from his students. "Welcome, reality check." Warm corpses in rain-filled bomb craters, approximate in age, similar in appearance to those comprising his fellowship. He observes his students'' reactions. "Hmm. Notice those on their backs, how many with their eyes still open, staring at the heavens, nostrils flared...Their last sights and smells in this world left on this very battlefield. New fathers, recently-married, friends, brothers...Us."

Tears flow freely; the students are appropriately bereft of shame or embarrassment. "They fought for the other side." Tolkien adds.

Click.

Back to the prior slide. The fellowship. "*They* fought for us. All four of them eventually joined the army, you see. And, one of *them* would not ever return home."

He *clicks* back and forth between the two images. "Ladies and gentlemen, dispel your romantic notions. *This* is war."

SOMME OFFENSIVE, WORLD WAR ONE, VILLAGE OF OVILLERS, FRANCE, JULY 14, 1916

"I had thought of our fellowship often during those days when peace was but an ideal. Though we all served, we did so in separate units. We would make it our business to remain forever in close contact. After all, a true fellowship stays together, always, despite the challenges of a great and terrible war."

"Let's go, solider!" They march on with the rest. Tolkien is shoved again as he inadvertently slows while fighting his own demons.

"A war in which I had come to believe that gentlemen were non-existent among the superiors...and human beings among them were rarer still."

Tolkien fires, misses. He is admonished, yet again.

"To some extent, the Somme offensive motivated me to write a novel.

Among fictional heroes shall be a reflection of the petty English soldier, of the privates and batmen I knew in the 1914 war...who once I too recognized as far superior to myself. You see, I've always been impressed that we survived, because of the indomitable courage of the "small people" against impossible odds."

He is particularly stricken by a German soldier, deceased, lying face down in the mud.

Click.

"This specific shot may well come to define my hero's view of the battle of men against men, as it has for me. Who had taken this photograph remains a mystery...but the image is precisely how I remember it. I have been ever-thankful I could not see his face. I have always wondered what the man's name was, where he came from...if he was evil at heart. What could have led him on this quite long march from his home? Would he rather have stayed there in peace?"

Click.

"He was but one of so many, as you see. Though I am neither pro-war nor pacifistic by nature, the sight of these tragic souls, regardless of allegiance...retain a deep, everlasting hold on me."

The clouds burst; the rain resumes. Tolkien prods on.

CLARIDGE HOTEL

Thomas types furiously into his search engine: "Beowulf Influence on Modern Literature." *Search.* Third on the page: "Beowulf and the Works of J.R.R. Tolkien." *Enter.*

He grabs a pen, and takes notes as he quietly reads: "Myth or reality? In some circles it is considered gospel that J.R.R. Tolkien believed since childhood that every soul was protected by a guardian angel. If true, this belief should be credited with guiding him through many difficult periods to follow..."

"On July 1, 1916, I lost one of my closest friends. I had mentioned one of the esteemed members of the T.C.B.S. never did return home. Lieutenant Rob Gilson was in his mid-twenties. He was killed by a shell on July 1. I found out on July 20."

Tolkien stands in the doorway of his Bouzincourt hut, reading a letter as rain falls:

If you are reading this, my dearest friend and brother, please see to it that the work of the T.C.B.S. goes on. May you say the things I have tried to say, long after I am not there to say them. —Rob Gilson, Lieutenant.

Tolkien bows his head, then looks to the horizon. He notices something, in the far distance, a disquietingly familiar form. She is small, the size of a stunted child, or a dwarf.

She is watching him.

"When my friend passed I no longer felt like a member of a complete body. I honestly felt in my heart that the T.C.B.S. had ended and yet, in his honor, I trod on. We needed a sense of 'hope,' a reason to persevere in the face of our unfolding English history. In his honor I remained a soldier, but a soldier better with words. I would be inspired to undertake the daunting of creating nothing less than a working mythology for England."

They lock eyes. Tolkien is about to follow, but the figure quickly disappears.

"Global cultures were in part built upon the tales of our earliest oral storytellers. Then they were written as epic poetry, and Beowulf *is one such example. These epics continue to define our notions of good and evil, of*

honor and war.

Tolkien reconsiders, and slowly approaches the area.

"Would I appear foolish to you if 'I' admit to a long-held hope? A hope based on a nagging suspicion that Beowulf, *as we know it, is not the full story?"*

Nobody is there, as he suspected. Before turning back he considers his letter, then lifts his head to the heavens in silent prayer.

"Regardless," he chuckles, *"wherever would we be without our epics?"*

MIRKWOOD

It has been eleven sunsets since the death of Eron, the great dragonslayer, and the beginning of a primal scream that resonates through time and space. Finally, the grief-stricken muse silences. She leaves the mountain. As she walks her hair gradually turns the most fiery shade of scarlet. She notices, and realizes...

The blood of spirit...

She then ignores the matter entirely. She has lost her remaining control and accepts her fate. *So be it.* The world resumes, and Ara watches passively as the dragons fly back to their caves over *smoking* wood. The flames have been extinguished. *As meant to be.* She turns to Eron, whose body rests on a calm patch of earth. The immortal's path is unobstructed. She walks to him, like he would have to her, and falls to her knees upon reaching her destination. She leans into his ear: *We will be together again.*

Nothing is making any sense. Nothing at all. To add to Ara's dismay, she realizes that there is something missing. Something, in its absence, that for a brief moment distracts her.

His weapon...Where is his weapon?

~~~

In the 21st Century, the theory of a pre-historical *Abeyance* will be published and ridiculed as "yahoo science" in a respected scientific journal. The event will be estimated to have spanned the equivalent of eleven nights, and the person who hypothesized the matter will be immediately discredited as a "wack-job," among other endearments.

There will not be, however, a public record as to the identity of this entity. He will be referred to only as *X*. He or she will remain an enigma and only prove significant later on, once evidence appears that an allegedly measurable second such event was documented by the U.S. government in mid-2014.

X would leak the findings to a skeptical yet insatiable media and immediately become an international cause celebre. The aphoristic *Who Is X?* would be adapted as a tee-shirt staple and spawn a cottage industry of the likes not seen since the prime of *Star Wars.*

X: No Name, No Identity...No Matter. The follow-up, and final catchphrase-turned-product line would then become an even bigger seller all around.

The concept of the Abeyance will be explained as follows: the universe, literally, suspends itself for an indeterminate period of time, then resumes with a correction. According to the findings presented by X, displaced pages from a confidential memo titled *Project Ara*, antecedents of such an event include a freak dysfunction of sundials and man-made timepieces. Though the pages will be made public in mid-2015, the memo's title will be intentionally redacted.

"History leaves clues," X had replied. X was grilled in a series of phone interviews. His voice has been altered and the line scrambled so as to be untraceable. X was challenged about the Abeyance and its plausibility.

"The theory is flawed by its very nature," the interviewer, himself a respected physicist, had contended. "Consider: would the universe suddenly stop if time didn't stop along with it?"

"Your first mistake is continuing to address this event as theory," X retorted. "My upcoming presentation will prove beyond a shadow of a doubt that what you consider science fiction is, indeed, absolute fact."

"Upcoming? Are you holding back on us?"

"Time will tell." replied X cheekily.

"If you are, then why?"

"*If* I am." X had scoffed. "My muse once told me that the truth would destroy you."

Ara runs her tiny right hand over Eron's body. What she would give to touch him, to feel him, to comfort him in his passing. She sobs softly over his prone shell, kisses him on his lips. There is no brush of contact. *If only.* She stands. *We were not meant to be apart.*

The muse sullenly walks away. She glances at a cave embedded at the foot of a mountain as she passes. It appears to contain nothing but darkness. She walks out of sight.

Inside, a prodigious eyelid opens, revealing a second, slightly-transparent lid that fills the entirety of the cavity. This lid closes, then opens to its orb as a diamond-shaped slit shyly peeks outside.

ST. PETER'S CHILDREN'S HOSPITAL, ICU

"She's weak, but she'll pull through. Fortunately, her vitals are stable."

Daniel and Samantha take a moment to process the doctor's optimistic appraisal. HIPAA, the Health Insurance Portability and Accountability Act that would otherwise maintain strict patient discretion for non-family members, was long-ago overruled in this instance due to Samantha's *office.* Though her official job description was then as now shrouded in shadow, she flashed the proper authorization regarding such matters and has since been treated by administration as kin. As has Daniel by association. That they have become trusted and beloved as long-term volunteers has further blurred any potential conflict of interest.

As Marlo once told them, "You two are part of the scenery now."

"What happened?" Daniel inquires.

"That's the issue. Her heart and other vitals are functioning exactly as they should with no visible reason for the arrest. No signs of arterial or cardiac damage at all. We ordered a battery of tests—"

"Can we see her?" asks Samantha.

The doctor looks at his watch. "Check back with the front desk in an hour. We expect—we hope—to have some answers by then—"

"How do we reach you?" Samantha persists, while cocking her head in Brikke's direction.

He looks her over. *This one won't quit.* He reaches for a business card from his pocket. "Call me directly." He hands her the card. "My direct extension is on there. Barring an emergency I'll pick up."

Samantha is about to respond, but he cuts her off.

"One hour," he reiterates, before nodding and returning to his patients. He passes Brikke as he enters through the swinging doors, whispering to him along the way.

~~~

Meantime, inside the ICU, Marlo slowly sits up. She looks around. The doctor signs forms on a clipboard while the nurses tend to other patients.

She takes a deep breath. *It's time,* she thinks, and silently counts-down:

Ten...nine...

She peels off her monitor patches.

...eight...seven...six...

She disconnects her IV.

...five...four...

The machines immediately react and she swings over the bed.

...three...two...

A station nurse notices. "DOCTOR!"

...one!

The Abeyance commences. Everything and everyone *freezes* in their last position, save for Marlo. And one other.

She exits through the swinging doors where Brikke has been waiting.

He takes her hand and they leave the hospital as the building crumbles around them.

FLAME

A young dragon, a male, who should be gone with the others, steps timidly outside of his sanctuary. He is small but still growing, three times the height of the average human and thrice its height from nose to tail-tip. Though his wings are nearly formed he has not, as of yet, taken flight. He is a crawler, ineffectual despite his present stage of development. He should minimally be able to fly short distances and messenger warnings to the others when danger is lurking.

He desires more than anything to be helpful to his own kind because he is wholly aware that this is what they expect and he has so far been useless. He is presently, also, lost and directionless, having taken refuge when the adult dragons froze in mid-flight after stopping the human.

He witnessed the Abeyance. He is not affected by the Abeyance. After, the other dragons flew away, or tried to, he was left behind. Then those other dragons got stuck in mid-air. In either case, he does not understand why he was singled out.

The dragon should be unable to see Ara and yet he can, and does, much to his confusion as she is quite far away and should be out of his eye-line. That was what she wanted him to think.

He has been watching. She believes that if she shocks him he will be awed and, if she is correct in her assumption, the dragon will be forever in her service. She savors the idea, which in the near-past would have been totally out of character. Her love has gone, his weapon—which may well hold the key to his passing and, she fancies, his eventual return—has been lost.

Self-control has become the least of her concerns.

Forever. He could aid me in my quest, so he will be used.

Ara sharply turns and glares at the interloper.

So close!

The terrified dragon scurries back into the cavern. He peeks from inside, however, as the muse's face contorts into a ghastly mask of determination before she again turns and walks on. The dragon should be unable to grasp the concept of a dire warning. Yet this too he can, and does.

Her face says all he needs to know.

He certainly should be unable to read her thoughts, yet when Ara is further in the distance the dragon *hears* her final *decision* on the matter and becomes cognizant as to why he has been spared.

She is responsible, because she has a far more important issue to resolve:

Do not worry, my love. I swear to you, we will *be together.* The muse follows with a request: *Taebal, join me.*

The dragon suddenly realizes he has little choice in the matter. He was named *Taebal* by Eron, who saved him from a *cleansing* and secretly raised him.

Taebal, meaning *Guide to Light*. *She* should not have known that.

Now, nothing makes very much sense.

Word had spread that the mystic S'n Te was seen exiting the king's castle, holding a scroll close to his robe as the gates closed behind him. This led to whispers from the inside that he and the king were engaged in a secretive, likely-illicit collaboration.

The dragons attacked the premises as S'n Te, on foot, safely departed.

The latest of the human-led cleansings against the dragons was plotted by Eron, but two sunsets prior to the assault on his father's kingdom. As with the two preceding cleansings, both of which drastically curtailed the older dragon population, the moats would be poisoned, thrawn would be located and strategically released for battle, distracting the dragons, and the humans would slaughter their shared food supplies and hoard the feed into the caves for their own consumption. In the end, the remaining thrawn would again scatter and the dead dragons would also be used as food for the victorious humans, while the young dragon population would be tamed and used as laborers.

The foresight that a hopeful, peaceful coexistence was integral to the long-term survival of the humans was Eron's alone, and he would curtail the anticipated outcries as necessary with means that he considered deserved; if successful, the laborers would be fairly compensated, and further rewarded, with a regular supply of meals and the occasional war games.

The hope was that, in the near future, the young of the species would fight alongside the humans when the need arose. New long-term threats had not yet been defined, neither outside nor within the human circle.

Not yet.

Cleansings were rare and impeccably-coordinated. The risk of human casualty was outstanding. Therefore, the planning and the execution of a single cleanse could, cumulatively, extend over a human lifetime. Eron did find it questionable that the young dragon would come to him voluntarily, following the death of his parents at the hands of the dragonslayer's army.

He must have reason...

The orphan was lost and wandered into their victory feast; when one of Eron's troops mocked him then drew a dagger to slay him, Eron stood in the way and instead leashed the dragon. Taebal would then subordinate himself to Eron by allowing a carry on its back, which delivered dragon meat and blood to the drunken fighters.

Later that night, the dragon led Eron near an infested area where the older dragons slept. Eron discovered that they had been counter-plotting their own cleansing. He would be prepared. The camp was raided the next day. Taebal's disclosure saved many lives.

Eron learned to trust him.

The dragon would be named by the dragonslayer as *Guide to Light* and remain his faithful companion to the end.

Both Eron and Taebal possessed a certain knowledge that bonded each to the other, though neither was aware as to the other's understanding: Taebal's parents were *good.* They did not engage with the other dragons in their conflict with the humans. They too believed that the species should work together against common enemies, and the father recruited others for that purpose.

Taebal saw what happened. His parents' deaths were inevitable. The damage was collateral; they were needed in the height of battle, both of them, and were pulled out of their cave by a warrior dragon as a powerless

Taebal was left to fend for himself.

Torn upon witnessing the death and destruction, Taebal's parents attempted to hide the injured but still living—both human and dragon—as opposed to fighting. When one of Eron's men caught the dragons moving the human casualties, he mistook their effort for aggression and slit their throats.

Eron saw it all, and he made a choice. He fought on for his own.

Taebal watched from the cave's mouth as he struggled to make sense of his loss. He also noticed Eron, once free, walk over to Taebal's father, climb atop the tail and close the dragon's eyes with his fingers. The killer of Taebal's parents watched in disbelief.

When Eron died, Taebal ran away, horrified, and hid in his parents' cave. He had intended to stay there until he too was taken. The third cleansing was not to be. The dragonslayer considered the timing of the assault on the king's grounds suspicious.

My recklessness will kill my father, he considered, tormented by the paranoia that he had been betrayed. *If it does not kill me first.* Reinforcements, led by the distressed Eron, arrived at the castle. Strangely, the dragons retreated at first sight.

~~~

Taebal looks up—and ahead. He is tempted to step outside, provoked even, but he is frightened as a helpless child.

Reluctantly, he complies with the muse's design. Somehow, he *knows* he has no choice.

Ara does not see the perceptive creature, however, first recover Eron's sweord from the cavern with a sweep of his right hind leg. Nor does she see him place the object into his mouth as he steps outside.

However, the weapon has been disabled. The implement's gauntlet, the profound power source that no living, breathing thing alone would be capable of dismantling, is gone.

This part of the weapon is relatively useless as is, save as a standard blade.

Taebal struggles to catch up to the muse, whose back remains to him as she strides on.

CLARIDGE HOTEL,

"5 DAYS POST-ABEYANCE" (ED. VERIFIED) PROJECT ARA

Thomas snores. He's fallen asleep sitting in his desk chair, yet again, the side of his head snuggled over his keyboard, his arms dangling. He stirs in response to a subtle *whoosh* as an envelope slides across his suite's hardwood flooring. Twilight sleep. When he dreams of her, which of late is increasingly frequent, the imagery comes in fragmented flashbacks that return him to a time before his heart was taken.

"Game and match!" she says triumphantly.

There was a time, a brief time, when he *did* play games. When he not only played, he looked forward. He used to be a rabid air hockey player until he started losing, constantly, to his late wife. She was so pretty and carefree back then, until the Sickness sapped her of body and spirit.

Sam is the spitting image of her mother in the prime days of of her health. Sam, though, was never carefree like her mother.

Thomas and Elizabeth are back in their first house together, inside of the modest rec room that could barely contain the table game they both loved as kids. Thomas suffers, as always, the chronic ass-whooping he regularly pretends his ego cannot tolerate. Back then, his ongoing strategy was to manipulate her pity in a bit to throw off her natural skill-set; the efforts never paid off and yet, secretly, he didn't ever mind. He reveled that he could only ever be his true self with her—a man-child who could be serious, humorous, moody and sophomoric, sometimes all at once—and she would accept and love him for being "human."

When they married, he decided that, in his world, games will be reserved solely for her. Gaming with anybody else would be *cheating*. And *now*, yet another *whoosh* of that infernal plastic red puck immediately precedes the even more horrible *ker-plunk* of yet another goal. One again, the winning point is the loudest.

"Gloating? I'm not gloating. I'm just good."

~~~

He awakens but she is nowhere to be seen. *Maybe she's teasing me?* He rubs the fatigue from his eyes and glimpses the envelope—which he can't reach. His sight is drawn to the floor-door clearance, and he realizes it was the sound of the incoming mail, slid under his door, that had roused him.

Now he'll have to stand up and then bend down which truly pisses him off as, once awake, he can rarely fall back to a restful sleep. Who knows the next time he will see her? He glances to his window. It's still dark outside. *Come back soon, huh?*

McFee swipes the envelope and attempts to make out the name of the addressee. A useless endeavor. He remembers that he wears glasses when no one is looking and never works with his contacts. He grabs his glasses from his desk. The spectacles bring his immediate future into focus, as he tears the damn thing and removes the note inside:

```
Apologies for missing our earlier appointment. STOP.
May I suggest tomorrow at 3? STOP.
```

A telegram? thinks Thomas, who is somewhat flustered by the eccentricity. *A telegram. Who the hell sends telegrams anymore?*

"Especially at..." he mumbles. He looks to his desk clock.

4:45 AM.

Are you for real?

BRADLEY AND SON BIBLIOTHEQUE

The writer has arrived lightly-encumbered. A folded computer tablet with an attached keyboard and an attached stylus. That is all.

Donovan shows an awed Thomas around the shop. Shelving and cases of antique books are, as expected based on his earlier window-view, everywhere. There is barely room to walk, and the guest is stunned by the sheer quantity of prime material.

"As a fellow antiquarian I do hope you found your invitation by telegram charming?"

"I was unsure what to think, actually."

"Internet, e-mail. Do you ever question, Mr. Bradley, how so much of the world's greatest masterpieces of music and literature were composed without the benefit of a computer?" Before Thomas could answer, Donovan continues—"If you have not, you should."

Thomas is preoccupied. "I don't mean to be rude but, as a writer myself—"

Donovan ignores him. "So frequently we confuse surviving with living, with...true discovery. How can we as a society expect to continue to break ground in terms of artistic creation, if everything we need is handed to us?"

"Some say that's progress."

"Poppycock. It's corruption if you ask me. My late son, rest his soul, was a devout homosexual who was once was sent home from school for digitally manipulating the figure of a woman on a Botticelli website—from his cellular phone. I have no idea—"

"Where did you find this?" Thomas McFee holds a book, its covers protected by mylar. *Songs for the Philologists*, by J.R.R. Tolkien.

Donovan snatches the book from Thomas's grasp. "Just because you could do something doesn't mean you should," he says, completing his thought.

Thomas nods in understanding.

Donovan continues. "I have no phone, Mr. McFee. My own special brand of protest." He turns the book to its back. "I found this one as part of an estate sale."

Thomas extends his hand. "May I?" Donovan gives him the book. Thomas studies the volume. "Leeds University Department of English," he observes. "Only 14 of these are known to still exist. You didn't find this in any estate sale."

Donovan snickers. "Of course not." He turns his back and walks away. "Shame on me for propagating such absurdity. The cheek of it all, this humble old fool believing he could get one over on you." The dealer's manner is nigh-flirtatious. He turns back around and looks Thomas square in the eye. "You passed *this* test."

A suspicious Thomas stares him down and returns the book to Donovan's hand. "With respect, please tell me this is not some kind of game?"

Donovan sighs. "Hardly," he answers, succinctly. "To the issue then. In point of fact this edition is one of the very few early Tolkiens to survive the Gower Street Fire." Thomas raises his eyebrows. "Or, I should say, the only copy *I* was personally able to retrieve." Thomas McFee is stunned, and Donovan notices the response. "This is one of the authentic, duplicated typescripts intended for the English Department of Leeds University but never distributed. It was stored at the Gower Press." He pauses. "Permission for its use had not been sought from its most important contributor."

"You spent so many years denying your presence at Gower Fire."

"I turned 90 this year." Donovan smiles weakly. "I confess my bullshit to you and you only and for that there is reason...as with the rest." Thomas keeps a game face. "McFee, where does all this go when I'm gone?"

"I'm afraid your legacy is secure—"

"Meaning what, exactly? That once there was a collector of words...whose life's work was dispersed or extinguished depending on the prevailing winds?"

"You won't ever be forgotten," McFee weakly attempts. "You are one of the world's foremost—"

"When one passes doesn't the world end?"

"Mr Brad—"

"Nothing lasts forever, Mr. McFee. That much I've accepted. What survives is most easily manipulated. Our technology has allowed the digital manipulation of...everything. What then becomes of *history*?"

Thomas concedes. "A fair question ..."

"Bullocks. It's the only question. Here I've attempted to preserve what it means to be human, if you will, and here belongs the documents you shall shortly review. My thoughts have become topsy-turvy. What I've believed all these years is now in question, and then I wonder if any of this purity will survive."

"You have amassed quite the collection but if you don't mind me asking—"

"Ask me anything you like."

"If the documents are authentic I could understand a vague change of perspective but—"

"You miss my point. When technology clashes with antiquity there is no history, don't you see? There is more out there and we've developed the ability to rewrite our past. I will not be around much longer, how the fates will stamp this *legacy* as you say has become a terrible obsession, a museum has yet to make any real offer to house these contents and I am horrified at the prospects of all this being lost."

Thomas is taken aback by the older man's passion. "What I'm hearing," he says, "is that you're expecting a calamity of some sort when you—"

"A calamity," Donovan plainly repeats. "Did you see the my son's obituary when you entered? Surely you saw his obituary. No one talks about him now and yet the fire was headline news at the time. Any personal significance there, hmm?"

Thomas' suspicions are validated; Donovan knows more than he's letting on. "You know, I've been researching historic literary fires for my book?"

"I thought your book was finished?"

"You been spying on me? Is that it?"

"Yes."

McFee waits for more. Donovan bites his lip.

"I guess I won't ask," Thomas says, giving in. "I thought I was finished too. Until lately."

"Call me curious."

"I'm carrying this nagging sensation that I've missed something. Between you and me, I feel like I'm being—pushed. By whom or what I have no idea..."

Donovan smiles weakly. "You"re a perfectionist."

"Are you disappointed? You want me to leave now?"

"No. All as planned."

"If anything happens to me, you can sic the authorities on my publisher, who's bound to kill me when she finds out—"

"A *paranoid* perfectionist," Donovan clarifies. "Do you believe you are being manipulated?'

"Anything is possible," Thomas responds. "Are *you* manipulating me, Mr. Bradley?"

"And that too is a fair question," Bradley responds, referencing Thomas's earlier comment. "May I change the subject? I apologize if I in any way upset you."

Thomas smirks. "A bit of a relief, actually. I'm not usually asked."

"McFee, are you familiar with *Ragnarök* and the *Edda*?"

Thomas presses and rubs his tongue against his cheek. Now he's certain he's being played. "So?" For the moment, the extent of his engagement.

"Allow me to share my very favorite quote from the newest trove of *Edda Lays*, dated approximately 800 A.D. as compiled by one Snorri Sturluson." Donovan clears his throat, and proceeds. *'Long-oared, dragon-crested, ice-flecked, the sleek ship crests high on the billows of the whale road and hwat! The door to Valhalla appears high within the soaring clouds. The time of Ragnarök has come and yet...Ara keeps her father chained and his tumult and chase in abeyance.'* End quote. What did you think of my translation?"

"*Ragnarök* is a Norse myth, included in the *Prose Edda*—"

"I thought you knew. I'd have been surprised otherwise. Why the game?"

"Nice try." Time to re-focus. "What does any of this have to do with *Beowulf*?"

Donovan smiles. "As you advance in your own work and other indulgences, Mr. McFee, you will, like me, find that there comes a point where the myths you live by become indistinguishable from the reality you swear by. You've looked to these myths for your answers, you've adapted them for your worldview and then—like now—you find that there is...more to the equation. And that those myths, those stories that became the tenants you and so many others based your lives upon? They were incomplete. Like *Beowulf*...Like life."

"I'm not sure I understand."

"Let's reverse-engineer, shall we?" Thomas rolls his eyes at Donovan's long-windedness. "I've lived a life of lies, you see, as have you, and yet...I've learned that I've held the answers all along." He turns and points to a shelf containing numerous older first-editions. "Here." He turns again, and points to various books and displays. "Here. Here...here. I call them *souls*, Mr. McFee. The ultimate truth, hidden in each and every one...For example, a new read of *Beowulf,* mindful of this consideration, proves on its own it could never be the complete story—"

"*Beowulf* by design began *in medias res*, in the middle—"

"By design? How do you know?" Thomas does not answer. "Nothing with nothing. Read it more carefully, then ..." Donovan pauses; his next words are carefully considered. "I said the *newest* trove of Edda Lays and you didn't question me. Why?"

Thomas nods, as if acknowledging he's somehow been exposed. "Must have slipped my mind," he calmly answers. "That, or I don't know you well enough and maybe I'm being overly-respectful."

Donovan smirks. "Nothing doing. I called you here because for these matters you are the only person I could think of who belongs here, yet you failed that test with flying colors. Or did you, I wonder..." Thomas looks for a sign, anything that would betray the older man's agenda. "No mind," Donovan continues. "I lied to you. Perhaps I'm just a simple old man horrified of dying—"

"Why?" the writer asks, straining to maintain calm.

"Why what?"

Thomas answers with a sharp glare.

Donovan sighs. "If you're asking me why I lied to you that's as valid a question as any, I suppose. Tell me, what *do* you know about *Ragnarök*—"

"Mr. Bradley, if I'm wasting my time here I have no problem turning back and—"

"And I promise to answer your question...Please. This is important."

Thomas, barely, remains composed. "*Ragnarök* is the end. The world begins in frost and fire and ends in the drowning of man and god and dragon which begins the cycle of rebirth. And then the new birth is the beginning of the new end. And so on. Is that good enough?"

"Something like that. I'm impressed. So then, to answer your question ..." Bradley says, stepping slowly to a bookshelf to peruse an old spine, "Since my boy's accident, I do confess I've been plagued by selfish anxieties of my own impending demise. My days are numbered and you...this history must not be lost, my dear McFee. The importance of my plea cannot be overstated, as you will soon see. *Ragnarök* holds special significance to me and to your visit here today. *Beowulf* was largely influenced by Norse mythology, which in turn influenced your Tolkien and—"

"Aside from the dragons I'm not getting *any* connection—"

"The dragons...Indeed." Bradley turns to face his visitor. "They are all the same, I am telling you, don't you see? Every myth springs from what was once a common reality. My contention is *Ragnarök* comes closest of them all to that earliest, common reality. If there is more to *Beowulf,* then, what more could there be elsewhere? What becomes of our world, our lives...*Creation*?"

"Mr. Bradley, I'm afraid I have no idea what you are talking about or where we're headed..."

"Sometimes us crazy old fools aren't as crazy as you think we are."

"I never said you were crazy..."

Donovan is disappointed. "Granted, it *is* all a bit elliptical, isn't it?" Thomas shrugs in response. "I get carried away sometimes." the older man admits. "I guess now's not the time for a history lesson then. Let's just say, for the time being, someone has to take all this over when I'm gone."

"You're asking for my help, that it?"

"Possibly."

"Because," Thomas placates, "the answers to life, death, and the nature of the universe are contained in your collection?"

"Likely."

"Is that the real reason I'm here?"

"Possibly. I sense you're not a stupid man."

"Is that a compliment—"

"We'll hit a pub for the rest. For now, why don't you tell me about the fires."

Before Thomas could answer, Donovan excuses himself to make a phone call. Their initial conversation had gone considerably longer than either man had anticipated, and Donovan empathized with his guest's impatience.

In the meantime, Thomas peruses some of the older material. Donovan re-emerges, still curiously holding Tolkien's book, and resumes the conversation.

"So?"

"Sorry?"

"You were going to talk to me about the fires."

Thomas re-focuses. "Right, the fires..." He inhales heartily and expires slowly, regaining his thoughts. "And then I can begin my work? I must insist on—"

Donovan laughs. "Of course. I understand. We've spent a good deal of time but we were getting to know one another ..."

Thomas resumes. "The fires seem to be a bit of a motif in my work I am not sure why." Donovan nods. The conversation hangs. To alleviate the dead air, Thomas points to the book the dealer carries. "How much?"

"So sorry?"

"*Songs for the Philologists.* How much?"

"Oh. Not for sale. Display only."

"You are aware I can pay top dollar—"

"Not for sale," he restates. "Too much sentimental value, I suppose."

"Maybe another time?"

"Not for as long as I"m breathing and don"t you get excited. Patience is a virtue." Thomas cannot help but laugh. "However, as I discussed at length with Ms. Watkins, everything here is yours to peruse. I set up a room downstairs and trust you will find it comfortable."

"I hope you didn't go to too much trouble?"

"Trouble is me flicking a light switch. It takes me two days to recover, and yet still I breathe! Don't start the countdown yet, just because I have."

Suspicions aside, Thomas is loathe to accept that he is, alas, struggling against the older man's charms. Donovan is sad and he's intellectually challenging. And he's old. Perhaps a more potent combination this writer simply cannot fathom?

Just don"t let down your guard, old boy...

"I trust you'll find the accommodations functional, at best," Donovan says as he turns. "Come with me."

Thomas follows two steps behind Donovan as they walk in the

direction of the stairwell. He is paused when Donovan quickly extends his arm to hold him back. "Surely you of all people are aware, Mr. McFee, of Professor Tolkien's 1970 visit to America? Not the most publicized event in his lifetime—"

"I'm aware of no such trip." Thomas is puzzled.

Donovan drops his arm. "How very disheartening." He stops walking and faces his visitor. "My boy said the same thing once." Thomas has no clue how to take either statement. He cautiously follows Donovan as the old man walks on. They are about to pass an active, analog black and white television set when Thomas' attention is diverted by a static-ridden newsflash. A stock image of St. Peter's Children's Hospital appears on the monitor.

"Can I have a second? My daughter and her fiancé do some volunteer work over there." Donovan steps back and observes alongside him.

A *scroll* follows the image, headlined by a title card: *St. Peter's Children's Hospital.* Under that is listed the names of *survivors.*

"Survivors? Do you know what's happened?

"I leave the set on..." Donovan watches passively as Thomas rushes outside. He then turns back to the TV. He notices, among the names now nearly scrolled off-screen: *Samantha McFee.* He glances through the window. Thomas is dialing, near-panicked. Donovan completes his thought, murmuring to himself, "... only to keep me company."

He turns his head to a nearby photograph, framed cheaply and hung as if at random on the side of a bookshelf. He did not want to be obvious about the thing, even if he had just attempted to force the issue. He had hoped Thomas would catch it, as the glimpse would have initiated a far more meaningful, and stirring, conversation.

The image was taken 40 years ago and is so labeled. Three men, standing in front of New York's Algonquin Hotel: a beardless Donovan in the middle, flanked by J.R.R. Tolkien and one *Franklin McFee*.

Thomas's father.

"AN UNDISCLOSED LOCATION," LONDON, ENGLAND

The same television news report in progress:

"...repeating for those of you just tuning in, an utterly *astounding* scene unfolding in London this morning. Local bomb-squad crews continue to canvas the surrounding area where mere hours ago stood the iconic St. Peter's Children's Hospital. Authorities now suspect the potentially tragic implosion to have been caused by a yet-to-be-identified domestic terrorist. However, in what could only be described as a miraculous turn of events, the BBC understands that there have been no human casualties. All children, staff and guests have been accounted for, and all have been safely transported to an undisclosed location. We have been advised that for as long as—"

Samantha fumbles with the remote. The sound continues: "The city remains on lock-down—" *Mute.* She drops the remote onto her lap as she sighs, and takes a call.

"The lines were down" she says to Thomas. "I knew you would try. We're all okay..." Tears, stifled as best as she can. "*Daddy,*" says Samantha, "now is not the time..." Her words trail off as she glimpses Marlo, holding hands with Brikke, stumbling as she retrieves a cup of water from a nurse. The girl turns and immediately unnerves Samantha with a sharp glare and a half-cocked smile.

"Sam?" Samantha doesn't respond as her dad's concern can be heard through the phone line.

She's faking it, thinks Samantha, who looks away. *Why would she?*

What's the reason? She turns back to the television, a modest, older set resting upon an iron stand.

"What's going on?" Thomas' voice rises to a panic. "Sam!"

A portion of a typed letter is highlighted on the screen, attributed to the authorities' *prime suspect.*

They say, "History leaves clues." They also say, "Those who ignore history are doomed to repeat it." What is happening now is clear as the sun but execrable to consider. The St. Peters Hospital incident and the survival rate that you and your associates consider miraculous? No accident.

It was a manipulation.

The letter is signed, not surprisingly:

The image fades, and is replaced by a highlighted postscript:

P.S. For those of you who prefer to face the unknown only from the safety of an armchair...Wake up! Ponder then why these classic flights of imagination have so-endured and, perhaps, you'll garner some insight: The Lord of the Rings, Pinocchio, Alice in Wonderland, Frankenstein, Dracula, The

Wizard of Oz, 20,000 Leagues Under the Sea, The Time Machine, Dr. Jekyll and Mr. Hyde, The Raven, At the Mountains of Madness, Hamlet.

Would any of you consider these authors to have been more enlightened somehow than the rest of us? Could there be more to the biblical concept of 'providence'' than we have been led to believe?

A quick dissolve and the letter's conclusion overtakes the screen:

With this message—that I trust you will frame as an admission of guilt; it is nothing of the kind—I have invited my capture. As you attempt to find me, realize The Truth is Nigh.

As Samantha finishes reading, she concludes that not only is the writer mysteriously aware, but that she knows exactly who he is.

He is on the verge, she considers. *Oh God—*

"Sam!" His voice is faint but she hears him. Samantha remembers the phone, and puts it to her ear. "Sam, are you still there?"

Samantha turns in response to heavy footsteps. She does not notice the new televised graphic behind her:

MANHUNT!

The Search for 'X'

Marlo stares, mesmerized, at the television from yards away. Brikke leaves her side. He approaches Samantha, alone.

"Sam, if you can hear me. I'm still your father and I love—" Samantha terminates the call as the giant's shadow overtakes her. "It's time to talk," she says.

PEMBROKE COLLEGE, OXFORD, ENGLAND, 1935

The professor bites his lip as the bell rings, interrupting his flow. Class is over. No one moves; they have been riveted, as usual, by his lecture.

He turns the projector off. The final image fades from the screen. It was of Beowulf facing the dragon whose poisonous blood would ultimately kill him. Tolkien faces his rapt audience.

"Ladies and gentlemen, if you permit me I shall now judge your worth as human beings for all eternity." Confused reactions as Tolkien deliberately pauses. His students glance at one another, shrug, laugh, some still wipe tears. "I have your papers to grade. Scurry." His students applaud, most nervously, and slowly disperse. Tolkien smiles as the last of them closes the door upon exiting.

He walks to the door, locks it and returns to his desk. Tolkien lights his pipe, and gets to work.

He ruffles through the rest of the papers. Though his eyes are somewhat strained, a particular composition captures his attention:

Against All Odds:

Influences of Early Epic Poetry on Global Thought

The first lines intrigue the instructor:

The heroic ideal, as defined and punctuated by our earliest literature, is the masculine ideal. Mindful neither of personal handicap nor of feminine constraint, the masculine hero's victories inspire awe and idolatry. His influence transcends cultures and creation.

Tolkien laughs heartily upon noticing what follows:

Blah blah blah. This is, of course, bollocks, proving only that chauvinism has existed since the beginning of time and that the roles of women have only devolved from there.

He smiles as he continues reading. Amused though he is, Tolkien is without warning seized by a sudden sense of despair. He looks across the empty room—so empty without those young minds, without their life!—and hearkens back to an incident during the War when he had last felt so alone.

That period, now again so fresh in my mind, he realizes. *Maybe I got a bit carried away today.*

It was in Bouzincourt, as he read Gilson's letter, but then he saw the strange figure *watching* him. When she disappeared, he was compelled to trod on in his friend's honor. And, before that even, when he was a child and the incident with the spider...the same onlooker perhaps saving his life...

The moment passes. Tolkien re-powers the projector, curious, and briefly looks up and behind him to the last slide. Beowulf and the dragon. He then looks down to the paper, and circles the word *beginning*. And circles it again. And then a third time.

He has an epiphany and scribbles a note above the top margin on the essay's front page:

In a hole in the ground...

He lifts the paper's corner, and admires the words. He resumes:

...there lived a hobbit.

"Humph," he mumbles. He considers the sentence:

In a hole in the ground there lived a hobbit.

Tolkien is unable to move onward, nagged by the sense that his compulsion was no accident.

He wonders which of his creative predecessors had experienced the same *moment*, this split-second euphoria of sudden inspiration, followed by a subtle wave of melancholy that nothing will ever be the same again.

"My my." He draws on his pipe. "So, what do we have here?"

FIRE (PROVIDENCE)

Bournemouth. Population: 400,000.

For John Ronald Reuel Tolkien, seventy-eight, and his beloved wife Edith, this modest, sheltered coastal resort town would be considered home away from home in their final years. Due to its predominantly older, professionally-accomplished populace of fifty-plus, J.R.R. adopted the community as a welcome respite from the ongoing attentions of Oxford.

A welcome respite, most of the time. His celebrity was muted in Bournemouth. He liked and accepted this. The residents, though eminently respectful of their esteemed visitor, rather took to him as one of their own. Tolkien, like them, was a figure who transcended the heights of his chosen profession and had earned his influence. On rare occasions, though, a resident would snuggle up to his wife, to get closer to him. They would both quickly see through the charade, but these instances were infrequent.

J.R.R. and Edith frequently visited the south coast for the holidays. In the late 1960's, they retired to Poole. Bournemouth was a retreat predominantly for *her* benefit. They were honored guests who would stay in the same suite at the Hotel Miramar. J.R.R. also retained a second, smaller room in which to write.

"Yes?" he responds, to a knock on his office door.

"It's time, Ronald, luv."

The former Edith Bratt's life with *Ronald*, as his closest confidantes called him, was not always a comfort blanket. Their first meeting could be called *serendipitous*, but during difficult times—to better appreciate the depth of the union that followed—Ronald frequently pondered the challenges of their early pasts.

Ronald's mother, Mabel, anointed him the new "man of the family" on his ninth birthday, five years following the death of his father, a time when, she thought, he would be willing to understand his lot. Though his immediate reaction proved less-than-noble, he realized soon enough that without his honest efforts they really may not be able to eat; he would work closely with his mum in her day-to-day and make sure his brother did too, whether either of them wanted to or not.

Ensuring his family's survival as they continued to straddle the poverty line would become Ronald's new priority. He was still too young to be a money-maker; as he couldn't support them financially, for his part he would be sure to not give Mabel any guff and complete any chores she asked of him. In other words, make it as easy on Mum as possible.

His dad would have been proud, anyway.

In 1904, Mabel took ill and was diagnosed with diabetes. She died within weeks, on November the 14th, leaving behind two orphans with barely a penny between them.

Ronald and Hilary were attended to by family friend and advisor, Father Francis Xavier Morgan, a half-Welsh, half-Spanish parish priest who received Mabel—and Mabel's sister, May—into the Roman Catholic Church in 1900. He had attended to the boys" material and spiritual needs and oversaw their welfare.

In the ensuing years the brothers were placed in boarding care and had become devout Catholics. It was in one such boarding house, run by a Mrs. Faulkner, that Ronald met Edith Bratt, a resident of less than a year. She was 19, he 16, and though any romantic attraction was gradual, they were inseparable from the beginning. Father Francis, a prescient man, forbade Ronald from seeing her until his 21st birthday, due in equal part to the young scholar's academic responsibilities and her opposing Anglican convictions. Ronald was not happy, though as a show of respect, and fear, of the man he would come to know and love as a surrogate dad, he acceded to Father Francis' interdiction and gracefully complied.

Besides, Father Francis promised to teach Ronald how to smoke a proper pipe if the young man convinced him of his sincerity. Not a bargain; the good Father would have none of that. He was asked.

"One day," Father Francis said.

"Can you be more specific?"

"Before I pass away."

"Father?"

"Yes?

"And when will that be exactly?"

Though Father Francis was enamored of Ronald and his unique humor, until the young man's 21st year he was rarely anything less than

103

authoritarian in his presence. Though the request was sincere (and would one day be fulfilled), Ronald was advised that he was too young yet for *that* diversion.

Little matter. The adroit Ronald understood their respective stations and he trusted Father Francis more than almost anyone.

He had greater concerns anyway.

Five years is such a long time.

Though he missed her terribly, Ronald applied himself to his studies. He developed a knack for Linguistics and languages, including Greek and Latin, as well as an easy fluency in ancient (Germanic) Gothic, Welsh and Finnish. Edith never strayed from his thoughts and he was confident that as long as he achieved scholastically, he would not stray from hers. She would hear about his accomplishments for sure. *She* would be proud of him.

And they would certainly wed upon their reacquaintance because he was falling in love with her and gossip had it that the feeling was mutual.

Ronald knew as much as she did about her father, one Alfred Frederick Warrilow, which was nothing. He knew that Edith was born his illegitimate daughter in Gloucestershire and raised in Handsworth, Birmingham, where her mother, the unmarried Frances Bratt, left her an orphan in 1908. He also knew that Edith was a classically-trained pianist.

As Ronald continued to temper his loneliness by attending to his schoolwork with near-obsessive abandon, he counted the days until they would finally meet again. During his immersion at Oxford's Exeter College, he discovered the Old English epic, *The Christ of Cynewulf,* and would be forever haunted by a couplet he found within the second of the poem's three parts (*Ascension*):

Eálá Earendel engla beorhtast Ofer middangeard monnum sended

Translation:

Hail Earendel brightest of angels, over Middle Earth sent to men.

Ronald would later write, in praise of Cynewulf's vision of the *Advent,* *Ascension* and *Last Judgment of Jesus*: "There was something very remote and strange and beautiful behind those words, if I could grasp it, far beyond ancient English."

Fortunately, he never could "grasp it." If he had been together with Edith during that time, he likely would not have found the poem that would compel him to explore *Beowulf* and so refine his life's journey.

Father Francis passed away on June 11, 1935. Whether interviewed by press or spoken with in private conversation, neither Ronald nor Edith would ever forget to credit him for his host of life-altering contributions.

"Leaving for New York is exciting, not difficult," she says. "We've been together over fifty years. Don't you think I deserve a break?"

"Hopeful for me, are we?"

"Lord, I hope not."

"I appreciate your best wishes." His right leg pushes his suitcase inches away from the couch, leaving him a bit of leverage to heel into the floor and wriggle closer to her. Much to her chagrin. His transportation is late; he will not have another chance to push her buttons for a week. "How is that flare-up of spirit?" he asks. "Do you need a doctor again?"

"Losing you for a week is exactly what the doctor ordered." Ronald winces. "Still, you just be sure to come back to me, you hear?"

"After all this you want me back?"

Edith's mouth curls up from the corners and breaks into a mischievous grin. She takes his hand. "I'm used to you."

"You're used to me?"

"I said that to you when you came back to me the first time, remember? I married you despite all that religious twaddle and I stayed with you when you *forced* your beliefs upon me. I was convinced we'd raise a beautiful family."

"I hope I helped. With the family, that is."

She ignores him. "Dear me, I'm becoming a tad mawkish—"

"A tad," he agrees.

"Of course I'm hopeful for you, you old coot. We both know you need to go. I just pray you find what you're looking for." She softens. "My husband's too damn important to me to be disappointed and that's the plain truth."

"I've handled disappointment before," he reminds her.

"Your heart is not as strong as it used to be."

He holds a laugh; she notices. "I believe I should thank you for your carefully-worded concern."

"Need I remind you of that horrid war in the Somme when we wrote letters in code? That was the first time. You always let me know where you were to keep me hopeful for your safe return." She shakes her head. "Unfortunately, I haven't changed a bit. Save for some weaker muscles here and there."

"I fought so we could resume our life together..."

"You have your good points." She playfully elbows him in the ribs.

"Ow! Careful! Remember, I'm a brittle old fool."

"What I put up with. Don't fret, I won't be lonely. I'll be feted as a society matron, they'll all feel sorry for me."

He favors his chest. "Poor dear."

"We belong in Bournemouth together, Ronald. When you return there's no reason to move around any more."

"I miss Oxford and *intelligent* conversation. I miss the company of Jack Lewis and our conversations about *Narnia* and religion. I miss my more intellectual associations. Perhaps I'll reunite with some of that brilliance in

New York—"

"You told me Bournemouth was an escape for you? Have you been lying to me all this time?"

"Not all. You couldn't go without food forever, could you?"

"Always the healthy ego. Maybe you're not so brittle as you say you are."

"Actually, you sort of said it first."

"Has the *legendary* J.R.R. Tolkien become too important to write a letter? We earned our solitude, don't you think?"

Ronald looks at his watch, then tilts his head for any sign of incoming transportation. Not yet. The debate is becoming uncomfortable. The truth is their doctor had given them both passing bills of health before he made his decision. His wife's fatigue is age-related, the doctor explained. Maybe Ronald's guilt is as well, which the husband would like to believe anyway.

"The rest then?" he expires.

"The rest?"

"Is there anything else?" he translates.

"Ah. You see, now you're getting me crazy. I was about to wax nostalgic about, let's see, your trench fever in '16," she vamps. Ronald looks to the floor and pinches the bridge of his nose, cannily hiding his face as he agonizes. "My poor baby, laid up in the hospital but writing. Always writing...and making a life for the two of us. Even while in the hospital, composing your *Voyage of Earendel* of all things, setting the *great Tolkien* on his way to glory and—"

"*Our* way." He peeks up. "You appreciate me most when I'm at my most helpless, that's it?"

"Something like that."

"Look who's reminiscing now. I guess that means you're gonna miss

107

m—" His last words are drowned out by the sound of an incoming chopper.

Edith closes her eyes, then opens them to a tear. She has gotten his message. "I guess. *Maybe* some separation anxiety. I told you I haven't changed a bit…Maybe I'll come to my senses."

He cannot hear her over the propellers. He taps his hand on her knee and stands. "You sure you'll be okay?" he yells.

"Second thoughts? You're right. You are an old fool."

The chopper lands. They listen, both reluctant to end the moment.

He turns to her with a comforting smile; she then stands up, struggling, behind him as he prepares to head outside. He places her hand on his shoulder and gingerly turns him towards her for a tender embrace.

She pulls back. "You know I love you." She straightens his shirt collar. He watches as another tear falls to her cheek. "If you don"t take this chance," she continues, "you'll regret it for the rest of your days and you"ll resent me." She laughs. "Now get going. And I promise I won't fight the concierge when he checks on me. I'll be fine."

Half-past-three.

Edith watches as Ronald is escorted to the helicopter by a black suit in dark glasses. It appears as though the force of the whirling propellers nearly prevents the author from proceeding. The escort gently pushes Tolkien's arm when the author suddenly breaks from him and turns back.

"Professor!"

The propellers had nothing to do with it. Ronald stumbles along the way as he returns to his wife.

They both laugh like kids as they again embrace. He rubs her face and she kisses his forehead. He's made his point. She cranes her neck half-heartedly, in a gesture for him to return to his chopper. In response, he bores into her eyes and brushes her hand. He then winks at her before allowing the escort to help him back to the copter.

Ronald is safely guided inside the three-seater, just behind the pilot, and buckled in. The escort sits to his right and affixes his own strap; the pilot turns with *thumbs up* to verify readiness. The escort nods; permission granted.

The copter ascends as Ronald waves to his wife, who returns the gesture until he is well out of sight.

The chopper approaches a helipad at Bournemouth Airport. The trip was short. The pilot was pleasant and spoke when he was spoken to, but he would not dare refer to his passenger by his first name even when requested.

As they touch down, *Tolkien* squints to get a better look at the clean-shaven gentleman stylishly dressed in tweed suit and silk scarf awaiting his arrival, hands in pockets, standing in front of a private plane.

Donovan Bradley...

BRADLEY AND SON BIBLIOTHEQUE

Donovan peeks outside the store window. The younger McFee bears little physical resemblance to his dad, maybe save for his gait. A distinctive, never-relaxed carriage that implies a life in perpetual chase.

Or in some such pursuit.

Donovan again focuses on the photo. He rests his arm on the corner of an antique music stand for additional support. Atop the stand is an open chapbook, red silk marker holding a special page. The right page is blank. The left reads:

Our deepest fears are like dragons
guarding our deepest treasure.
- Rainer Maria Rilke, Austria

His palm grazes the book. As he looks down and peruses the words, he is troubled by the growing suspicion that he is being *guided* and is no longer in control of his actions.

He has heard of this phenomenon before and more than once, which adds to his discomfort as his thoughts on the matter are very assured and specific.

Why me? he wonders. *Why now?*

MIRKWOOD

Taebal is exhausted, having maintained a safe distance from her for what seems like forever. The dragon's sole distraction had been thoughts of his last sun. His had caught a rare glimpse of the blood-red star through Mirkwood's impossible cloud cover. He had hoped his view would continue unobstructed but the clouds patched up; the orb descended back to purgatory and the downpour began.

It was when she screamed that the sun disappeared. When the scream ended, the downpour did as well, stopping mid-flight just like the dragons. With the exception of Taebal.

He used to welcome the night. Now, he's haunted by the image of that last ray before the darkness returned—in a predictably fierce display—and of the flashing lightning that briefly illuminated the night sky, exposing at once the dearth of immediate shelters and his suspended brethren.

Presently, the clock of the world is in Abeyance. His kind, as with all other living, breathing thing, is stilled. So too is the weather. The dragon follows blindly, until he can no longer.

He's had enough, and collapses in a heap.

Ara stops. She turns and gazes at Taebal, who has awaited and dreaded this moment. He lifts his head, though he barely has the strength to stay awake. Through the course of today's excruciating journey to nowhere he would not dare travel ahead of her, because if she considered his act an attempt to escape, the punishment would have far outweighed the innocence of his intention. The intense boredom of maintaining a controlled distance was all-the-tougher and it wore him out. But he persisted. He couldn't conceive of the *other* torture, whatever that *may have been*, and he played it smart.

He played it safe.

Ara notices the *sweord* for the first time. Her first impulse is to snatch it from him, but she cannot. She approaches slowly, not from any fear but, rather, from what has been driving her since Eron's death: her elemental ambition to cross worlds and connect with her fallen warrior.

This dragon was her only link. And now, this sweord. She will no longer be reckless.

Where is the rest? she questions.

Taebal is guarded as she appears in front of him. He reconsiders his options. He will extinguish her and hurriedly fly away if she takes another step.

She takes another step.

The sweord falls from his mouth and he breathes his fire. She doesn't move. He breathes and breathes and the flames don't penetrate. He gives up, hesitantly, and his mouth closes. Then his legs give way and he falls flat on his stomach. His eyes close. His head convulses. Snot drips from his flaring nostrils.

And he snores.

~~~

Dawn.

Ara has remained in her position. Taebal is just awakening. On the ground, the sweord reflects his shadow. His eyes focus; he sees her. As before, she turns her back to him and walks.

He struggles to stand, shaking off sleep. Again, he lifts the sweord into his mouth. Taebal is not a happy dragon. When his parents were alive he was protected. He had dreamt he was back home, with them, and the entire experience from their deaths onward was a nightmare.

And now? Though he barely understands anything that has happened since, the muse's presence frightens him like nothing has before. This much he does know.

He also knows that he would kill her if only he could.

If only he could.

As he follows, his fear mounts. Taebal understands that this may well become problematic if he acts on instinct. He is conscientious, an evolving trait which in itself defines him as *different* and gifts him with unusual insight. In her, he senses the loss of control but also the sadness. Though he identifies with both he also realizes that he must be maintained, for now, if he is to survive.

This appears to be the difference. He is guided. She clearly has direction, which he lacks. Each respects that the other is unique.

He may learn something. But he doubts he will overcome his fear.

~~~

Taebal's judgment had once almost killed him. When his parents were attacked for sport by a laughing, drunken band of slayers, he hid in a mountain range at the behest of his father. He protested but his parents returned shortly thereafter.

The slayers were killed when they invaded the range to slaughter the young dragon. In his protestations they had noticed him. Taebal's father trapped and extinguished them.

He knew that new groups would surely come, and soon, to exact revenge.

Taebal rested on his father's back as they escaped to another home, a distant cave. In the midst of their flight he looked down. Below them was a body of water, one of Mirkwood's rare seas.

The storm hit with no warning. Suddenly, the skies lit with bolts of fire and the land shook with fierce thunder. The sea below was fraught with waves and it was there he glimpsed another dragon, no older than he, battling the seas, drowning.

The dragon beneath them cried; he could not breathe his fire and he could not take to the skies. He saw Taebal. With his eyes he plead with Taebal as his only hope. But Taebal's parents, also noticing, flew onward. If they did not find shelter soon, they too would die.

Taebal watched, helplessly, as the other dragon was overcome by the rapids. He turned to his father, who maintained his course. He looked back upon his parents passing the sea and resuming the flight over land to check on the dragon. He saw the dragon's scales go under, followed by the loudest blast of thunder he had ever heard. Taebal tucked his head in a scar on his father's back, crying softly, as they travelled to the cave that would shortly become their new dwelling.

Taebal's great secret is that he has been plagued by nightmares since that day. He believed he could have saved the other young dragon. In the passage of time he came to realize that his parents saved *him* that day. Until then, he blamed them.

He loved them. He blamed them. He has never felt *whole.*

On this day he is not afraid to die. He is horrified as to the *manner* of his death.

It was the eyes. In the muse's penetrating eyes he sees, surprisingly, much of the same panic so he cannot help but be restless.

As they continue to wander, he promises himself he will maintain his guard at all times, regardless of cost.

He is convinced that there will come a time when *he* is in charge, and whatever he is experiencing now is happening for a *reason*. He is also convinced that once he is able to properly fall asleep the fear, as ever, will plague him in his dreams. The fear is that he is being led to water, and that he too will drown. And, before he goes under, he will look up and see others who could have saved him, but who stayed their course and flew onward. This *will* happen. If not now, or soon, then one day for sure.

He does not know *why,* but of this he has no doubt. None whatsoever.

SOHO ARTS DISTRICT, NEW YORK CITY

When he paints, he dreams. *This one*, he considers, *will become my legendary lost masterpiece.* He considers those who have come before. Artists who, throughout history, *hid* a work that would be *discovered* years later. They all had their reasons: providing for family, the prevailing public sentiment, *legacy...*

His own reasons were not so highfalutin. *This* painting, *this* bit of therapy was for his own edification. It barely took a day to complete; no conceptualization was necessary. He had no idea what would transpire once his brush touched the canvas—and yet he is convinced that this work is his best. He admires the result. *There are no accidents*, he thinks. *I've painted her watching over me all this time and she must have inspired this.*

He will make sure no one sees it for a long while. He is convinced that he's receiving a message and first needs to figure exactly *who* she is. *May take a lifetime*, he considers.

He is quite elated; his sense of accomplishment is substantial. He is also worried. He's considered himself an *intellectual cripple* since his NDA—his *near-death experience*—of last year and has been generally miserable since. Only at work is he able to relax. *This* work. He is a single gay man who has dreaded being by himself since the accident.

He has not been with a man since. He hasn't been with anyone, in fact, since his significant other, scion of a prominent London-based book dealer, perished in a fire months ago. The younger man loved New York and frequented the city for business; once-monthly he would arrive at JFK fully-planned for the week. "Loaded for bear," he would say. In the days following they would spend quality time as a couple hunting for books (the Londoner was the *expert*, Matthius his companion) and then together discover new after-hours haunts.

Matthius thought about his ex frequently but, of late, his deceased cat more so.

Still, today he is experiencing a high that he has not felt since he met the legendary J.R.R. Tolkien so many years ago. Tolkien was his inspiration back then. No longer, apparently.

Guess I graduated.

He remembers the words of Franz Kafka, words to live by: "Don't bend; don't water it down. Don't try to make it logical; don't edit your own soul according to the fashion. Rather, follow your most intense obsessions mercilessly."

He did. Maybe that has something to do with it. He does not generally take to pretension and so prefers to follow his soul. As he always does when painting the face that so haunts him.

These paintings of the *woman*—the eight he has completed so far—will be all for the time being. He returns to his job at the hotel in less than an hour and, until his next week-long vacation, he will no longer have the luxury of basking in these sudden bursts of creativity.

The first painting, more accurately a *paint-over*, came the quickest until this last. He saw her in a photo online, clip art of all things, and appropriated the image as his own. She looked like a model, early to mid-twenties. He would cover her false eyelashes, the lip gloss in as much as he could...add the disquieting red hair that stood out in his quick glimpse of her before the incident with his cat...incorporate in the hair images of paintings, books, and other creation.

But it was the face that so gripped him. Surely, this was *her.* As to the representation, the flaming red hair against the stark, dark background worked best in his opinion. If he had more confidence he would have completed the portrait in a day. It took him two.

For this last painting, he notices a quick touch-up is in order. *Blue.* Then a brush stroke or two of *gray* and a few well-placed scratches of *white* for the foam and...*done. And that's that. It's been real.*

He grabs his suitcase and rushes from the studio apartment. The door locks from the outside. He rushes to catch a bus but then realizes he's forgotten something. He feels his pocket. No phone.

"Shit!"

He turns to head back to the rent-controlled two-story building, but looks at his watch, then to the driver who, without saying a word, gives him what for. She closes the doors and is about to leave.

"Fuck it," he says. He waves to her, signaling his intention. The doors open. He enters. The bus pulls away.

The light turns green at the nearest crosswalk. X patiently watches the bus pass, then crosses the street and heads toward the artist's hovel.

He cracks the lock and enters with caution. He closes the door behind him and stares at the latest painting. The image portrays a dragon, identical in appearance to the young Taebal, fighting crashing waves in the midst of a horrible storm. He appears to be drowning. The faintest image of the muse's eyes watch over him, glaring, superimposed within harsh gray skies.

MIRKWOOD

Taebal's fatigue is perilously close to overwhelming. He will not be able to keep up much longer, but he does not protest. That time is coming and very, very soon.

Meanwhile...

In a castle not very far away, an old, grizzled warrior-king sits on his throne. He is surrounded by stacks of documents. Each contains an irregular placement of symbols carved into the thinly-sliced fatty tissue of slain dragons. One such pictogram reads, skewed to the right-side of tissue:

The documents are protected by a removable covering of the original flesh. Some are partially—or fully—*peeled* from a corner, exposing the *writing*.

Though the symbols are unrecognizable as characters of any known language—in the event of a successful attack against the kingdom these meanings shall *not* be translated—they indeed comprise a language of their own. This language is for his family only and shall remain indecipherable to all others. Eternally.

How it was meant to be.

*Now our seed has been erased. There is no hope for succession, and yet...*He turns past his collection of so-recorded stories and human interaction, to the closest window, peering into a far distance. He regards the dragons, rooted in the gloom above.

Where are they? he wonders. *She should be here.* The pensive king, Eron's father, scratches his long gray beard as he awaits his visitors. *Have my thoughts deceived me? In my vision I was to receive a visitor, and S'n Te said she would bring another.*

The similarities in his look and physique to another *collector,* someone who eons hence will wrenchingly lose a son—his only son—is remarkable. *I am cursed. I am resolved to the Fates. My heir is gone. The world has stopped, and yet I remain, alone, tormented by grief?*

He rubs his face, feeling every line. *How much longer must I suffer?*

BRADLEY AND SON BIBLIOTHEQUE

As Donovan regards his younger, handsome self, he instinctively rubs his face, feeling every wrinkle, every nook. The lines run deep. *How much longer must I suffer,* he thinks.

"May I see my quarters?"

Donovan snaps out of his trance, turns and forces a smile upon the younger writer. "Is everything okay?"

Thomas digs for the most apt response. "Peachy."

The old man is confused. "I'm afraid I'm not familiar..."

"Forget it. My daughter. She's fine...or so she tells me." Donovan is unaware though he nods in approval.

"Hmm," he says.

"May we continue?"

"Are you sure? We can always—"

Thomas bristles. "I've come a long way and frankly, right now, I'm not sure of anyth—"

"Follow me."

~~~

They descend the spiral stairs into the basement. Bradley grips tightly and nervously onto the bannister. As Thomas turns his head and observes the old man's trepidation, he is assured a fall is inevitable. The writer steels himself, just in case.

"A contemporary author such as Rowling is a rare thing," Donovan decrees, as if speaking to an audience from a stage. "Excuse my fervor but her prose has influenced the world. These kids who ten, fifteen years from now will be responsible for upholding our laws, running our governments...so many of them would have never dreamed of opening a book on their own. She touched upon something, that one."

"And now they're inspired to be wizards, that it?"

"In a matter of speaking." affirms Donovan.

"I agree. It'd be a pleasant change having educated adults running our governments."

Donovan ignores the remark. "Like your old *Star Treks*, remember? What's a cellphone, really, but—what did they call it back then?—a *communicator*? Our best speculative fiction inspires the creation of our greatest technological advances." He pauses. "It's the horrors I rarely bother with. Too dangerous for the more fragile truth-seekers among us, I believe." He's again testing the younger man, who doesn't respond. Dismayed by the lack of a retort, Donovan summarizes his thought. "If stories don't dictate our course, I don't know what—"

"I'd like to believe our future is dictated by our present. And our present, the past. And the past...the far past is irretrievable. Beyond recorded history and the earliest surviving documents...anything prior must be considered nothing more than a game of *Telephone* until proven otherwise."

"I know Telephone! Ha! The memories. I used to play this game with my schoolmates when I was a lad." He shakes his head in a wave of nostalgia. "Telephone—Splendid!" In his excitement he releases the bannister and grabs Thomas' shoulder for support. "I acknowledge, my dear McFee, the words of our earliest oral storytellers have been re-told and translated over so many generations. By the time they were immortalized in writing, their original forms and meanings surely were lost. I agree with you. I further acknowledge the Library of Alexandria fire in 48 B.C. destroyed much of *those* early writings, but so what? There's nothing we can do about that now. My life-long mission has been to salvage whatever knowledge we have left from the refuse heap, and discover our truths from there."

"Too many variables." replies Thomas McFee cryptically. "I have to admit though I expected more from you than *so what—*"

"Say again?" Donovan pauses.

"No difference. I believe you speak to my point. The world's shaped on a foundation of fantasy."

Donovan is amused. "Perhaps. Do you believe in the collective unconscious?" he asks, attempting to distract them both. "You may as well answer because I have nothing better to do until I get downstairs."

"I trust in the human condition." Thomas McFee slows in his descent as he responds. "Archetypes, primality—all that pretension I tend to toss out the window. If that's where we're headed."

"Pretension?" Donovan raises his eyebrows.

"Was it Hawking who said that God is an invention for those who are afraid of the dark?"

"It may very well have been. Would you agree with him then, Mr. McFee?" They have almost reached the bottom. Six steps left.

Which could take thirty minutes at this pace.

"I know the dark exists; that much I'm sure of. Or our perception of it anyway. I can prove to myself that I can't see in the dark."

"You don"t think this a bit cynical?"

"Every species shares experiences common to itself," Thomas responds, with a shrug. "But can anyone explain it all, really?"

"You didn't answer the question."

"I'm an agnostic Republican," replies Thomas as Donovan chuckles. "Clearly I don't have the answers either so who am I to say?"

They leave the last stair and step into the basement.

"There's nothing more hellish than attempting to grasp the inexplicable," Thomas adds, as awed as he was when he arrived.

Donovan drops and extends his hand, inviting Thomas to freely explore his new surroundings. The desk, the documents, the cobwebs even. Here, in this new environment, everything within eye-range represents an attempt—or an opportunity—to lurk among the shadows...and prove to Thomas that he could, indeed, see in the dark.

"Well, then—" says the writer.

Donovan once again places his hand on Thomas" shoulder, cutting him off. "Welcome to hell," responds Donovan.

MIRKWOOD

The king sits, gazing through his elevated throne room's window to a gray smokestack in the far distance. *The dragons have come yet again*, he thinks as he mourns the loss of his only child and heir. *It's been barely a fortnight since they took his life and they will not allow me even the dignity to mourn.* He watches passively as the smoke rises still higher. *Will this madness ever end?*

He had been warned of the tragedy in vision, *witnessing* his son's extraordinary battle from the vantage of a mountaintop and perspective of another's eyes.

Surely he will dream no longer.

The king has lost his hope. The expected visitors have not arrived.

As he can no longer look forward, he looks back.

Back to his recent, desperate efforts to save the life of his son...

The king waits. All is still. S'n Te had warned him of the cessation; but all the same, the absolute calm is maddening. "Compose for me then," *S'n Te requested.* "Compose for me this fear your tongue cannot articulate."

He had prepared; he shows the mystic:

"I am plagued by visions. What you see—" He extends his arm towards other etchings. "What you see is from the record following an unbearable loss."

"These are Eron's?" S'n Te asks.

"The skins had been given to me by my son following his conquests. The composition is ours together though this one has troubled me greatly from the beginning and I have not received another since—"

"You wrestle with the essence of tragedy," S'n Te replies, nodding gravely. "The unknown. Your son is a most courageous and skilled warrior." *He ignores the documents. "And you seek to reconcile your expectations while you have the capacity to do so. This is natural."*

"But I have lost men before. You must tell me, is he next?"

The mystic is taken aback. "My role is to advise you, not to convince you to alter your course of action."

"You must tell me!"

S"n Te is not used to such displays of vulnerability, particularly from the king. He trembles as he informs him: "Should Mirkwood lose its future king to the fire-breathers...the immortal who watches over him most certainly will suffer as do you."

"To every man an immortal, S'n Te. Even in death." The king calms. "The natural order of things has always been thus. The immortals neither abandon those they lead nor do they grieve as we."

"You are correct, of course," replies the sage.

The king regards S'n Te with skepticism. "But you are convinced. How do you know this?"

The mystic pauses. He is pondering an escape from the query yet does not betray his intention.

"I resign to my intuition," he says. "You are correct, save for this: If not for your son's god-given gifts, he would have been extinguished long ago. Lately he is getting...sloppy. I sense a very dangerous distraction."

The king is resigned. "You have answered my question."

"And you have displayed weakness!" S'n Te scolds. "You have yet to master your sensitivities. They will be your undoing but for now—"

"She will come."

S'n Te smiles to break the tension, and detaches the document. The king does not stop him. "And then you impress me, dear King." S'n Te holds up the writing. "The distraction is mutual, and my best assumption is indeed, she shall act upon her grief. A...temporal event of some duration, at the precise moment of your son's passing and I ask you, who but an immortal possesses the power to reset the pulse of the world?"

"The Abeyance you infer is an invention of our scops..."

"You do not extend their due," S'n Te advises. He regards the king's symbols with amusement. "You compose as the minions on cave walls, in sign. Only the characters differ—"

"Each symbol, a word..." says the king.

"I sense that soon the storytellers you so insult will share your compulsion and etch their tales for permanence, in their own syntax, if they have not already—"

"But that would be unlawful."

"Righteous intent be damned, have you not broken your own law?" The king doesn't respond.

"You enforce a position of universal tongue only to tighten your grip over those you rule." He turns his back on the king, testing him. "The most truthful of the scops will become immortalized as masters of invention. They will build new worlds, all under her influence, and by so doing new beliefs, which will not and cannot be contained. Their carvings will be adapted as speech which itself will spawn new marks that eventually will be too numerous for any one man to master, empowering them beyond—"

"She will come to see me..." the king realizes.

"...their mortal binds. It is they—not any royal bloodliner—who will influence our direction, insofar as they themselves are manipulated...by this corrupted muse." S'n Te again faces the king, continuing to hold the document as if he is awaiting permission. Or judgment. The king nods. He can keep it. *"She will not be alone..."* the mystic confirms.

"Eron requires your help."

"This is against the will of the gods. I cannot interfere any further!"

"This is a direct order. You must build Eron a device, a gauntlet, that can defeat the dragons once and for all. You must save the life of my son!"

An unsettled S'n Te realizes a continued argument with the king is not in his best interest. *"Eron shall have his weapon, my Lord,"* he submits. He bows to memorialize his promise. S'n Te leaves the castle, head nestled in the hood of his robe. He scrolls the king's document as he walks toward the mountains, considering this most troubling matter.

The onset of dusk turns to an overcast dawn. S'n Te has been walking the night through. He arrives at his destination. S'n Te stands above a hole in the ground—a passage—large enough to contain the shoulder-to-shoulder width of an average-sized man. The hole is fitted covered entirely in copper, including a handle for lift and entry.

He elects to walk onward, barely four hundred paces past it. S'n Te has made his decision.

Once his shadow looms against fallen rock, at the base of the largest mountain, he stops and peeks back to make sure he is safely out of range of the kingdom.

He is.

The mystic adjusts his stance and lowers his head. He methodically raises the king's scroll to the sky and holds it until a dragon wail reverberates from the mountains. First comes the cry of one dragon, then *another. And another. Satisfied, he points the scroll in the direction of the castle as a dragon swarm rises behind him.*

Taebal sees the faraway castle as a wayfarer glimpses Mirkwood's kingdom from a distant shore. The haze of barely-penetrable fog obscures his view. They pass flooded, dank swamps littered with the viscera of deceased warriors both human and dragon. Their path has been long and will continue for longer still. Treeless miles of plain grass and mountains abound. The castle, though, is in sight. The dragon sees that he will follow her to that battle-scarred domain ahead. They will face whatever happens when they get there.

Taebal will determine the course of events. He holds the weapon. Not her. Though he does not comprehend why she allows his guardianship, he will, so long as he can, maintain possession of the sweord.

"An Undisclosed Location," London, England

Samantha peers across the room to her fiancé, who sits on the ground cross-legged as Marlo and another group of children—again—listen to his stories. "He knows nothing," she says to Brikke.

"Why should I believe you?"

Frustration mounts. She pinches the bridge of her nose with her thumb and forefinger. "I'm willing to talk. I'm not the poster child for third-degrees."

"Well then?"

She stares at him before giving in. "Because otherwise I'd be considered a threat to national security, as if you didn't know."

"Doesn't mean I trust you."

"I'm not asking you to trust me."

"May I speak plainly?"

"I can't stop you." Brikke glances at Daniel. As before, Marlo rolls her eyes while the others, in wheelchairs, laugh.

"Such a shame," Brikke relays. "He makes them forget about their fright—as I'm sure he does you. If you lose him, what's left?"

"Bigger pricks have pried me for information. They couldn't break me either"

"Watch him," Brikke advises. She complies with some difficulty though she manages to keep the straight face. "He once told me he wanted nothing more than to be a dad." Samantha strives to maintain her cool. Though Brikke is pushing her buttons, they both know he's right. "They adore him. A born scop and a natural father. You haven't had that since you were a child." She looks away. "Don't you think, if the opportunity arose with someone else—"

"What do you want?" Samantha demands.

Brikke pulls back. "Let me be clear. The next time—"

"The next time?"

"We may not be so generous with our warnings."

"*We?*"

"Myself. The girl—"

"I assume I couldn't stop either of you if it came down to it, now could I? I couldn't before."

"We've hacked into your hard drive in the past, but we were locked out during the Abeyance. How?" The news report airs in the background. X is still onscreen. "He can"t run forever."

"Not unheard of in these parts," she deadpans. "He had nothing to do with any—"

"He's a truth-seeker, he disseminates dangerous information but he's never bothered to explain the pending...war." Samantha looks to the ground. "Otherwise, what do we know, really? The public ridicules him and yet he's the most wanted man in the world right now. Meaning, he's not nearly as innocent as you say he is, and I want to know what you're both hiding and why." Samantha looks back up and glares at him in defense. "In the meantime, you want to save your fiancé?" Brikke pushes. He leans in to her; her back is against the wall. "I want that gauntlet." Sam is shocked. "Oh, don't be so surprised," he adds. "I always know more than I let on. You of all people should remember this."

"You're making a big mistake. He's not holding anything back. Why would he possibly risk—"

"You know what to do."

Daniel looks up. He is unclear as to 'fiancé's body language and attempts to capture her conversation. He is tugged on his sleeve by a young boy.

"Finish!" implores the child.

"Come on!" says another, as a distracted Daniel forces a smile and—for the moment—gives in. "You can''t hear them anyway," he adds, as Samantha and Brikke continue their tete-a-tete.

"No," Sam answers softly. "As I've told you, he's done nothing." She peeks over towards Daniel. "Thank God for those kids."

"He's coded your program," Brikke continues, "so the rest of us could no longer access the report. His talents must be utilized. He will need to be protected."

"You have a warped sense of justice, don''t you think?"

"I will not *deliver* him. I will attempt to *turn* him, to set him free. I alone will be responsible for the gauntlet. It will be out of his hands, as is the sweord. One is useless without the other. Together—"

As he again gets close, Samantha spits in his face. Brikke's gesture was not misinterpreted. "Where is the sweord?"

Brikke eyeballs her. He turns to Daniel, who, engaged as he is with the children does not notice. Or so Brikke believes. Brikke casually lifts his hand to wipe his eye. "Let me remind you," he seethes, "that this world and those in it are molded in shades of gray. There is no such thing as purely evil or purely good. There are reasons for everything."

"No."

He turns his back to her, facing Daniel's direction, whispering, "If you don"t deliver him to me, then here's your option. If you rest on your pride, you lose not only your fiancé, your father, your dog—"

"And if I do? Deliver—"

Brikke smiles. "You buy time. And we figure out a strategy to escape from this rut."

Daniel excuses himself and stands. He straightens his shirt and, sternly, approaches his fiancé.

"Did Ara send you here? For the gauntlet? For Daniel *?*" she asks, before he gets there.

"Worse," Brikke answers. "You did. Only, poor girl, you don"t yet know it." Police officers arrive, wearing gloves, body protectors and gas masks. They inform the staff of the end of the shutdown, and of the beginning of decontamination procedures. Brikke disregards them, and concludes his moment with Sam. "It's no different than before. We didn't trust one another back then either so I ask you now, for the final time: Where do you stand, *Ms. McF—*"

"Sam." Daniel angrily takes her by the arm. "This conversation's over."

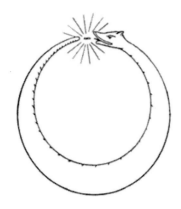

CONVERGENCE

ADIRONDACK NATIONAL PARK, UPSTATE, NEW YORK

Fresh, misty air, mountains for miles and astounding greenery—of no importance whatsoever. He lurks, where he is most comfortable, in the gloom.

Or, maybe *comfortable* is not the right word. Maybe *confident*. On second thought, he does prefer the latter.

More accurate. I think I think too damn much.

Typewriter keys strike paper:

An Open Letter to the Media

You know...

He does not proceed. He's not in the frame of mind to write any further. For now. His new communication must still go out later today for beginning-of-the-week delivery. There is no mailbox for miles but that's become a regularly-resolved quandary. As planned, the letter will run in Monday's print *New York Tribune*, where he has lately morphed from ridiculed cult-figure (who has regularly popped sales) to the far more titillating *international fugitive* (who has nearly doubled circulation). The new entry, as typical, will be published concurrently on the *Tribune's* website. The search engines will then pick up *X's* message which will go viral by Tuesday; this time, bigger than ever to be sure considering recent events. Several online science journals will likewise reprint the letter but continue to lambast him…no matter; it's the exposure that counts.

He is honest—Professor Searle's favorite word when describing his protege—in his intentions.

How foolishly lofty, he reflects. *An honest fugitive with noble intent trapped into exile by the very people he alone has the ability to save. I'd see that movie.*

In this regard, Samantha was right.

~~~

Snail mail is always X's first step, sent from different boxes based on his location. Final effort is to copy, paste and e-blast—in the body of the email—from existing web carriers to intended sites who still ignore his words once the letter has already multiplied, exponentially, online.

For that, he discreetly breaks into homes and uses other people's devices (from which he also plans and executes his hacks) as he does not own one himself. He never steals computers because the ISP numbers would give him away.

This way, he earns the time to escape the scene, rendering him nearly impossible to track as his messages are successfully placed.

He will relegate his message on those high-traffic sites—that do not legitimately publish him—to the *Disqus* or comment sections of existing articles, frequently above and/or below those for money-making schemes and mind-blowing sexual kinks.

Whatever it takes to make sure everyone is properly warned.

I've come too far. Bully for me.

When not running, he gets bored easily and most frequently daydreams of sleep. He's safest there, where he can escape from reality and dwell in a world of Lewis Carroll-type nonsense. He is a long-time fan of Carroll's, one of his very favorite authors. He's long admired him for his particular ability to convert inexplicable nonsense into accessible entertainments and, as such, attaining a rarefied influence. X's words are not meant for entertainment purposes, though if he could *get through* to his readers like the author did to his, he believes he would be taken more seriously by those who still doubt him:

The majority.

During those rare instances when X does not daydream, his human interaction is limited to practicing street magic on unsuspecting insolvents. He"ll draw his crowd, including the occasional cop, and by so doing effectively remain in the public eye.

TIMES SQUARE, NEW YORK, NEW YORK, YESTERDAY

"Hold the cup," X requests.

"Coffee?" The homeless man, once a poet, has no legs. He's filthy; on an average day, very few would go anywhere near him.

Today is not an average day. A crowd begins to form, beginning with a husband and wife, who wave their friends over, who in turn...

X ignores them. He's not impolite. He's keeping with his focus. The homeless man motions to sip the coffee, but is stopped. "Is it not good?" the vagrant asks.

"It's delicious." Some of the growing crowd laughs. Others are disgusted. X places his hand under the cup.

"You"re taking it from me?" asks the homeless man.

"I wouldn't do that to you. Keep your eyes on the cup." X rubs it and coins overflow from its top. The crowd is aghast.

The homeless man, at first silenced, cries out in elation. X stands. Many applaud. As he walks on, he cherishes the response. A rare feel-good moment. The trick was simple and has become a staple on television magic specials. The coins were in the cup all along, pushed upward and over the minimal amount of coffee from a simple break and press of his finger underneath.

X loves magic. The world of illusion holds a peculiar, almost fetishistic fascination for him, as he believes everything is illusory anyway. But with magic, if he sees a trick performed once, he figures out its secret within a minute. X's primary interest lies not in the strength of the individual illusion, however, but in the passion of that audience response.

'They are so easily fooled,' X thinks, as always.

He turns away and walks on, hiding in plain sight.

ADIRONDACK NATIONAL PARK, UPSTATE, NEW YORK

The area in which he hides is no larger than an average two-car garage. Exposed wiring dangles dim lightbulbs from the electricity he's managed to generate so far. The typewriter is evenly balanced on a base of rocks, supported in its middle by a block of wood under the keyboard that has been wedged between stone. The walls and floor are predominantly sediment. An old metal folding chair is embedded into the sand below where to its right rests his raggedy travel sack, which only partially hides the gauntlet.

His mindset changes, several times daily usually, regarding the device. He will keep it here, safely hidden in a special spot, when he hitches into the city. Or he will bring it wherever he goes.

He'll regret either decision without fail.

Thankfully, though, the usual concern is not a concern at this moment. X stands and shadowboxes to keep the blood flowing.

Mentally and physically exhausted, he decides to check out the day.

He takes to an iron stepladder and enters a tunnel. He reaches the end and wedges a familiar copper, pothole-like cover up and aside. As he slowly sticks out his head and peeks around, he shields his eyes from a blazing morning sun and opines that he is likely the only human present for miles.

Or whatever reasonable equivalent, he considers, half-serious.

~~~

All he perceives are the mountains and canyons that surround him.

There's nothing in the skies either. Not a copter or plane in sight. Or a dragon, for that matter. He runs his hand over the copper cover, recalling the name he asterisked in his notes when he last hacked into Samantha McFee's confidential document. This was the entity he believes is responsible for his current station. And, where there is responsibility, there is *reason.*

S'n Te. He has done his homework and comprised a rough translation: *Mage of the Mountain.*

X takes the chance and exits the hovel.

As he steps outside, he immediately tenses upon realizing something he had not previously considered—

I'm pretty damn far from New York City.

He looks back to the tunnel below, then again up and around before focusing on a soaring black bird, none too far away.

"That a raven?" he asks himself. The bird comes closer. "That's a raven..."

No shit...

"You're not supposed to be—"

As if summoned, the creature lands on a rock. It sits and silently observes the awestruck boy—the attention is mutual, as it appears is the question of the other's presence—and a few seconds later abruptly flies away.

X watches as it goes. He shakes his head. *How did we get here?* he ponders. And then he briefly considers his new *toy*, the gauntlet...and just as quickly dismisses *that* intrusive and incomprehensibly horrifying thought.

Dismisses, that is, in favor of another:

But this is not the first time I've been here...

TIMES SQUARE, NEW YORK, NEW YORK, YESTERDAY

X wanders off and the vagabond cherishes his windfall. Another transient, who had been watching from a safe distance alongside a nearby bricked supermarket, nervously deliberates. He approaches, cautiously.

"Hey," he says, tapping X's shoulder.

X turns, startled, then looks the transient over.

"Please don't touch me."

The transient removes his hand. "Matthew was wrong."

"Do I know you?" X asks suspiciously.

"I sleep there." He points to the opposite side of the building from where he had been hiding.

"Usually..."

"I do know you. You were wandering the streets the day the bodies were found in the subway. What did you just say to me?"

"Matthew was wrong."

"I remember, you said that then."

The vagrant regards him with pleading eyes. "No one believes me. They all think I'm crazy."

X nods. "I've been there."

"What day is today?" the vagrant asks.

"Monday."

"No, I mean—what date?"

"April 14."

"And-"

"2015."

"Do you know what tonight is?"

"I'm sure you gonna tell me."

"Tonight is blood moon." he tests. "Lunar eclipse. First of four. The evangelicals say it's the end of the world. What does that mean to you?"

"Do you believe that?"

"They''re close."

X becomes irritated. "What does that mean, 'They''re close'?"

The vagrant grins. "Time doesn't exist. Matthew 25:13 warned you. He said, 'Watch therefore, for you know neither the day nor the hour...'" I watch."

"Apologize to him for me."

"But he was wrong about something else. The Bible was close to the evangelical version but it's not the red moon that matters. Promise to listen?"

"Not promising a damn thing."

"Like the evangelicals," the vagrant continues. "They listen to no one but themselves. Do you know why Matthew was wrong?" When he opens his mouth and smiles, X notices his missing teeth. Save for his crooked two front bottoms, there are none remaining.

"Why?"

"You know why. I know you. It's not the moon they—or you—should be worried about. Did I just tell you that?"

As the vagrant makes sense of his ramblings, X spots a contingent several yards away, staring, but not at him. The other vagabond, newly-flush, untapes his bent legs from behind him, manages to balance first on his knees, crumble and toss away his black tape restraints. He straightens, stands, and walks away counting his coin.

"Friend of yours?" X asks of the other.

"Yes."

"Come with me."

~~~

Several blocks uptown, traversing 72nd Street. "I'll buy you a pack." he says to the vagrant, both now far away from the crowd that just minutes earlier applauded X's efforts.

"Don"t smoke."

"A beer?"

"Don"t drink. Ain"t I got enough to handle without losing control?"

X stops. "Where do you live?"

"I told you—"

"No. No bullshit. Where?"

"I told you where." The transient faces X, taking offense. "He's a friend, yeah, he is. A group of 'em, they run ads—"

"Where?"

"What?"

"Where do they run ads?"

"Craigslist." He takes note of the skepticism. "Actors Wanted. They stand on my street corner, collect my money, give a percentage of their commission to the nutsack who hired them. Big business. No wonder I'm always broke." X's forehead crinkles. "Ever notice every day has a different vagrant standing on the same corner?"

"No."

"Shifts. Look, I used to have a computer too. I wasn't always homeless."

X refocuses the conversation. "You said he was your friend."

"You have any idea how lonely it can get out here without anyone else to talk to?"

"You just asked me if I noticed the different people—"

"That guy works full-time. He's there twice a week."

A brief staredown, and X gives way. "Why''d you follow me?"

"I didn't. I live near here."

"Why''re you with me now?

"Because you asked me to follow you."

"Was that a foregone conclusion?"

"What do you think? I can out-wrestle you and turn you in right now."

"Why was Matthew wrong?"

"Who?" And then, as if suddenly remembering—or conning—the transient's eyes widen, and he panics. "Matthew! Matthew was wrong!" X is taken aback by the sudden change of mood. "Why did you ask me, we were getting along so well!" The transient backs away. "No. I told you he was wrong. Matthew, the evangelicals—the Bible—all wrong and you don't believe me!" He turns and runs, as quickly and as far away as he can, nearly getting hit by a taxi as he crosses the street.

The cabbie stops short in a screech of brakes and jumps from his vehicle.

"He didn't believe me!" screams the vagrant.

Meantime, the cabbie's raring to go, to fight the son of a bitch he could have killed. The vagrant, however, is already well out of sight. The cabbie is short of stature, perhaps five-eight, 50-60 pounds overweight and about 70-ish years old. Caucasian, mustachioed, with a full head of died-black hair.

NEW YORK, NEW YORK, 1970

Tolkien and Donovan grasp their respective door handles in the back seat of a taxi, as the cab speedily accelerates from JFK International Airport onto the Belt Parkway, Brooklyn's major thoroughfare. Donovan turns to the author.

"We can still call for the limo service I planned. I can ask—" They hit a bump. "I can ask him to drop us off back at the terminal—"

"Nothing doing," Tolkien replies. "When in Rome..."

Donovan looks to the driver. He's young, almost a kid.

"Can you please slow down?"

He's ignored. It's nothing intentional. The driver is intently focused.

"Why worry?" Tolkien asks. "We"ll get there."

"It's the 'in one piece" part of the equation I"m worried about. Boy!" The driver turns. Short in stature, caucasian, black hair. "Sir?"

"How old are you boy?"

"How old am I? Why do you ask?"

"Is this your first job?"

The driver smiles. "How did you know? My dad got it for me, and—"

"That's quite all right. May I ask you a favor?"

"What's that, sir?""

"My associate and I would appreciate it if we could survive this journey. Would you mind slowing down?"

"Was I going too fast?"

Donovan bites his lip. "No. I just wanted to start conversation."

The driver does not process the sarcasm. "What is it you would like to talk about?"

"Did you think that if you engage me you will get a larger tip?"

"I would hope so, sir." No guile, no attempt at deceit.

"Never mind," Donovan says.

Tolkien laughs. "I heard New Yorkers were a dangerously honest lot."

Donovan nods his head, reluctantly accepting the present circumstance. He looks at his watch. "If we get to the city alive, we should be at the hotel within the hour."

Tolkien slaps Donovan's knee. "Settle down." He smiles at the blaring car horns from the next lane over, and the exchange of flashing middle fingers. The drivers'' windows are up so their curses are muted. The author laughs as they speed over another bump...which really is no bump at all.

~~~

It's a jolt. Turbulence. The men have yet to arrive in New York City though they are not far; they are still over 20,000 feet above ground.

"I'm having a grand old time!" Tolkien exults, as the clouds below part during a fit of rough air. Donovan jumps from his nap. The antiquarian blinks rapidly to clear his vision, and he checks the spellbound author. "Time to take a bite of the Apple," Tolkien adds, softly, without turning his head from the window.

But the author cannot help but be bittersweet. *Edith, my dear, if only you were here...*

From the cockpit: "Gentlemen, please fasten your seatbelts as we begin our final descent into JFK. It's gonna be a little choppy."

Professor Tolkien doesn't hear the announcement. He remains glued to the window, captivated by the sprawl below. Donovan observes his travel companion with both idolatry and envy. *As if the plane ride isn't enough,* he ruminates, *within the hour I will be riding with John Ronald Reuel Tolkien in a limousine in New York City.* He peers over Tolkien's shoulder. *I could have sworn I got off the LSD nine years ago.* All the while Tolkien sits and stares, his sense of wonder remarkably vibrant for a man approaching 80. *I'm still hallucinating,* Donovan concludes. He motions over the lone flight attendant.

"Can I get a good stiff drink before we land?" he asks.

One hour later. In the limo. Mid-town.

"When I was first informed of the *Beowulf* documents, Professor, I—"

"Bradley, old boy, please understand that these days it takes a virtual act of God to separate me from my dear Edith. Even if only for the week."

"I don't quite know how to take that, Professor. Do you have regrets?"

"I am complimenting you, Bradley. Congratulations on your conviction. It is quite contagious."

"I'm at a loss, Professor," Donovan stammers.

"This, coupled with your stellar reputation," Tolkien compliments, "makes me quite hopeful." Donovan smiles, properly gratified. Tolkien turns to the passing New York streets. "I would be an old fool, Tolkien considers, before correcting himself—"Okay, I *am* an old fool, but I must admit to having a time processing the geography of this city." He is disarmed by the lights, the sounds, the noise. "How I wish she was here to see this. She was willing. But, alas, she was not healthy enough to travel...Tell me, is all of America this flamboyant?" Tolkien asks, innocently.

"I imagine not," replies Donovan with a smile.

"I am not very inclined to travel, much like my hobbits. But, I believe now that we've made it here, safe and sound..."

They pass a hooker arguing with her pimp. Donovan is embarrassed. "I anticipate no problem, Professor."

"I will be at your disposal, Mr. Bradley." He's a bit distracted but quickly gathered. "We"ll have plenty of time to study and discuss *Beowulf* together, I am sure." They turn a corner. To Tolkien's perspective, every store in the vicinity displays its name in impossibly-glowing neon. Donovan points ahead to the epicenter of Times Square and its brilliantly-illuminated tron. "Oh my," gasps Tolkien. "I must say, I find this fair city morbidly fascinating but couldn't imagine living here."

"No?"

They slow to a crawl. Smoke rises from a pothole, dead ahead. Tolkien's fascination abruptly turns to disapproval, and not because of the city workers enabling the gridlock.

He notices something troubling, just beyond the roundabout. The frontispiece of *Ralph's Camera Store* hosts a three-dimensional, lenticular-type recreation of one of history's most well-known photographs: *Life Magazine's* 1945 V-J Day photo of the sailor kissing his woman in this very area.

Times Square, a lifetime ago.

It's not the image itself that bothers him so; it's the *manipulation* of the image, as the lenticular version alters from black and white photo-real to a colorized bastardization of the *woman holding the sailor.* And back again. *There and back again.* And again. And again.

"Dear me." Tolkien shakes his head in disapproval. "I shudder to consider the manipulation of history thirty years hence."

Donovan attempts to re-focus the conversation. "It's been a pleasure getting to know you, Professor Tolkien. But Sir, please..." Tolkien turns his way. "A few moments ago you honored me though understand it is I who is at your disposal."

Tolkien becomes calm and offers a comforting smile. "I had hoped for that response."

"Is there anything I can do for you now, before we get to the hotel? I trust you will find the sleeping accommodations at the Algonquin as sublime as their cuisine."

Tolkien thinks the question through. "Perhaps we can start with canceling those dinner reservations, Mr. Bradley."

He knocks on the divider. After a moment, the limo turns into an alley before backing up for a quick U-turn...

Ten minutes past the hour, the limo is parked on a side street. Its lights are off, so as not to cause attention. Inside, a box of pizza lies on Tolkien's lap. He is utterly triumphant as he eats.

"Magnificent!" he says. "Ha! Magnificent! New York pizza is everything they say and more." He finishes his slice with one more bite and grabs another. He carefully but sloppily folds the piece as cheese and oil leak to the sides. He hands the sauce sandwich to a none-too-willing Donovan. "Please."

Donovan studies the mess before taking his first bite, hiding his bitter disappointment at the sudden alteration of his meticulously-planned evening.

"Oh, how I love this fair city," Tolkien cheers.

"An Undisclosed Location," London, England

Four dedicated portable decontamination cylinders have been erected throughout the inside perimeter, respectively denoted *Patients,*

Staff, Visitors, and *Emergency Personnel.* Separate lines form in front of each unit. Emergency crews escort the less- or non-ambulatory patients to their markers.

Daniel stands behind Sam. He stares at an increasingly unnerved Brikke standing directly across from him—on the line to his left—but does not say a word.

Brikke does not return his glare though he does sense it and suppresses a growing compulsion to respond. Instead, he remains obdurate and focused straight ahead, to where medical staff is administering blood tests following completion of decon. This he had not anticipated.

"It's been a day, huh?" Sam cautiously offers, before leaning over and kissing Daniel on the cheek. A weak effort to evade any questions.

"Is that the best you can do?" Daniel blurts.

Or any trouble. What Samantha is certain of is that she is neither looking forward to tonight's drive home, nor the surprisingly fast shortening of the line on which she herself stands. "Maybe you should go ahead of me?" she asks.

Immediately suspicious, Daniel takes his eyes off Brikke. "I don't think so."

THE STRAND BOOKSTORE, DOWNTOWN, NEW YORK CITY

Discreet in a backwards *Yankees* cap, hood down, X becomes just another New York Soho-ite skimming *miles and miles of books* on a Wednesday Wall Street lunch hour. No different than most shops near the downtown financial district, restaurant overflow spills into this one as a panorama of suits and fashionistas give up on the long eatery lines and run away anywhere else. Now, they're here for books. Or to be noticed.

They'll grab their food later.

Sometimes, neighborhood bums like X drop by and hang because the library is too fucking quiet.

Lunch. The busiest time of the day to be a downtown New York book buyer.

~~~

X adores bookstores. He remains especially comforted by the musty smell of the older books, which he has associated for much of his life with an unsuccessful decomposition of eternal mind and history. Unsuccessful and eternal because "words and ideas will never die as long as we continue to ingest them," a pithy statement he frequently makes to those on the street less fortunate than he. With the joyful response to his magic tricks comes such wisdom and naturally so; though dependent on his mood, which can certainly detract. X is disposed to offer hope to the hopeless whenever he is emotionally free to do so.

Though he's been *one of them*—the derelicts, the hopeless—when he repeats this philosophy of late he is bold-faced lying. His work continues to prove, to his chagrin, that the concepts of *eternal mind and history*, indeed, have a shelf-life.

He'll continue to repeat the words, however, to comfort those he figures need to be comforted. Most will be street people, and most of them will snicker behind his back. Especially those who respond to the *craigslist* ads.

Very few realize his *heart* when they mock him. Even less care.

X knows the deal. He may be complex, he may be guilty of many crimes—as most would consider his day-to-day affairs—but he considers himself a good guy. If he becomes a *bad guy*, it's only because he's been driven in that direction.

He misses the days of the independent brick-and mortar-booksellers. So many literary-minded *mom and pop* shops were forced to shut down when the economy crashed. The Strand is one of the few left in New York and he cherishes his infrequent visits.

"The big chains miss the point," he once had said to Searle. *"Reading's not meant to be a communal experience. Reading should be a private matter."*

"What do you mean, 'private?'"

He contemplated his response before answering. *"I look at a dirty book, I don't want to be ashamed. Know what I mean?"*

He never looked at "dirty books," but Searle got his point.

"The customers could still look over your shoulder, you know," Searle countered, before a sudden wash of curiosity got the better of him. *"Chains don't sell dirty books now. I don't think…"* He was unsuccessful in fighting his curiosity for too long. *"Do they, though? I get everything on my tablet so I really have no idea…"*

"Do 'any' corporations respect the spiritual connection between the product and the consumer?"

Searle didn't expect a direct response. *"Getting religious on me?"*

"I said 'spiritual.' The chains will get theirs one day. Watch." X was like that and still is. High-minded, concerned, indignant when moved to speak up. More often than not he keeps his opinions to himself, except when they're related to his work.

In that latter circumstance, he doesn't know when to quit.

~~~

Upstairs and down, X traverses the shop's selection as one would eye-candy. Early-editions of work by his favorite authors are here, notably those whose bleaker writings have influenced his studies. New books are here too; but the older ones, especially the signed volumes that long-deceased authors have actually touched, are for X the most special of all.

Today, though, is a day for bibles. *Too bad*, he thinks, *I can't find a signed one of those.*

"Matthew was wrong! Matthew was wrong!" X has been unable to simply discard the words as he would smoke from the occasional, troubling cigarette puff. The vagrant was onto something, he suspects. No, he *knows.* He has no clue, however, precisely what passage the nut was warning him about.

"Wrong about what?" X asks himself. "What?"

He grabs a *King James*, sits cross-legged on the floor and leans his back against a shelf. As he peruses, he dog-ears several pages—folding a triangular sliver atop various pages of interest—while searching for the passage in question.

"I'm sorry, sir." X looks up. "We don't allow sitting on the floor." The employee smirks. Very early-twenties, male. "Fire hazard." He holds under his arm a stack of books to be re-shelved. On the top is something that catches X's eye. The boy stands, and points.

"Are those going back on the shelf?" As he asks, he pockets the Bible.

"These? Yeah."

"Can I see that one?"

"Which?"

"That one right there. On the top..."

The employee peeks at the cover as he hands the book over. "Peter Levin? I've not heard of this author. Familiar with his work?"

"No. Mind if I hold on to it for a minute?"

"Go ahead. You just lightened my load. Probably a self-published thing. We get those all the time in here. Are you interested in self-publishing?"

"No."

"Anything else I can help you with?"

"No. Thanks."

They nod, and the employee goes back to work. X examines the cover: *My Week with Tolkien.* He pockets this tome as well and casually leaves the store.

~~~

X walks, calmly, toward the nearest subway station. The air is crisp, offering brief moments of whistling wind and biting cool amidst the melodic scatter of falling leaves and, pulling it all together, the embrace of a forgiving, modest sun. He loves these harmonious New York autumns, when the unpredictability of the weather and the crunch of grounded red leaves align perfectly with the turmoil of his own inner symphony.

He looks up; not a cloud in sight. *Magnificent,* he thinks. *Just an amazing day.* He turns away from the train station, feeling pretty damn positive—for a change—and instead heads uptown on the power of his stride. *Exercise won't kill me any sooner.*

As he walks, however—passing the shops, the smoke rising from open potholes and the litany of parked cabs—as is typical of his troubled soul he begins to question his uncharacteristically positive outlook. *It's all good, though. I like this feeling.*

"I like this feeling, but I don't know why I feel this way," he says to himself. "Something's not right..."

X suddenly becomes fearful. When he turns his head at the faint sound of a police radio, emanating from yards away, his nerves take hold. Fear devolves into paranoia and his day is ruined.

X walks on, quickening his pace with every step. He nearly falls as he sprints downstairs into the West 4th Street subway station while *casually* peeking over his shoulder.

One cop, becoming two, joined by a third. None of them is doing the greatest job of being as discreet as he. X is not mistaken. He is being followed.

Not nearly as discreet as I thought I was, obviously...

He stays hooded as usual. Once inside, he hops the bannister and quickly paces under the sign for the *D* train. To its immediate left is a second sign, containing a white down-arrow, reading: *Port Authority.*

He heads down another flight of stairs. Platform. The *D* arrives nearly a minute later. He enters.

"Stand clear the closing doors." The bored tones of the conductor, through the intercom system. The doors close. The train leaves the station. X takes an empty seat in the half-full car.

As the train enters the tunnel, the last image he sees upon entry is the glare of flashlights. Three, four of them aimed in his direction. Those holding the lights are dressed head to toe in blue.

~~~

Dark. Nothing can be seen through the windows as the tunnel is traversed.

X illuminates his watch's digital display. "Three-minute warning," he mumbles. The train's inside lights turn off. The train sways; the brakes screech. A typical New York subway experience.

"Move over. It's not you they're after." The voice is sturdy, male. The lights turn back on.

~~~

He wears a New York Mets cap, plastic black-rimmed glasses and is covered neck-to-toe in a paint-splatted white smock. He is no more than five years older, also African-American. His features are stronger, more pronounced than X's though there is a superficial resemblance. The notable differences are starker: his nose, particularly, most notable during the flare of his nostrils is quite larger from the bridge downward, and his jawline is similarly sturdy. He looks very similar to the police sketch of X, rather than to the teen himself.

"What?" asks X. He doesn't need this. Not now.

"You hard of hearing?" X tries to stand. "Please. Don't go. We don't have time."

"What do you want?"

"It's not *you* they're after."

X is unsure but betrayed by a pass of confidence. "You're not exactly inconspicuous. What'd you do?"

"By design."

"I notice that word is thrown around a lot—"

"What they think I did, I did. And I didn't. Don't believe everything you hear. Nothing is what it appears to b—"

"Yeah, I've heard that before also. I'm an expert and just who the hell are you?"

"I'm fucked. Nice meeting you."

"You're getting on my last nerve—"

"I know who you are X." X is shocked. "We're on the same side. Don't worry, but before we conclude our wonderful time together, I must say I'm sure it's hell going through life with just an image and no identity, huh?"

X doesn't answer. The train turns track and sways once more.

"I'm fucked," the stranger repeats. "And I have a last wish, you know."

"What's that?"

The stranger reaches into his pockets. X prepares to strike if need be.

The next station is in sight, viewed through the windows of the two connecting cars in front of their own. The brakes screech.

X and his unwanted companion—along with a suddenly nervous group of passengers—glimpse a group of cops coming into view, maybe a dozen in formation, standing on the platform awaiting their arrival. Suited Feds surround the perimeter. The officers stand side by side, right hands clasping their holsters, separated by the length of the train doors.

One cop to each entry.

"Give me your hoodie?" the stranger asks.

"Hell nah—"

"Give me your hoodie; they'll never guess to look at your skinny ass. I promise—"

X weighs his options, glances at the awaiting officers, and complies. "Why you doing this for me?" The stranger puts on the hoodie. "Why?"

"Really, I never thought you were deaf or hard of hearing. Take my glasses." X takes the glasses. "Put them on." He does. "Now you're jus' another NYU nigger-"

"I should kick your ass."

"Yeah go for it," the stranger patronizes. "I'm doing this because you're right. *They're* not. I admire your work. Don't stop."

"Why you antagonizing me then?"

"You need to get your focus off this b.s. and get back to what you do best. You need to stop running." He reaches into his pocket and hands *X* a rubber-banded stack of lined index cards. "Here." X takes the cards and flips through them. Handwriting is scribbled on each.

"You never told me who you are," X asks.

"Doesn't matter. You'll know, oh, within five minutes? But let me ask you this. Who looks more like the police sketch, you or me?"

X checks him. The sketch does *not* bear the strongest resemblance...

"The only way the cops wouldn't track your ass down," the stranger resumes, "is to do what they're about to arrest me for. In the meantime, be sure to read what I gave you. I'd hate to think my months of planning were wasteful."

The train stops.

"Ladies and gentlemen," begins the conductor, "we ask that you please remain seated until further word. Thank you."

"What is this?" X asks.

"*The other version*," he cryptically responds. "The *lost* version not lost. There's more than one of you too, you know."

"More than one?"

"You'll figure it out. Incidentally, I prefer *'The Lost Chronicles'*...Of what, not a damn clue, but I trust you'll come up with something."

"You a fucking martyr, that it?"

The stranger, simply, smirks in response.

The doors open; the cops rush in.

The stranger is forced to the ground by the officers with guns drawn to his head, as passengers scream and one of the FBI's Most Wanted fugitives watches helplessly.

"I'm innocent!" he screams. I'M INNOCENT!!" It's an act, but he's highly effective. He struggles, his eyes widen and fill with tears.

"Let him go! He didn't do anything!" says an elderly woman nearby. Others also argue his cause.

"We got 'im," X overhears an officer speaking into his walkie. "We got the London bomber." And then, the coup de grace—

"We got X."

CENTRAL PARK WEST

X, the real deal, left the train, along with the other passengers, two hours afterwards. He was questioned, like everyone else, insisted he knew nothing, and was summarily dismissed.

I wouldn't have minded visiting London at least once, he thought, as he walked through the last banister. *Life can be so unfair.*

Not that he believed he was a free man at all. He didn't. He did believe that in time the authorities' gross mistake would be discovered, and he would be found, properly identified, and ultimately sentenced to life. If he was lucky. *It'd be a PR nightmare though. Maybe they'd cut me a plea.*

As he exited the station and breathed the fresh air outside, he sprinted to Central Park West, took a bench, and perused *"the other version."*

Could the writing be any smaller? he wondered.

X leans back, squints. He remembers that he's wearing glasses and tosses them into a trashcan. *Much better.*

The top card immediately captures his attention: *I'm not strange, weird, off, nor crazy; my reality is just different from yours. It was your hero, Lewis Carroll, who said, 'You used to be much more...'muchier.' You've lost your muchness. Get it together, X.*

"Screw you too," he says in response.

He places the card once read on the bottom, as he will with them all. *Ever consider that maybe Alice knew more than one rabbit? If not, consider this:* As X begins to read the rest in earnest, his own tenuous reality quickly unravels. *The two hares, with huge upright ears, stand next to a ring-tailed cat with immense eyes of iridescent yellow. A great black squirrel looks around pensively. Rats are there, of a size and ferocity to empty a medieval village. They are arrayed around a singular figure, a fox standing upright. Soon they are, all of them, engaged in a Babel-like exchange of squeaks, chirps, rabbit-foot thumps, squawks and hisses, punctuated by brief, eerie whistles.*

What is this? X questions. He reads on, fascinated.

There is a Writer nearby, asserts the next card.

A writer? ponders X.

Not a scop. An etcher. He wanders on the other side of this great forest and is engaged in his own business which, for now, might be described as bored disengagement. He had hoped he would find her, to express his gratitude at least. She is the invisible angel on his shoulder who has enabled him to be useful and further ensured a good life for him and his family.

Was the trek worthless? thought X.

"But the first writings were on cave walls..." X whispers to no one, suddenly questioning his efforts as he is wont to do at the occasional *inconvenient* disclosure.

He impulsively looks in Ara's direction, deeper into the forest.

X pauses. *Ara.* He stares dead ahead. Joggers and dog-walkers pass, and he does not notice a thing. He shakes his head, sighs, and resumes...

The animals scramble. Ara is undeterred. She moves to the clearing and steps into the firelight, her small figure captured in lonely silhouette.

The Writer, adjusting his position so he could see through the clearing, sees the fox shape-shift and take human form. And then he finally sees her and she is, though a halfling, which surprises him, as beautiful as he had hoped.

He is as compelled by her as he is by that which stands in her stead, opposite the fire pit. Her inquisitor is almost certainly an incarnation of the Crafty and Malicious One. Son of a giant known for cruelty, father of monsters. Described as far back as the Icelandic Eddas and the earliest Germanic lays. A promiscuous shape-shifter. Devourer of the hands of gods.

The mouth that opens and now speaks with Ara bears hideous scars. Remnants of stitches once commanded by the gods. The Writer is mystified. What could impel Ara to stalk this monster, leave behind her stewards, and walk up alone to face him?

And The Writer wonders 'How do I save her?'

However, in response to crunching leaves, The Writer turns forward. He too shall now be challenged; he shall face his own confrontation.

By his raiment and manner, his broadsword, his helm with crest of boar-bristles, The Writer knows well the legend Beowulf when he sees him in flesh and blood.

Which way does he go? Does he save the muse? Does he fend off his own challenge?

~~~

He's read this far, but X realizes that the remaining cards are either not in order, or there is something missing or withheld. The rest does not seem to make much sense, on first glance.

He just as quickly considers that perhaps he is making a wrong assumption.

The Writer's story has abruptly ended, with no resolution.

X gives up and reads the rest of the cards, in the order received.

The Writer's outcome is up to you. You see, within this other version is yet another. And another after that. A hall of mirrors, if you will.

A reconciliation of these matters will one day enable a common man to soon peek into the Infinity Pass.

I am certain that man is you, X.

"Gee..."

Thing is, no god or mortal has yet gotten that far.

Ever.

Ara's Curse, as it will soon come to be known, was visited upon her by the shape-shifter who stood before her. You well know his name, X. It is a name of legend. It is a name of myth.

But I will not share that name in these notes as you need to stay focused!

Single-worded card to the bottom and X furiously reads the next—

"Your feats, your sneaking among us in your mortal incarnation are over," he said to her.

'Mortal incarnation?'

"A future?" he utters in disbelief. "A future?"

"Your history, all tales of your vain heroism, will be erased. Just as autumn leaves scatter in fragments before the next season's harsher gales. Thus your mortal existence shall be forgotten, save for one account. Written in our own language, impossible to render into other tongues, always as uncertain as the shifting paths of Mirkwood. Tantalizingly out of reach of mortals. Your vaulting ambition to do good shall remain in check, a spell of lingering shall envelope you. Not immortal, you shall yet linger in life, past the moment of your mortal bones, alone, adrift and becalmed in a sea of time without horizon. You may be a teller, a scop, even a provoker of great feats, but never again shall you by action be an instrument of change in this world."

X, skeptical as he is, has never felt so consciously removed from the human race as he does at this moment. While others in the park may be free of these annoyances, they are ignorant and he feels sorry for them. Not a typical burden.

As to the 'wheres' and the 'hows'...

Ara's life was recorded in the demonic language of the Dok Kalfor, the Dark Elves.

'C'mon, now..."

Yet even that history would be persecuted and harassed into oblivion by the inheritors of this world, men and their meddlesome wizard-allies.

But I am convinced that there have been other men and women, unsung, their names and fates forgotten, who would have stewarded and preserved these obscure lays.

The rest of the answers you seek lie in the physical evidence they left behind, the words they passed in secret from generation to generation, and one very special survivor who I will get to in a second.

But first be warned, my new friend. Proceed with caution, lest you suffer an unimaginable retaliation at measure with your hubris, your delving.

"Great..."

Don't kid yourself. Others before you attempted to inhale the Mirkwood mist and were infected with its contagion. You see, Ara's existence was to remain forever erased from the memory and record of all mortals. Forever erased, with one perverse exception. This exception is the name you must now search for, the 'special survivor' earlier referenced:

Aragranessa Flameleaf.

X laughs. *This is absurd...*

It is Aragranessa Flameleaf's doing, not yours, that the truth behind Ara's existence continues to unravel. Regarding her name, simply note that this is no coincidence.

That said, I am loathe to admit, you have been nothing but a pawn to now.

"I'm nobody's pawn."

The last card:

Remember, for better or ill, X, you have taught those of us who would listen that The Truth is imbedded in the words. The words make the tales. The tales make the world and you, my friend—by virtue of your intellect and your knowledge—you are the guardian of the tales.

"Joy."

The guardian of the tales, save for the most important of all: those that are lost. We are convinced of Aragranessa Flameleaf's return from the bloodstorms of the Ragnarök cycle. You must find her, hear her words and record the rest of her story, and determine her allegiance.

"*Bloodstorms?* Aw, come on, now. What do you take me for?"

The Great War is upon us, X, and she will be the key to continuing your momentum.

"I must be dreaming. *Ragnarök?* Isn't that a video game, or ..." He returns to the card.

I've listened. I've taken you seriously.

"You're the one."

As if in response, the final lines on the card read: *Yes, I'm the one. We cannot depend on Thomas McFee alone.*

"Agree there, but how the hell could you have possibly known about..."

We cannot depend on anyone but you.

And that...is all.

X rubs his neck, frustrated, then re-bands the cards. He shoves the words into his back pocket as he stands.

On course with today's habit, he talks to himself, this time before quietly slinking away—

"As if I didn't have enough to worry about...I'm a damn fugitive, fuck all. Why do I put myself at such goddamn risk?"

An hour later, as he scouts locations for his next sleep, he realizes two things. First, that Peter Levin's book was left in the pocket of his hoodie. And second...the possibility exists that he truly is a pawn.

In that event, based on his recent compulsions, he would be *Ara's* pawn.

Which would, at least, answer my last question, he contemplates. *But, if so...does that really matter now?*

X understands that any new inconvenience will assuredly figure into his next major set of problems. He is cognizant that he has reached out for help before and has received less than his expected share. He knows well that an important delivery was recently fulfilled in a place he would love to visit one day and he was assured the contents of the package would be read.

He also realizes that his work is approaching critical mass and he'll need to contact Thomas McFee directly.

This game is over.

BRADLEY AND SON BIBLIOTHEQUE

Night.

The sign on the entrance door is turned to "Closed."

Sonorous snoring emanates from a private side room upstairs. The alcove's total square-footage is barely larger than that of a confessional.

Donovan has fallen asleep in a recliner, the space's sole piece of furniture. *The Holy Bible* is clasped face-down and open on his chest, supported by his left hand which presses against its spine. His other arm hangs, knuckles inches from the immaculate green shag carpet.

When the shop was conceived, Donovan had planned for the idea of a personal reading area as a getaway; therefore, when built, it was of the most imperative nature that the carpeting and light brown walls reflected an environment distinct from the store proper.

The larger downstairs office, in which Thomas is presently working, reflects the workspace that was intended to support Donovan's *other* dream. A long-held dream that he had thought died with his son.

Lately, he's been troubled by the resumption of his old inclination, the attainment of which has fast become insatiable.

He had wanted, almost more than anything, to be an author. But Donovan Bradley had never been published. He had never applied himself; the extent of his writing was confined to signing his store's receipts.

When good-naturedly asked by patrons, he blamed business obligations for his lack of creation, even as he aged and his boy was doing most of the work. In truth, he was terrified. He believed he knew too much based on his voracious reading, and any real exploration of his own soul would likely prove personally, professionally or even *globally* disastrous.

He once admitted as much to his son, in the store, two weeks before the fire.

"What if it doesn't go well?"

"What if what doesn't go well? Why don't you come out with it and tell me what are you so scared of—"

"I never said I'm scared—"

"Then what? You want to write a book; write a book. My father's turmoil doesn't require a proclamation," admonished Donovan, Jr. *"God knows you have enough stories."*

"Maybe I know something the rest of them don't. Maybe I need to be careful with my thoughts—"

"Is there no limit to your overreacting? I mean, really..."

"I guess not," Donovan, Sr. defended. *"But understand, there are reasons—"*

"Then what are you hiding from me?"

Donovan, Sr. never answered that last question. He excused himself to make a phone call, a typical *out* when a conversation does not continue as preferred.

When he returned he simply informed his son, who was bored with the hassle, that he'd keep reading and ingesting as many books as possible.

"It's the safer pursuit," he said.

~~~

Since the arrival of his visitor was planned over a month ago, and for the first time since his son's passing, Donovan, Sr. has been reading for ideas. For ideas to address and expand upon in a work that he is finally ready to put to paper. At 90, he accepts that the recent disquieting forces that have been pushing him to proceed as planned can no longer be fought.

It is not unusual for Bradley, thus, to fall asleep when reading. Much like Thomas. Nor is it unusual for him to read or skim two or more books at once.

For now, *The Holy Bible* is joined by mythologist Joseph Campbell's *Hero With a Thousand Faces*, which rests on his upper leg. Its back cover contains a single blurb, a quote by George Lucas as taken from a *National Arts Club* speech he delivered in 1985.

On *Star Wars*:

"I went around in circles for a long time trying to come up with stories, and the script rambled all over and I ended up with hundreds of pages. It was The Hero With a Thousand Faces that just took what was about 500 pages and said, 'Here is the story. Here's the end; here's the focus; here's the way it's all laid out.' It was all there and had been there for thousands and thousands of years."

Thomas McFee sits alone, downstairs, at a desk with the *Beowulf* documents spread on its top. He is beguiled by the wealth of material, particularly the pages closest to him. On either side of each are symbols. His index finger *reads* the two groupings right to left, which he gathers to be contextually correct based on nothing more than a whim.

One, two...These are ideograms, he thinks. *Right, left, one, two...*

His finger touches the first grouping (right):

Each symbol...

"Each symbol, a word..." as once explained an old king to his mystic.

Then, the second grouping (left):

ΣΗΘμαθΙσθισξ θ[αιθδησωοα ζφξ εξλαμδγωε

Just as it appears. Each symbol, a letter. Each group of symbols...

"A word, then three to watch over me..." as young J.R.R. Tolkien said to himself many years ago, upon scribbling these *letters* in the dirt.

A cursory scroll of other pages exhibits horizontal pictograph combinations similar to the latter.

"The first set on the right, a syntax I've never seen." he mutters. "Why then do both groupings appear...on the same page?"

ΣΗΘμαθΙσθισξ θ[αιθδησωοα ζφξ εξλαμδγωε

A few further moments of study, pointing and an epiphany...

In combination the characters take shape...as a sword. He runs his finger over the outside area.

But two distinct parts...forming one.

"*Hrunting?*" The possibility quickly strikes him. "The sword...Beowulf used unsuccessfully on Grendel's mother?" Again, he traces the shape with his finger. "Or *Nægling*...the sword that failed against the dragon in final battle?" He shakes his head, giving up. "Or...the product of an exhausted imagination?"

As he leans back and rubs his temples, he notices his name on a brown paper envelope, a delivery, that had been placed atop a small, vague stack on the right corner of the computer. He looks to the stairwell—*Why didn't he say anything?*—then, curious, reaches for the package as he turns back to the desk.

NEW YORK CITY, 1970

A paperweight is excitedly slammed atop the same *Beowulf* document. The hand placing the paperweight belongs to Donovan.

"A gauntlet and its blade," he says.

"Looks like an arrow to me." Franklin McFee, mid-40s.

"How about an electric guitar," Donovan sarcastically retorts.

Tolkien, meantime, is mesmerized. He strains to bend and review. "Gentlemen, sometimes a cigar is just a cigar."

"With all respect, Professor," Donovan adds in an unguarded moment, "you're about as convincing as my ex when she'd swore she'd never leave me. As soon as she realized I was more interested in my life's work than I was her, I knew it was a matter of time—"

"How rude of her," Tolkien says facetiously. "That occurred when?" he asks, his eyes remaining on the document.

"Minutes after the Rabbi said, 'For better or for worse.' At our reception—I'll never forget this—she whispered in my ear, 'I'm going to save you, you know. I'm going to take your nose out of those books and re-introduce you to reality. We'll be so busy, we'll hire someone to run the store and you and I will travel around the world.'"

"And you said what?"

"I said, 'Do I need you for this?'"

"Charming. Familiarity breeds...familiarity, does it?"

Donovan laughs. "I have no idea what that means."

"Neither do I," Tolkien admits.

"More importantly, gentlemen," interrupts Franklin, "have I delivered?" Donovan turns his attention back to the document.

Two armed police officers guard the doorway, ignoring the visitors' words as the potentially invaluable material is perused—within a confined, impenetrable bank vault.

Wrought-iron, electrically-charged bars separate this room from another, adjoining, of equal size. The area of each is approximately twenty by twenty feet . A single desk stands in the room's middle, upon which the documents are splayed.

A third armed guard wheels a chair towards Franklin, who guides it to the desk.

"Professor, please," Franklin gestures to the chair. A distracted Tolkien takes the seat.

"Thank you, my friend." Tolkien swivels and scoots the chair with his foot for the best possible vantage. He resumes his review the manuscript. "Extraordinary." He runs his fingers across the document, pointing out but not yet calling attention to various characters and marks of interest. "The concept of a *pictograph* may not be so far-fetched as I let on," he says. "McFee," he continues, "I would like to hear from you directly how this document came into your hands. My friend and I are rather curious."

Franklin approaches them. "Professor, I returned from your fair England little over a month ago."

"You don't say? Bradley, why didn't you tell me?"

"I thought Franklin would be the best man to explain the provenance..."

"No matter, Bradley. Remind me to receive anything you explain to me from here forward as a half-answer." Donovan turns his head in embarrassment. Tolkien smirks. "Go on, Mr. McFee." The author is enjoying himself, glint of mischief and all. He winks to Franklin, who smiles as if he's in on a great rib.

"As part of a tour exchange," Franklin continues, "I visited the site of an old monastery..."

CARMELITE MONASTERY OF THE MOST HOLY TRINITY, NOTTING HILL, ENGLAND

One Month Earlier.

A spired dome presents atop the main chapel, which itself is conjoined by two corridors of four open-arched entranceways on either side, surrounded by acres of immaculately-coiffed brush.

A bored Franklin McFee stands with his tour group, eyes averted, pretending to be captivated elsewhere. He attends without a guest; a Nikon F Photomic camera is strapped around his neck. He backs up and away as the tour guide goes through the motions.

"Founded in 1878, an homage to the spirit of Saint Teresa of Avila..." Her horrid monotone is engulfed by an emissary of God, in the form of a low-flying plane in late-stage descent.

As the rest look up, Franklin notices a potential happening in the far distance. He lifts his camera to magnify his view. The plane passes; Franklin follows his hunch, focusing his camera as the tour guide resumes. "Where was I?" she asks. "Oh yes. Founded in 1878, as an homage to..."

"I was distracted by a newspaper boy. He was pedaling, pretty hastily, and appeared to have some difficulty breathing," he explains to his companions in the vault. "I thought this because of the way he gripped his bars, how he was hunched and the frantic up and down movement of his shoulders."

Franklin escapes the scene. He walks brusquely away from the tour and approaches a nearby storefront, watching the boy with his own eyes as the kid tosses a paper. The tabloid hits the front window, behind which is displayed a host of operating television sets.

The boy rides away.

"Either this was the last delivery of his route, or he only had one paper as I noticed his sack was completely empty."

Franklin swipes the newspaper, unfolds, and glimpses the headline:

ENGLAND COURIER

ORIOLES TAKE SERIES, ROUT REDS IN 5

"It was a slow news day in England. Or so I thought."

As he watches the newspaper boy pedal onward, Franklin is taken aback when the boy quickly turns and regards him, before again quickening his pace and disappearing on a decline. Franklin is troubled but does not know why. He is tempted to somehow follow, but he quickly realizes the futility of that pursuit.

Franklin turns away from the decline and immediately notices a burgeoning crowd approaching the store. He follows their gaze and turns to the screens behind him.

Canadian Prime Minister Pierre Trudeau, so identified by a band at the bottom of his image, speaks to his country, a simulcast of which presently airs throughout the world.

Also on the band:

OCTOBER CRISIS: CANADIAN PM INVOKES
1914 WAR MEASURES ACT

The crowd cannot hear the Prime Minister, but they follow the on-screen captions:

"At this moment, the FLQ is holding hostage two men in the Montreal area, one a British diplomat, the other a Quebec cabinet minister. They are threatened with murder."

Franklin walks closer, his growing visage reflecting in the store's window.

Trudeau continues. "If it is the responsibility of government to deny the demands of the kidnappers, the safety of the hostages is without question the responsibility of the kidnappers."

Others from the tour group notice the crowd and break off to join them.

Franklin has seen enough. He again backs away, but catches Trudeau's next words before turning:

"If a democratic society is to continue to exist, it must be able to root out the cancer of an armed, revolutionary movement that is bent on destroying the very basis of our freedom."

As Franklin walks alone away from the store, the cyclist returns and rides straight towards him.

"Hey!" the boy exclaims.

Startled, Franklin jumps out of the way...and again watches the boy ride off. Once the biker is out of view, Franklin looks to the ground, having caught something from the corner of his eye. His face tenses. He looks up and around; no one is watching. He looks down. Just inches from his feet, a silver briefcase stands, upright. He taps the case with his shoe, listening intently.

Repeat.

He moves the case with his foot, judging its heft. Satisfied, he kicks the case to its side. He's safe.

Franklin takes hold of the case and walks away.

"And, gentlemen," he resumes to his associates, "as the rest of the world was exposed to a new firepower...I found my own dynamite."

Back in his hotel room, Franklin opens the case. He has no idea what to make of the contents inside ...

"It was a set-up, clearly," says Franklin. "I have no idea who was responsible nor why the work was planted. And so here we are."

"Here we are," Donovan repeats.

"Mr. McFee?" queries Tolkien, his eyes affixed on the documents. "Forgive me. You are adamant this work was *planted.* How could you be sure?"

Franklin nods in acknowledgement."Perhaps I'm guilty of a questionable word choice," he corrects. "I have no idea why it was passed to me and I can only assume—"

"Never assume," advises Donovan.

"Remind me where you teach, Franklin?" Tolkien asks.

"There is teaching and there is *teaching,* Professor Tolkien. Brooklyn College English Department. Classics of Western Culture, though I'm but a journeyman in your esteemed company—"

"Indeed you are," Tolkien teases him affably. "Would your response, however, not appear to at least partially answer your question?"

"I don't understand..." Franklin responds.

Tolkien reaches into his pocket and removes a pipe. He stands, with difficulty. Donovan and Franklin walk to his side for support. Tolkien smiles and waves them off. He turns to Franklin—

"At the risk of appearing immodest, you are, still, a fan of my work?"

Franklin is surprised. "Very much so, Professor. Are my seams showing?"

"Yes."

"If you remember, I had once planned to compose a definitive biograph—"

"I kept copies of our correspondence."

Franklin pinches himself. "I don't know what to say..."

Donovan finds the issue curious. He turns to Tolkien. "Why didn't you tell me?" he asks.

The professor faintly shrugs; for the moment, his curiosity rests with Franklin. "Why did you not proceed, then?" Franklin shirks. It is now his turn to be embarrassed. "I agree to cooperate and suddenly, my boy, you become quite silent," Tolkien continues. "Go on," he presses. "It's meant to be an awkward question."

"Well-deserved, I'm afraid. But I'm a big boy..."

"I hope I didn't bite."

"No. The question is as fair as my response simple. My wife—now my late wife—and I learned that we were expecting our first child." He smiles, half-cocked. "And I realized we couldn't all be as fortunate in our paid literary pursuits as you, Professor."

Tolkien takes it in, and nods. "As grateful as I am, how I pine at times to regain that freedom..."

"Life is a matter of perspective, it appears," says Franklin.

"You think so?" Tolkien asks, not so innocently.

Franklin pauses. "You disagree?"

"Of course I disagree." Tolkien tilts his head to the documents at hand. "You refer to your find as...dynamite, yet your status in life in the present tense as something less than free. Would not your discovery once announced buy you the freedom you seek?"

"I'm sorry, Professor. I didn't mean to offend—"

"Don't be daft. I disagree with you. I'm not sending you to bed without any supper."

Donovan intercedes, noting the tension in the face of the unnerved Franklin. "You seem very strong on the matter, Professor. Please explain..." he says.

"Mr. McFee...Mr. Bradley, I am proud of my achievements, and fortune has shone upon me. But now...as I encounter these documents in the autumn of my years, and find myself reflecting on the entirety of my life's inspiration—you'll both get there, trust me—I can only think of an expanded Middle-earth that could have been. Or worlds of my creation that never were."

"But Professor, so many of your readers consider you an architect of sorts. The influence you've had on world mythology and culture is immeasurable," Franklin says. "The hippie movement loves you and certainly that has to account for something major—"

"And I appreciate the hippies but understand, McFee, assuming your find is verified? Your biographical effort would have been an exercise in futility."

Franklin is surprised at Tolkien's somewhat regretful tone. "Professor?"

Tolkien turns to Donovan. "But I also doth protest too much, methinks." He cocks his head towards the exit. "Please." Donovan nods to the guards, who open the vault doors. Tolkien pauses, before exiting. "We are prone to become targets. All of us. Regardless of who you think I am. We must continue to be discreet." He reaches into his pocket for a pipe. "Perhaps I've spent too much time with Sauron's Ring, gentlemen, but treasures can be perilous in the wrong hands..." He lights the pipe. "Excuse me."

And he steps out.

BRADLEY AND SON BIBLIOTHEQUE

Basement.

Thomas McFee, deep in thought, holding position with head in hand and elbow on desk, scrupulously reviews the contents of the package.

He holds the five sheets of paper that were included therein; there was nothing more. The envelope has been folded and rests standing in the wastepaper basket below.

And he reads again; this time, as he promised himself, he'll make it to the *bitter end* with neither anger, fear nor interruption ...

CRIBBED AND RE-FORMATTED FROM
THE NOTEBOOKS OF MATTHIUS ALEXI
(THIS HEADER AND MY ANNOTATIONS IN CAPS;
MARKUP 6/9/14)

———

Biblical refs and other misc, for the record:

Genesis 1:1

הָאָרֶץ וְאֵת הַשָּׁמַיִם אֵת אֱלֹהִים בָּרָא בְּרֵאשִׁית

When in the beginning God created the heavens and the earth, the earth was untamed and shapeless...

The Fourth Day: Genesis 1:14-19

1.   And God said, Let there be luminaries in the expanse of the heavens, to distinguish between the day and the night; and let them be for signs, and for seasons, and for days, and for years.

2.   And let them be for luminaries in the expanse of the heavens to give light upon the earth; and it was so.

3.   And God made two great luminaries, the greater luminary to rule by day, and the lesser luminary to rule by night; and the stars.

4.   And God set them in the expanse of the heavens, to give light upon the earth;

5.   And to rule in the day, and in the night, and to distinguish between the light and the darkness; and God saw that it was good.

6.   And the evening and the morning were the fourth day. -JUST HOW LONG WERE THE DAYS PRIOR? DAYS 1-3 WOULD NOT BE 24 HOURS?

Exodus 23:13-32

Thou shalt not bow down to their gods, nor serve them, nor do after their works: but thou shalt utterly overthrow them, and quite break down their images. (v.24) - OTHER GODS IMPLIED?

Psalm 82:1-2:

In the divine council, God holds court in the midst of the other gods: "How long will you judge unjustly and show partiality to the wicked?" - YET ANOTHER OF SEVERAL REFS OTHER GODS.

Psalm 82:6-7:

I said, "You are gods, sons of the Most High, all of you; nevertheless, like men you shall die, and fall like any prince." - MISC: DURATION OF DAYS 1-3 NOT DEFINED IN ANY BIBLICAL VERSION, PRESENCE OF OTHER GODS AND, FINALLY, AN EXPLANATION:

Excerpt From Inherit The Wind

Play by Jerome Lawrence and Robert Edwin

Based on Scopes Monkey Trial (1925)

Evolution vs. Creationism

Drummond: Then you interpret that the first day as recorded in the Book of Genesis could've been a day of indeterminate length.

Brady: I mean to state that it is not necessarily a 24 hour day.

Drummond: It could've been 30 hours, could've been a week, could've been a month, could've been a year, could've been a hundred years, or it could've been 10 million years!! - A PROVOCATIVE QUESTION. WHAT EXACTLY WAS THE STATE OF THE UNIVERSE IN DAYS 1-3?

CONCLUSION

WHATEVER THE DEFINITION OF A "DAY," THERE WAS ONCE A TIME BEFORE TIME. THIS MUCH IS CERTAIN. WHAT IS LESS CLEAR IS THIS: THE ORB THAT THEN BURNED IN THE SKIES, SUSTAINING LIFE ... IF NOT THE SUN, THEN WHAT?

STRATEGY SUMM

"MY PLAN" EXPOSED:

TURN A BELIEVER, TURN A SKEPTIC. SOMEONE WHO ONCE BELIEVED AND DOES NO LONGER.

NOTHING IS EVER AS IT APPEARS. YOU ARE MAN AND MAN IS LIMITED. UNLEARN WHAT YOU HAVE LEARNED. ADDRESS THE BIBLE AS A LITERARY CREATION ONLY, CONSIDER ITS INCONSISTENCIES AND BE SURE TO TROLL THE MOST SOULFUL INVENTION OF OTHER INFLUENCERS TO TRIGGER YOUR SOLUTION.

I TRUST YOU'LL KNOW WHO THEY ARE WHEN YOU GET THERE. I'VE GIVEN YOU A HEAD START.

REMEMBER, ONE BELIEVER, ONE SKEPTIC TURNED TO MY SIDE, CAN MAKE THE DIFFERENCE.

LOOK OUTWARD AT MYTHS TO FILL THE GAPS.

CULTURAL MYTHS ARE NO LESS VALID THAN ANY OTHER.

CONSIDER: CREATIVES INSPIRE CULTURES. WHO INSPIRES THE CREATIVES?

THE MUSE.

HEADS-UP. SHE EXISTS. IN <u>EVERY</u> MYTH IS A SEMBLANCE OF REALITY AND THAT, MY FRIEND, IS BOTH THE NATURE OF OUR WORLD - YOUR COSMOLOGY, AS IT WERE - AND OUR CRISIS.

THE GREEKS WERE WRONG. THERE HAS BEEN BUT ONE MUSE THROUGHOUT HISTORY. WE HAVE BEEN IN HER SERVICE FROM THE BEGINNING. SHE MUST BE WEAKENED. SHE MUST BE DENIED. HER INFLUENCE MUST BE IMMINENTLY DIFFUSED LEST SHE DESTROY EONS OF PROGRESS AND, BY EXTENSION ... YOU KNOW THE REST. SO, MY FRIEND, YOU WILL FIND THAT OUR NARRATIVE BEGINS, CONVENIENTLY, IN A HERETOFORE-UNCONSIDERED PERIOD I REFER TO AS

THE PRE-GENESIS ERA (A BLATANT BIBLICAL INFERENCE TO REDLINE A TIME PERIOD OF UNKNOWN DURATION – AND ATTEMPT TO CAPTURE BELIEVERS, WILLING ATHEISTS AND AGNOSTICS OF ALL MINDS WITH NO PREJUDICE.

THAT IS, IF YOU DIE OR SOMETHING WORSE AND YOU CANNOT FOLLOW THROUGH.

SO ... HOW TO PROCEED, YOU MAY ASK?

REVERSE-ENGINEER THE MYTH TO PROVE HER EXISTENCE, THEN PROCEED WITH YOUR EVOLVING PARANOIA -- DESPITE <u>ANY CONCERN</u> THAT YOU ABSOLUTELY WILL BE OSTRACIZED ...

OH, AND ONE MORE THING:

PROVENANCE.

ALEXI KEPT HIS NOTEBOOKS, OF WHICH FOR OUR PURPOSES I CONSIDER THIS THE MOST PERTINENT OF HIS ENTRIES, FOLLOWING HIS NDE - THE NEAR-DEATH EXPERIENCE THAT (HE WOULD WANT YOU TO BELIEVE) CRIPPLED HIM INTELLECTUALLY.

AND WHY THE RESULTING HANDICAP, YOU MAY ASK? BECAUSE, DURING WHAT SHOULD HAVE BEEN HIS FINAL REST, HE SAW HER FOR THE FIRST TIME.

AND SO HE ALSO TOOK BRUSH TO CANVAS, AND HIS

PAINTERLY EFFORTS TO <u>MAKE SENSE OF IT ALL</u> BY RENDERING PORTRAITURE OF THE MUSE, AS HE SCRAPPED VALIANTLY TO KEEP HIS WITS, TRIGGERED THE REST OF THE PROCESS.

(HIS IMPRESSIVE RESEARCH ASIDE, ALEXI WAS NEVER MUCH OF A WRITER - AS AN AUTHOR YOURSELF YOU MAY FIND HIS WRITTEN COMPOSITION FAIRLY AMATEURISH - BUT THERE IS, SAY, "CONSIDERABLY MORE" TO HIS PAINTINGS THAN MEET THE EYE. THEY TOO WILL COME TO YOU, AND SOON, YET YOU WILL HAVE NO IDEA <u>WHO</u> SENT THE WORKS, <u>WHEN</u> OR <u>WHY</u>. YOU WOULDN'T SURVIVE THE DISTRACTION.)

IN THE MEANTIME, CHECK THIS OUT:

ALEXI DISCOUNTED NOTHING AND QUESTIONED EVERYTHING.

YOU AND HE - TWO BODIES AND ONE MIND, REGARDLESS OF HOW WELL-PROTECTED YOUR OWN SECRETS SO ... YOU WERE SCRUPULOUSLY SELECTED TO UNCOVER THESE NOTES.

IN OTHER WORDS, YOU HAVE BEEN "SET-UP." SORT OF LIKE YOUR DAD TOO, A LONG TIME AGO, BUT I THINK THAT'S A STORY FOR ANOTHER DAY.

WE'RE MEN OF LOGIC, YOU AND I. I'VE BEEN WATCHING YOU TOO. IF YOU DON'T LIE TO YOURSELF WE MAY

WELL PROCEED.

IF I CONVINCE YOU, THERE'S STILL HOPE.

BUT THEN YOU MUST CONVINCE ARMIES. I BELIEVE IN YOU AS I TRUST YOU HAVE SOMETHING I LACK.

CREDIBILITY.

I TRUST YOU HAVE THE CREDIBILITY TO FINISH THE JOB. SO IT'S YOUR MOVE NOW.

THE WORLD NEEDS YOUR HELP, TIME IS RUNNING OUT, AND THESE NOTES CAN BE YOUR MOST POWERFUL INSTRUMENT IF YOU CHOOSE TO BELIEVE.

SO WHO WILL YOU CONVINCE FIRST ... MR. MCFEE?

(YEAH, IT'S ME, THE INTERNATIONAL FUGITIVE YOU'VE HEARD SO MUCH ABOUT. DON'T BE TOO SURPRISED; YOU HAD TO SUSPECT AS MUCH. THAT ADMISSION SHOULD AT LEAST ANSWER SOME OF YOUR QUESTIONS AND, TAKING INTO ACCOUNT THE TIMING OF THIS LEAK, MAY WELL ALSO SERVE TO, IN PART, HASTEN OUR INEVITABLE CONFRONTATION. I'M AVAIL ON TEXT, EMAIL ... I DO HAVE YOUR CELL NUMBER FOR EMERGENCIES. WHEN THE TIME IS RIPE FOR MUTUAL COMMUNICATION I MAY CHOOSE ONE OR ALL THREE DEPENDENT ON THE CIRCUMSTANCE. I TRUST WE'RE GETTING THERE. MY PLEA TO YOU IS TO UNDERSTAND

THAT, DESPITE APPEARANCES, THIS GAME IS ENDING. BY NOW, DONOVAN BRADLEY AND I BOTH KNOW HOW YOU LOATHE GAMES, THOMAS.)

BUT I GET AHEAD OF MYSELF. TYPICAL. FOR NOW, JUST BE AWARE THAT, FOR GOOD AND PURPOSEFUL CONSIDERATION, 'X' IS COUNTING ON YOU.

(ONE MORE ASIDE, IT'S BEEN A DAY AND I'M SPENT. WHEN THE TIME COMES, YOU MAY WANT TO FIND AND CLIP TODAY'S E-BLAST WITH THESE PAGES. FROM THERE, I'LL EAGERLY AWAIT YOUR WELL-CONSIDERED RESPONSE.)

Thomas is roused by incoming footsteps, accompanied by a sudden, unwelcome *glow* on the wall in front of him.

He quickly turns the disquieting papers and discreetly covers them with his own notes. In the moment, he decides that he will not volunteer a word about the matter. Not to Donovan, who assuredly hid the delivery in plain sight—he'll try to piece together his possible motives later—not to Denise, Samantha...anyone. In his review he's come to the quick conclusion that he's well-steeped into something he did not bargain for. He'll proceed over the days and weeks in *business as usual* fashion. He'll probe here and there but, until which time he has no choice, he'll simply keep his mouth shut until he figures what the hell is going on.

Or unless someone says something to him first.

Donovan arrives, penlight in hand. He leans on Thomas's shoulder for support, reaches around and shines the thin, bright beam directly in the writer's face. "Miss me?"

180

NEW YORK CITY, 1970

Tolkien has returned. He sits at the desk; the documents have remained unmoved. Donovan and Franklin stand behind him.

"I must admit to a sense of resentment," he says. "And relief, at once." They hinge on his every word. "If this is a forgery, gentlemen, it is of itself a magnificent work of creation. However, if you were to ask the opinion of this occasionally idealistic old man...I believe we are sitting at the foot of literature's Holy Grail."

Franklin beams. He slaps Donovan on the back. "Professor," he says, "I expected nothing less—"

"Validation is a funny thing, McFee," Tolkien replies. "Under just circumstances, the result proves its own reward while in the negative, it is a tool, and the annihilation of all that is just and correct may be justified by the extreme, as extreme consequence."

The others digest his words. "I don't think either of us has any clue what the hell you're talking about..."

They all laugh. "Don't plan your celebration just yet, gentlemen."

"Not yet?" Franklin asks.

Tolkien continues. "My great friend and brother, Jack—*C.S.*—Lewis, and I have shared several similar explorations over the concept of *biblical justice*, but I digress." His eyes moisten upon reflection. "I miss him as I miss my youth, but nonetheless...as you know I was a code-breaker in the Great War. Within these papers and this mysterious language, which I will consider Elvish for wont of something...convenient, allow me to indulge in a simple translation..."He carefully places another document to the right of the other.

"Why not that one?" Donovan points to the original page.

"I'll get to it. Patience, my friend."

"I have to admit, Professor, much like my ex," he jokes, "patience and Donovan Bradley were never agreeable bedfellows—"

"Sshh." Tolkien points to a particular grouping:

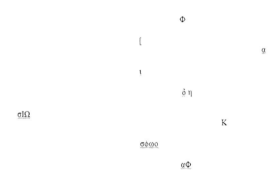

"This is the opening sentence, of the *opening* page."

He's left little room for embarrassment. The other two move in, over his shoulder.

"These characters that you see throughout this work," Tolkien continues, "in the midst of the Middle-English text, do not represent single letters. This is subtext, *meaning upon meaning*. Such sections throughout these papers…" He sorts a few pages and points out specific examples. "Such sections are not Middle-English. They are code." He waves his hand over the *words*: *"Of all beliefs and actions, a vow is the most precious as it is the giver who must believe and engage."*

"Fascinating," says Donovan, eyeing Tolkien with a new respect. "Can you explain your method of translation, Professor?"

"It will be my pleasure but please, these formalities are tiresome. Call me Ronald."

Donovan ponders the request. "I'm sorry. I can't do that, Professor."

Tolkien sadly regards Franklin, who looks away. "Nor I, Professor. I'm sorry…" Tolkien sighs in obvious disappointment.

"When in Rome..." responds Donovan.

"We will stay professional then. Pity. I was hoping we could all be friends." Donovan and Franklin both grimace, immediately realizing their mistake. Tolkien rubs it in: "I don't have many...*friends.* Mostly acquaintances, you see. People think I'm from another plane, or something...They judge me only by my books. Oh well. Too bad—"

"We didn't offend you, did we?" Donovan asks, anxiously awaiting Tolkien's answer.

"Yes," he tersely replies.

"We would be honored to be considered your friends ..." Donovan states.

"Of course, Professor—"

"Moving on, gentlemen. *C'est la vie.* So, are you interested in how I derived my translation or not?"

Franklin steps up, despite the raging instinct to apologize profusely in the hopes of thawing the Professor's good side. "Please..."

Tolkien touches the top character: Φ.

"My interpretations are based on historic habits and adaptations. On the basis that the author was a genius poet and not necessarily a sophisticated coder...this circular form is universal. *All, everything...*But it's broken in half, into two spheres, to represent something further. *Of all, everything* contextually..." He looks up. "Remember the word *half,* gentlemen, in my description of this opening character...We will get back to this."

He points to: δ η.

"An *s* and an *n* derivative. The physical likenesses later utilized for our King's English is not accidental. Something I know about, as a child would experiment or play with mixed letters based on familiar letters or symbols, or in my case subliminal symbols, to comprise a new language. New words. These characters representing two plurals...*beliefs, actions*...which taken as a piece within this grouping comprises a sensible translation."

φω.

"*Precious*," he goes on. "*My precious*—I've obviously encountered this one before—though not contextually correct in this case, rather, *most precious, more precious...*"

Φ.

"*Vow*. Later adapted, or *retarded* based on your point of view, for Coats of Arms and other such insignia, frequently representing a vow to uphold a family legacy. And on it goes..."

Tolkien taps each individual character and translates, in their proper order—

"*Of all inspirations and actions, a vow is the most precious as it is the giver who must believe and engage.*"

He pulls back.

A few moments of silence, then he continues:

"Do you notice that the grouping on this page, this *first* page, are smaller by half than other groupings we've seen? For instance, compare this...

Φ

[

α

ι

δ η

σιΩ

Κ

σφωο

αΦ

"...to this, and tell me what do you see?"

"The symbols are considerably smaller," Franklin answers.

"Indeed. And our first symbol, divided in half?"

"*Of all,* in itself, would be not only universal in usage but also representative of the known...and unknown, universe?" Donovan hypothesizes. "In half, the page is referring only to the *known*? Or...*unknown*?" One or the other?"

"No, but an admirable effort," Tolkien responds. "It is because these first words, and some others throughout, are attributed to a most special narrator. She is a *halfling*."

"A *hobbit*?" asks Donovan.

"No, something much else...But, subconsciously, as an inspiration...I venture to say that anything is possible." He appears to be uncharacteristically guarded in his response.

"Does...she have a name?" Again, Donovan.

"Oh, she has a name." Tolkien grins broadly; his eyes twinkle as if he's returned to the effortless wonderment of his childhood. "The words are attributed, on the very next page, to a halfling...by the name of *Ara*."

"*Ara?*" Franklin labors.

"Professor," prods Donovan, as Tolkien winces, "the name has been associated with you before—"

"Indeed. I had for some time considered the existence of another book of *Beowulf,* as told from the perspective of a *female.* I had spoken of this once at University as a theory, based on some scattered notes and loose ends from the original poem, but had summarily dropped the idea when nothing further was found on the matter. It broke my heart, you know."

"What can you tell us about *Ara?* Franklin asks.

Tolkien considers his best answer. "Truth be told, gentlemen, I've known her all my life…"

ALGONQUIN HOTEL, NEW YORK

Donovan escorts Tolkien through the lobby. The author, on a high from recent events, admires the decor as they await their elevator, particularly a wall mural immortalizing the storied *Algonquin Round Table.*

"They all made me laugh. Still do," he says, as he names a few of the figures portrayed. "Groucho and Harpo, Dorothy Parker, Robert Benchley…in that very dining room…they swapped tales, jokes…worldly opinions on just about…everything, you know."

"Wistful, Professor?"

"Somewhat. Would have been most flattering for Jack and I to have been held in such esteemed company, even once."

"Your humility never ceases to surprise m—" Donovan Bradley manages, before he's interrupted by the elevator bell. The doors slide open; they enter. "Penthouse," he informs the attendant.

The button is pressed; the doors close.

~~~

Tolkien sits, peacefully, puffing his pipe, his chair alongside the window that oversees the lights and theaters of The Great White Way.

And he ponders...

Flash.

Middle-earth, an expanse of greenery, mountains and lakes...

Flash.

Tolkien removes the pipe from his mouth, and disapprovingly stares outside...

Flash.

Night. The trenches of World War 1 in the height of battle, suddenly morphing into Middle-earth in the dark, in the midst of a mythical war.

Flash.

Tolkien resumes puffing his pipe. He bows his head in further reflection...

Flash.

A background image from Middle-earth—a silent observer, a woman—joins Tolkien's troops on the battlefield of The Great War. She stands in the distance, and watches his every move. He isn't certain if he sees her or senses her but she appears to be wearing a robe, and a hood. She comes closer. And closer still. She appears quite small, dwarf-like. She pulls down her hood.

Ara.

Flash.

Tolkien stands, and slowly walks toward the television. On the way, he places his pipe atop an astray and removes his shoes.

Flash.

Ara physically struggles as she drags an eight year-old Tolkien to safety, following his encounter with a tarantula. She sits on a rock, and rubs an ashy substance—from a small bag that hangs around her neck—on his forehead while patiently waiting for him to regain full consciousness.

She is beautiful, disarmingly so, as she watches over him.

Flash.

He's done.

~~~

Back to reality, he contemplates.

Tolkien manually turns on the television. He stays on a specific channel, amused as he watches a feature on magician Doug Henning's *The Magic Show* now on Broadway.

He walks to the bed and lies down, still clothed. The show captivates him.

Tolkien smiles as he watches clips of Henning sawing a woman in half, among other tricks—

The screen suddenly goes black, followed by: "We interrupt this program to bring you a special bulletin."

Tolkien sits up. His eyes glaze at a horrifying scene, caught on tape, as two warring New York City street gangs rumble with guns, baseball bats, knives and chains in the midst of graffiti-ridden 10th Avenue, just blocks away.

"The Italian East Harlem Purple Gang has encountered The Black Spades..." Tolkien huddles to the window. Business as usual, no criminal element there. Yet.

He turns and stands in front of the set, intently watching the report. It's not fear that grips him. That's a non-factor. He's disappointed...

"...and in a rout, during an apparent heroin deal gone wrong—"

The phone rings, stunning him. He walks over and picks up, doing his best not to expose his coming tears.

"Oh, Edith. My darling." He wipes his eyes. "The highest of highs, suddenly the lowest of...No, I'm just tired. What a d—Yes, dear, you don't say..." He glances back at the television: The fighting continues. He turns away and sits at the foot of the bed, bringing the phone wire with him. "Nothing but a momentary free-fall back to earth, I'm sorry to s—No, I'm fine now...Well...No, not at all. These gentlemen and that treasure far surpassed my most optimistic—" He does not finish his thought. He does, however, take a much-needed breath. "Good Lord, it is so wonderful to hear your voice..."

ENGLISH COUNTRYSIDE

Thomas, speeding like a spitfire in a rented BMW.

As he drives, he contemplates the pages forwarded by X, written by Matthius Alexi. *If this is a prank,* he considers, *I'm out for bear.* He immediately follows that thought with a hopeful association: *May have been something I heard from Denise once. That she's going to get me one day 'cause she's 'out for bear.'* However, he really doesn't believe it. Not even a bit. He knows the contents of the package are authentic for several *hard* reasons, none of which are worth the effort to presently review. As always, Thomas goes with his gut. *Okay then. No need to waste time any more there,* he figures.

"Warp Factor Ten," he says, as he accelerates towards his targets...

He slows and stops at various points that inspired Tolkien, holding up and matching individual photos where *Mirkwood-green* and farmland once abounded. He scribbles notes of his findings.

There has been but one muse throughout history, read one of X's supplemental markups. Thomas had not planned on traveling the countryside today though the side trip had been scheduled in his itinerary for later in the week. Something *he* added. Not Denise. But then the package, X's notes...

No better time than the present, he concluded, *to return to the beginning.*

When he turns and lowers each photo from the perspective of their various angles and locations, Thomas's resulting views of the country are striking: skyscrapers, shopping malls, vast urbanization surrounded by nuclear plants...all hosted by a dull gray sky, in part wrought from rising black smoke of faulty auto exhausts.

Thomas exits the vehicle on his last stop. Here the green remains. Here he leans against his car, before walking to the closest tree and resting his foot on its base.

Here he sits and stares upward at the single ray of sun that barely manages to escape and envelop him.

He thinks of his wife, Elizabeth. When she died he wanted nothing more than to be at her side. His way of getting there was a stereotype: an orgy of self-destruction. It was something dramatic that most alcoholic, drug-addicted suicidal writers would appreciate.

A *Bacchanalian feast.*

He said this to Denise once. She responded, "You're important. You're not that important. Going *La Dolce Vita* on me isn't gonna register a blip." He knew she was full of shit but it didn't matter. Whenever a writer of any prominence passes, *blips happen.* If he did himself in, his posthumous book sales would briefly spike thanks to the curiosity from readers looking for clues. But when she followed up with, "You wouldn't want me to sell more books, would you?" in that bitchy manner of reverse-psychology only she could engineer, he gave in.

"Of course not. What was I thinking, huh?"

He didn't have the guts to engage anyway. Any of it. He didn't drink, he didn't believe in drugs after the first Reagan administration—and prior, only the infrequent joint as acid made him sick to his stomach—and he considered suicide selfish.

He had a unique identification with Nancy Reagan as she reminded him of his late mother. When Nancy Reagan said to *"say no to drugs,"* he listened.

He did, though, keep a scheduled speaking engagement the following week at Brooklyn College, his dad's alma mater.

"Heaven," said Thomas, "whether an invention of man—physicist Stephen Hawking once called heaven a 'fairy story' for those who were scared of the dark—or not, is based on...something. Whether an idea...a misdirection...or otherwise something quite real as returned to us from one who peeked...heaven is an ideal. Hell, by contrast...the origin of the concept notwithstanding, is something to be avoided at all costs. How then can we possibly live our lives freely, or happily, when outside circumstances conspire to force our actions?"

The session did not go over well. Thomas was widely accused of being "indulgent" to the point of boredom. He was expected to discuss his books. Though most did not know about his wife, he did not defend himself against his detractors.

He accepted the fact that he would never be invited back, and so he would move on from there. A loss of nothing compared to the prior week when Elizabeth breathed her last, so a ban didn't matter a whit.

When he returned home, Samantha met him at the door.

~~~

"Mom, she had a DNR?" Samantha holds up the paper. "Why didn't you tell me?"

"Where did you get that?" He was not expecting the confrontation, but nonetheless—"We didn't want to put you in the middle." He was

embarrassed by the weakness of the answer. He loathed lying to her. Truth is, he signed it and claimed to the doctor that he forgot about it. He couldn't bear to see his wife suffer.

"Doc Conroy called, looking for you. He asked me if you wanted this. I told him you weren't home but I would pick it up for you."

"You shouldn't have done that."

"Did you write this?" she demands.

He didn't know where to go. "You shouldn't have done that," he repeats.

"I know you signed her name to this! It's not even a good forgery." She followed as he walked into the kitchen. "WHY? Why did you do it?" He's about to answer, when she says, flatly, "Don't lie to me again, Dad."

~~~

"Don't lie to me again, Dad." The single sentence that has defined his actions, and inactions, since Elizabeth died. These days he would sooner avoid his daughter entirely than take the chance and squirm out of another uncomfortable scene. Which he's done. Out of another uncomfortable scene and out of her life. Samantha said she would never trust him again.

He threw himself into his work. He belongs to the world now.

Samantha has been on his mind more than ever of late. He misses her horribly. Her phone call was a wonderful, necessary distraction.

~~~

The tendency to work and then reminisce on the final days of their *proper* father-daughter relationship was becoming an all-too-familiar pattern. He strives mightily to immerse himself in his writing, but the legend of his favorite author has been so tightly-fraught within the McFee family to a degree where traps of reflection are often inescapable.

Which is why so much of his professional life revolves around Tolkien. This, and the other matter of his own father having met the man himself.

192

Franklin once told him: "He was as real as you and I and sometimes I think surprisingly insecure. When J.R.R. Tolkien entered a room it was as if he was guided either by a marvelous light, or else by something quite melancholy." Thomas clasps his hands, rests his elbows on his knees and stares above at a misty, shallow moon.

As he looks, a quick question comes to mind and he utters it aloud:

"But it's only three," he says. "What's with the afternoon moon?"

MIRKWOOD

Taebal is enraptured by the moon, now wreathed in fog.

As he and Ara enter the open castle gates, he pauses and turns back to what may be his final glimpse of the world outside. His fate is uncertain, and he wants the moment to last. These things he ponders as the gates grind and close behind them.

"AN UNDISCLOSED LOCATION," LONDON, ENGLAND

Brikke sits on a stool as a doctor pricks his finger.

His blood runs through a tube attached to an auto-sampler; the doctor analyzes the numbers. He nods and thanks Brikke, who stands, glares at Daniel and approaches a decontamination chamber.

He is in and out in seconds, and is cleared to enter an awaiting yellow school bus. Marlo has been saving his seat. She waves to him from the window as he approaches.

Samantha watches him go. *This should never have been so easy—*

"Samantha McFee?"

"McFee?" Samantha didn't hear the attendant the first time—a stern, overweight woman reading from a clipboard. Her surname is written, in black marker, on a sticker-tag affixed to her right breast: Esme. Samantha turns. Upon noticing the woman, and then the name, she thinks: *But that would be impossible.*

Charade on.

Samantha hides her concern and says, admonishingly, to Daniel: "I told you there was nothing to worry about." She bites her lower lip and takes her seat on the stool. She completes her procedures five minutes later and steps outside. She waits, apprehensively, for her fiancé; together, they will enter the second of three school buses.

Daniel joins her and tightly clasps her hand as they walk towards their transport. "Settle down, would you? It's over," she says.

"Sam, right now—"

She knows what will happen next. He'll question everything: her job, her position...her strict confidentiality oath which, of course, has no place in a marriage. All of which will lead to the usual fibs, guilt...

No different than dear ol' Dad.

Daniel will go on an overnight bender—hopefully soon—and *then* put his suspicions behind him. Until next time.

"Don't worry about it. There's always tomorrow." she says.

"It's a dead issue."

Wishful thinking. Both, at once.

They've reached the bus and enter in stone silence. Samantha takes the window; Daniel, her immediate left. The buses leave in ascending order, accelerating onto a dirt road as they enter a miles-long countryside path.

Barely yards beyond a sign—

LONDON

434 km

—Samantha dials on her cellphone.

194

"Who are you calling now?" Daniel needles. *"Hercules? Frankenstein?"*

"I'm calling Denise."

"Oh. *Katness.*" Samantha scowls. "Then again," he resumes, *"she* shoots straight. You both could learn a lot from Katness."

"Letting her know we're okay. Please—"

"You don't think she watches the news?"

She ignores him. The call picks up. He listens in as best he can. "Well son of a bitch, Sam. You couldn't get me back?" Samantha crouches closer to the window, muffling the call from Daniel. He doesn't care all that much. He closes his eyes.

"I've been a little busy," says Samantha flatly.

"I called you yesterday! Then ten hours ago, five hours ago." Denise persists.

"Sorry. I appreciate the concern—"

"Thank God for your dad. He didn't want to speak to me either."

"It's not that—"

"He didn't want to speak to me either but he had no choice. He let me know you were still in one piece."

"Then why are you calling?" Daniel butts in.

Samantha cups the phone. "I called her!"

"You still there? Sam—" Denise can still be heard on the other end.

"I'm here."

SCARP PUBLISHING

Denise paces nervously.

"Well, good," she says. "The last thing I need is for two McFees to make my life miserable."

"Denise?"

"How can I help you?"

"This isn't a good time but I did want to at reach out and let you know

195

everything is fine."

"That's mighty kind of you but everything is not fine." She settles slowly. "You said you spoke to your dad?"

Daniel elbows her. *Not now.*

"Briefly. Look, Denise, I really have to go."

"Did he say anything to you?" she asks, slyly.

"No. What are you talking about?"

"Who's with you?"

A brief pause. "Exactly."

Nothing more needs to be said. Denise retreats. "You promise to call me later?"

"I promise."

"I mean it. We need to talk."

"Is it a matter of life and death?"

"Not yet."

"What then?"

"It can wait." She exhales, for a change. "Honestly. I'm glad you're well. Call when you can."

"If it's important I can talk for a couple more minutes. What's going on—"

Denise hangs up, disgusted. She walks to the closest window. They are all closed. She looks upward. Black smoke is billowing from the rooftop, and is rapidly expanding.

~~~

Sitting on the roof much as he did days ago at Denise's brownstone, X watches the fire trucks down below. The gauntlet covers his right arm and hand and he is consumed by its power. Proving his newfound strength as far beyond his greatest imaginings, he casually manipulates the torridlyspreading fire that should already have killed him.

Elemental, my dear Watkins, he thinks, before snickering at the all-too-obvious pun.

ENGLISH COUNTRYSIDE

"How about we do something different this time?" asks Samantha, placing her hand on Daniel's knee. "Whatever happened today, we were in it together. There's no reason to be mad. How about we end the big freeze now and start fresh?"

"Do you know him, Sam?"

She shakes her head. "Yeah, I do," she offers. "But you'll need to trust me on the rest because you know that's all I'm going to give you."

"Look. I'll ask you again. I know you're not playing around behind my back—" He catches her suppressing a laugh. "That's funny to you?"

"No, it's not funny. You're just so goddamn ridiculous sometimes."

"I'm glad I amuse you."

"Why don't you finish?"

He tries his level-best to remain stoic. She doesn't see him crack a smile, from which he quickly *recovers.* He can't help himself either. "You're such a c—"

Their bus suddenly swerves, as the bus in front of them loses control.

"Jesus—" Samantha gasps.

They pass Thomas walking back to his car. He is clearly visible through Sam and Dan's right-side windows, though in the fracas neither notices. And then it happens again. This time, the impact is far worse.

Screaming.

Or the equivalent—some sort of dreadful noise cocktail like that a terrified child complains about to Mommy or Daddy when they're not crying wolf. It's no concoction but the parents are never convinced. Maybe it really is a horridly-clogged earful of crickets or bees or locusts. Or all, one legion, collectively, close enough to be heard harping a sing-song of life or whatever is the opposite—maybe dying. The complaints are not always an excuse to stay home from school. Sometimes, children really are more perceptive than the adults, and only they know it. Only they hear the incessant buzzing, whistling, chirping—all together now!—and it feels like it will never stop.

This is the sound that presently emanates from the bus that is rapidly spinning out of control in front of them.

~~~

The second and third buses following have managed to stop and swerve onto grass to avoid a collision. The side of Samantha's head is split and has broken the window. She is conscious but shaken. Daniel grabs her cell and dials furiously.

"We need help!" he shouts. "I don't have time to hold!" Furious, he keeps the phone to his ear while removing an old, stained handkerchief from his pocket. He presses it against Sam's gash.

"Ow. God," she mutters.

"Hold it and press hard," he says. "You'll be okay. It's just a bad scratch—"

"Damn it. Fucking hurts—"

"Do as I say for a change, please, and sit there. Don't move." She reluctantly leans back in her seat and follows his directive. He gets up to observe the damage. The rest of the passengers seem okay. Minor bruises here and there but a lot of crying. Everyone is, as expected, shaken. He pats the head of some of the kids, reassuring them. Sam watches, and through the trauma is again reminded why she wants to spend the rest of her days with him.

Emergency gets back on the phone. "Where is your location?"

"We're in the country, we're..." he looks for signs. He's lost. "We're about ten minutes out from—" He looks over at Sam. Their prior location was "undisclosed." He's become used to confidentiality issues, and for a moment he considers that Sam may be possibly *exposed* in some way if he discloses too much information. And yet, these kids...

What would she do? he ponders.

"Call choppers," he decides. "Many injured. We're in the countryside, approximately ten miles west of ..." He sighs, giving in. "About ten miles west of The Carmelite Monastery in Notting Hill."

Thomas runs to help as the first bus tumbles into the grass, stopping on its passenger-side. Once it stops rolling, Brikke holds onto the driver's panel, standing over the driver who is now unconscious. The rest of the passengers are also blacked out, save for Marlo, who joins the giant. She is no longer limping when she walks over and reaches into a bag lying just under the driver's seat.

She unzips the bag and removes its *glistening* contents.

SCARP PUBLISHING

Rooftop.

X opens and closes his fist, experimenting with the gauntlet. He's realized that the ancient device can be controlled by his movements, rendering his new strength all the more impressive. When he closes his fist, the fire retracts. When he opens it...

For now, he maintains the presence of mind not to be responsible for any lives.

For now.

Emergency personnel evacuate the building. Half of their battle is maintaining a sense of calm for those escaping down the open stairwells.

Elevator service has been discontinued from floors 21-40. Everything below operates as usual. Denise is forcibly escorted by her arm as she reaches for a manuscript to bring with her.

McFee's.

As he tugs at her, the fireman looks up and out her window. He's momentarily distracted, as the smoke dissipates and pulls away, and expands again. He clicks his walkie: "Orci. Sergeant, do we have an air team on the roof, over?"

Over the radio, in response: "Orci, your team reported on location less than ten minutes ago. Awaiting your report if air is necessary."

"Roger that."

Denise pulls away, rushes to grab the manuscript and leaves on her own as Orci shakes his head and follows.

ENGLISH COUNTRYSIDE

Eron's sweord is nearly as long as Marlo is tall. She knows exactly what she has unearthed and clearly expected as much. She straightens her frame and stands the weapon to her side. *So close.* Marlo then lets the sweord fall into her palms and presents the implement to Brikke.

SCARP PUBLISHING

X continues to open and close his fist, and yet the fire extinguishes, on its own, regardless of his efforts. He stands, waves the hand wearing the gauntlet...removes the device...attempts to adjust it...Though the power source seems to have terminated, a shadow abruptly hits the gauntlet's back. And then another.

Coordinates? On a whim, X removes a few stolen cellphones from his pocket, finds a *GPS* app and begins to play.

All right. Seconds, if that...

Brikke's cellphone rings from his pocket. Marlo is as surprised as he is. He looks to her for advice and she nods.

He initiates the receiver but doesn't say a word. He puts the phone to his ear. After an extended pause, X discloses: "I have what you're looking for." Seconds pass in mutual consideration, and X terminates the call.

Brikke gently holds the sweord, running his hand over it, studying it. He sighs, as if his efforts have personally culminated in a great victory. Or partially so. "Halfway home," he says to his companion.

"The gauntlet survives," Marlo acknowledges. "You were right. Yours is the hand who will save us." Brikke is deep in thought. He looks to her, at this moment the only person in his universe that he can trust. "I'm sorry?" she adds, weakly.

Brikke wields the sweord, though bereft of the gauntlet the implement itself is relatively useless.

"You can make yourself bleed," she adds. "You can live as one of them and guide them with grace." As Brikke figures his next move— "Taebal is coming," Marlo warns. "And he—"

Blood seeps from her mouth and she gurgles, choking. She falls; eyes wide-open, staring at the man who has just slain her. Or freed her.

Regardless, the point of the sweord is still sharp enough to kill...just another mortal. He freezes; the realization is gradual. "Oh no, please," he desperately pleads. "Oh, not y—" He sweeps her head and cradles her in his arms, sobbing hysterically. "My sweet girl, our work is not done! You *swore* to me you were one of us." Brikke wipes his shirt with her blood, then gently rests her head atop the rubber flooring. "I let you *see* me," he cries. "I let *them* see me..."

Her eyes remain open. And he affirms what he has long denied: She is who she's always been. A young, physically-impaired human girl, who compensated for her disabilities with a particularly active, hopeful imagination. A dreamer of faraway lands and races, where she could assert her *being-ness* and be accepted as *normal.*

Nothing more.

Although ...

I never told her of Taebal, the dragon.

She told him once that she loved him. They were the best of friends, and he was her personal bodyguard of sorts, which was most fun whenever the hospital kids traveled off-grounds. Marlo believed that every day was a small part of a larger *epic,* that she and Brikke were on a great *quest* together and that they were meant to be inseparable.

But Marlo does not remember a life before the hospital. She does not remember her real parents nor her birth name. He called her "Marlo," from *Marlow* in England, where once was written the preface to "Frankenstein."

"Are you calling me a monster?" she asked him.

"No," Brikke responded. "An angel."

She cannot recall how she met Brikke and he never told her.

He just aways...was. And *is.*

Like a *muse* they once talked about in a *make believe* land known as Mirkwood.

He was as *different* as she.

As was the muse, from her family. Different from them all. This they continued to speak of, now and again.

And Brikke ignored the obvious—the logic of it—as there were signs all along. The fatal act of moments ago was intended as a *confirmation*, not a killing.

Inconsolable, Brikke turns the weapon on himself; the implement penetrates his stomach and exits through his back. He still stands.

Losing a well-fought battle of restraint, the giant bellows in frustration, a guttural, horrid wail. It is an unwelcome affirmation of his own miserable existence, and a stark reminder of his responsibility that, upon the gir's passing—as she herself had reminded him—this grave battle will be his alone.

He didn't believe she was capable of passing, this angel who was capable of being his friend.

He is briefly distracted by loud *bangs* emanating from outside, towards the rear of the bus.

"Can anyone hear me?" Thomas yells.

"Hello! Is everyone okay in there!" He hears nothing. "Is anyone okay in there?"

Thomas looks up. He notices, above breaks in the fog, that the sky has shifted suddenly to what appears to be a darker shade of hell. A disquieting, reddish hue.

Passengers from the other buses leave their transport to help.

Dan helps the kids; Samantha stares in disbelief upon noticing her Dad.

He sees her as well. His reaction is identical.

The strobes of flashing sirens project and dissolve into a firmament now very nearly as red as Marlo's death.

The authorities are on their way.

203

Scarp Publishing

X has left the roof and discreetly wanders the streets. The evacuation appears to have been successful. The gauntlet has ceased to function and no fire remains.

Minutes ago I was a god …

He looks to the increasingly red clouds above, punctuated by a second layer of fire that is slowly breaking though.

Asia, Africa, South America, Antarctica, Australia

Worldwide. The skies are becoming more than a curiosity. They are becoming a concern.

Global newscasts *create* and track the *event.*

"一份 烦扰的 大气的 异常的人或物"

"…an atmospheric anomaly…"

"…of as-yet unknown cause. To repeat, we…"

"…are covering a breaking story…"

"…dismissed by one controversial purveyor as, and I quote…"

East Village, New York, New York

Dante's tenth ring of hell:

Inevitability.

Another home—a studio loft—and another computer. The room's television is on, the volume is low. X is astounded by the tenor of the current syndicated report.

"'Dismissed? Sons of bitches," he mutters in disbelief. *What will it take?*

The report continues: "The enigma known only as X, who is now a suspect in the Scarp Publishing Fire…"

That captures him further. "An eyewitness, who wishes to remain anonymous, claims to have seen what appeared to be an older, dark-skinned, possibly African-American teenager, descend from the Scarp's rooftop at approximately 4:58 P.M. this evening."

X walks towards the television. "Police have sketched the man, based on the eyewitness report." The reporter holds the etching to the camera. The likeness is uncanny. Sirens approach. Someone has called the cops. X panics. His breath becomes faster, shallow. He peeks out the window.

They have arrived.

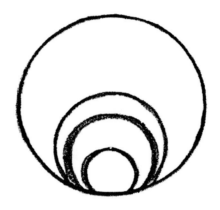

THE FIRST FALLEN

The king. A muse. A dragon.

Eron is dead. The king has no heir. There is still but one kingdom in Mirkwood and the king awaits its imminent fall. He has never been one to deny inevitability. Hence…

The king hosts the duo in his throne room. The room is faced by open windows that frame an intimidating cover of brilliant red sky. He explains to his visitors the urgency of their gathering.

"The gods are preparing my final passage," the king says. "Yet the heavens are bloody."

A brief regard outside and Ara is further angered. "We were summoned," she says, "and I do not understand. This dragon has traveled by my side with little food or water from afar and you state the obvious? This is your message?"

"You use your companion as an excuse?" Ara doesn't answer. "The universe turns and no matter of god—nor mortal, I'm afraid—yet comprehends all of its mysteries." The king refuses to waver. "It has been foretold that the answers shall attend many, many sunrises hence but for now, confessing to a certain ignorance...yes, I was expecting *you.* I swore to the gods. You alone have heeded my cries. I desired an audience with the entity responsible for my son's death." Ara scowls. "Perhaps I am emboldened in my present state," he continues, "speaking thusly to an immortal but no matter. Time—"

"Time is yours to waste," Ara flatly responds. "I am responsible for nothing."

"Time," returns the king, "is no longer a luxury. My instincts tell me that Eron is solely responsible for our meeting and I feel confident in addressing you as his murderer. And that what happens here is his will."

"What is it then?"

"Did he ask for your help?"

Ara seethes. "I must confess to you a terrible anger, a hatred of all things known and unknown as I look into your eyes..." She is barely able to continue. "You are selfish. You are blaming him for my actions, which—"

"Quite the contrary. To the extent of my son fighting for the greater good, he has become a martyr."

"Though you imply as much, *you* are no such thing."

"Then allow me to begin again by disclosing to you what I know," he continues, speaking over her. "I am keenly aware of your exile...my dear *Ara.*"

The muse cannot speak. Taebal observes her reaction and growls at the king in response. The dragon finds himself vacillating and becoming protective of her. He understands that she could have killed him at her whim. He does not understand his contradictory impulses. What is most unusual for him, however, is that she has never appeared so vulnerable, so helpless.

"In truth *you* have been self-serving from the beginning," the king resumes. "The very thought of a muse and a mortal, together, is an unconscionable sin. Eron sensed your presence. He acted upon his instinct ...and you killed him." Ara is about to object, when— "I'm telling you nothing you don't know."

"A goddess," she says, containing her emotion, "a true goddess such as I...does not comport so. How—"

"You believe yourself to be a *true* goddess do you?"

"How dare—"

"You killed him," he repeats.

"No..."

"*You* were selfish and he lost his focus. And, very soon I'm afraid, I will join him—"

"You are already spirit..." she realizes.

The king suddenly transforms into a regal image of his son, taking his place on the throne.

Ara breaks into sobs...

"The natural order, as it should have been...Will I convince you with this more pleasing image?" the king asks, before quickly transforming back.

Ara reclaims her senses. "The other gods really *are* tricking me..." She stops herself, forcing the thought away...

"I had no reason go on," the king continues. "I left this coil mere moments upon hearing of my son's demise, though we have not yet rejoined. It appears I am being held in this...*purgatory* to deliver this message to you..." He turns away in regret, peering to the red outside. "My blood boils much like the clouds in your presence. Soon they will part and the dead shall remind us that their fates too have hinged on this outcome...You have become *dark*. Once The Truth is known and my son is implicated as the cause of...all this..."

"The actions were not his. They were mine. I admit—"

"Do you not then hold any account aside from your own?"

"I just—"

"This discourse grows tiresome. My bloodline will be identified and you will have sullied my son's name! The natural order must be restored and—"

"Only another god would know such. Only another god would dare speak to me as you do—"

"You are but a child," the king sighs. "As you know...I am no god. Your confusion will be your undoing as it was with Eron." Ara listens, ashamed. "If you were mortal and I was able to draw my sword, I would strike you where you stand for your actions. And then of course your dragon would attempt to destroy me. This dragon, which I remind you is your only surviving connection to my..."

Taebal growls; his head motions up and down, as if nodding in agreement.

The king resumes. "To avenge my greatest loss shall re-start the clock of the world. It is the only way—"

"But the dragons—" Taebal scowls at her, though she pays him scant attention. "See for yourself. The dragons—"

"Suspending the dragons is...inadequate," he explains. "Eron could never see nor grasp the source of his obsession then." He closes his eyes, as if admitting to a truth he is loathe to confront. "Yet now, I know that he's watching. His hostility with you has transcended boundaries of time and space, and from the netherworld he is sending me a message—"

"You are bluffing."

He ignores her. "By returning to dragon-scorched earth...a time before recorded time when the dragons were once dominant, only then would you have the opportunity to meet again—"

"I do not understand—"

"Then return to your family for the answers you seek ..."

"That's imposs—" She reconsiders. "And you are asking me to set loose the dragons that destroyed your son—"

"I am begging for a return of the natural order. That which survives, survives. Releasing the dragons and every living thing is the only way—"

"Why?" This time, the king does not answer. "And my cost?" Ara asks instead. "What is my cost—"

"Your cost is the entirety of the world. On your shoulders..." He realizes that neither does she grasp this meaning. "You have two, very real choices. You can standby and do nothing and the universe remains in permanent suspension. Or, you can reverse your actions, obey your exile and allow Eron and the rest of the world—as you say, 'both known and unknown'—a peaceful, *natural* passage..." He considers his words. "There truly is but one decision. In my son's honor, you must free the dragons, you must free them all—"

"But Eron...he was a dragon *slayer*—"

"Eron's spirit shall visit safely with your companion. What does *Taebal* tell you?" Ara glances at the little dragon but does not engage. As she ponders, the king regards the world outside. "Time is bleeding and only you can restart it—"

She peers out the window, to skies the color of her hair. "The spirits of the dead are restless, as you." She gives up the prior questioning. "We are making no progress. There is a third option."

"If you believe as much you are tragically misguided."

"The skies settle when I bathe my hair in the blood of spirit."

"Meaning?"

"*You* will not understand." She sets to go. "I see nothing more—"

"But neither do you *see* the actions of your sisters as you are imperfect." The comment was well-timed. Ara's being goes limp. Her head bows in quiet submission; she has heard these words all-too-frequently from her sisters who ridiculed her, and she must finally acknowledge the truth. "You are imperfect and your thinking is as cloudy as it is beyond this window. But those clouds have not yet broken either. There is still hope. Once they do...it is too late to turn back. The natural order must be *immediately* restored," the king follows. "With no further interference by the likes of you—"

"I will not abide you addressing me thus as I *am* a god you speak of—"

"Though you *were* a god. A god condemned to relive a great loss over and again throughout the ages as you too have the ability to die—"

"This is not possible—"

"—is a god no longer. Not only possible but true, I'm afraid." To compliment his point: "You are aware, of course, that not all the dragons have been suspended. Where there's smoke—"

"I *cannot* believe you..."

"You were cursed by your sisters...you have been sentenced by the other immortals and then you interfered in their design." The king's ghostly-visage begins to fade. "Ara, you truly are imperfect but only you can make it right—"

"No ..."

"Only you," the king continues, "but in so doing you must never again attempt to reach my son. To do so will destroy everything."

She speaks softly. "I don't believe you." The king's form shimmers. "I will help only Eron," Ara continues. "We are fated to be together…" she responds, waging a personal war of indecision.

"You *are* misguided. If there is any hope I shall leave you with this: Taebal must remain by your side at all times. Watch him always. If my son is not in his presence to keep him tamed, he is as impulsive as his ilk. Quite easily turned and not to be trusted…"

At that last, Taebal breathes his fire. Ara doesn't stop him; instead, she allows him the freedom to act on his impulse. The king vanishes into the ether.

"He lied, Taebal," Ara adds. "It's a trick and there are too many questions. If the spirit of my beloved watches over you, as the king has suggested, he would never warn me to stay away. If the dragons are freed and they destroy the mortals, how then could we ever be together? His words are empty…"

In response, Taebal turns and enflames the curtains, the documents. The castle proceeds to burn to the ground as the dragon and his muse turn and walk outside.

~~~

Many, many eons later, Brikke escapes with Marlo as St. Peter's Children's Hospital crumbles around them.

Ara glimpses the far future event as she and Taebal approach the foot of the nearest mountain. Taebal is dazed from the stench of rising smoke, streaking the scarlet troposphere that has been carried by the winds from the fallen kingdom beyond even this considerable distance.

My immortal brothers and sisters, she ponders, *would not—or could not—stop me. Do I sense the presence of another force, of an intruder…stronger than I?*

Indeed, they are not alone. Rising, Phoenix-like from the castle's remnants, eyes affixing on both as he stands, S'n Te dusts himself off but does not yet advance.

He does, however, track their every move.

Futures upon futures but there is no witness to this period, Ara considers. *If it were not for this intruder, there would be no future at all.*

Once they leave his sight, S'n Te slowly lags behind. Ara amends and punctuates her final thought: *If Eron and I cannot be together, there will be no future at all.*

The first drops of blood are released from the clouds...

~~~

She has ignored the king's wishes. The other dragons remain suspended as the muse and her companion disappear in the distance and the clouds finally break and threaten to flood the *murky wood* with scarlet reminders of the world's restless deceased.

Over-dwellers.

So-regarded as they do not allow themselves to pass and reincarnate peacefully. They *dwell*, actively, as opposed to *resting* until which time the gods would return their souls into new living forms. Invariably, they are fighters, most with families, all with reason for the wars they continue to wage, all who have died before their time and have unfinished business to attend to.

They will—ineffectively—swing and punch and kick and spit and blind and...Whatever it takes to recover their prior lives. For many moons have they been conspiring for their release...Which is exactly what would have happened—the calamity, less the threat—had the blood rain not suddenly ceased before touching ground and the skies returned to their normal shade of dull.

And had S'n Te not quickened his pace, allowing Ara the vaguest notice of his robed frame...she would not have suddenly reversed her intent and spared the downpour just a split-second before the first drop touched ground.

There will be another time. The right time...

But first, she must solve the enigma of this mystic who continues to prod on despite the cessation...and whose existence has, until now, never crossed a god.

So again she breaks the gods' rules and intervenes, ridding herself of a primary distraction. The world resumes and spins again yet, with the lone exception of Taebal, all of the dragons are vanquished. Though the king had mentioned the presence of other, active dragons, Ara chose to receive his words not only as bluff but also reinforcement that she controls her options. The muse will leave nothing to chance; she would immediately slay all the dragons herself if she followed her impulse, likely including her present companion...but in the event of a freak, unforeseen circumstance, maybe a possible act of sedition by her sisters, she realizes that she may one day require their help.

As with Taebal, for other reasons.

Ara has carefully considered the rest as well: *For every other manner of flesh and blood life goes on as usual; eventually, the extended hibernation of the fire-breathers will lead to questions and concerns, and a fierce debate between two opposing factions that shall now come to the fore and position for a new monarchy.*

All of which hastens the outcome of her grand plan. In all events, she will remain focused on her endgame and do what she must to get there.

NEW YORK, NEW YORK, 1970

Scattered voices from the vault. Today, the three gentlemen have been joined by another.

The guards stand by, their eyes darting back and forth from the table where Tolkien presently holds forth. Ink bottles and test strips rest to his side. "McFee," Tolkien says, "the *Nowell Codex* that survived Ashburnham is a single manuscript. *Beowulf* as we know it was but one of its books. The others are unrelated. Which means, to my admittedly fractured sensibilities—age, you know, may be kind to wisdom, not sense necessarily—that if these pages are authenticated by Mr. Levin here, we are likely in the presence of the fabled second book of—"

"No." The baritone Professor Peter Levin surprises them all with his curt response. Mid-sixties, bearded, well-dressed in sportscoat and slacks he is, clearly, nobody's fool.

"No?" asks a forcibly polite Donovan.

"Gentlemen," Levin answers, "and I confess my appreciation of you all is immeasurable...this is *not* the missing *second* book of *Beowulf*." As the others allow for the beginnings of horrid, personal disappointment, Levin smiles. "*This* is the heretofore unknown *first* book."

Tolkien stands, on his own power. Donovan and Franklin reach to support him but he waves them off. "The *first?*" he stammers.

"An *introduction,* actually, as opposed to a separate book. If I may amend my answer, these pages were intended to be digested *before* the common text. What we've considered through the years as the unique version of *Beowulf,* Levin explains, "was included in the *Nowell Codex* as you've stated. Also included, as you know, Professor ..."

Tolkien finishes the sentence:

"...*The Life of Saint Christopher, Letters of Alexander to Aristotle, Wonders of the East* and *Judith.* Only the first was a fragment," he says. "The others are complete. Or *were*—"

"Until now," Levin concludes. "Apologies for the interruption."

"Not necessary."

"In the context of storyline, these initial stanzas ..." Levin runs his hand over the pages, "comprise the tale of the dragonslayer as told from the perspective of the muse who inspired him, or otherwise of the author who invented it."

"The muse who inspired him? Perhaps, but in this context, as you say, maybe we should leave the *hidden meanings* for others to decide?" asks Donovan. "In some circles, such a reference would be considered blasphemous. Why take the blame? A reconsideration of one of the iconic texts—"

"In point of fact," Levin defends his point, "a reconsideration adds bulk and, I daresay, a bit of clarity to the already-epic proceedings."

"Professor Tolkien, what do you think? Donovan asks.

"Another opinion?" echoes Franklin.

"Please," Tolkien replies. "I accept Professor Levin's expertise and I suggest you both do the same."

"In that case, I have another idea," Franklin adds. The men turn. "I say we go to O'Malley's down the street, slam a few, and decide how we're going to hide the windfall from our dear wives." They all laugh. All, except for Tolkien.

"Perhaps, if you leave me back at the hotel, then?" Tolkien asks.

"Nothing doing," Franklin answers. "I wore a hat when I checked in. We're about the same size. No one will notice."

"You are comparing your head to that of J.R.R. Tolkien?" Donovan ribs.

Levin gets them back on track. "If I was to be serious for a minute, I don't know whether to celebrate or hide," he says. "This is...historic and...and, um, I'm quite speechless, actually. Much unlike me, which you'll find hard to believe the longer you know me—"

"You're right. Let's drink."

"Franklin...my friend, we'll get there. I think first, to formalize these proceedings...The entirety of your document is authentic, gentlemen." Donovan is more demonstrative than the rest. He beams, and pumps his fist in victory. Tolkien, for the moment, is reserved, pensive. "I've been thinking, as we've been gathered here," Levin adds, "about Beowulf himself. The character. He would always go it alone, my friends. Victory and glory would be his and his only; he's a man forever in exile, but why? Whom or what was he hiding from? I would ask those questions of the present party. Now that we can better appreciate his motives, perhaps?"

"Can we get to the point?" Franklin asks, impatiently. "Not to be rude, but..." He motions taking a quick shot of alcohol.

"Franklin, your imbibing will have to wait. And may I suggest that you allow me the pleasure of a complete thought before interrupting again, thank you." Tolkien chuckles at Levin's manner; Franklin sinks his teeth tightly upon his lower lip so as to remain quiet. "To speak to your earlier question, Beowulf attained everlasting legend though he was slain by the dragon. I was merely curious is all. In the meantime..." Levin changes course, "we have found what may be most accurately described as literature's *holy grail.*" He turns to Tolkien. "Your inspiration—which I am inclined to believe also served the original scop of this work and was adapted as a motivator for our protagonist—what does your muse tell you now? I would be very curious to know."

Franklin whispers to Donovan. "He certainly can be a divisive sort, don't you think?" Donovan smirks in response.

"Certainly." Tolkien proceeds carefully, responding to Levin. "Monetarily, the value of this piece...well, this is a priceless find. A priceless find." Franklin and Donovan are surprised. Levin remains attentive.

"With respect, Professor Tolkien," Donovan inquires, in the form of a statement, "these pages are so much more important than the money they would command—"

"My friend, your predilection for stating the obvious only adds to my fondness," Tolkien replies, as Donovan shirks away.

"You two go to the same charm school or something?" adds Franklin, immediately regretting his knee-jerk reaction.

"You cannot call me *Ronald* and yet you are throughly entitled to insult me, that it?" Franklin looks around, fraught with embarrassment. There is nowhere to hide. Tolkien slaps him on the shoulder. "Relax, my boy—both of you. We're making progress." Franklin cautiously turns back. "I will stand by the majority. My larger interest now is that speculative. What else is out there?"

Levin picks up the strands: "Do you believe in magic, Ronald?"

Tolkien notices the men hanging on his every word. "Do I believe in magic? Or are you asking me if I believe in the possible realization of other worlds such as Middle-earth?" He laughs. "Before I get to my stock answer, gentlemen, let me tell you a story. The best advice ever given to me came to me in a dream. In this *moonlight sonata* during my very early youth, a hooded vagrant—further shielded from the blazing sun by a friendly branch or two—said to me, 'Never be afraid of the trees.'"

"The trees?" asks a confused Levin.

"I understand," Franklin concedes.

"You see," rejoins Tolkien, "you should have completed that book! Perhaps you can explain it."

"Professor Tolkien was frightened of trees as a boy. And then years later, having power over all things—"

"Oh, hush," says Tolkien.

"Having power over all things," Franklin continues, "he incorporates symbolically the trees throughout his Middle Earth cycle. Our esteemed visitor here has long since become a lover of nature. He abhors out-of-control technology."

Tolkien motions to the papers on the table. "The trees became my friends. Because I learned to believe and trust in the—yes—the, *magic* of trees, I gained the freedom to explore. This, in turn, opened so many creative doors for me..." He points whimsically to his noggin.'Here. Many of my characters continue to be defined as either good or evil depending on how they treat my trees."

Donovan is awestruck. "Outstanding..." he murmurs.

"So," Tolkien concludes, "in summation of my long-winded response, what I will end today's *lecture* with is...don't ever break the spell. *Always* believe. And that is the best advice I could possibly give to you." The men nod as one, entranced, like a well-choreographed Broadway troupe introducing the very first move of a new dance. "As to the rest, my dear colleagues, I leave it in your hands."

"Do you think we can handle it?' Franklin asks, earnestly.

"What choice do I have?" Tolkien laughs. "I've done what *I* needed to do. I've seen what I needed to see. And, within seventy-two hours I shall enjoy that drink, but with my wife and my wife only." Franklin laughs, but behind the gesture is a certain tension, in his face, that belies a crushing frustration. "My friends," Tolkien continues, "I shall spend the rest of my days loving her and, one hopes, creating new worlds with *this* newfound inspiration." He and the others turn their attention to the contents on the table. "Thanks to you all, *Beowulf* lives again." He smiles, like a sprite.

"Ara's will, Professor?' Donovan asks hopefully.

"My dear Bradley, I *believe* I already answered your question." Still

219

smiling, he extends his hand to Donovan first, then the others. Handshakes all around. "Gentlemen..."

~~~

Minutes later.

The material is being translated into English. There are now four chairs in the vault; all of the men sit.

A typewriter has been removed from an open bag and is now also on the table. Tolkien points and transcribes as Franklin types—

"Listen!"

The author of *The Hobbit* and *The Lord of the Rings* is enraptured, his imagination transporting him as an observer into the faraway land and ancient events he breathlessly discloses—within *Middle-earth*.

Beowulf's Middle-earth.

"In the darkest days," Tolkien resumes, "after angels once tread, then first came Ara, who led a race of seers, to keep watch over the dragons and the kings. And Beowulf, the future king. And then the adventures of the future king and his tragedy, to sake a record for the world. Listen!"

He continues to read, but in his mind's eye Tolkien *watches* as they compare their find to the existing, accepted work...

Beowulf attacks the creature Grendel.

Beowulf's mother attacks the grand hall and is defeated by the opposing army.

Beowulf returns to Sweden and becomes King of the Geats.

Beowulf slays a dragon but is fatally wounded in the process.

Beowulf's great funeral, during which he is buried with the dragon's treasure hoard, is attended by commoners and dignitaries.

"A pesky reminder that my *Smaug*," jokes an invigorated Tolkien, "didn't corner the market on dragons and their doubloons."

Franklin looks up. "The gold was Spanish?"

Donovan crumples a piece of paper and tosses it at Franklin head. "Why don't you get back to work, McFee," Tolkien advises. "As will I..."

~~~

The impromptu break has long-concluded; the work has resumed and, in the process, illuminated the poem's primary addition: a framing device, solving the mystery of the epic's true *author...*

Ara orally composes the story of Beowulf, alone, while sitting under the giant tree that surrounds her, as...

A scop awakens from a dream.

Meanwhile, as he continues translating...Tolkien *flashes back* to his youth and the hooded vagrant from his dream, who was "shielded from the blazing sun by a friendly branch or two."

The *vagrant's* two hands reach up and remove *her* hood. Again, Ara.

And young *Tolkien* awakens from his boyhood reverie.

As Franklin keeps pace, Tolkien vacillates from *Beowulf* to his own life:

The scop excitedly gathers a group of children and together they head to the trees, where he shares the new tale as a bittersweet Ara watches...

...and continues to watch, centuries later, *standing* in a corner of Tolkien's Oxford classroom as the confounded Professor writes the first words of his first novel.

"My, my," says Tolkien. He tokes on his pipe. "So, what do we have h—"

"Franklin?" Donovan looks worriedly to Levin, who nods as he too notices Franklin struggling to stay on track but falling woefully behind.

Levin places a hand on Tolkien's shoulder who, despite the marked enthusiasm, manages to pause. Levin, though appearing curiously preoccupied, points and Tolkien glances over.

"McFee?" Donovan nudges.

No answer; Franklin still struggles to catch up...

ENGLISH COUNTRYSIDE

It is minutes *before* the crash of the buses. Thomas McFee, his hands clasped and folded, his elbows on his knees, sits against a tree, staring above at a fog-shrouded moon.

Reflecting...

BRADLEY AND SON BIBLIOTHEQUE

Two days earlier.

"McFee!"

Thomas continues to work, voraciously, downstairs. He ignores Donovan, who is inching towards him from the stairwell. No rudeness intended; Thomas is intently focused. Donovan walks still closer, tossing a crumbled piece of paper at the writer's head. Not the first paper toss of his lifetime. In fact, many years ago, Thomas's father was a recipient of a similar Donovan Bradley fastball.

Thomas swats the paper aside like he would a mosquito.

"Would you like a spot of tea?" Donovan asks.

"I don't think so, thanks." Thomas doesn't so much as turn.

"Do you ever take breaks?"

"I tend to fall asleep on top of my work; those are my breaks. Is there a problem, Mr. Bradley?" He puts down his stylus, holding back his frustration.

"I didn't mean to interrupt. Well, yes, as a matter of fact I did."

"Can I help you with something?"

"I was thinking maybe I could save you some time. Maybe some trouble."

"I promise you, I'm just busy. Doing as *you* asked. There is no trouble."

"You haven't yet followed up with me about Tolkien's New York trip. Nor have you asked me about my participation in it."

McFee shuts his tablet, and locks it for good measure. "I thought, when the timing was right, that you would—"

"I need some fresh air. Why don't we hit a pub and I'll tell you all I know, huh?"

Thomas agrees. If there was anything that could pull him away from his work, it was this.

Unknown Tolkien. Privileged information that he may be able to add to his book.

He stands and helps Donovan to the stairwell.

JONESIES PUB, LONDON, ENGLAND

A nondescript establishment on a busy downtown street.

Inside, at a table and over drinks, Thomas taps and stares at the bottom of his glass. "He was a wonderful man," Donovan says. "I also found him to be quite sad and sometimes overzealous." Thomas taps as if he is unnerved. "Like father, like..." Donovan chances, bending his neck slightly and regaining eye contact.

"No. You see, my dad used to tell me that about Tolkien."

"With apologies to your dad, that's poppycock."

"Why do you say that, I wonder?" Thomas taps faster. Donovan looks to the writer's hand. Thomas notices the gaze and stops, self-conscious.

"Precisely. Your father was gregarious. You are far more private, I gather, though neither one of you could help but over-compensate for your disappointments. But then, perhaps I'm being cruel, which is not my intention..."

Thomas flips the backs of his hands on the table, as in, *Can you explain?*

"Franklin so wanted that evening to share a celebratory drink with Tolkien, his literary hero," Donovan continues. "Your father couldn't accept the response but it was all so innocent, you know. Tolkien wanted to save that drink for his wife. He was not being unkind. He confessed this secret to me, that any potential last round must be a toast from him to Edith. I didn't ask and I didn't question his wishes—"

"You didn't tell my dad?"

"I was told in confidence, so no. I assume it was a promise of some sort. For a hiccup, this non-issue became something of a joke among the other three—Levin, myself and even Tolkien, who felt a tad guilty when he was told about your father but was also a bit of a pixy—"

"A pixy?"

"He had a healthy sense of humor." Thomas nods. "So that night Levin and I took your Dad to a bar rather like this one. He got quite, how do you say it, *shit-faced?*" Thomas goes back to his tapping as Donovan goes on. "He was very upset until the morning Tolkien left. He found it increasingly difficult to be in his presence; it was quite out of proportion to the rejection to the point where it wasn't funny anymore." The tapping is quicker, more nervous. "I'm not trying to make you uncomfortable—"

"Don't mind me. I do have a question, though." Thomas does not look up.

"What's that?"

Thomas slows his tapping. "You said Tolkien's vow to Edith was a secret between him and you."

"That's right."

"Then how did Levin know?"

"Levin?"

224

"You just told me the secret became a joke among you three?"

Donovan for a quick but notable moment glares at his drinking companion. Thomas peeks and notices. He is struck by Donovan's suddenly harsh demeanor and the old man catches Thomas's curious gaze. Donovan then smiles, broadly, as if he was under a terrible spell and had just been freed. "Nothing of it!" he defends. "You may be correct. After all, the ravages of age...You do know I'm 90?"

Thomas lets it go. He had hoped for more, for answers he's been awaiting since he read the package sent by X.

Not yet...

"May I ask *you* something?" asks Donovan.

"Of course."

"When did you see him last?" the old man furthers. Thomas pauses. "Did you not hear me?"

"I heard you. I was thinking of a smart-ass answer," Thomas admits, "but nothing came to me. It's fine. My dad loved me. I know he loved me, but, goddamn him, when my Mom died—she had just turned 70—he changed. And then my Elizabeth got sick a few months after...We were in the hospital. My father was a wreck. He kissed Elizabeth, he kissed Sam—Samantha, my daughter—he hugged me and whispered in my ear, and this I'll never forget: 'I'm proud of you but *she's* our only hope now.' He was speaking of my daughter." Thomas wipes a tear. "Never heard from him again. To this day I have no idea if he's even alive—"

Thomas is probing but Donovan doesn't directly respond. "I'm sorry. I didn't mean—"

"—or what he meant." Thomas nods, and tries to force a smile. "The whole Tolkien thing with my family...I always felt that I was obligated to continue the work he never completed. I hope somewhere he's still proud."

"I'm sure." Thomas flicks another tear then laughs in embarrassment. "I understand loss," Donovan adds.

"Your own son, of course. That was selfish of me—"

"Nothing doing. We'll consider the venting mutual."

"Not a bad thing, huh?"

"Never," says Donovan. Thomas nods in approval. "Which brings us to this wonderful pub here on the West End."

"Yes, it does." Seconds pass. "So!" Thomas slaps the table. He takes a shot, squeezes his eyes closed in response to the alcohol, and slams the glass. "Ahhh." Another couple of seconds, and, "Where do we go from here?"

"You wanted to see the trees, the countryside?" offers Donovan.

"Ahhh, yes!" Thomas motions the waiter over for another shot. "I'm not used to drinking at ..." He looks at his watch. "7:34 in the morning."

"Life frequently takes one on unexpected journeys, no?"

The waiter returns, with another shot glass. "To unexpected journeys." Thomas swigs, and— "Waiter?" The waiter spins around. "I—"

"My boy wanted you to know that he is now cut off," Donovan interjects. His manner is nothing if not patronly. "He has a long drive this morning to look forward to." The waiter notices Thomas's surprise, but nods, takes the glass and leaves.

"I was just beginning to have fun," Thomas objects. "It was only my second."

"It was your third, and that's enough."

Thomas pulls back. "So," the writer says, "I guess this is the part where wisdom fills me in on the rest of my *hero's journey.*"

"That would be a correct assumption. To wit—"

"Do people actually talk that way here? '*To wit*'?"

"No."

226

"Didn't think so."

"To wit," Donovan continues, smirking. "Do they not say that insanity is doing the same thing every day and expecting a different result?"

"I think I've heard that somewhere."

"You can disagree if you choose to, of course." There is no objection forthcoming. "Tolkien," Donovan continues, "left his comfort zone and arrived in New York City. Surely what would occur from there would be substantially different than anything he had experienced before."

"What is it, exactly, that I need to know?"

"What's that?"

"There are, to my thinking, no real accidents in life. My deepest, my gut instinct tells me as much but I'm not a religious man. I'm practical. Do you understand what I'm trying to say?"

Donovan shakes his head. "Not at all."

"Neither do I." Thomas laughs, in a rare unguarded moment. "I told you I'm not used to drinking so early."

"But it's probably too late to change course, don't you think?".

"Maybe. How's this: Why me?"

"Very good. A question I can answer." Donovan studies Thomas for a moment before responding. "I received a letter from your dad. We began to a correspondence. After several weeks of questions, I came to trust him. I called Tolkien. It took many weeks to receive a return call. We started from there."

Thomas takes it in. "What don't I know?"

Donovan glances to Thomas's hand which, for now, remains still. "To be continued after a suitable interval." He swigs his own drink. "Tolkien chose to believe he had a guardian angel. Mind you, I say *chose* to believe..."

ALGONQUIN HOTEL, NEW YORK, NEW YORK, 1970

Lobby.

Franklin holds the silver briefcase as he stands at the front desk and helps Tolkien check out. The Professor wears a cap, hiding his features. Franklin is careful not to have Tolkien sign a thing; all signatures in care of both the Professor and Donovan are his.

"We'll be just another minute, Mr. McFee." Franklin grimaces; clearly, the concierge is taking his time. He cannot help but aggravatingly peek up at the author and smile upon meeting his eyes.

Time passes. "Will that be another of today's minutes, or...?" Franklin asks, losing patience.

"Very good, Mr. McFee. Groucho would love you."

Franklin nods, unsure of the concierge's intent there.

It's like a comedy show, he judges.

The concierge tears a piece of paper—the bill—and hands the mimeo page to Franklin. "Good to go," he says. "Please come again."

Franklin turns, tightening his grip on the case. "Come on, Sir," he says to Tolkien.

"Sir?" The concierge hurriedly grabs something from underneath his desk—a book—and leaves his post, motioning to those standing behind the duo to give him *just a minute*. "Before you go?" He rounds the bend and corners the two men. "I'm...truly sorry. A bit embarrassed, really. But, um—"

"Get on with it, then..." Franklin requests.

The concierge fawns over the author—

"I understand you don't want to be recognized and mum's the word—between us—but I have to tell you..." He removes a tattered paperback copy of *The Hobbit* he slipped from his desk into his jacket pocket, replete with author photo prominent on the back cover. "*I* recognize you." The author is a bit discomforted, but he smiles politely. "If I were being honest, Mr. Tolkien, and I hope you don't mind me saying this, the first is still my favorite of all your books..."

Tolkien nods, politely; Franklin forces a smile and quickly escorts Tolkien away without a word.

"This has been a pleasure beyond compare, sir!"

Donovan is elsewhere engaged, on a couch, with Levin. Franklin again tugs his arm; his sleeve shortens; the case is attached to his wrist via an iron band, which is secured by a chain.

He and Tolkien join the other two. The guards from the vault sit casually across from them, reading papers but each maintaining a keen eye on the proceedings.

Two suited gentlemen, late-twenties, take seats at a small coffee table just feet away. The concierge walks back to his post.

Tolkien watches him and, surprisingly to the rest of his party, stands and walks back to the desk. The concierge is stunned. He beckons a younger underling to take his place, and cautiously approaches his favorite writer.

"I'm a bit embarrassed, really," the concierge admits. "But, um...Have I been unprofessional?" Behind them, the two suited men stand, and exit the building.

Franklin joins Tolkien and attempts to return him to the couch. "I'm sorry, I really am. We have to get the Professor back to the airport—"

The author holds up his hand. "Nonsense."

"Professor?" Franklin asks.

"Ha! Nonsense!" Donovan and Levin stand from the couch, and watch nervously. Tolkien faces his admirer. "I appreciate your kindness," he says.

The concierge is star-struck. "I'm...Matthius, Professor. Matthius Alexi. My uncle is one of the owners here, and I...I hope you enjoyed your stay..."

"Oh, I did." He notices the others watching closely. Tolkien leans in, a private moment. "I did very much, thank you." He pulls back. "May I see your book?" Matthius nods—the book is still in his pocket—and he gives it to him. "Do you have a pen?" Tolkien asks. It was already in Matthius' hand. "May I?" Tolkien grabs the pen, and scribbles an inscription on the inside front cover.

"Keep the pen," says Matthius. "I have dozens..." Tolkien returns the book.

Franklin, Donovan, and Levin surround them but keep quiet. Matthius is intimidated but makes his point:

"I just wanted to let you know, I've...I mean you...your work makes such an impact in this world, and in people's lives, and I...I..."

"Matthius?" Tolkien asks kindly.

"Sir?"

"Call me Ronald." Franklin shies away, and sulks on his way back to the couch. "I have great respect for what *you* do, dealing with people all day long, keeping everyone happy..." Levin and Donovan remain, as Tolkien extends his hand.

Matthius is near-overwhelmed. He shakes Tolkien's hand. "I know you don't travel much," he says. "I just wanted to say thank you for staying at the Algonquin...*Ronald.*"

Franklin overhears the words. He does not quite understand why but he finds the younger man's use of Tolkien's proper name inappropriate. Distasteful, even.

"The pleasure was mine." He lets go. "And now," he says, "my bodyguards await..." He smiles, and the men return to the couch as a bittersweet Michael returns to his post.

The concierge taps his co-worker, who makes way. "He asked me to call him *Ronald,*" he says in disbelief. The underling clearly has no clue as to what he's referring. She nods disinterestedly and walks away as Matthius opens the book and reads the inscription:

Matthius,

I rarely sign books but history must leave clues. Only you shall hold the proof of my "top-secret" visit to your fair city. But let's keep it our little secret. I promise you, the universe rewards good men.

Your Friend and Admirer,

Ronald

Back on the couch—

"Time to leave Mirkwood and return to the fates," says Tolkien.

A disarmingly quiet Levin shakes Tolkien's hand, pats him on the back, and heads out the front door.

Trembling, he lights a cigarette and takes a much-needed drag.

Inside, Donovan feigns offense. "Mirkwood? Is that not a bit dramatic, Professor? The efforts of our band of merry men didn't meet your expectations?"

"Your efforts far *exceeded* my expectations, my new friend." Their limo arrives; the doorman waves to them. "This has been an immensely rewarding excursion, but how I miss my Edith…"

They stand to head outside. The guards follow.

Levin drops and stomps on his cigarette.

Matthius stares at the exit, for a moment ignoring his line. "One exits, one…" he whispers plaintively to the air.

On their way out, Tolkien leans in Franklin's ear—"What worries you so?" Franklin is taken aback. "He was a harmless enough boy—"

"Maybe I would like you all to myself?" It's an attempt at a joke, though neither he nor Tolkien buy it. Both know the words are less frivolous than the manner in which they've been delivered.

Levin says his goodbyes and walks back into the lobby.

Donovan has overheard Franklin's words; he disapproves but says nothing, and enters the awaiting limo as the driver holds open the door. Tolkien follows, tipping his cap to Franklin before the door shuts.

The author mouths to him, 'Choose to believe...'

The door is closed. The driver takes the wheel and pulls away. A confused Franklin watches them off...

JONESIES PUB

The story of Tolkien's New York trip comes to an end...

"Tolkien was cut-and-dry about returning home," Donovan says. "He was looking forward to his Edith. Period. His week-long New York adventure had come and gone. She was always his priority. He planned to return to her as a conquering hero, and when we hit ground and said our goodbyes...And so it goes."

"But what of our *Beowulf* papers? What was the plan? And what happened with—?"

"As to your first question, the plan was fairly elaborate. None of us were to say a word about the find to anyone, per Tolkien's wishes, until both he and his wife passed on. His fondest desire was for the both of them to live out their final years in solitude. In the meantime, I would bear—on paper, which would be finessed so as to avoid needless disclosure—the burden of guardianship of the documents once your father was no longer capab—" He stops, briefly, a sudden, awkward break of phrase that, again, Thomas immediately notices. "To decoy any possible intel on the matter," he resumes, as Thomas looks on suspiciously, "my son became custodian until the fire that...took his life, after which all this came back full circle. To me."

"Your son *became* the guardian, past-tense, so what happened to my—"

"Unlike your father, I frequently contemplate that Tolkien led his life—from that point forward—just as he wanted. And, poor man, his dearest Edith passed on scant months later. John Ronald Reuel Tolkien and I never spoke again once we arrived back in London...but I've always wondered one thing. I've always wondered if he and Edith had the opportunity to share that one last toast..."

McFee knows something else is forthcoming, something he may not want to hear. "'Unlike your father'...why did you say that?"

Donovan draws a breath, and exhales slowly. "As to the rest of your answer..."

NEW YORK, NEW YORK, 1970

Tolkien's limo is gone, and another takes its place. The door is likewise held open by the driver. Franklin enters first, the guards behind him.

As the door closes, the two suited men from inside the hotel rush the vehicle. The first smashes the back passenger window with a pipe, while the second shoots Franklin square in the chest.

He bleeds profusely.

JONESIES PUB, LONDON, ENGLAND

"Thing is, though, he died in an instant," Bradley relates.

An incensed Thomas turns away, hiding his face as a sympathetic Donovan allows him time to process the reveal.

The younger man elects to listen to the rest and not yet take up the matter.

NEW YORK, NEW YORK, 1970

Franklin is dragged from the limo. The guards exit from the other side. In the melee, the chain is shot off Franklin's arm, disconnecting the briefcase which drops to the asphalt. One of the guards is immediately shot and killed. The other shoots and kills an assailant.

Levin, meantime, stands in the hotel lobby, benumbed as guests and pedestrians duck for cover.

Police officers join the fracas, approaching from surrounding streets. Sirens follow; backup is en route. The getaway car—an unobtrusive, brown Dodge Dart easily camouflaged in street traffic—speeds to a halt alongside the limo. Emergency sirens become louder, closer.

Levin cautiously rushes from the hotel and enters the vehicle, backseat passenger's side. The remaining guard is shot in the leg and he falls. The surviving assailant retrieves the suitcase and joins Levin, who scoots over.

"Go!" Levin orders in a panic, before the passenger's side back door is fully closed. The getaway car screeches as the driver floors the gas pedal. Yards behind, the fallen security guard manages to retrieve his gun as he pushes himself on the ground with his elbows. He shoots and blows a tire on Levin's vehicle. The getaway car spins and crashes into a dumpster.

Police arrive and immediately handcuff the perpetrators. Levin watches woefully as one of the officers confiscates the briefcase. He closes his eyes as he's shoved into the police car. As he sits in the back, behind the fence, he meditates as an escape.

Levin thinks of his wife, who gave him a family. He thinks of his twins, who are about to enter college. He thinks of his career that feeds his family, how she's always wanted the best for them and how *fortunate* he's been.

He shakes his head in desolation. His eyes remain closed.

"What have I done?"

JONESIES PUB, LONDON, ENGLAND

"The arresting officer told me as much. He was speaking off the record, mind you. 'What have I done? What have I done?' Levin kept repeating, 'What have I done?' He had lost his mind. I wouldn't be surprised if he was still in a sanitarium."

"The case?" Thomas asks, half-heartedly.

"When I returned to New York the following month, that's when I took possession of the briefcase. I held on to it all this time as, to a man...there was so much bloodshed associated with..." Thomas bows his head, immediately drawing Donovan's sympathy. "The same officer returned it to me," he continues. "That's when I asked him questions." Thomas has again has turned away. Donovan gives in. "I'm sorry."

Thomas waves him off. "It was a long time ago," he shrugs. The ensuing silence is uncomfortable, at best.

"He was a good man, Tom." Thomas nods, then changes the subject—"And what of Tolkien? Did he know?"

"No. Not unless—" He catches himself. "No."

Thomas keeps his attention on Donovan. However—

Why is he lying to me? Minutes ago I told him Dad was with me and Sam when Elizabeth was dying before he disappeared...Why is he so obviously ignoring me? His entire story is inconsistent...What more is he lying about?

HOTEL MIRAMAR, BOURNEMOUTH, DORSET, ENGLAND, FALL 1970

Dawn.

John Ronald Reuel Tolkien and his wife Edith hold hands on their doorstep, sipping tea, silently welcoming the new sun and crashing waves of this morning's brilliant blue sea.

JONESIES PUB

"What else could possibly matter to him at that point?" Donovan asks. "And if he was informed, considering everything, what would he be expected to do, really? In the end, history was preserved. Which spoke to his mind—and a place in his heart not reserved for the mother of his children—and I never heard anything more..."

"Was he, honestly, convinced that a muse named Ara had delivered this material to him?" Thomas will stay the course, hesitantly, to find out more. "I mean, you reached out to me—rightly so—and this may make good copy but—"

"Honestly? What do I know? I *do* sense that, to a degree, his life's purpose was validated by this found material, but, as I said earlier...he believed what he chose to believe. And I will stand by that conclusion."

"I'm sure you will."

A rare silence permeates the gathering. "Speaking of...may I ask you an honest question?" Donovan broaches.

"Sure..."

The antiquarian dabs his mouth with a table napkin, then places the napkin onto his lap. "My dear McFee," he says, "Why are you *really* here?"

"Why am I...here?"

"I believe that was the question—"

"You reached out to me. Did you not? Am I missing something?" He laughs, uncomfortably, defensively. "I'm here because my publisher—"

"Crap."

Thomas's patience has been exhausted. He will not answer the question. He stands and excuses himself to the bathroom.

"Before you rush off?" Thomas pauses, curious, but does not turn back. "What are you hiding?"

"What are you not telling *me?*" Thomas retorts.

"Trust must be earned, Mr. Mc—"

"Why don't you get the check?" Thomas intervenes. "I don't mean to be rude, Mr. Bradley, but it's been a hell of a long day."

Donovan takes note of the writer's gait as he walks away. Thomas's shoulders are hunched and he makes a concerted effort to stand straight. Donovan believes the younger man knows he may have been exposed. He also believes the younger man has no idea what's given him away. But Donovan acted upon a hunch; he was unsure Thomas had been hiding anything. Now, he knows.

"You can run, but—" The waiter arrives. Donovan stops mid-sentence and asks for the check.

English Countryside

Still seated against the tree, Thomas's eyes glaze over as he looks down from the moon onto a cheaply-framed photograph that lies on the grass in front of him: a beardless Donovan, Tolkien...and Franklin, standing together in front of New York's Algonquin Hotel.

Thomas swiped the portrait while Donovan slept.

He is reminded of Donovan's explanation of Tolkien's gift signature for the Algonquin concierge. He ponders specifically the written comment about *history leaving tracks.*

This could have been something Tolkien said, Thomas considers. *Not a remark that sounds wholly out of character.*

He breaks the frame's glass on a rock, removes the photo and turns it on its back. No inscription is present, to his disappointment. *So much for that.* What is present, however, is a typeset poem. He reads it:

Be advised thus

When the skies turn to red

And from there a graver shade of scarlet

Engulfing your world in shadow

Mother Nature has ceased to exist

It is a new order

There is only the bleed above

And the bleed to be

The dead

And the dead to be

A man may run and deafen

And invoke meaninglessness and still

Or he may fight and adopt

And chance victory and change

But it is the most fanciful of man

Who is the most dangerous of man

In his blasphemous challenge

Nothing shall be as it appears

Either within the Infinity Pass

Here too

- Goddess Ode

He cannot make sense of the poem, nor, at this moment, does he care to. He flips the photo face up. Tolkien's face is no longer there. In its place is the visage of the young concierge, posing in front of the hotel with Thomas' father, and Donovan. A white, clumpy substance appears under his eye. Thomas touches it, smells it, rubs his fingers. On the grass just under Thomas' hand is a neck-up shot of Tolkien—from another photograph.

A cut and paste job. Why?

"Again, the lies..." he says, as the the realization penetrates. "That son of a bitch." Thomas presses the image of Tolkien back in place. A perfect fit, immaculately-cut. He lets go, and this time the wind takes it.

He touches the face of his father. "Were you really there or did he lie about you too?" He fights tears. "Why shouldn't you have been part of that history, Dad?"

Donovan did get his personality down, from what I remember of him.

Thomas holds the photo to his heart. But only for an instant. He flips the image to its back, looks quickly, and gives up. Sick of the world, he pockets the snapshot, stands and walks back to his car.

But Donovan also asks too many damn questions...

~~~

The bus is down.

After a brief argument and ensuing threat of arrest, Thomas allows the authorities their position. He gathers that they see him as too old to be of any constructive use and, otherwise, Samantha has been waiting. He is asked by an EMT to leave and is led to a rubber slide.

The official statement is he was "getting in the way."

Once on the ground, he brushes off a sea of distraction and approaches his daughter for a hesitant embrace.

"What are you doing here?" she asks, striving to maintain her calm.

He ignores the query, which she immediately forgets. "You're safe. Thank God," he says. He gently pushes her back, and brushes hair out of her eyes. "Is Daniel with you?" She nods and nods again in her fiancé's direction.

Daniel turns away and offers his help to the lead officers. They accept his aid. Thomas snickers.

"Do you know what's going on?" he manages, before he is interrupted.

239

"No," Samantha answers, having anticipated the question. "My best guess is that I know about as much as you do." They turn to the damage. A fire crew struggles with a small brush fire. "They'll handle it. You've been crying," she observes.

Thomas says nothing. If it takes a tragedy to return to his daughter's graces, then so be it.

Samantha touches the side of his face, pitying him, but not sure why. He grabs her hand as she pulls away and returns her touch to his cheek, allowing for a few more seconds of contact to make up for lost time.

"I've only seen you cry when Mama died," she says. "Your tears are not for *them*. What's going on with you? Why are you here?"

"Babe." Daniel, curtly nodding to Thomas in acknowledgement. "I think they could use your help."

Samantha is torn. Thomas clenches his jaw at the uninvited intervention.

"Go," he advises. "If you can help; he's right. They could probably use you."

Daniel takes her hand, nudging. "C'mon Sam. He'll be all right." Thomas grimaces. Permission granted.

Daniel and Sam head to the buses. She peeks behind her only once. Thomas's back is turned. He is walking to his car. He arrives, opens the door, and takes the driver's seat. He stares out the front window as he takes stock of the chaos.

It's madness—

"You didn't lock the door," Brikke admonishes him from the back seat.

Thomas squints to get a look from his rear-view mirror. As he is about to turn around, he cautions him. "No. Don't look at me." Thomas can't help himself.

"Who are you?" Thomas asks.

"I'm not going to hurt you."

"You're not what?"

"There's no time; I need you to listen and not ask questions. They're going to be looking for me. In minutes, that bus will become a designated crime scene. Your daughter will identify me as a likely suspect."

"Sam? What will you do to my daughter?"

"Nothing. If you listen, she'll be safe. Your daughter is caught up in something with which she never should have engaged. If I allow them to find me, I will have no choice but to commit to a greater insanity than anything you've experienced today. I will also take her down with me. Do we understand each other?"

Thomas takes his time, weighing his options. *Any options.*

"Do we?"

"Of course we do," Thomas answers as his anger rises. "Of course. Just don't hurt her, please."

"She'll be safe as long as you listen to me." Thomas reaches discreetly toward his dashboard. "I know who *you* are," Brikke resumes. "I've read your books; I've known your family." Thomas trembles as he withdraws a pocket knife from the side pocket. Otherwise he remains compliant. "Good. Respond from here. Yes or no. Do you know the identity of X?"

"No." The knife is hidden. Thomas would not be able to explain why if asked, if he survives, but he anticipated the question. Thomas opens the knife. Brikke does not appear to have caught the action.

"Do you understand who I am speaking of?"

"Inasmuch as anyone."

"Yes or no, please. Has Samantha ever, *ever* mentioned anything about him to you?"

"No. What's this all about?"

"Do you know who *I* am?"

"No."

"The muse is dead. Do you understand who I am speaking of?"

"I'm sorry? The *muse*..?" he bluffs, straining to maintain his calm.

"You've never been a good liar. Be careful." Thomas tries to locate his daughter. "Ara is dead—"

"I don't think so," Thomas tests.

Brikke continues, furious. "Ara is dead! Rest her soul. At any minute, they will discover that she died by my hand."

Thomas's frame of mind slips to dangerous. "You're sitting in my car," he says. "You threaten my daughter and you confess to murder all within the span of a min—"

"I've never been a good liar either."

"—a minute," Thomas finishes. "Why are *we* having this conversation?"

"You are correct in your suspicions—"

"My suspicions?"

"Have you come this far for Mr. Bradley or is your quest little more than a convenience to reunite with your daughter?"

Thomas pauses, before responding. "How do you—"

"No time. You have been troubled by many questions since your wife's passing." He's reaching inside, awaiting a reaction; Thomas does not play. "Specifically as it relates to your daughter. You're a writer. Your writer's natural curiosity has led you to become very much aware that she is involved in something *unnatural* and very likely dangerous, and you do not trust her...I need your help—"

"What do you know of *Ara*?"

"There's no time, as I said. I—"

Thomas tosses his keys out the window. "Then I guess we'll have to wait for the police to arrive and you tell them everything you told me." He raises his hands overhead. "Let them figure it out." Thomas motions out the window.

A gaggle of police officers cautiously approaches his car. Their guns are drawn. Brikke notices. "You have no idea what you are starting."

"Then why don't you tell me?"

The officers are yards away. Four of them, all in ready position, breaking into groups of two to cover either side of the vehicle.

"Mr. McFee ..." Brikke pleads.

As in a chess game, Thomas asserts his next move as he preps the knife's blade with his thumb. "Where is this going?" he asks. Brikke is surprised by Thomas's nerve. "You threaten my little girl," Thomas reminds him. "You tell me where this is headed or you're going to have to kill me too. And then you'll still have *them* to deal with—"

"If they take me," says Brikke, "*she's* next." Thomas's knuckles turn pink as he tightly grasps the door handle. "Look above," Brikke continues. "Look at the clouds, the sky. Have you seen anything like this before?" Thomas doesn't respond. "The Over-dwellers return." The police are just feet away. "That's no accident but of course you know this too. They're back—"

"Leave the vehicle with your arms up!" one of the officers shouts...

"It's too late," Brikke chastens. "I warned you." He looks up in horror. The clouds have broken. Red rain falls, followed by furious, incessant thunder. The officers cease their efforts.

The fallen bus slides further down its slope in response to the slickened grass.

As the bus proceeds on its course and the officers disperse for cover, Thomas reluctantly admits to Brikke that *nothing is as it appears* and he needs to be trusted...but in the fracas Brikke does not hear another word.

NEW YORK, NEW YORK

The thunder repeats, each successive blast louder and longer than the one before. Denise rapidly draws the blinds of her office windows. X escapes through the muck as police vehicles line to take cover in the nearest parking garages. At this late New York hour, none of them are able to yet make out exactly what is falling...

ENGLISH COUNTRYSIDE

Daniel grasps Samantha. She fights him, struggling to pull away. She screams that she needs to reach her father but Daniel holds on. He'll protect her for as long as he can. There is nowhere to run.

The grass under Thomas's car turns quick; the downpour is torrential as the vehicle begins to sink.

As the blood from the skies becomes unbearable in its force, Brikke takes a final opportunity. He reaches forward and smothers Thomas, hand over mouth, until the writer loses consciousness. "You are going to forget everything that's happened today," he says. "It's the only way," he adds as Thomas slumps.

Brikke leaves the vehicle. He rushes to rescue Daniel and Samantha, who is herself barely conscious. He drags them to the car, helps them inside and slams the door. On his own, he lifts and pushes the car away from the sinkhole to what is, for the moment, a safer haven. He gingerly lets the vehicle down, then stands away.

He strains his neck upwards and unleashes his own, unyielding *force* in defiance of the gods. "NOW!!" he shouts. The elements coalesce and a new Abeyance begins.

The effort has weakened Brikke, who crumbles to the ground. Once again, the world suspends; though the immortal responsible fears the resilience of the Over-dwellers, he hopes his action is timely. Unfortunately, the fear he expressed to Thomas was, in this instance, well-founded.

They were out of time.

Brikke was too late. While the others may still be trapped, one form has, indeed, escaped from the repugnance of stasis and returned successfully to earth.

The fight has been won. The form advances upon Brikke, limping, falling, crawling...

Brikke loses consciousness before he could see the face.

The form lifts its scarred, burned head and manages to regain *his* footing. He stands over Brikke, as in celebration of his great victory.

Eron.

INFERNO

An Open Letter to the Media

"I TOLD YOU SO"

And we awake. Me, maybe earlier than most.

We did not have a "collective nightmare" last night. What you remember is what we left off with.

What you've awakened to is the correction.

I've warned you and I've warned you. And then I warned you some more.

I've watched new dawns for as long as I can remember. I never expect to live until the next morning so each daybreak gives me reason to put one foot in front of the other. I walk onward like the Christian soldiers you may have learned about in Sunday school. Today was no exception, though I knew the second I opened my eyes what had happened.

How many of you right now are scared or confused? How many of you have convinced yourselves that last night was merely a dream. If it was, it was one you experienced more vividly than you would have thought possible.

It's only been weeks since "the last one." It was far worse this time though, wasn't it? We really came close this time, didn't we?

But how many of you have already recovered sufficiently to prod on? The blinds have been pulled. You see that the sun has risen in its full glory. The television is turned on; breakfast is waiting.

Most people will keep their "dream" to themselves, embarrassed, until drawn into conversation with someone who "just needs to talk."

The cover-up has already started.

"What a gloriously perfect day!" they say on CNN and all around the world. Or they will shortly, depending on your location.

Well, this is just one of those days. And it will be for everyone else. It's one of those days where, for now, everything is perfectly calm.

And yet you didn't listen. You didn't listen. What a surprise (sarcasm obviously intended).

You chose your way and I chose mine and what this means—to all of us—is that, despite today's wonders, my repeated warnings have failed and now we will all suffer the

247

consequences.

I get it. I read—past-tense—that line after I wrote it. Over the top, yes? Much like some of my other letters; maybe that was my foolish mistake. Maybe you didn't take me seriously because you couldn't take me seriously.

Even if my heart was in the "right place." Even if I, repeatedly, risked my life for yours.

Unfortunately, the horrors that are now about to be unleashed are more terrible even than the hyperbole you probably processed from what became my own ongoing, one-sided dialogues.

Right?

Because the skies were bleeding. The skies are no longer, so certainly this is best explained as nothing more than one of nature's infrequent "freak shows..."

Except for the fact that none of us can remember the clean-up. Nor recall an iota of damage. Nor find even a stain yet we all remember the "blood rain," nor...

FUCK YOU ALL!!

Do you see what you did?

Do you see?

Do you care? Right.

FUCK YOU!!

I know. I'm "bitter," I told you, I get it. I'm bitter because my fifteen minutes will soon be over and back into the annals of obscurity I will be...But only once this "terrorist" serves his time, of course. Any arguments?

Sometimes, I wonder if you're even reading me at all anymore. But it doesn't matter, really. Not in the end.

And, lest I remind you again...this is the end.

You see, nothing here is, or was ever, hyperbole. Not even "...horrors that are about to be unleashed..."

That one was an understatement.

Folks, today's bag o' fun is stream-of-consciousness all the way. The writing has become habitual; I had to send you something and I'm not in the mood to polish.

I tried. I really did. Whether I've remained a harmless crackpot to you, or something worse...or even a non-entity, I wanted to help. That was my sole, and my best, intention.

Now I'll do you all favor and move on. Watch for me on the news reports, call your friends in the event of a highway chase. It may be me, it may not.

But never stop watching. Certainly, one of you—or your readers—will win the lottery based on providing information that leads to my capture.

To the the lucky winner, spend impulsively as if it's your last day. And I will do what I need to, as you have killed me too.

What's done is...

Done. Now you can only watch.

Go on, tell your viewers, your listeners or your readers that it's a delightful day to ignore their problems.

And watch.

It's also a delightful day to make a killing. :)

Catch me if you can. At this time, I'm wrestling with a mounting contempt for each and every one of you so I may not be all that nice when we actually meet and you find out who I really am.

Just don't say I never warned you (double-negative be damned).

P.S. Do I have your attention now?

X's finger hesitates, then presses *send* on an anonymous computer. ISP information has been disabled, per an electronic note on the bottom of his email client.

He then enters his blog information, and off the message goes to the rest of the cyber-sphere.

Facebook. Pinterest. Twitter. Linkedin. All in one click. A mock-up painting of a ravaged planet earth, found online from the cover of some public domain science fiction book, is attached to the posting.

At 16, X is an old soul, and he privately acknowledges that the world is getting smaller by the day.

I can reach everyone. I can convince no one.

Though he's a prodigy, like any other so young and gifted he does not always have a firm control over his emotions.

This is the rub. Today, he borders on a near-complete loss of his senses.

Those that enable him to get by anyway.

I've only ever had two people in my life I could trust. One died, the other betrayed me and I'll stick with those conclusions. Who cares? They're both gone.

He's reminded of the last time he felt so angry. It was at the end of that abhorrent week last year when Professor Searle, having accompanied the boy for a series of medical tests to determine a possible organic cause for his extraordinary intellect, sat across from him in the doctor's office and explained away the source of his greatest insecurities.

Which, expectedly, did not go over well.

X had overheard Searle asking the doctor to leave, 'just in case," so he could be alone with his student. The doctor did, following a few objections of "going against AMA regulations" or some bullshit. Searle convinced a leery X that the tests would be in his best interests. When Searle relayed the diagnosis of Asperger's, however—a form of autism underscored primarily by a retardation of the processes that enables in-person social interaction—X lashed out. He cursed Searle, accusing his mentor of being jealous and holding him down; in reality, X perceived the diagnosis as both confirmation of his inferiority and reason for his disquiet.

He never admitted to his mentor that the admission was actually a favor. He preferred to play the blame game and remain, unreasonably, upset.

A saddened Searle continued to work with the boy, despite the shift in attitude. "You can still be proud," the Professor explained, "but acceptance is a virtue."

Searle disappeared shortly thereafter. X convinced himself that he killed him, that Searle felt as though their relationship was irrevocably damaged and that the consternation destroyed his health.

X has been blaming himself ever since.

Game lost.

X's greatest frustration has continued to lie in his inability to relate to anyone since. He leans on the idea that he simply does not have the skills. He's learned to accept that much, thanks to his mentor. So he acts when he has to—portraying various roles when around others, including street magician—and primarily takes to the computer to be *heard*.

And nobody listens. They're always just amused. The hell he promises cannot arrive fast enough.

I wonder if I can speed the process. They deserve as much after all my work.

X removes his flash drive, stands with the gauntlet that he sacks over his shoulder. He prepares to exist for yet another day, on the loose, somewhere in the state of New York.

He leaves the Underwood behind. It has outlived its usefulness.

He is alone, as always, with his thoughts but this time is missing the last of his emotional attachments. Making him a very dangerous man. "They got what they wanted," he says to himself as he walks out the door.

BRADLEY AND SON BIBLIOTHEQUE

Six hours later, on the other side of the Atlantic, Thomas sits at the basement table, sleeping. He stirs in response to Donovan Bradley's thinnish hand pressing on his shoulder.

"I'm sorry to bother you." Thomas awakens, and nearly jumps from his seat. "It's almost noon. I was wondering if you could help me upstairs?"

Thomas' composure does not return without protest. He straightens, still seated. "Is she safe?" he stammers. "Saman—Samantha. Is she safe?"

"I don't know. Who's Samantha?"

And Thomas is reminded who he's dealing with ...

"What are you doing here?" he says. "Why the lies?" He looks at

Donovan from head to toe, as if in a challenge. "Why am I back here?"

Donovan steps away as the younger man regroups. "My, my. Are you quite through?"

Thomas takes a deep breath, holds it then slowly expels. He strains to convince himself—

"You were with me."

"Surrender Dorothy, would you?"

"Dorothy?"

"Click your heels three times and you'll return to sanity. I promise..."

~~~

Back upstairs, Thomas is toweling his face in the washroom after cleaning up. He's fine. He comes out. "All of this *Beowulf* stuff and Tolkien. It's enough to make one bit...off-center. Don't you think?

"You know what I think? I think you need a good stiff drink." returns Donovan.

Thomas is ashamed of himself. He almost blew his guard and for that he must hurriedly compensate.

"Jonesies?" he offers.

That catches Donovan by surprise. "I thought you told me you'd never visited the pubs here."

"I haven't."

"How do you know Jonesies?"

"Wretched memories of my recent past." says Thomas. He takes a couch, cozy even for him. "Five minutes.

"Pleasant dreams, hmm?" Donovan probes. "Would you care to share?"

"What's that?"

"The wretched memories of which you speak, of course," says the older man.

"You're a busybody today?"

"Along with the couch." He squeezes alongside his guest. "Excuse my laziness. Walking to my private room is a distance when the vessel is breaking down."

Thomas shifts, none too willingly. "In answer to your question, not at all. I'm 90 years old. I care as much about your personal business as I do last night's hangnail but I am interested in what ails you. Maybe I can help, if you need to vent—."

Thomas smirks. "Do I remind you of your son?"

"Nothing doing."

Thomas immediately regrets his question. "That was improper of me. I hope I didn't cause offense."

"No, but you didn't allow me the opportunity to answer."

"I guess not."

"I do have my reasons for asking the question I asked," Donovan says, attempting to refocus. "If you're uncomfortable, I understand."

"I'm not uncomfortable. Maybe *you* remind me of my father, I don't know." Donovan accepts this as a compliment. Thomas continues. "I lost my my dad, my wife, and my daughter at about the same time, you see—"

Donovan struggles to stand, waving off help. He gets there, a back crack or two along the way.

"So," he says. "How 'bout that drink?"

JONESIES PUB

Donovan discusses Tolkien's New York trip, shares anecdotes about Thomas McFee's father...

Deja vu.

Thomas can recite line and verse from this script but keeps his dream to himself. As does his host. There is, though, one *tweak* in the present version. As they speak, Donovan lightens the tone of the conversation and casually hints at his shop's newest acquisition:

"Allow me to be the first to tell you, I had a visitor today. I've been presented with the secrets to *Wonderland*." Thomas rubs his neck, hiding a grimace. Donovan senses the writer's frustration. "Maybe another time, then."

English Countryside

Re-tracing his visit, Thomas sits under the tree...and walks back to his car. And then...nothing. No buses, no photo, no clues. Yet the images have retained their unnerving lucidity.

Wonderland, he thinks. *How much more of his eccentricity can I take?* Discouraged, he stands to return to his car. As he takes his first step, shards of glass crunch under his shoe. He looks down and lifts up his foot. *Well surprise, surprise.*

Thomas arrives at his vehicle. He enters, keys the ignition and U-turns back toward his hotel. The glass—the *red herring*—was all he needed. Against all semblance of logic, Thomas is steadfastly convinced that what he experienced *yesterday* is something far more notable than a nightmare and far less innocuous than, say, a genocide plot.

Samantha's life is certainly in jeopardy. Among God knows how many others.

As he drives, Thomas accepts that any attempt—from here onward—at shunning related nags will fail miserably.

Claridge Hotel, London, England

Thomas sits, shoeless, on the king-sized bed. His legs are crossed; his tablet is on his lap. His back is supported by two pillows.

He listens to a *Wikipedia* entry:

"...his identity, though not in question, was said to at times deliberately mimic the traits of several influential artists—which caused him considerable ridicule in his later years.

' Professor' Randolph Searle was not a degreed or licensed professor. He was, however, a teacher, a martial artist and life-long admirer of author J.R.R. Tolkien—whom he considered 'beyond reproach.'

Thomas pays particular attention.

"When terminated from his last teaching position—as a high school special education instructor—Searle simply said he was 'carrying the torch of a respected tradition.' When asked whose tradition in a televised investigative report, he rolled up his car window and refused to respond.

Allegations of improper conduct were never proven, however, upon his firing, several students came forward—with their parents—and filed a class-action suit against the beleaguered Professor, and the New York school district that employed him.

He regrouped and funded his own private academy for runaways and other troubled youth, which he described as the 'culmination of a life-long mission.' The suit subsequently failed due to lack of any tangible proof, and he was closely monitored in his new school for which he had received a controversial permit.

He remained out of trouble until his disappearance.

Searle was considered 'well-off' financially due to strong investments in the futures market. His Artist's Academy was entirely self-financed; his students were taught the 'safety' of constructive self-expression through writing and other artistic endeavors. 'Necessary skills that are woefully lacking in public school instruction,' he wrote in a Daily News editorial.

'Encourage self-worth, help extract the students' natural abilities— their potential—and your crime problem drops exponentially.'

He was the Academy's sole instructor. His administrator, Esme Chaconte—a certified teacher's assistant and former pupil from his public school tenure—worked with Searle and his students for the duration of the Academy's operations. Only ten students per semester were accepted for admission in the scant Greenwich Village studio.

Searle considered himself a 'cosmologist,' and credited Tolkien and other 'visionaries,' such as H.P. Lovecraft, Michelangelo, Bruce Lee, The Beatles for 'showing him the way,' which he defined as 'nothing in this universe is what it appears to be.'"

Thomas chuckles at the irony.

"'They all broke from staid tradition and delivered their messages with an impact reserved only for those of us brave enough to peek outside of physical or emotional limitation. Huxley, The Doors...'"

The writer laughs, and wipes his eyes. "Aarrghh..."

Quite the maddening day. Thomas mouths the following, a favorite passage:

"'Blake: 'If the doors of perception were cleansed, everything would appear as it is—infinite,' he quoted in the same editorial."

Thomas accepts the most troubling aspect of it all: Much of it makes a good deal of sense to him. "Maybe I never should have quit the drugs," he says. He finds himself wishing he could pick Searle's brain; maybe he could learn something.

"'Therefore,' he concluded, 'we must account for the sheer variety of personality-types as we teach our students. One method most certainly does not fit all. Our influential leaders of artistic expression see it; why can't the rest of us? Why is it that some artistic works reach the reader, or the

viewer, or the listener, on a visceral, gut level? Why is it that so much else falls by the wayside collecting dust? Because those who were brave enough to see, maintained a much firmer grasp of The Truth.

"*That's* a comment..."

"*Searle has been missing since mid-2013 and is presumed deceased but, to date, no body has been discovered.*

His greatest claim to fame is several of his students had since achieved substantial degrees of stardom, at a still-young age following their 'graduation' from the Academy, yet 'flamed out'—as one investigator said— in a rash of drugs, alcohol, or suicides following the announcement of Searle's disappearance.

"'Tolkien was right,' he added in his Daily News op-ed. 'He was one of the most inspiring of all teachers because he encouraged his students to dream, as he did.'

For Thomas, the ending is a kicker:

"*Those who seek The Truth may not like what they see, but nor will they be able to turn back...'*"

Thomas is exhausted. The tablet is still on his lap, still open, still on the same Wikipedia entry. He must have been staring at the screen for minutes, as if in a daze.

He notices the image of a *flashing envelope* towards the bottom left of his screen:

YOU HAVE AN INSTANT MESSAGE

He doesn't move. "Wonderful. Denise. I don't need any grief from you today..."

He clicks on the image and reads:

What do you think of this addition? Some say the terrorist 'X' was a student of Professor Searle.

"*Not* Denise. And not now, please." Thomas stares at the screen. And he types:

If you're a fan, I appreciate you reaching out. But I don't have the strength right now to

Response:

They would have been right, you know.

Thomas realizes who, and what, he's dealing with. He props himself up, and googles an article about X, the alleged *terrorist.* He replies:

Why are you contacting me?

Response:

We read the same websites. McFee, did you read my package or did you forget because of the Abeyance?

Thomas:

I repeat the question. Why are you contacting me?

Response:

No answer, then. Have it your way. We'll be in touch.

Thomas:

X?

Nothing. He continues:

Is this you, really?

As he awaits a response, Thomas checks the *typing* notification. No movement.

I can turn you in.

It's a bluff. Response:

You do that.

Thomas notices that there is no ID on any of X's messages. He types—

Why me?

Response:

Why Searle?

Thomas is dismayed by the simplicity of the reply—

He was a good man. What are you searching for?

Thomas:

Not him.

Response:

What does that mean? Not him?

Thomas carefully considers his next answer. He writes:

Means to an end

Response:

What end?

Thomas takes his time. X, though, takes the initiative:

Nevermind. We'll be in touch as I said. Searle always told me "There are no accidents" so right about now I don't trust you...really never did anyway.

And that is all.

Thomas takes a moment to ponder, then tosses the tablet to the foot of the bed. He turns off the light but keeps his eyes open, gazing at the ceiling.

Dark.

No more than thirty seconds later, as Thomas attempts to relax, his cellphone rings.

Lights on.

"Yes?" Thomas asks.

"Why did you stop texting?"

"I thought *you* did—"

"I had to go to the bathroom. That okay?"

"I needed to hear that?"

"No—"

"How did you get this number?"

"Don't worry about it."

"What do you—?"

"You've been reading up on Searle. I would like to know why—"

"What business is it of yours?"

"I've been reading up on *you*. Would you like to know why?"

Thomas pauses. "Not particularly—"

"I'll tell you anyway. You're a smart man, Mr. McFee."

"What can I do for you—"

"Nothing, but here it is. Stop sniffing."

"I'm sorry?"

"You don't have to sniff any longer."

"I have no idea what you're—"

"Did you know Peter Levin adopted my father? He wasn't too popular back then, right?"

"Wasn't—"

"Do you know Peter Levin?"

"No," Thomas answers nervously.

"I'll rephrase my question. Do you know of Peter Levin?"

"Yes," he sighs.

A beat, and then—"Donovan Bradley knows my identity. And only Donovan Bradley knows my identity since Searle…" Thomas struggles to stand, his legs limp. "Do you believe me?"

"No."

"Has Mr. Bradley ever mentioned me to you?"

"No…"

"Don't lie to me. If I've gone here, it would be prudent to assume I'm far more informed than you believe. Has Mr. Bradley *ever* mentioned me to you?"

"No...No."

"Has he mentioned his son?"

Thomas withholds his nerves. "Yes..."

"The fire ..?"

"The fire...Yes—"

"That I was once sent to live in London on a special exchange program but I only lasted a month? That his son—*Junior*—once did something very bad to my Professor and then there was a fire—"

"Where is this headed?" He wants to hear it from him...

"The books, all that history...should have been destroyed. There are *reasons,* you know."

Thomas feigns stupidity. "What books?"

"Nice try. You'll know the reasons soon. Everyone will know the reasons soon—"

"Anything else—"

"Yes. Your daughter," X continues, "Samantha, is an...acquaintance of mine—"

"What do you want?" Silence, from the other end. "Just...tell me what you want—"

"Do you have any idea what she's involved with?"

"That's not your—"

"Yes, it is. If it weren't for her I'd be anony—"

"If you harm her, if she's in any danger I'll find you and I swear to God I'll kill y—"

"You really should read my work. I put everything into my work...and nobody pays me any mind—"

"Why is that *my* problem?"

"The reasons I just referred to? Same applies here...To answer your question—"

"That's no answer—"

"I refuse to lose my temper anymore today," X decides. "It hasn't been a good morning in New York."

"What do you want?" Thomas reiterates. He awaits X's reply, but hears only heavy breathing, and what distinctly sounds like the holding back of explosive emotion.

"Have you read my work?"

"I looked at it. Tough to avoid lately..." Thomas voice trails.

"Well that makes me happy. I'll ask you again. Did you read what I sent you?"

"I don't know what you're talking about."

"Are you bluffing?" X asks. "If you're bluffing, this conversation's over—"

"That's it?"

"No. But you've read my work."

"Yes."

"If you read my work, tell me what *Abeyance* means," he tests.

"I'm not into games—" Thomas stops himself. *Oh my God...*

"Are you still there?" X asks. "Don't be rude, I hear you breathing like you heard mine."

"I'm not dead yet." Thomas resists the temptation to run, and is loath to admit that the boy's statements are resonating. "If what you've been saying is true, then why didn't—"

"I did, fuck! What does it take? I tried. You have no idea how much I tried. Even about the goddamn books—"

"You sound like a kid."

"I'm no kid!"

"Getting under your skin?"

"No. I'm better than that, don't you think?"

"Why should I believe you?"

"Mr. McFee, please," he laments. "You can't have it both ways."

"Why not?" says Thomas obstinately.

"Ara exists." Thomas can barely take another word. "Okay? Do we understand each other? Ara exists. They all do."

"All? Who else are you—"

"Let me ask you this: Did you dream last night?"

"Why?"

"Was the sky *red*?"

"Who the hell are you?"

"Where were you? In your dream?"

"I don't have to answer this."

"Was the sky red?" X repeats.

Thomas's stomach drops. Nausea wells up. "Where are you?"

"Exactly where I was nine months ago."

Thomas runs his hand through his hair, and scratches the back of his scalp to distract from his aggravation.

"It's impossible, all of it."

"Why?" asks X.

"It's absurd! All of it."

"Why?"

"You're implying that this theory you've put forward."

"It's no theory. You're just like the rest. No one believes me."

"You're implying that this *event* lasted nine months. Is that what you're telling me?"

"Finally."

"I know where I was yesterday. I know where I was a week ago. A month—"

"Prove it."

"You're out of your mind!"

"Everything would be so much easier if that were true."

"Are you familiar with *Ragnarök* McFee? It's all in there."

"I'm getting off the phone."

"Another imbecile," X mutters under his breath. "Tell your daughter that in certain circles she's as wanted as I am."

Thomas catches him. "What does that mean, exactly?"

X is deliberate with his response. "It means that you should have paid closer attention. Because I'm done."

X clicks off his line. Thomas throws his cell phone full-force against the closest wall. Both break into many, many pieces.

KINGS COUNTY HOSPITAL, BROOKLYN, NEW YORK

Esme had been warned that the delivery would be high-risk. She worked until the day before, and then collapsed on Denise's stairs. The publisher, as usual, was not at home. Fortunately for Esme, the mailman saw her lying, prone, through the glass window. He called the ambulance and waited with her until they arrived.

Esme stirs in her bed. Her wrists are strapped to the posts at either side. Oxygen is fed through her nose. The cannula is nearly knocked out as she starts to thrash.

"Doctor," the nurse summons. She carries a clipboard and appears to be in a hurry. Doctor Michael Katz rushes to Esme's side. He's in his late-thirties; the nurse is old enough to be his mother.

"Verbalizing?"

"No. Not yet."

"Antecedent, Nurse?"

"She cried first, like now."

A tear drops from the corner of Esme's eye. "How long?"

"If the same as before, less than a minute."

"Time?"

"5:31 P.M."

The doctor leans his ear to Esme's mouth. Nothing yet. He presses *play* on a hand-held digital recorder so as not inadvertently to erase anything important. He times the device to five seconds of dead air, then *stops* and *records.*

"*5:32* P.M." he corrects.

The nurse glares at him. The bastard wouldn't even accept her *time.*

"Patient exhibiting unprecedented antecedent volatility through coma induction," the doctor states. "Labor expected to be brief and anticipatory." *Stop. Play.* Five more seconds. *Stop.* He turns to his nurse "Do you have the transcripts with you?" She hands him her clipboard.

"Thank you. Dismissed." As she walks away to prepare sedation. "Please close the door behind you—"

"Doctor? Dismissed? Aren't you going to sedate the patient?"

"Nurse?" he pauses in place, as if insulted. "Please don't question me."

"Shouldn't I bring additional hands?"

"Nurse!" She's surprised; she's not surprised. More upset than anything. This new perinatologist, Katz, has been brusque with her since he started not even a week ago. She's been a well-regarded employee for over twenty years. Kings County is her home.

He should praise me for my ambition. And also for putting up with his shit.

She snaps her gloves before removing them to get his attention. She fears jiggling her hips wouldn't have the same effect, and is likely right. She walks out the door.

Dr. Katz doesn't give her a second look. He'll report her later. For now, keeping close watch on Esme, he again *records* as she mumbles through her sleep. "The gauntlet survives," she says. "You were right. Yours is the hand which will save—"

Esme screams, agonized, cutting off her sentence. Katz is unsure whether she is reacting to the labor pains or to something gone very wrong with the induction. The machines surrounding them exhibit no unusual activity. The screaming subsides.

Katz holds a moment, then listens again.

"I'm sorry..." Esme intones. "You can make yourself bleed. You can live as one of them and guide them with grace..." Seconds go by. "Ahh!" Esme, still under, struggles to escape from her shackles. Her voice has diminished to a whisper. Katz leans his ear and recorder to Esme's mouth, making sure all of her words are captured. "Taebal is coming..." Esme says through tears. "Taebal is coming, and he—"

She gasps and her eyes abruptly open. Her lids flutter; her breathing becomes dangerously spasmodic. Esme's electronic measures rapidly descend. Her doctor hastily grabs the intercom from the wall. "Need backup, stat!" The nurse is the first to arrive. She curses the doctor, who turns his back to her as Esme flatlines.

U.S. EMBASSY, LONDON, ENGLAND

On the screen is an email, still in draft form, which is located within the secure file, "Project Ara."

The communication has not been sent to a specific address. It has been sent to a folder, stamped with time and date of entry: November 27, 2014. 5:35 P.M.

Samantha.

She completes the action, swipes her keys from her desk and exits the room. Upon the close of the door, her monitor shows the email as *retrieved,* and *reading.*

EMPIRE STATE BUILDING OBSERVATORY, NEW YORK, NEW YORK

A hooded X, integrated with the other visitors, reviews from his cell what he can of Samantha's email. As new pages load, he glances out and about. *So high,* he ponders. He looks down. *And so small. No wonder they still have no real idea what I look like. The last artist's rendering did come pretty close though.*

Samantha has been feeding him information all along. He again checks the phone. *Any day now—*

"Oh! Excuse us. So sorry." X watches as the immaculately-attired seniors—husband and wife, he figures—force apologetic smiles and walk quickly away.

"No big deal. I don't get *banged into* nearly enough, that's part of my problem." He addresses his phone, not them. When he looks back up, they're already out of sight.

Amazing. I'm all over the news but what's the best way to keep people away? Be black and wear a hoodie. Hide in plain sight and stay to yourself. Obviously this works.

He observes the rest of the crowd around him, including the three strategically-stationed security guards, and exaggerates his inner voice:

And they frontin' I don't even exist! No niggaz out here, cuz, just me. They all too scared to even look at me!

He glances back down as the email loads, and resumes his self-talk:

Outnumbered as I am...I told them downstairs in the X-ray that the gauntlet—one-half of the most powerful weapon known to man—was a toy for my son. And they believed me! But I get it. Man is not meant to be God— or god. But I'm not a man, as the doctors so charmingly informed me before ruining my life. He taps the gauntlet with his free hand. Still there, still in the sack. The drawstring is tight. *I should be wearing it, not holding it,* he bemoans.

"It's him again," the husband murmurs. He nods to X as he and his wife step hurriedly aside.

So this is why 'most wanteds' take so long to find. They're avoided.

The wife nervously looks behind her. She doesn't intend to make eye contact with X, though she does. She turns back and leans her head into her husband's chest, hastening their pace. "Harve, come on!"

I shouldn't care anymore. Doesn't matter. They'll manage their weakness—for now, I'll manage mine. He glances at the email. It's almost downloaded. *Soon,* he thinks, *the blade will be returned and I will meet my destiny.*

He laughs to himself as he echoes his melodramatic thoughts. *And I will meet my destin'—I think you need lessons on real-world verbiage, son. Maybe I should adapt my drama to the modern stage.*

X notices that the email has fully loaded. *Anyway, like I said, they should have listened.*

As he walks to the corner, he reads from the email:

Yes, of course. Acknowledged that Esme Chaconte did not "literally" work until "the day before" her delivery. Short-hand: I remind you again, as illogical as it may seem to you, the narrative must be driven by the inner workings of those featured at any given time. They're all tapped. We're privy here. Agreed she worked up until the day she conceived nine months ago which, based on my estimates of the Abeyance from your figures, would work out time-wise to correlate with my vision of the bus accident.

Minutes before. Samantha types:

Here is the sequence of events best as I can tell: Esme had a one-night affair with Searle. When Esme tearfully admitted her indiscretion to her husband, he slapped her in the head. He broke a blood vessel in her temple. She collapsed and fell into a coma. Searle heard what had happened and disappeared. He most likely doesn't know he impregnated her. How can he? Esme doesn't know he went away. How can she? Nor could either know the death of a hybrid named Marlo would spark her conception. (Let's go with "hybrid" here, defined in this case as still part-immortal. Brikke never thought anything other but when she "died" he lost perspective. Yes, Marlo "was" Ara. She knew of Taebal and the history. She could only know this by having retained some of her gifts. It may only have been the gift of knowledge, but that was enough. Her intentions were "not" noble. More on that later.) Her new incarnation, through Esme, fulfills her sentence. Ara is now mortal. The child must be protected.

X scrutinizes the last sentences.

Ara is now mortal. The child must be protected.

This is no longer my problem.

He reads on:

You were right, X. You were right all along, which isn't too surprising. Esme died in childbirth. The baby lives. She is Ara's final incarnation. Ara has become mortal. And it's up to us—and to her—to reverse the course of her vengeance. (Pardon the bad horror-movie parlance.) My question to you is what are we talking time-wise here? Eight years? Ten?

X responds:

DOESN'T MATTER ANY MORE. I THINK WE ALL GOT WHAT WE WANTED.

He sends, then waits for a response. Nothing. Which means she either left right after she submitted the email or she's being cagey. Or both.

X retrieves Samantha's words as he heads to the elevator. "Always in caps," he mutters. "Maybe I should've asked if she was angry with me or something while I had the chance." Satisfied, he sends a quick postscript then powers down his cell.

Wonder if she ever noticed mine were in caps, too, in response and my letters were bigger.

U.S. EMBASSY, LONDON, ENGLAND

Samantha left right after she submitted. There was nothing cagey about it. She didn't want to wait for his response is all. If her day was going to be ruined, considering her almost-exclusive awareness of precisely when the world was going to end (assuming her and X would be unable to work with the child to somehow alter the present course), she would rather wait until tomorrow for anything new.

Tomorrow, defined as: following a good night's pill-induced sleep, some yoga, a shower, a 15-minute car ride to her favorite coffee shop—and the ritual evisceration of peanut butter on a stale multi-grain bagel downed with the aid of a large brew. Ten minutes more to the office, five to her computer...and utter panic for the rest of her life.

Tomorrow, for sure.

Samantha had long-ago concluded that a muse could only influence and never alter. Hence, the first Abeyance where she broke the rules and was sentenced for her crime. X had convinced Samantha that only in mortal form would Ara theoretically be capable of reversing events, as her occasionally-conflicting agendas of revenge, mortality, and *happiness ever after* would be decreased by at least a third.

271

Samantha believed most of it, not all. She feared the enigmatic Ara may have been more powerful than either of them realized—based upon the extreme actions taken by her immortal family—and she expressed her thoughts to X.

"You're a pessimist," he told her.

As today, apparently, X will have none of it.

Samantha didn't respond.

That'll cause some sturm und drang.

A minute has passed since X sent his last email, and now...

The entirety of the confidential *Project Ara* slowly disappears from Samantha's computer display.

The words 'File T*ransfer' flash.* When completed, her monitor reads:

PROJECT ARA: CONFIDENTIAL

File Transfer Complete.

File Deleted From System.

The words fade from the blue screen, and are replaced by the following:

TOUGH F'IN LUCK.

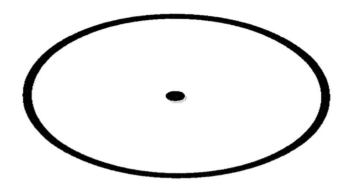

BREATH

English Countryside,

Nine Months Earlier (Estimated)

Brikke has not moved.

Pondering through the elements, Eron turns to the car; the blade awaits.

He is in weight and frame as he was as a dragonslayer. Flame and force from his final battle, however, have robbed him of both flesh and bone. He is nigh-fleshless from belly to chest and lower back but skin remains here and there. His body is unclothed. His face has largely been preserved. The hair is mostly singed and the scalp heavily scarred; the teeth remain. He is still, identifiably Eron. Though his hardened features define the severe look of a dutiful warrior, through his scar tissue remains a man many would consider, conventionally, handsome.

He retrieves the blade, paying no mind to the car's three current inhabitants. He grips the blade as tightly as he can. He looks up. Down. To the edge. Checks one side: flawless, unmarked. Checks the other:

ΣΗΘμαθΙσθισξ θ[αιθδησωοα ζφξ εξλαμδγωε

He runs his partially-shredded fingers over its point. Despite, or perhaps because of, its identification, he prizes the return.

Out the car window, the sun's luster returns as the color of death dissipates.

The ground returns to its former finery.

The car is now empty. Neither Thomas, Samantha, nor Daniel is present.

Eron carries the blade and walks away.

KINGS COUNTY HOSPITAL, BROOKLYN, NEW YORK

Fairly recently, maybe a year ago, Esme read an internet post analyzing the quantum concept of *biocentrism*—the notion that consciousness created the universe, not vice-versa. More engaged by religion than science but ever-mindful of Hawking's idea of heaven as a *fairy story*, she was especially taken by one commentator's analogy: "As electricity powers a computer, energy-derived consciousness powers the soul, which in turn builds the world."

The post explained the contention in layman's terms, which triggered Esme's interest. While the body eventually dies, it read, the soul lives on throughout infinity within a new *vessel*. Hence *deja vu* and other peculiarities.

This piece, and the subsequent book written by Dr. Robert Lanza, created quite the stir—and made a hell of a lot of sense to Esme. The existence of *multiverses* notwithstanding, a concept which she could not quite comprehend, biocentrism and the *eternal soul* became keystone articles of her faith.

They'll all think I'm nuts, she thought.

Regardless of Esme's concern, The Truth is that Lanza had come closer than any other mortal to solving life's greatest mystery. But he still had a ways to go, because the immortals never figured in his equation as they did with X, who knew that much more.

The answer, which will soon be known to all, lies somewhere in-between.

Not surprisingly to Esme, it was X who calculated the *Ten Measures of Creation.* She has prayed Lanza would read X's work and take him seriously.

Though X may have been privy to hidden information, and he and Esme were *connected* as associates of sorts, as her body ceased its function she knew what was happening.

She watched.

When she looked down at the team of doctors fumbling to resuscitate her and save the baby, she clearly heard Katz's instruction before she drifted away and allowed *God* to play his hand: "We can save one, not both."

There was no tunnel and there were no lights. There was only dark and then she woke up.

Dead.

~~~

She made it.

She had no idea she *made it,* other than the vaguest memory of looking down and suddenly becoming very confused—

"*Call it.*"

"*5:36 PM.*"

"Name?"

"Esme Chacont—"

She watched in wonder as Doctor Katz cut the umbilical cord and blanketed the baby as his nurse reached for a cap and covered the child's head.

Esme did not see the child's hair but did notice the sex.

A *girl...*

She watched in horror as Katz's nurse escaped through the swinging doors with the newborn cradled tightly in her arms.

The dark followed. Along with a lifetime of recall.

SHEEPSHEAD BAY, BROOKLYN, 1970S

Esme knows she'll be married to Carlo for the rest of her life. She'll never let him go because she can never fully trust him; he's a bad boy. She also knows, already, that she loves bad boys.

Esme is five years old.

Carlo Monetti is a year older, and his parents just moved to the U.S. from Abruzzi, Italy, in search of opportunity. A journey similar to her own family. His parents were staying with his cousin, he told her, until his dad found a good job.

He said there was nothing going on in Abruzzi, but his dad's idol—the pro wrestler Bruno Sammartino—was doing well enough in America. World champ. Defeated the loathsome *Nature Boy* Buddy Rogers in forty-eight seconds with a backbreaker. Made Abruzzi proud.

"It's time for the Monetti family," his father said, "to be like Bruno."

Carlo's family is Jewish-Italian. He heard the term "cheap wop" once. He had no idea what it meant but he knew inside it wasn't good. Whenever he feels insulted, he becomes angry and violent.

Where he diverges is in his equal defense of his friends, which Esme thinks is sweet. Carlo finds himself a great deal of trouble, but his alibi is always the same:

"Just like Bruno. Quick in, quick out."

Esme thinks he's the cutest thing she's ever seen.

~~~

Esme's parents relocated to Brooklyn, New York, from Paris, France when she was four. Mom was a housewife; Dad worked in the Garment District. When in Brooklyn, she veritably grew up with Carlo. Throughout high school she chased him. He paid her no mind as he was "too busy" with the other ladies. Esme, he thought, was not one-night-stand material.

He respects her too much. And he doesn't respect her a whit. To alleviate his guilt—he valued their friendship and really didn't want to hurt her—he once told her that if they ever did sleep together he wouldn't be able to perform.

He said it, as in a secret-like, between them. Like he had a medical problem or something. Psychologically, he would be affected because he'd fear they'd no longer be close, that their relationship would never be the same afterwards...that sort of thing.

She felt he cared, which he did. That he was putting her on a pedestal and really saying that they'd be together when the timing was right. Maybe when they were older.

His response when she revealed this to him: "Um hmm."

Carlo's true agenda wasn't that far off but his perspective was another matter. He told his friends he had a jones to pound Brooklyn's punani pavement while in his prime and keep a pin in Esme, just in case he required marriage material in the future. "It's not the sex in your life," he advised anyone who would listen, "it's the life in your sex. Get it out of your system and *then* settle down. *That's* the secret to a successful marriage."

Alienating her really was out of the question. He really did care. So he'd sow his oats for as long as necessary. *The best of both worlds*, he reminded himself whenever guilt tipped its hat.

All of which drew him to her even more. She saw his explanation as noble but ill-informed. She swore to him she'd be willing to try anything— "almost, as long as it's not too painful"—but to no avail. He reiterated his concerns.

So she told him she'd wait. For as long as it took.

1980s

The week after graduation, Esme was housekeeping when Carlo called her. He registered for adult education classes and needed money for materials.

"You did? For what?"

"Classes. I told you."

"What kind of classes?"

"You're not giving me the third-degree, are you?"

"You know I would never do that to you."

"Can I cry bullshit?"

Esme laughs. "You know me too well. What kind of classes?"

"I'm not off the hook?"

"*You're* asking *me* for money."

"You won't laugh again?"

"Pinky swear. Over the phone."

"Fine. Three nights a week and two Saturdays a month. Physics, Philosophy, Abnormal Psych. You can make fun of me now."

"Do I know you? Where did all this come from?"

"What do you mean?" He plays along coyly.

"All this. You didn't even know how to pronounce *philosophy* a year ago."

"I read this book."

"What book?"

"A book. Do you have the money or what?"

"Does the book have a title?"

"You didn't think I could read either?"

"No, I mean, yes! I'm thrilled! I'm stuck cleaning house and you—you're all big shot now going to night school. Maybe it can help me too? What's the book?"

He picks crud from his teeth with his pinky nail, feigning arrogance. He *thinks* he's feigning arrogance—

"What's the book?" Esme repeats. "You're gonna make me beg for the name of a freaking book—"

"*Mein Kampf.*"

She almost drops the phone.

Hitler? This is who's inspiring you now?

The conversation went from there; it lasted an hour. She loaned him money she didn't have.

The transaction took place on the corner of Nostrand Avenue and Avenue Y. Across from the Batchelder Street Projects. Drug haven.

Esme held the cash but she pulled her hand back at first. She said, "I never said something to you because I thought you wouldn't speak to me again. Hear my story and reconsider what's influencing you."

"I can't," he said, honestly. "How can I reconsider something I don't even understand?"

"What do you mean you don't understand?"

279

Carlo expected this and his hands begin to twitch, an old nervous habit that usually signaled the beginning of a fight. He buries his hands in his pants' pockets and looks away from her. He had hoped the conversation wouldn't go this far, now he doesn't have a choice but to continue his honesty when some half-explanation would be so much easier.

"He influenced the world more than anyone else this century." Esme doesn't flinch. Carlo cannot hold her gaze. "I'm not the first person to be inspired by a book. It's not like I'm going to go out and kill anyone."

"You have a choice. Hear my story or you take my money and don't even so much as call me again." He wanted to hear the story. And they didn't speak for nearly nine years because her Jewish mother was captured during the French occupation and barely survived Drancy transit camp.

She hated Carlo. She still loved Carlo. When she hated him, she was so angry she could barely work. When she loved him, she couldn't stop thinking about him with other women. After their meeting, every day was a battle with jealousy. Self-loathing, then on to cutting, which required several hospital stays.

Esme dropped out of public life after high school. She knew her parents would never be able to afford college and she...she just couldn't take it any more. So she read too. Classics, mostly. Some art books. She devoured culture and visited museums. By herself.

Between reading she worked and went home, where she took care of her ill mother.

When her mother was admitted into an old-age home, Esme became a recluse. She heard that her mother died soon after, but she couldn't bring herself to see her in that condition. Her dad passed a month later, of a heart attack. Sixty-seven years young.

Carlo read about the passing in the local newspaper, and was the first—

and only—person to reach out and call Esme. They met again, this time at a diner on Emmons Avenue. She didn't hesitate.

His parents amassed some wealth in the stock market, retired and moved back to Abruzzi, he told her. Esme told him she started a housekeeping business. "I have three employees right now. I clean too."

"So you're an entrepreneur?"

"Something like that. I guess."

He unexpectedly takes her hand. "I changed my name…"

"You changed your name?"

"I needed a fresh start. I begin my second doctorate next week."

"Amazing. I don't know what to say to you any more."

"*Professor Edward Searle.* Psychologist. Physicist."

"Why *Edward?*"

"Had a ring to it."

"Had a ring—" she begins to repeat. Before gasping.

There is was, glittering from the overhead lights. *Professor Searle* knew this was a long-shot but it was now time for marriage material. He stood up, dropped to one bent knee in the middle of the restaurant.

He said all the right things.

1990s

She had met another man she fell in love with, this one a bit more consistent in his *lower achievement.* She was not intimidated with him as she was with the brainy Searle. He owned a pizza joint in the city. A simple man; she knew she had a thing for Italians. He worked hard—and beat her harder.

But Esme married him. He always apologized and she blamed herself for any trouble. She gave birth to twins—a boy and a girl. They stayed together through thick and thin as their relationship quickly devolved into a co-dependent morass of apologies and acceptance. Then the bad: more apologies, makeup sex, more fighting...

2000–2014

She stayed in touch with Searle and they spoke daily. He did not begrudge her the rejection of "second chance." She said to him she couldn't bear being hurt by him again. He understood.

But she gave up her none-too-successful business and went to work for him anyway. He opened up his school and their prized student became a young runaway today's world refers to as X.

Only she and Searle knew him by his real name. Searle had insisted. At the boy's request they would never tell anyone else. The thing is, though, he had lied. He had given them a fake identity. The boy near-idolized Malcolm X; he understood that *X* was not the revolutionary's given name and yet the particular letter held great power.

Uncompromising, influential, persistent, passionate. Powerful.

X.

Just like his predecessor. Just as Alex Haley, who assisted Malcolm on his autobiography—years prior to *Roots*—had helped to assert the icon for all eternity. What X could never understand, however, is just why that single letter held him in such a grip.

Even more so than the man he admired, the letter meant that much *more...*

Early on, X had suspected the possible presence of a supernatural force that led him to adapt the moniker. But, long before his research, his findings...he was a devout skeptic. What was...was the here and now. Only.

Translation: *Survival.*

All of which he confided to Esme. He also told her, in an unguarded moment, that his worship of Malcolm X was owing to the bravery of adopting the name first, and his work second. Nonetheless, Esme agreed with Searle to protect X's secret, as they were   convinced—both of them—that there would be consequences if he was betrayed on the matter.

They earned X's trust.

<div align="center">~~~</div>

Esme and Searle slept together only once. Despite his other shortcomings, her husband never cheated on her.

Abeyance.

Esme's husband killed her that night. It took about 24 hours for the death to take hold.

Searle disappeared. Her baby was stolen; the nurse was arrested. Chaos.

"5:36 P.M."

<div align="center">~~~</div>

Black.

Stars.

In her passage through the cosmos, Esme realizes a few things:

My consciousness has not left me.

And—

I never should have betrayed that wonderful boy.

Esme considers the moment X approached her for a second opinion on his *findings*, and her subsequent destruction of his computer equipment.

X had written about this episode early on:

I temporarily withheld the fruits of my labors and continued the study for several months in silent dread. I then submitted my new findings, in-person, to a trusted associate for a second opinion. But, while away, my office was ransacked; my hard drive was compromised and my portable back-up platforms stolen.

As to my associate? Never heard from her again.

Esme remembers how sick she became when she read about his letter because all she wanted was to save him from a life of ridicule.

Esme's final realization:

Time is space. Many said this.

Her mind wanders ...

Events he spoke of, so close apart ...

Enlightenment.

Abeyance.

I understand.

Two pauses, one lifetime.

My lifetime.

Why was he never effect—?

She enters the void as the gods swallow her whole in preparation for her next matter of business.

HOTEL MIRAMAR, BOURNEMOUTH, DORSET, ENGLAND, CHRISTMAS DAY, 1971

They had been married for over 50 years.

When Edith passed, less than a month ago on November 29, Ronald relocated to Oxford. Merton College would be his new home; the school accommodated Oxford's prodigal son by extending room and board for as long as he needed.

He would return to Bournemouth on Christmas Eve—last night—but only for a whisper. His intent was to break his cardinal rule and privately raise one more glass to his wife.

Which he did.

He then lit the fireplace and went to bed.

And he had a dream.

He had a dream of a faraway time when he wasn't so brave—or inspired—in real life, a time when he walked through a taboo forest.

If only they could talk.

The trees, that is. Always, the trees.

His friends. When he slept.

But on this night the dream *turns.* The trees, spontaneously, catch fire. Ronald stands, stilled in disbelief. He runs as the flames come closer and he panics, trapped in a horrific maze as the trees—his friends and guardians—topple and collapse around him and threaten any chance of escape.

And then he sees her.

Ara!

She motions to him. He follows her lead...only to incur the wrath of the *little dragon* who swoops overhead and enflames the last remaining timber. Young Tolkien looks up in response to a terrible noise.

He is about to be struck by a falling monster oak, so-conditioned by the dragon, when—

Tolkien awakens, panting, drenched in sweat.

Before, when he set to sleep, he had hoped he would *find* his wife, as if they were playing a simple game of *Hide N' Seek.*

Wishful thinking.

Tolkien rises from his bed. He wipes sweat from his brow, straightens—in as much as he can without breaking—turns on the end table lamp, swings his feet into the white cotton slippers that rest on the floor...pushes himself up with his arms and stands.

Hell. Pure hell.

He takes a moment to breathe, peeks at the snowflakes falling in the darkness outside his window illuminated only by hotel light—then hobbles over to the antique desk at the room's opposite side.

Okay then.

He grabs a pen from a holder and scribbles on the yellow legal pad.

Just as you say, my dear, 'Ronald, time for more constructive pursuits.'

Pen works; he gets to business.

My Dearest Mr. McFee,

I pray this correspondence finds you in prime health and welfare. As for me, I cannot sleep. I am certain you have read by now, my beloved Edith passed away on November 29th. Though she was quite ill and her death was expected, my present state of loneliness reminds me of those early days when I was a boy with no friends and an overabundance of neediness. My father was gone. My only association then, aside from my surviving family, were the trees.

Remember the trees? Surely we spoke of my trees.

By the way, I do hope that you resume your efforts on my biography, if my modest life (how I wish I could have lived my literary adventures!) still inspires you so. I am quite honored, actually. I have always been keen on you, though I admit I may have given you a tough rub here and there.

Please take the compliment in the spirit intended, as I would never trust "just anyone" with my story. You were never anything less than authentic with me and that was such a welcome quality. A person true to others and himself is a person I admire.

I have since moved back to Oxford and have been spending a good deal of time with my grandson. The best of times compensating for the worst of times. For now, I am in Bournemouth for what is likely my final visit, desiring to be alone with my thoughts. Edith's favorite retreat hosts me once more.

We did a remarkable thing last year. Really we did. All of us, and for that I am forever grateful. We became merchants of history and realized, collectively, that all was not as it appeared. Yet, who else knows? No one else (I believe, based on the lack of any credible news), save for our motley group.

I have long been compelled to write these words to you, to both commemorate our discovery and remind us all of our responsibility. Firstly, I appreciate the discretion of you and Mr. Levin, and, of course, our dear Bradley. I understand fully the enormous temptation to tell the world and shout from the rooftops one and all, as to our miraculous find.

Thank you again for not acting on impulse. You've waited, as agreed. When I am called to reunite with the only woman I have ever loved, the decision shall rest exclusively with you and the remaining 'fellowship' as to how best to direct this material.

Shall I confess to you, however, an apprehension of mine? I am nagged by the fear that we have been guided to this find by a larger force, that our ensuing fortune was no accident but...in translating the work we may have unlocked a portal to the past that should not (yet) have been unlocked. If my concern is well-regarded, may I suggest to all that you hold off until which time the world *needs* to know?

I place my trust in your awareness when that day comes.

If you do resume your book, may I also selfishly request no mention be made of our gathering in that context? Unfortunately, I cannot explain any further. I do not have an explanation as to my fear, other than my dreams have always served me well and, of late, I am consistently warned that my muse may have deceived me.

Such inescapable unease threatens to engulf my spirit, and I fret over my own passivity as I am not the most capable during this advanced state of affairs. Perhaps I should have expected to encounter some late-life demons without Edith by my side, but nonetheless, I beg your prudence as one can never be too careful.

Allow Ara to remain an enigma. For the safety of you and yours, the very concept is a fiction, as Beowulf is a fiction, and that is all. Let it rest.

You are a good man, Franklin, and you will certainly set a fine example for your boy...as I am sure my own father intended for me.

Just be ever-mindful that you are the architect of his universe.

He carefully considers his salutation—.

Cheers, Ronald

287

He nods, satisfied. He stands and walks over to the closet, where he removes a money clip from a pair of old trousers.

Tolkien tosses the clip onto the desk. He removes a note, handwritten on an Algonquin Hotel napkin—Franklin's—from the mess of bills and cards. He copies the address onto an envelope from Hotel Miramar's stationary, seals it and places it in his door's outbound mail slot. He again passes the window—*still so dark out there*—wriggles off his slippers, and lies on the bed.

Once more, though fairly terrified, he will try to sleep.

Light off.

He stares at the ceiling.

Not ready.

Light on.

He reaches to the nightstand on the other side of the bed, and grabs a book: *Complete Poems of Robert Frost.* His finger runs the red ribbon—his bookmark—and he opens the book to his last saved page.

The Road Not Taken

He reads for but a moment, then places the book, spread, on his chest. "With apologies, Mr. Frost..."

Tolkien clears his throat. He stares at the ceiling, then closes his eyes and recites from memory:

"Two roads diverged in a yellow wood, and sorry I could not travel both and be one traveler, long I stood and looked down one as far as I could to where it bent in the undergrowth..."

He settles in. The poem is relaxing him. And he *glimpses* the English countryside, the same where Thomas McFee will years from now attempt to help a group of children involved in a bus accident.

But first, a much younger Tolkien, in his early-thirties, *visits* a time past...

~~~

Yesterday.

Professor Tolkien has been roaming the landscape, on foot, taking mental note of areas Thomas McFee will visit decades from now. For the moment, he has stopped. A fork beckons, the dirt paths themselves nearly identical, save for a degree of grass on the other. One route, though, leads in the direction of habitation. Civilization. The other—*who knows?* Hills dead ahead block his visibility.

Two paths, likely two distinct ends. He makes a decision.

"Then took the other, as just as fair, and having perhaps the better claim..."

He climbs atop a grassy incline and admires the panoramic beauty over which he presides. Nothing but green.

"*Mirkwood!*" he proudly exclaims.

He has found his setting, for his book...

~~~

Tomorrow.

Present day. The author is long-deceased.

From the confines of his bed he peers into the future and he walks onward, though deceased his age appearing the same as now, envisioning ...

A beautiful sun. The slightest gusts of wind. A familiar locale.

"*... because it was grassy and wanted wear...*"

The locale of an immortal's last stand and a dragonslayer's return. In Tolkien's minds-eye he *knows* of these events, and related future events, and does not question his cognition.

As with Thomas—Franklin's son—Samantha and Daniel before him, now Brikke is no longer present.

And neither is Thomas' car.

"... *though as for that the passing there had worn them really about the same...*"

All is as it once was.

Save for the lone exception:

Eron has entered the road.

And, on this new day, he is being watched. An older man circles him on a motorbike. He approaches, passes, skids into U-turn. He repeats this action several times, each instance looking in his mirror when he passes for closer observation.

He is Professor Searle.

Tolkien is curious. His brow furrows; he squints his left eye. This is all very familiar...though he has neither an explanation for the vision, nor an identification of either entity.

Still, he recites:

"... *and both that morning equally lay in leaves no step had trodden black...*"

~~~

Yesterday.

Tolkien looks first behind him.

"*...Oh, I kept the first for another day!*"

Then he descends from the incline.

"*Yet knowing how way leads on to way, I doubted if I should ever come back.*"

He walks on, and does not look back again.

Tolkien turns off his light.

He falls asleep in seconds, book still on his chest.

~~~

Tomorrow.

As REM sleep overtakes him, Frost's poem is concluded in his reverie:

I shall be telling this with a sigh somewhere ages and ages hence.

A single ray of sun sparks the grass. The spark begets smoke. And then the smoke begets flame, which in turn attracts a sleeping dragon who he believes is named *Taebal* who breathes his own fire which begets...a raging inferno, destroying everything in its wake.

Tolkien shifts in his bed, unable to escape this unrelenting phantasm.

Two roads diverged in a wood, and I—I took the one less traveled by.

From there...come the *armies.* Short, sudden glimpses of sides taken and a world under siege, lines drawn and battles fought by all sorts of mortal and god and monster and spirit and—

And that has made all the difference.

~~~

Tolkien awakens with a start, barely able to control his shuddering. As his mind clears, however, so too does he steel his resolve. He refuses the demons another win. It's been a night. He reaches for the comfort of his wife's touch...and he remembers that he is not only quite alone, but that he's also trapped in the dark. This time he refuses to panic.

"I'll be brave, my dear Edith." He sobs, softly. "I'll be—Edith, how I miss you." He is overtaken by emotion. Tolkien glances out the window. The lights are now off and he can no longer see the snow. "Are you safe, Edith? He continues. "Have you touched His hand?" He closes his eyes and leans on his pillow. "Please..."Tears stream down his cheeks. His final words, before choking and crying himself back to sleep. "Please take care of her." He pulls up his blanket, settling in. "My dear, I will see you soon." He wipes his eyes. "I may see you sooner than you think," he yawns, interrupted by a half-hearted chuckle.

He adjusts his position, prepping his sleep.

~~~

"I promise, my dear…"

"Taebal is coming."

A *female's* whisper.

"Hmm?" he says aloud. Nothing more. He stretches. "See you…" he says, barely aware.

"Taebal…"

Tolkien's mouth opens; his orientation is lost and he slips from consciousness.

"Tae—"

Black.

~~~

Morning.

Tolkien stirs and rises, as if he slept through the night without interruption. He remembers nothing, save for the letter he wrote to Franklin McFee.

He swings his legs over the bed, to the floor. Slippers on. He stands, then walks to his closest. Removes his bathrobe. Robe on. He looks to the mail slot.

Sent. Bloody good.

Tolkien enters the *toilet.* He prepares for a shower.

Everything is in order. Soap, shampoo. He squeezes toothpaste onto his brush. Brushes, gargles, rinses. Looks in the mirror. As he silently curses his aged reflection, his immediate second thought will remain with him until his final breath:

She will not allow me to complete another book in my lifetime.

BOOK TWO

ON THE SECOND MEASURE OF CREATION

LEWIS CARROLL

ALICE LIDDELL, A CHILD

A PORTAL BEYOND THE RABBIT HOLE

As a man, I am enlightened by passion.

As a creator, I am ruled by fear.

I fear my muse cannot be contained.

She guides me toward the brightest of lights.

She leads me to the pitch of hell's dark.

And I am forever consumed:

Shall I become an influencer of good, or of madness?

- Anonymous

A SACRED PROMISE, AND
ANOTHER

SCARP PUBLISHING, INC.,

NEW YORK, NEW YORK, SUMMER 2016

Denise sits, feet atop her desk, immersed in a newspaper.

She suffered for his visit today—hair, nails, facial—and looks damn good. Thomas attempts, valiantly, not to notice. He needs to keep a clear head.

But those legs...

Thomas moved back to Brooklyn six months ago but intentionally avoided Denise until last week. Prior to his return, they did not speak for over a year—since the book release. He was not angry; the book sold better than his others and Denise did a hell of a job in marketing and promotion. He needed to vanish for a while, to get away from all things business for his own mental well-being. He also needed to get away, specifically, from her.

Denise was used to his eccentricities. "He's a writer. It comes with the territory," she would say, when she found herself in the unenviable position of turning down requests for book signings.

She was always honest as to why. He always had reason. Every time. A legitimate reason; as his proclivity was to sequester himself at the completion of a project, he insisted from their first contract a condition-precedent: No questions asked, self-promotion of his work would be at his sole discretion, she was not to interfere in his time off. The clause was necessary if they were to undertake any business relationship.

"It's just the way I'm built," he would say, diluting the question whenever it was asked.

Thomas and his publisher have skirted their boundaries alarming frequency over the years, which has—almost—everything to do with his most recent absence.

Almost, because he had begun to wonder if she had anything whatsoever to do with his adventures in London, specifically, if she had any connection to...anything he found himself dealing with while visiting Donovan Bradley.

What Thomas could not tell her regarding his most recent sojourn was this: Just after the publication of his book, he had spoken to a local priest in the lobby of the Claridge about his late wife, Elizabeth. The meeting was accidental and the conversation impromptu; Thomas asked if the priest would be so kind as to give him some advice. The priest complied. Thomas asked the priest if he should continue to wear his wedding band. The priest asked him if he still loved his wife, regardless of her passing.

'Of course I still love her. That's why I approached you."

"Would you still love her if you removed the ring?"

"Of course."

"Why then are you questioning whether you should remove your ring?"

"I need an objective opinion."

"Why are you questioning whether you should remove your ring?" he repeated.

"Father, I have no religious convictions, but—"

"Why the difficulty answering my question?"

"Father—?"

"Please. Try to answer my question."

"Am I allowed to move on?"

By the end of the conversation, with the priest's blessing, Thomas promised that if he could get it together, emotionally, he would give the ring to Daniel, who would then bequeath it to Sam for their wedding.

~~~

When Denise peeks and catches his eyeline, Thomas pretends he's studying the headline:

ENGLAND COURIER

EXTRA

Friday 2 September 1973

RINGS AUTHOR TOLKIEN DIES IN BOURNEMOUTH

LITERARY LEGEND AND CULTURAL INFLUENCER WAS 81

"I love the old papers." She sniffs. "Even smells different." She back-folds to the front page and places the paper, face-up, atop her keyboard. "He told the Miramar's registry that his '71 trip would be his last. I'm sure he meant it at the time."

"If we're going to do this," Thomas interrupts, "maybe we should get down to business."

"Didn't mean to be disrespectful. It's good to see you, you know."

"No disrespect taken."

"Well...thank you for the gift anyway," says Denise. "Would it be ghoulish if I framed it?"

"Yeah, probably."

"I thought so. Why I asked."

"Yeah."

Some clumsiness, as expected. It has been a long time.

"That's all?"

Thomas smiles. "It's good to see you too."

"Okay, enough. You're busy, I'm busy—"

"You haven't changed a bit."

"Appreciate it," she says drily.

"Only thing with that story, and I was reminded when I found it," says Thomas, "is that it implies Tolkien returned to Bournemouth to visit friends."

"He did."

"I maintain that he returned to Bournemouth to die."

"That too. Who am I to decipher his deeper motives? That's *your* job." She changes frequency. "So, how do I convince you to follow-up on our biggest seller, huh?"

"Lots and lots of money. You can't afford me any more."

"Try me."

"I'm officially retired, remember?"

Denise stands and walks to the front of the desk. Modest skirt, pumps.

"No?" she asks. "If you're retired, what do we have to lose?"

He takes his time. "Probably my sanity."

"So what?"

"Right. So, tell me what he wants."

"Sanity is highly overrated."

"What does he want?" he repeats.

"What does *who* want—"

"Donovan."

"Ah. Him."

"Yeah."

Disappointed, Denise returns to her desk. She falls into her chair. "I called Sam."

"She told me."

"How are you both doing?"

"What did she say?"

"Me betray a confidence?"

"Nah."

"Back to the subject at hand. When you changed your number, Bradley couldn't reach you."

"I changed my number. That was the point."

"He wants to sell you the store." Denise smirks. She has passed the gatekeepers, as ever, and has gone directly to *go*. She adores his flummoxed reaction. "So?"

"The bookshop?"

"He needs a buyer. Just can't do it anymore."

"His age?"

"No, his shoe size."

"Ask a stupid question—"

"Get the only sensible response..."

"No."

"No what?"

"No, I'm not interested. I have no experience in running a shop—"

She appears legitimately surprised. "Really?" He takes the opposite seat.

"Let's strip away the b.s. for a minute, okay?" Denise slowly nods, curious. "Let's forget that we've done...relatively well together."

"We've done very well, Tom."

"And let's forget the fact that you desperately desire me and have spent the last week preparing for my visit. Nice perfume, by the way—"

"Gee, thanks."

"You're welcome. Why is he selling?"

"He's old, Tom. Anyone home? You were right the first time. Hello?"

"He could close the store. He has more money than God. He can put the books in storage. Or he can donate them to a museum, better yet, or—"

"He tried that. Didn't he tell you—"

"He may have. No buyer?"

"Bingo. You're his only hope."

"Well, Hope doesn't always spring eternal."

"What's your point?"

"My point is we've made a pretty penny together but I can't possibly afford—"

"One dollar, Tom. Can you afford that?"

"And the riddles continue..."

"He's not interested in selling. Only in getting out. He trusts no one else. His son is deceased and his health hasn't been the best lately."

"What's the catch?"

"No catch."

"What's his agenda, then?"

300

"You know, Tom, your paranoia will get the best of you one day. Don't you trust *me*?" He doesn't respond. "My turn for the stupid questions."

"Of course I do," he fibs. "I mean just...the responsibility..."

Denise types on her computer. "Hold on just a second."

Skype.

"You can't wait five minutes?"

"He's old, Tom."

"The bait less taken, remember? No impulsive decisions. You taught me that when you negotiated my second book deal."

"Funny. I'll fuck you right now if you say—"

"God No."

She shrugs, waits a couple of seconds, records a voicemail. "Donovan, Denise Watkins. It's not going to happen overnight. Call me."

She disconnects.

"Yeah," Thomas says. "You'll fuck me?"

"Not anymore." He shrugs. "What are you hiding from, may I ask?"

"I'm hiding. It means I'm not ready to relocate—again—and change my life. I won't walk away from the retirement I earned."

"Retirement. Bullshit. You know you'll be back."

"On my time. Sorry sweetheart. Let him know I appreciate the offer, yeah?"

"Again *yeah*." As she types—"Your vocabulary has slipped a bit since your last book I see."

"Really?"

"Hold on." She spins her monitor so Thomas can read it. "You're right. There *is* an agenda. Just not necessarily *his*. Check it out," she says, showing him a filename:

An Open Letter to the Media

1/3/15

Suddenly, Thomas is *very* uncomfortable. "He had no entries last year that I know of. How did you—"

"Don't ask questions." Denise clicks on the file. The entry appears, filling the entirety of the screen.

"Shut up and read. And then we'll talk." Thomas puts on his glasses, and scoots in.

"Sexy," teases Denise. "Never saw you with your specs..."

"And you never will again..."

About now, Denise may as well be invisible.

An Open Letter to the Media

1/3/15

I spoke to Thomas McFee recently.

"Where did you get this?" Thomas demands

"Keep reading."

"Who's seen this?"

"Keep reading!"

With trepidation, he turns back to the screen.

An Open Letter to the Media

1/3/15

I spoke to Thomas McFee recently. We didn't get on well, which is too bad as I really am something of a fan. How I so wanted to discuss the finer points of Tolkien's "The

Silmarillion," which the author never completed, you know.

But of course you do if you are at all literate. Stupid me.

Anyway, regarding Thomas and me, we got sidetracked. We discussed other things, issues of varying importance. I think I need to make up for that lost time so I'm reaching out once more to you, the world at large.

Let's talk. Let's talk for a minute about my new friend, shall we? You all know my friend, the one with the love-hate relationship with his publisher, a sordid state of affairs which the gossip rags froth over? They could never be, unfortunately, like Luthien and Beren, the names inscribed on the Tolkiens' gravestones, the 'great loves' of "The Silmarillion"

"He's sick, Denise. Why should I engage this garbage any furth—"

"Would you please? Not answering you. You need to finish."

... of "The Silmarillion," his (well, not all his) unsung final work? Because he was married before and I understand their ending was quite tragic and—

And...

You know what? I just thought of something. I'll do all the talking. You don't know him like I do. Pressure's off. Onward and upward.

McFee's publisher is one Denise Watkins, of Scarp Publishing, in New York. When I say "represented," I mean she is his agent. He's very successful; I don't know why he needs her anymore when he can write his own ticket—well, actually I do; see above—but...

I must admit, by the way, that Ms. Watkins' building does contain a fairly homey roof. I can only imagine the morally reprehensible goings-on after hours, especially on Friday nights during 'Happy Hour' (which, as brilliant as I am, remains a concept I could never understand). But I digress.

"This doesn't scare you at all? What does he know?" Thomas asks. "Do you know where he is?" The missive answers for him:

Don't bother. Further police efforts to find me are best targeted elsewhere. Been there, done that, as they say. Now, on to business.

Thomas McFee's father was an associate of Mr. Tolkien's.

"We'll talk when you're done. No! Close your mouth. You may catch butterflies."

Maybe a 'limited associate' is a more accurate descriptor. They didn't know each other all that well, but they did have some dealings.

So, the writing of Tolkien's "The Silmarillion" actually commenced well before The Hobbit. The stand-alone tales that would ultimately comprise the posthumously-published work began to take shape in 1914. Consistent with the author's abiding ambition to—paraphrasing Wikipedia— 'create an English mythology that would explain the origins of English history and culture," Tolkien mined various world myths to create nothing less than a pre-history of the planet Earth. He had just returned from France after taking part in the First World War. He was in the hospital, recuperating and presumably reflective, when he put pen to paper.

He composed his most famous books in the ensuing years, and attempted now and then to go back to "The Silmarillion." He strived to complete the work before he died but was unsuccessful.

The completion of this book was, metaphorically, a life-long ambition. I believe his compulsion to create a 'pre-history' was much more urgent than we have been led to believe.

But who am I to say? I'm just a 'crackpot.'

And so we go on...

"The Silmarillion" was published in 1977 with no small amount of assistance from others.

I reached out to Mr. McFee to share some information about this—I have some unique insight, you see—I wanted to help with his book but he was quite rude.

In the interest of fair disclosure, here were my observations regarding Mr. Tolkien, vis a vis "The Silmarillion" and my faithful protagonist.

Thomas tenses. "When did I become his 'protagonist?' When did I become anyone's pro—" He looks to Denise, who turns away, then reluctantly resumes his read—

1. A scarcely explored but notable theory as to why Tolkien was unable to see "The Silmarillion" to its completion is that

he simply didn't have 'all' the answers he was looking for. He may have thought he did; who knows? Certainly not Thomas McFee, as he ignored the question entirely in 'his' book. Nice job of playing it safe.

2. If "The Silmarillion" had been foisted upon a gullible public in Tolkien's lifetime, in a half-assed, fragmented manner, which was not this particular author's wont, the cultural repercussions would have been...upsetting. His reputation would have suffered—imo—due to the ensuing unfavorable response. And 'that' would have been problematic in the long-term.

3. His other, more established work would have been re-examined. Much like anything else that becomes wildly popular, a wave of backlash would have been inevitable. The question then becomes, "How big the wave?" See Lucas, George.

"He's deliberately misleading..." Thomas fumes.

"What do you mean? What don't you understand?"

"If he's talking *Star Wars*, the OT has never been more highly-regarded...And I'm not referring to the *Special Editions*. The prequels only served to enhance their popularity—"

"Thomas, OT?"

"*Original Trilogy*, Denise. Come on."

Denise shrugs. "Where's my head?"

"Do tell."

"You didn't like the prequels either?"

"The Force is spiritual, not biological. You want me to get back to this or not?"

"Such a glad-handler—"

"I'm partial to *Sith*, okay? But not the point. If he's misleading here, then where else? He's pushing my buttons deliberately, and—"

"Preliminaries recognized, genius. Yes, he's misleading everywhere. Endgame still to be defined and, despite every instinct in your body, he can't be trusted. Which, at this very moment, you are having a hell of a time accepting." Thomas is about to respond but he is fairly stunned. These last comments by his publisher actually make a good deal of sense. "So I repeat my question. What is it that you don't understand?"

"I had only hoped you would spell his motives out for me. As well as give me a formal explanation of the mysteries of life, death, the nature of the universe—"

"Why?" he deadpans.

"You serious? So I can sleep nights, sweetheart."

"Ask a—"

"Who is he, Tom?"

"Sorry?"

"Who is he—"

"I know as much as you or anyone. What makes you think—"

"I believe you, settle down. You told me you two spoke, I read this. I had to ask."

"Well...don't."

"Tom." Her manner turns to serious from something less. "You seem to forget it's not a twenty-year reunion here. It's been barely one. We did correspond. We spoke, on occasion."

"You wanted me to get through the rest of this?"

Denise tenses. "You know, Tom, this used to be fun. But you're acting like a damn robot. I wasn't expecting warm-fuzzies here but Jesus H. Christ—"

"Are we done?"

"Like hell. I'm not finished. So I suddenly forget everything that happened to you? To Sam? Seeing you back here means *nothing*, especially considering everything we've all gone through since we've last seen each other? I have a newsflash for you, Tom. Put the banter on the shelf for a second. I thought we were friends."

"That's your newsflash?"

"What?"

"That we're friends? Must have taken an awful lot of therapy to get you there."

"Tom—"

"This is why I came back to New York? To resume a perpetual battle of wits—"

"Fuck you too." She relents, and returns to her newspaper.

Thomas returns to the email:

So here we are.

McFee wrote a good book. Not a classic, by any definition, but an informative-enough tome for those less-critical readers, if not a bit dry. 'Dry' being a euphemism for boring...Who am I kidding? To be honest, I'm somewhat ashamed of Ms. Watkins for passing muster on the new work.

"What is *muster*, anyway?" Thomas asks to no response.

Unfortunately, since he didn't take advantage of my best

intentions, McFee missed the boat on delivering anything new.

And then some.

So why does (any of) this matter?

It matters because he came close.

Mr. McFee came very, very close—damn close—to what I call The Truth.

From this point, Thomas will not allow his attentions to be diverted again, regardless of any conflicting circumstance.

His book became Scarp's biggest-seller yet, which only reinforces my thoughts as to the ignorance of the general public.

When you offer pablum, they eat pablum.

It also explains why they never believed a word I said. Because I challenged them and they didn't want to be challenged.

That said, I would like to introduce you—and, you know what?—only you, Ms. Denise Watkins, to my new reality. 'Our' new reality.

Denise does not look up. Thomas is already feeling pangs of guilt, but he continues reading.

I don't want to be too much of a hypocrite. I said before that I had sent the last of my letters to the media. I'll stand by that. We'll reserve this one for you, and you alone. Therefore, when—and not if—you warn Thomas, please inform him of the following:

He's right. It ain't nuthin' but a game right now. It's a 'wild goose chase' (not that I ever quite understood that one either; what do wild geese have to do with anything?) and do you know why? It's because I'm bored. But we knew that already.

Tell your friend there that—no manipulation whatsoever (I swear!)—he could be surrounded by all the answers he seeks, all of them...if only he takes advantage of the opportunity you've no doubt already introduced.

I'm going to sign off in a moment. I'm feeling rather manic today.

Donovan Bradley is selling his business. He has no heir, which I may or may not have had something to do with. He is in his nineties, and he is surrounded by a literary record that— no hyperbole—is second in its comprehensiveness only to the Library of Alexandria. Which, need I remind you, was destroyed by a fire.

I may, or may not, have had something to do with that one too.

But let's not delve into those questions right now. Let's focus on the big picture. Remember, there are reasons, there are sources, for my knowledge.

As there are reasons for everything.

Denise surreptitiously observes Thomas's reaction. His eyes dart furiously; he rushes to get through the rest.

Random thoughts, transitions be damned: Smarten up your boy, Ms. Watkins.

All the history Mr. McFee, or anyone else, would ever need

to turn back the clock of the universe...(and I do hope you enjoy my dramatic spacings, em-dashes, carefully-placed parenthetical asides and ellipses, btw) is his for the accepting.

He needs to accept Bradley's offer.

Otherwise, we will not survive another Abeyance. Everything that came before has already been <u>corrected</u>.

No more chances.

For proof, his daughter and everyone in the country that day survived. As did he.

None of them remembers anything, but they will now start asking a bunch of questions.

Because—

I've said it before. They are realizing of late, and Thomas is finally beginning to accept, that nothing is what it appears to be. This includes Samantha, who is certainly not who she appears to be.

The gods are done. Except for one.

He may want to ask his daughter.

I think he knows why.

If not, I'll help him out.

Today, the world rotates as if nothing has happened. As if there were not two abeyant events within the course of a year.

That's worrisome, don't you think? An honest question.

(And, by the way... again? When I refer to "the world" I may also be talking, as I stated earlier, 'metaphorically.' Maybe there's more than one. Ever consider that, genius? May well put things in a different perspective, don't you think? Hint.

Hint. Idiot.)

Thomas rubs the back of his neck, aggravated. But he continues before Denise says a word.

I ever say publicly that I'm tired of being called a "crackpot?" Of course—though I can't prove a thing.

Woe is me. More worrisome.

So, to conclude...

The best of my estimates? From today forward? Till the universe implodes? Based on my scrupulously-calculated Ten Measures, as inspired by the works of Pythagoras and Lewis Carroll?

Five years.

McFee glances at the close—

Say 'goodnight' now. It'll be a while before we communicate again.

P.S. If either of you speaks to Donovan, may you be so kind to ask how he's enjoying Wonderland? Many thanks.

"Still love me, asshole?"

Thomas turns away from the screen. "Why the runaround, Denise?"

"There's no runaround, Tom. What the hell's this *Wonderland* reference all ab—?"

"Why didn't you just tell me on the phone? Don't you think I'd have answered?"

"No. You would have stayed in your cocoon."

Thomas accepts her words as truth. "You know me too well." He stares out the window.

"You need to fill me in, Tom." She stands and approaches and, shyly—which surprises him—places her hand on his shoulder. He doesn't fight it. "I still don't bite and I suspect I'm still the only friend you have."

"Denise, I—"

"Accepted. And you're still an asshole. But I have questions." Thomas nods, at an utter loss. He pats her hand.

This is what it takes? Denise wonders. "What's with *Wonderland?*"

"No idea. Something Bradley said in passing. That's the next thing that scares me." Tom steps away. She's not surprised.

"What's next?" she asks.

SAMANTHA AND DANIEL'S APARTMENT, CAMBRIDGE, ENGLAND

Three weeks later.

Samantha sits in her bedroom, in front of a full-sized mirror, alone, wearing a flowing white wedding dress. She holds an antique leather-bound photo album. It is a tied with a pink bow. She removes the bow, uncovering the title which had been obscured:

What If?

Her dad's name appears in smaller letters on the cover's bottom right corner. The pages are turned. She cannot look away; she is wholly immersed.

Photos abound of Samantha posing with her parents, from birth through college. The pages are all dated; no photographs are included past 12/25/2010 yet there are plenty of sheets remaining.

The final photo is particularly poignant. Thomas, twenty pounds heavier, stands with his arm around his daughter's shoulder. They are in Elizabeth's hospital room, and the smiles are forced. Elizabeth smiles weakly in her bed, undergoing a chemo treatment. They all wear Santa caps. A Christmas tree is blurred in the background.

But where's Grandpa? He was with us on that last Christmas...

Samantha forgets her question when she turns to the next page. And the next, and the next. *Sketches*, filling in the gaps of time Thomas and Samantha have been estranged. Just the two of them, standing in the stead of the Eiffel Tower, the Vatican, the observation deck of the Empire State Building...his final book signing. Samantha's eyes are made up and she struggles not to glaze over. She flips to the last page—

A final sketch of a baby, held by two faceless parents. The image could represent an infant Thomas with his own parents, Sam with hers...or a future child of Sam's with Daniel. Under the sketch:

P.S. Open to Interpretation.

Samantha laughs, truly touched. She closes the book, and fans her hand in front of her face so as not to become a crying mess. She is distracted by a knock on the door.

~~~

Thomas, dressed to the nines in a tailored black suit, white shirt and red necktie, awkwardly motions for her to stay seated. She doesn't move. Her back is to the door.

In reflection, she watches as he walks behind her. Sam shuts her eyes, not knowing where this is headed. Though she had hoped he would show.

"Keep your eyes closed," he says.

"Dad—"

"Please," he insists. Her eyes remain shut. "And open your hand."

A nervous laugh and then she meekly asks, "Which one?"

"Doesn't matter, really." She opens her right. Thomas reaches into his pocket, carefully removing the rabbit's foot which she once gave to him in honor of a sacred promise. It is now attached to a chain. He places it into her palm. "Open your eyes."

She knows right away. "You didn't."

"I'd understand if you want me to leave." he begins.

Sam opens her eyes. "No."

He pulls the chain and places the rabbit's foot back into his pocket. "Never," he says. "Recent events in my crazy life, well, reminded me..." They are both visibly relieved, each embracing the calm in the other. He carefully places his hands on her shoulders. "You like the gift? The book, I mean?" She nods. Thomas stares at her reflection. "I tried, you know."

"I know," she responds. She notices right away the absence of her dad's wedding band, but she stays mum for now.

"Sam..." He fights for the right words. "I...I don't want to take up all your time, especially today, but..." She taps his hand. His relief is welcome, but fleeting. "I only wish your mom were here to see this."

"She is," she says with conviction. She's always been more spiritually-inclined than he is.

"You look so beautiful," he says.

"Yeah, I know." They share a laugh.

"Sam?" Thomas continues. "I need to say something to you. Something I've been practicing..." She smiles at his effort. She understands how immensely difficult this rapprochement must be for him. "My issue was never with him—Dan—or—"

"I don't think we have to do this *now* but I appreciate what you're saying..."

"Sam, please?" Thomas continues. "Let me finish? If you don't I'll forget all my lines." She laughs, takes his hand from her shoulder, and squeezes.

"Permission granted," she says.

"I won't take too much of your time. I've always been proud of you, Sam. I looked for any excuse to reject him because, when Mama died, I wanted my baby girl all to myself. I was...lonely. I think it's a trait I have in common with my own father...I couldn't bear to be alone. Is that so bad?"

"You never took the time to know him. Dan's a good man."

"He let me in." She's not surprised. Double-meaning there. "We'll talk later. I swore to him he had nothing to worry about."

"Can I be there?"

"This isn't tough enough? I think it'd be best if—"

"Glad to see my dad is still my dad. Like I said I appreciate what you're doing. I know it's not easy."

"Did I give myself away?"

"Yes...But I have a question."

"I figured you'd have more than one..."

"Where did you think I would go?" She laughs but would certainly love to hear his response.

"I'm sorry. I'm selfish...And I can't answer your damn question." They both laugh. "Like Samwise, your namesake, I guess, like I already sort of implied I just didn't want you ever to leave home."

She pities him. "We lost so many years."

"Guilty."

"I get it..."

Hasty change of subject. So unlike him. "I never told you your

316

grandfather named you."

"Oh? No, you didn't."

Thomas tilts his head towards the book. "A foolish man's effort to make up for lost time." They both pause to allow the words and thoughts to penetrate, then—

"Smile!"

The wedding photographer, appearing out of nowhere. "Not quite candid," he says. The photographer checks the image in his screen. "But good enough. Nothing better than father and daughter on her wedding day." He readjusts his equipment. "One more. Show me all your teeth. Big smile!"

Snap.

~~~

Backyard.

White chairs with white bows line the grass. A similarly-designed platformed stage, reachable by a single step, stands feet away from the front row.

The apartment is part of a complex. Neighbors peek out their windows. The friends present are maybe 100 strong, gabbers and gossips among them, all having a great time.

Thomas wanders by himself. He has made headway with his daughter; he is present at her wedding, as he'd promised her mother he would be.

X's words persist in his thoughts:

This includes his daughter, who is certainly not who she appears to be.

But Thomas is determined not to give in today. Not if he can help it.

He hears the announcement. "Please take your seats. Turn off your cellphones...We're going to get started, ladies and gentlemen."

Thomas is surprised as he places face to voice. It is the priest from the Claridge, standing atop the stage, who helped him with the agonizing decision to stop wearing his wedding band. The priest recognizes him as well. Thomas lifts his chin in a gesture of greeting. The priest returns the same as Thomas smiles and hurriedly leaves the scene.

~~~

The service starts with a chord played on a violin. The remainder of the five-piece band readies *their* instruments with one-note strikes. In response, the chairs are quickly occupied.

Mendelssohn's *Wedding March* commences, amplified through the surrounding speakers. Daniel is escorted, by his parents on either side, to the priest. He is resplendent in his tux. He kisses his mom, first, and then his dad before the parents step down to their assigned seats in the reserved front row.

The apartment's back door opens. The music transitions to *Here Comes the Bride*. The crowd stands as a ravishing Samantha enters the yard to gasps and applause. She is escorted by Thomas...and Denise. He, especially, cannot look happier. Denise kisses Sam and returns to her seat. Her mascara is already running. Thomas kisses his daughter on the cheek, then unexpectedly adds a warm, loving embrace.

They hold each other until the priest intervenes—

"Dad..." he announces into his mic, "we do have a service to perform." The guests laugh.

Thomas pulls back from his daughter, and rubs her cheek with his hand. As he pulls away, he whispers into her ear, "Always believe." Samantha smiles, though she is not entirely clear as to what exactly he is referring. Thomas turns to Daniel, and shakes his hand. Daniel casually reaches into his pocket and flashes the ring. The gesture is one of thanks. Thomas replies with a gratified nod. He joins Denise, who good-naturedly elbows him in the ribs.

"This is all the matters right now," he tells her.

The music ceases. Tom, despite his better instincts, grimaces. "Dearly beloved," the priest begins...

As with the wedding, the reception is a flawless affair. Daniel introduces his parents to Thomas. Thomas dances with Daniel's mother. Denise feigns jealousy and dances with Daniel's father. Samantha watches, grasping her new husband. She is by turn shaking her head in disbelief and laughing hysterically.

Through the frivolity, Thomas watches Samantha closely. Whatever it is that X has been fretting over in regards to his daughter...for now, at least, he senses in her a sincere inclination to move forward with her *new* life and leave the past very much behind.

Four hours later.

Carelessly-stacked gifts spill over to the hardwood floor in random tumult.

"Sorry," says a flustered Denise, as she returns from the washroom, her face still wet with water. "I think I broke a heel."

"Jesus. You okay?" asks Samantha, about to stand.

"Don't get up. I'm fine..." Denise assures. She returns to her love seat. "Where's my cup...? Oh!" It is still in her hand.

Most of the guests have gone. Only the newlyweds and Thomas and Denise remain. The publisher furiously sips her coffee to stave off tomorrow's hangover. They sit in the apartment's spare livingroom. Thomas sprawls on a couch. Samantha and Daniel share a recliner. Denise's backside rests on the love seat two feet from her date. She extends her legs, which had been hanging on the furniture's side, to Thomas' knee.

"Wow. You two seem so comfy together," Samantha teases. Thomas moves over. Denise's feet fall to the cushion. She doesn't notice.

"Sam, you're not going to open anything? I wanted to see what you got…"

"I think, Denise, we'll get to all that mess later," Samantha says. "Anyone else want a drink?"

"A drink?" says Denise. "I don't think I could stand if I wanted to."

"You're already covered. Dad?" Thomas smiles, despite Denise's foolishness.

"No, I'm fine."

"Hon?" Samantha asks her husband. Daniel waves her off. *No.* A brief pause.

He breaks the silence. "Well, my parents liked you both," he says, looking at Thomas. "Very much."

"Good people." Thomas stands. He stumbles a bit himself on the ascent. "We should get going. You guys must be exhausted."

Samantha joins him. "Stay a few."

"You really should be alone—"

"No, it's okay." She turns to Daniel. "Hon, is it okay they stay for a little while longer—"

"Sit down, Tom," Daniel replies. "Majority rules."

Thomas shrugs, and sits.

"Move over." Samantha scoots next to him.

"Thank God," says Denise. "Don't want to offend anyone. Did I say I'm not ready to walk?"

"You relax," says Daniel. "If you want you can stay on the couch tonight. Both of you."

"Thank you anyway. I'll carry her back to the hotel if I have to."

"Finally," Denise adds. "This is what it takes?"

As the others continue to gab, about nothing very important, Denise falls asleep.

~~~

At half-past nine, once Denise sits, passed-out, in the cab and Daniel walks into the bedroom, Thomas rejoins his daughter at her front door.

"Well," she says.

"Well," he echoes.

"Are you glad you came?" she asks.

"What do *you* think?"

"You looked like you were having a good—" Thomas smothers his daughter in a hug, cutting her off. They hold for nearly a minute, until he takes both of her hands in his. "Does that mean you did have a good time?"

"I want this," he says. "I do. I want this for us."

"I do too."

He bides his time, then—

"Okay look," he says. "I have to give you something."

"You don't have to give me anything. You made that beautiful book that had me in tears. I'm wearing Mom's ring—"

"No, I do."

"Please don't feel that you have to overcompensate for—"

He hands her an envelope from his jacket pocket. "What's this?"

"This may be a loaded response. If you have it in your heart to forgive me, then I need for you to trust me..."

She chuckles, nervously. "Now you're beginning to worry me a little bit."

"I need for us to be honest with one another. I need for you to understand how difficult it's been for me to stay so distant when I thought about you *every* day."

"Dad?"

"You know something? When you call me that you sound just like that little girl I loved so much."

"I *am.* Just older."

"I'm going to call you tomorrow. I expect..."

"You expect? Expect what?"

"Just read it tomorrow?"

"How about when you leave—" she tests him.

"Please? Trust me?"

"I'll read it tomorrow."

"Promise?"

"You know I will." She bores into his eyes. *Why?*

"Because today was such a beautiful day." He's read her thoughts. She gets it. The letter or whatever it is will upset her.

"I promise," she says. "I promise. Why don't you go." Thomas nods and kisses her on the cheek.

No more words. He rushes to his cab. After briefly arguing about the time, he peels some bills and pays the driver. The vehicle swiftly pulls away.

Samantha opens the envelope immediately upon her dad's cab turning right at the end of the street. She is actually not surprised. The contents are exactly what she expected.

What she was *told.*

The letter, to Denise, from *X.*

"Nice act, Denise," she says to the air. "Thanks for the tip. You were right." She turns and heads back inside, reading along the way.

THE "UNDERGROUND"
CONFIGURED

ADIRONDACK PARK, UPSTATE, NEW YORK

Fresh, misty air, mountains for miles and astounding greenery...

As previously defined.

The hovel has been abandoned for a year. Its former occupant, the boy known as X, planned to leave a facetious handwritten note—for reasons only he could articulate—but a sharp wind gust blew it from his hand on his way *back* from the city, where it stuck under a particularly moist section of grass and rock for who knows how long:

The bulb is temperamental. My tenancy would have been so much easier if I didn't keep forgetting my flashlight. Words to live by.

Trust me.

It might once have been true, but no longer. Things, it appears, have changed.

The hole.

And that has made all the difference.

~~~

Inside the hole, a two-year-old wails. Her cry softens in response to a comforting voice. "Yes," says the voice. "Your mother would have loved you. And your father loves you very much. I only wish I could convince you."

Save for the absence of X's personal belongings, nothing much has been altered. Except for the recent inclusion, has to be, of *pictures*, dozens of them, tacked to the walls.

"Do you dream?" continues the voice. "Maybe not yet. Maybe one day, when you're older, you'll be able to answer a pressing question for me. That is, you look at a clock. The clock says...5:30 A.M. And then you dream—an epic dream, something that spans a lifetime of thought and adventure. The sum of your life experiences, my dear, all contained inside your subconscious mind for what seems like forever. Then, you wake. You look at the clock. It is only 5:35 A.M., and you've only been asleep for five minutes."

Professor Searle watches, curious, as the child becomes increasingly restless in her stroller. Her feet are kicking, her fingers flailing wildly no particular target. Her hair, a rare shade of crimson and already near-shoulder-length, stands out strikingly against the white of her pillow.

Searle has become a recluse since winning custody of his daughter from the state. He had refused emphatically to allow them to sentence his child to a foster upbringing. She has become his life. His responsibility. His reason. He is charmed as he watches her.

Thank God for DNA testing, he thinks once more. Above the stroller, nailed onto the wall, is a litho of an 1864 Charles Dodgson sketch of a young girl. The subject of the etching had been the object of inspiration to the artist. The work is of particular importance to Searle.

Charles Dodgson
1864
ink drawing of head

"Ahh." Searle nods understandingly. "Is *that* who you're trying to see?" He turns the stroller. The child does not look up, but she continues to point. "Who is that?" Searle asks. She stops crying.

"Her name? Alice. Alice Pleasance Liddell. Do you know the name of the artist?" He chuckles, rather enjoying the one-sided conversation.

The child again begins to whimper. "Charles Lutwidge Dodgson, who would one day become much better known by his nom de plume, *Lewis Carroll.* I must read you *Alice's Adventures in Wonderland* when you are a bit older. I have a feeling you will find it quite fascinating, and, perhaps, apt."

Finally, the child drops her arm. The arm. Searle is captivated. "For these and other reasons, I've always pined for a child of my own." he continues. "I am not a religious man, but if I may be permitted the indulgence, you are indeed a godsend. I thank you for entering my life." The child becomes restless, but grows calm again. "But I didn't answer your question. I'm so sorry!" He looks at the litho. "As for little Alice there, she's just a copy, unfortunately. The original is housed in a museum somewhere."

Her eyes glaze over. Sleep is imminent. "A very young girl inspired his greatest creation," says Searle. "Whomever will you inspire, my dear?" Her eyes close. As he turns and wanders through the hovel, he passes photos, numerous photos of the girl tacked to the walls in no noticeable order. So many poses—sleeping, walking, posing on chairs and smiling—all taped to the walls which are artful, not perverse, though one cold easily get the wrong impression as innumerable others had with Mr. Carroll himself.

An old, 1800s *wet-plate* camera rests on a stand near the desk. "Sorry to bore you. You see, Alice was so important to Carroll that her name would live on in infamy. Not her fault, I don't think. He was a controversial figure, no doubt. Some thought he was a bit dangerous, or, at the least, questionable when it came to his young friend."

She snores. "I guess I understand him well." He examines the signature on the etching. "But that's a whole other story."

CHRIST CHURCH COLLEGE, OXFORD ENGLAND,
APRIL 25, 1856

His head is hidden under a black cloth, which enables him to focus and eliminate unwanted light as he preps his wet plate camera. The church's cathedral looms in the foreground. The image, once taken, will be exposed and immortalized.

"It's becoming second nature already," he mumbles to himself. "Not many understand photography now, but they will soon enough."

He takes his shot, stays still for a moment...and ducks back under the cover and feet away from the camera to return to the fresh air outside. He ponders the cathedral from this more natural perspective, away from the camera's tripod, when—

"Dodgson."

Startled, Charles Dodgson turns. Tall—well over six feet, and reed-thin, he is a wisp. A stammering wisp of nervous energy and, some would say, eccentricity.

"Dean Liddell. An unexp-pected pleasure." He notices several young people surrounding the dean. Most of them he has met before. "My ear m-must be acting up. I didn't hear you approach." Liddell is not as tall as Dodgson, though he can certainly be an intimidating force when he chooses. Today, he wears a formal gray suit and tie. Its simplicity is severe and somehow enhances his importance.

Dodgson fights a sudden wave of anxiety. He has never felt fully comfortable in the dean's presence. Perhaps the authoritative voice carries some sway as physically he is not in any noticeable way threatening. Or, maybe the simple fact of his authoritative position induces fear. Still, the man himself is quite kind, and known throughout campus as a devoted husband and father. But he is not one to be manipulated, and he is one of the very few Dodgson considers an intellectual equal.

Dodgson looks to the other visitors who enjoy themselves just yards away. Liddell catches his eye. "My family, Dodgson. Permit me to introduce you?"

"Certainly, Sir."

"Harry you know." Nine years old, tall and lanky for his age.

They shake hands. "We met last year on the train ride over."

"That we did. G-good to s-see you again."

"My wife, Lorina."

"It's a pleasure to see you again, Mrs. Liddell."

"And my little ones, scurrying about like crickets—Children!"

"A little loud, Henry, no?" interjects his wife. "They can hear you in France."

The dean shrugs, and turns to Dodgson. "I run the school but only you and I know who's really boss."

"Don't forget it," his wife adds.

Three young girls, Lorina (seven), Edith (two) and *Alice* (four) frolic in the grass. They are all dressed in long white skirts and matching ruffled button-down tops.

Lorina has heard her father. She taps a laughing Alice on the shoulder, who turns and runs over to join him.

Dodgson's response is, at first, nothing out of the ordinary, though he takes particular note of Alice. He scrutinizes her as if he were planning a future composition. She stands out from the others. *Perhaps it's her hair,* he speculates wonderingly. While the elder daughters' hair falls freely, Alice's style is similar to a *pageboy* cut. Her dark bangs kept neatly-short and well over her eyebrows, and the sides long and cascade just above the shoulders.

Then again, he thinks, *maybe it's her smile. She appears serious and yet still is a happy, well-adjusted child.*

"Dodgson." The future Lewis Carroll snaps to attention. "These are my girls," Dean Liddell continues. "Lorina, Edith, Alice."

"Hello." he says to them politely.

"Alice I don't believe you've met before" the dean observes. "She was not with us on the train."

"Can we go back now?" asks the eldest. Henry is about to respond, not happy at the interruption.

"Go on," says her mother, noticing her husband's glare. "Just don't get too dirty!" Young Lorina takes Edith by the hand. Alice follows closely behind.

"Very nice to have met you, sir!" Alice says. Dodgson laughs as she sets off. "Very charming, sir." says Dodgson of the departing girls. He is scrupulous not to pay any one more attention than the others.

"Thank you, Dodgson. I'm blessed." He chuckles. "I don't take kindly to rudeness, but they're kids after all."

"That they are, Sir."

"Would you like to have kids of your own one day?" Henry asks.

"Oh, not anytime soon, I'm afraid—"

"They scare you, do they?" asks Mrs. Liddell, straight-faced.

"No, actually. N-not at all. In fact, I-I m-must admit, I feel much more comfortable around *them* than anyone my age."

"Really?" she asks.

"Or older," he acknowledges.

As Mrs. Liddell takes in his response, Henry admires the camera. "So," she says, "I'm told you have seven sisters and three brothers."

"This is true—"

"Wherever did your parents make time to...eat?"

"Well—"

"I am so, so sorry, really, I don't know what just came over me—"

"No offense, taken, Mrs. Liddell—"

"If it makes you feel any better—"

"I'm fine. Truly, Mrs.—"

"I have a feeling there will be several more Liddells running about by the time we're all done. Right dear?"

Henry circles the camera. He has not heard her. *For the best*, she thinks.

Henry is dubious. "Some would consider photography a frivolous pursuit, Dodgson—" he says.

"Some do not understand," Dodgson defends. "Photography is the art of the future."

"Wherever did you find this camera, Dodgson?" Henry bends his head under the cover. "Did you build it yourself? How did you learn to use it?"

"My un...uncle helped teach me the wet collodion process, Sir. And my friend Reginald Southey helped me acquire the camera—"

"I've seen him and you here before. I don't know why, perhaps I am working too hard. I seem to recall that you once tried to have my daughters stand in the foreground for this very shot, but they were very restless that day."

Dodgson is surprised. "Perhaps in another life, sir?"

"Perhaps...Where does one look, Dodgson?"

"Through the *looking-glass*, sir." replied Dodgson.

"I know that, but I don't see...Oh! *There*...Hmm. And, don't you make your prints out of egg whites, or something?" His voice is increasingly muffled but Dodgson hears him.

"They're called *albumen prints*...The egg whites are processed to hold silver salts on a coated surface. This allows for the wet collodion negatives, once fixed and dried, to contact with the paper."

Liddell rejoins Dodgson. "I get it," he bluffs. "And you didn't stammer once during that highly technical explanation. Curious." Dodgson looks to Mrs. Liddell, embarrassed. "Lorina?" Henry resumes. "Would you like to..?"

"It's all right. I'll keep my eyes on them." The girls are playing an impromptu game of *chase*. The youngest falls and begins to cry. "And...that's that. Girls! Let's go!"

"Honey, they can hear you in Venice."

She smiles and turns to Dodgson. "This is why I love him. He's quite original, isn't he?"

Dodgson nods, and smirks in return. He looks out to the girls, the youngest is being escorted by the oldest. Alice is picking a flower. "Come on, Alice! We have to go..."

Her mother attends to Edith. She wipes dirt off her daughter's bruised knee, then lifts her, and carries her off. "Nice seeing you again, Mr. Dodgson," she says. "Alice, stay with your brother. See you all inside."

Alice turns around, and smiles at Dodgson. She rushes over, holding a daffodil.

"For me?" Dodgson asks innocently.

"For my daddy," she says, handing the Dean the flower.

He kisses her. "Let's get going," Henry says. He nods his head. "Carry on, Dodgson."

"Thank you, Sir."

The Dean walks away. "Next time for you." Alice says as she follows.

Dodgson is captivated as she goes...

~~~

Later that evening, in a makeshift Church *darkroom*, Dodgson manipulates a sensitized plate of glass. The plate is wet. He develops the images. He is in his element and the artistry is therapeutic. Still, try though he may, he cannot shrug his first impressions of young Alice.

Why? What is it about her that is so motivating? So endearing? These are the issues. Charles Dodgson is no different than any other when unexpectedly confronted with the suddenness of *inspiration*. For now, he will subscribe to this: A merely human mind, such as his and regardless of its gift, can rarely ever quite get to the bottom of things. Nevertheless, he presses on with his reflections.

~~~

Weeks pass.

Dodgson sits at his desk in his office. Alongside a stack of private journals is a small stack of books. They stand beside his ink bottle. The titles include *Alton Locke* by Charles Kingsley, *Maud* by Tennyson, Charles Dickens's *Little Dorrit* and Bronte's *Wuthering Heights*. On top of the stack, opened, is a prized edition of *The Train*, a literary journal. He grabs the issue, from 1855, the year before. He opens it and finds the poem:

Solitude by Lewis Carroll

I LOVE the stillness of the wood:
I love the music of the rill:
I love to couch in pensive mood
Upon some silent hill.
Scarce heard, beneath yon arching trees,
The silver-crested ripples pass;
And, like a mimic brook, the breeze
Whispers among the grass.
Here from the world I win release,
Nor scorn of men, nor footstep rude,
Break in to mar the holy peace
Of this great solitude.

Here may the silent tears I weep
Lull the vexed spirit into rest,
As infants sob themselves to sleep

Upon a mother's breast.

But when the bitter hour is gone,

And the keen throbbing pangs are still,

Oh, sweetest then to couch alone

Upon some silent hill!

To live in joys that once have been,

To put the cold world out of sight,

And deck life's drear and barren scene

With hues of rainbow-light.

For what to man the gift of breath,

If sorrow be his lot below;

If all the day that ends in death

Be dark with clouds of woe?

Shall the poor transport of an hour

Repay long years of sore distress

The fragrance of a lonely flower

Make glad the wilderness?

Ye golden hours of Life's young spring,

Of innocence, of love and truth!

Bright, beyond all imagining,

Thou fairy-dream of youth!

I'd give all wealth that years have piled,

The slow result of Life's decay,

To be once more a little child

For one bright summer-day.

His first and middle names are written in a notebook that is presently open. A Latin dictionary rests, open, at his side. He translates, casually scribbling:

Lutwidge = Ludovicus (Latin) = "Lewis" (Anglicized).

Charles = Carolus (Latin) = Carroll (Anglicized).

Lewis Carroll.

He mutters to himself, amused, "Yates, my editor, you are a clever bastard when you want to be." He places down his pen, and stares at the result. "It took two years for me to convince you of my brilliance," he says. "But Edgar Cuthwellis? Edgar U. C. Westhill? Lewis Carroll. Your creation among four, not all fair the four to be fair though fairer than two not as fair and the third. No choice in the matter, though I may have doubted you at first. And now *Lewis Carroll* shall embark on another journey and become the artist he always knew he could be."

Satisfied, he kicks his feet up on the desk, tilts his head back and closes his eyes, but he cannot sleep. He again takes his pen. He contemplates his next effort...and sketches an image of a young girl.

Her hair is short, similar to the girl who had so unexpectedly captivated him weeks ago. As impromptu as the effort is, he finds himself *drawing in*, improvising, lengthening her locks to fall below her shoulders. The facial features will be completed at another time, however, as he is startled by an unexpected voice:

"Your door was open." Dean Liddell walks forth. "Do you mind if I come in?"

Dodgson discreetly turns the etching, face-down. "It appears you are already h-here." He is not sarcastic, though his sincere attempt at comedy falls flat.

"You called upon me, remember?"

Dodgson stands. "I do. I'm...um, I'm going to be traveling, during inter-session."

"Oh? Where to?"

"The Lake District and North Yorkshire first."

Over the summer holiday, Dodgson visits the theater, delivers a magic, singing, and comedy show for families at the Croft School—which he later describes in his diary as "one-man entertainment." He begins to mix in high society and generally experiences a lifestyle, and a passion to perform, that most who know him would consider out of character.

Liddell had wished Dodgson well on his time off. However, it would take another few years for Dodgson to ask the dean to grant him a very specific request.

ADIRONDACK PARK, UPSTATE, NEW YORK

Searle glimpses the photos on the wall as he passes. There are provocative posed shots of Alice Liddell from ages six-ten. Young Alice, dressed formally in white with black shoes, sitting on a draped table next to a small plant, her feet dangling...Alice, just a bit older, standing in a garden in front of a tree, in white casual wear, shoulder barely draped, barefoot and looking very serious.

"They would all get the wrong impression sooner or later," Searle says to the sleeping child, "though it was all quite innocuous. Her mother or another family member was with them whenever he shot..."

He turns and retrieves a folding chair that had been standing against a far wall. She snores again. "Excuse me?" he inquires politely of the girl. He opens the chair and sits across from her. "Dodgeson," he resumes, "would become very close with the Liddells. He would take Harry and young Lorina—'Ina'—on boating trips and picnics about scenic Oxford. Mrs. Liddell, especially, was quite fond of him. Then, when Harry went back to school and Edith and Alice were old enough to ride on the boat, that's when the history began," he says. "The genesis of *Alice and Wonderland*, that is."

The girl doesn't move a muscle.

"But I digress," he says. "We were talking—I was talking—about what, I don't remember. But I can tell you, sure as I breathe, that young Alice's spirit lives on." The girl turns, but remains asleep.

"'Why?' you ask. 'Do you believe in spirits?' Answer: I do. I know they exist. *She* exists. There's no supposition here." She sleeps through every word. "How do I know? Do you feel them yet? Do you sense them yet? There are *many* spirits, here, Right here in this room, yes?" The slightest cry emerges from the child but she doesn't awake.

"Yes, of course, this will be *our* rabbit hole. *Hers* was in England, you see. Me—I never cared for England, particularly. Much too stuffy but really it doesn't make any difference. You know why I'm here. I came back home only for you...I had no choice in the matter, to be honest. I only fled overseas to escape."

He looks to the child. *Not a care in the world.*

"We are safe with the spirits here. Do you know that? We have that in common because we are both protected by angels. I, you, and *you*—your mother. Here's something else we have in common, you and I. Neither of us knew her very well. And now she serves the gods.

He is charmed by his daughter. *So peaceful.*

"Nonetheless." He moves his chair closer to the carriage. "My dear *Adriel*, we have an issue. There's an urgent matter that I must bring to your attention. Where there are spirits and gods, you see, there are also *counterparts.*"

He stands, folds the chair and returns it to its proper wall. Troubled, he paces throughout the tiny hovel.

"I saw the blade, Adriel. The blade, which I'm afraid is now held by a *malignant* spirit."

BERKSHIRE HUNTING GROUNDS, BERKSHIRE, ENGLAND

His intellect has remained. As have his survival instincts. He walks— cautiously, not stupidly—in the mist-shrouded woods. He is comforted by the cleansing light drizzle, because this afternoon is not optimal for hunting.

It's optimal for killing—in the event any sort of defense is necessary. The other prey is hiding from the elements, not him. He still has four of his senses and all of his confidence. What he's lost is his voice and physical acuity, which he *senses* are temporary deficits.

But the *malignancies* among the spirits, as Searle so adequately christened, have up to now been nothing but folklore. In the *fairy stories* of old, *restless* spirits played by an entirely different set of rules. Though the world of today is no fairy story, Eron's return changes everything. *He* is the malignant spirit of whom Searle speaks.

"Despite his return," Searle says to Adriel, *"he will remain spirit forever and never evolve."*

In truth, Searle is certain of very little concerning this matter. However, Searle has grown adept at studying cosmologies and will stand by his theory until something better comes along.

This is what he knows:

That a returned soul has no place.

That no over-dweller had ever returned successfully to earth, whether

337

in physical or any other form.

Eron was the first.

That no human had ever seen a malignant spirit before.

Searle was the first.

A recipe for a mutually unintended kinship...but still sometime in the future.

There have likely been many others since who have spotted Eron, but certainly they have no clue as to the importance of his presence.

"He may be dangerous. He may not. Why he has returned—assuming I am correct in identifying him as I do—is not a simple question. My great fear, Adriel, is that his restlessness will lead to a successful quest. I fear that he will somehow endanger you."

Clothed in fox and deer flesh, his face a literal mask of animal hide, Eron walks amidst the wild. The blade may as well be attached to him; it is held by its handle and dropped only when he *skins.*

"I do not know his present whereabouts, and neither do I have the slightest indication of who he once was."

Eron is skilled, uncannily so, in compensating for what he has lost. Over the past year, he has (re-)learned how to stand upright by modeling the other hunters.

"He must have been someone of substance, I guess. Why else would he be here?"

He is compelled to hide when he has to, which is strange to him as he is fully aware he's already dead. Searle is correct. Eron has been spotted repeatedly since the Professor's first watch. He has been sighted, but nothing more. Six days before, a reward was offered "for the capture, dead or alive, of *The Berkshire Beastie."*

Eron is aware of this as well and does not care. He is single-minded, as ever, and will stop at nothing to capture that for which he has been hunting. What he does not know is that he is also being guided towards something far, far greater.

ADIRONDACK PARK, UPSTATE, NEW YORK

"I should stop now, my dear. You haven't heard anything I've said." He glances at the etching of Alice as he continues. "She looks upon you as my protege—X, as he's called, my friend—" Searle says, with some regret, "once looked upon me. To him, as he concluded from his research, Carroll's *Alice's Adventures Under Ground* represented a *mathematical* response to our place in the universe. My apprentice contended, much like Carroll, that nothing was ever what it appeared to be; but that there has always been a single Truth. He gifted me with this image drawn by his *hero*, as it happens. This was for the last day—my birthday—that we had spent together. Then I abandoned him." His voice drops. "Such was *never* my intention, you understand."

He relents to the futility of using a two-year-old as his sounding board.

"I guess I needed someone to talk to for a minute. If there's anything to the concept of a subconscious process, you'll filter my words later. As did the character *she* inspired." He bends, kisses her cheek and grimaces on the way up. "I remember what it was like to be young once."

CHRIST CHURCH COLLEGE, OXFORD, ENGLAND, JULY 4, 1862

Men's room.

Dodgson straightens shirt, pulls down his sleeves, and checks his beard. There is no beard. All good there. He splashes water on his face, dries off, looks once more at himself. Then he leaves.

Barely an hour later, he rows his usual scenic route with Edith and Alice, regaling them with his special sort of *nonsense* as the girls laugh hysterically. "There was once a girl. Her name was Alice," he begins.

"That's me!" Alice exclaims.

"No," Dodgson says. "Another Alice. An Alice with long, silky hair who once came across a rabbit hole."

"A rabbit hole?" she asks.

"She then *fell* into the rabbit hole."

The girls gasp. Alice is first, then is mimicked by Edith. And so it goes...

BREACH

Night.

The mystic S'n Te stands atop a stone, nude save for a wrap of hide around his waist. He is safely ensconced in the cave that once housed the family of Taebal. A fire burns near the cave's turn, closer to its mouth, illuminating the interior. Above the flames is a spit upon which cooks a slab of meat.

He has been engaged thusly: carving symbols on the walls, etching pictographs similar to those once inscribed on Eron's sweord:

ΣΗΘμαθΙσθισis^

ξοα   ιθδηα-1\[a7a
-.`~'alz   iqσωοα
ζφξ
εξλαμδγωε

He drops the rock, his instrument. Done. He uses his arm to wipe off sediment, then walks towards the fire. He tears a piece of meat for the taste. Could be better. He peeks outside.

Still the slight drizzle...

S'n Te retrieves his robe, which had been drying on a stack of twigs near the flames. He fans the fabric, and feels for moisture. When he turns his back to the cave opening, satisfied, S'n Te does not notice, or he ignores, the two travelers who had been watching.

The muse and the dragon, looking into the cave. As S'n Te had watched *them* earlier. Ara is shaken when she glimpses his back. The mystic is scarred—grotesquely so. Tracing from both anterior shoulder blades connecting to the right and left lumbar spine are horrific carvings scored deeply into S'n Te's flesh. There is no presence of blood, dried or otherwise, on his person, nor would it appear that there is anything other than randomness about the design:

S'n Te slips into his robe and attends to his meal.

~~~

Ara slowly lifts her head to the skies, as if she has suddenly encountered a matter of great urgency and has little choice but to summon the other immortals for intervention. She then grows angry at her own vulnerable reaction—but does it again. Her response implies that there is meaning in S'n Te's scar, a meaning which alarms her greatly.

You were right. All of you. I am nothing. Take me back. The gods must align.

In a moment of clarity, as she realizes that no godly response is forthcoming, she wanders off. The dragon snarls but, for the first time, he does not follow. He remains transfixed by the new presence, by this mystic who has claimed Taebal's former home. The home of his beloved and departed mother and father, both of whom he dearly loved. He considers his master, who no longer appears as powerful as she did just a memory ago.

He follows his inclination and he enters the cave.

ADIRONDACK PARK, UPSTATE, NEW YORK

A shirtless Searle, deep in thought, washes himself with soapy water from a pot as Adriel continues to sleep. The scarification on his back is identical.

The single letter, *X*…

When he's done, he gently slips on a T-shirt and sits back in the chair. He stares at the image of young Alice, and clasps his hands in great concentration.

There he stays until he too falls asleep.

SEARLE ASTOR ACADEMY,
GREENWICH VILLAGE, NEW YORK, NOVEMBER, 2013

X sits alone in a cramped office. He is engrossed in his work. He scrolls a pdf of 'Alice's Adventures Under Ground' from his computer. He advances the text and he reverses. He reviews passages he may have missed, and scribbles notes with a black marker on a yellow legal pad.

Some of the text he highlights, and then analyzes in pen:

"Let me see: four times five is twelve, and four times six is thirteen, and four times seven is—oh dear! I shall never get to twenty at that rate!"

~~~

343

Chapter Two: The Pool of Tears.

Variant mathematical base notations = compounded surreality beyond base imagery.

He scrolls to the last page, to the story's closing poem:

A boat beneath a sunny sky,
Lingering onward dreamily
In an evening of July—
Children three that nestle near,
Eager eye and willing ear,

Pleased a simple tale to hear—
Long has paled that sunny sky:
Echoes fade and memories die.
Autumn frosts have slain July.
Still she haunts me, phantomwise,
Alice moving under skies
Never seen by waking eyes.
Children yet, the tale to hear,
Eager eye and willing ear,

Lovingly shall nestle near.
In a Wonderland they lie,
Dreaming as the days go by,
Dreaming as the summers die:
Ever drifting down the stream—
Lingering in the golden gleam—

Life, what is it but a dream?

Close: "A Boat Beneath a Sunny Sky." Carroll's celebrated play on words in honor of his inspiration: the young girl, Alice Pleasance Liddell. Marker: Computer highlight first letter per stanza.

A *boat beneath a sunny sky,*
L*ingering onward dreamily*
I*n an evening of July—*
C*hildren three that nestle near,*
E*ager eye and willing ear,*

P*leased a simple tale to hear—*
L*ong has paled that sunny sky:*
E*choes fade and memories die.*
A*utumn frosts have slain July.*
S*till she haunts me, phantomwise,*
A*lice moving under skies*
N*ever seen by waking eyes.*
C*hildren yet, the tale to hear,*
E*ager eye and willing ear,*

L*ovingly shall nestle near.*
I*n a Wonderland they lie,*
D*reaming as the days go by,*
D*reaming as the summers die:*
E*ver drifting down the stream—*
L*ingering in the golden gleam—*
L*ife, what is it but a dream?*

Eisenberg and Hillard

X points his finger to the screen, following the first letter of every line. The check is cursory; as is his quick follow-up on a Carroll tribute webpage that validates the well-known factoid.

However, second later, another computer check of the same poem yields something quite extraordinary:

A *boat beneath a sunny sky,*
Lingering onward dreamily
*In **an** evening of July—*
Children three that nestle near,
Eager eye and willing ear,
Pleased a simple tale to hear—
Long has paled that sunny sky:
Echoes fade and memories die.
***A**utumn frosts have slain July.*
Still she haunts me, phantomwise,
Alice moving under skies
Never seen by waking eyes.
Children yet, the tale to hear,
Eager eye and willing ear ,
Lovingly shall nestle near.
In a Wonderland they lie,
Dreaming as the days go by,
Dreaming as the summers die:
Ever drifting down the stream—
Lingering in the golden gleam—
Life, what is it but a dream?

The highlighted letters, however, begin to blink. First individually, slowly; then in tandem. Then finally in an uncontrollably-hastened pitch.

X watches. He doesn't panic.

'She's...communicating...?'

The letters, a-r-a, flash still quicker.

He sits back, and taps his space bar in response. The flashing slows. X was correct in his assumption. The muse has been acknowledged. He grabs his pen. The lettering pulses as if the speed of a heartbeat, slowing substantially but continuing to flash.

The odds are not high that the common letters a-r-a would appear in a line-by-line. Where the odds falter is any combination of letters RANDOMLY flashing on any system. Any system.

What does she want?

But they're not just any combination.

The pulse quickens...

U.S. EMBASSY, LONDON, ENGLAND

At the same time, Samantha's unattended computer flashes the same significant letters in the same onscreen poem. The pulse continues to hasten; as if in overload, the illusion becomes that of a single word flashing, as opposed to single letters:

ara—ara—ara...

As the pulse reaches its zenith, the computer vibrates. Lightly at first. The walls follow, setting off the alarm. Samantha's desk follows; papers slide. On the monitor's bottom right, a Red Alert signal appears and blares through the speakers...before the computer falls to the floor in response to a fierce blast.

Outside.

A series of explosions, each successively larger than the last, rock the Embassy.

SEARLE ASTOR ACADEMY, GREENWICH VILLAGE, NEW YORK

X stares at his monitor, which has frozen. ARA. All other words onscreen have disappeared. ARA. He attempts to reboot. Unsuccessful. No shit.

He takes his pen, and for now jots the last of his notes:

November 10, 2013. She exists. And she has my attention.

AGENDA

Bradley and Son Bibliotheque, Summer, 2016

Donovan stumbles toward the stairwell in response to a *beeping* Skype signal. He flips the light switch—the basement bulb *sizzles* and lows.

"Damn it all!" Grabbing the wall for support, he walks to a nearby drawer and fusses through the mess. He grabs a small support tray, a candle, and a large matchstick. Donovan struggles as he walks downstairs. "Hold your damn horses. I hear you."

He barely manages to make his way to the desk before collapsing in the chair. The *Beowulf* papers have been long-since removed. The computer reads: "One missed call." He catches his breath and opens the program. The beeping ceases. "Haven't used the infernal thing in five years and this is the second bloody invasion today."

He hears the message: "Donovan, Denise Watkins. It's not going to happen overnight. Call me."

He's disappointed but not close to surprised. "Shocking." As he motions to carefully place the candle down on the desktop, he twinges and clutches his heart in response to a sharp, stabbing pain. He remembers what the doctor told him. "Stay calm," he said. "Place one pill under your tongue, let it dissolve."

Donovan opens the desk drawer for his pill bottle. It's empty. He reaches into his pocket. Also empty. When he panics and tries to stand, his legs give way and he falls. On the way down, his arm flails across the desktop, dislodging the computer.

The candle falls with him. He glimpses a smallish pile of books to the immediate right of the desk, blocking the computer's extension cord. This pile is the first to ignite, along with a sprawl of plain notebooks marked on the top page as *Journal Entries* of Lewis Carroll, *Volumes 1, 3, 6,* and *7.*

These are original volumes that have long been considered lost. A slip of paper is rubber-banded to the side of *Volume 3.* The handwriting reads, familiar black marker, excessive line spacings and all:

Mr. Bradley,

Wonderland. Recompense.

As promised.

Beowulf was only the beginning. Many more treasures to come.

You will have your answers shortly. One little secret: Your son will live on. Nothing stays lost forever.

If you believe.

If not...

This is followed by his typical flourish:

P.S. I will see you soon.

On top of the book pile is a first-edition fine copy of *Alice's Adventures in Wonderland.* The last of the title lettering to burn on the cover: *a* from "Adventures," *r* and *a* from "Wonderland."

Donovan then peeks to the letter as it too burns. All this he sees—or thinks he sees—and curses as he loses consciousness. "*Why?* You...son of a...bitch..." Once overtaken by flame and vanquished with the rest, the computer's electrical outlet is the next to catch.

TRIAL

Dodgson is alone with his thoughts at long last. He is carrying a fairly ponderous stack of texts and papers scooped hastily from his desk. He is on edge. He escapes down the impossibly-steep, winding back stairs in the main hall. He departs through a bleak, disused tunnel and into the light.

Class is over. His students have been properly challenged. He deserves the break. Fresh air is calling. Calmer now, he strolls the finely-coiffed greenery of the sprawling English campus. He pauses here and there to gaze at the brilliant sun, then downward and around at the breathtaking beauty of his environs. He feels himself *at one* with the company he most cherishes. He nods in acknowledgment as others pass. He recalls now something he's heard, that is of his reputation as something of a snob. He is not much bothered by the assessment and does not make an effort to redress it.

Dodgson even responds to one query. "Sir? I'm lost, I'm afraid. Would you be so kind as to direct me to the way of the Main Hall?"

Without so much as a breath, Dodgson replies: "Read the directions and directly you will be directed in the right direction." He walks on. He will continue to walk and take in the crispest air of the year. He hears the bell and returns for *Godly* reasons rather than his own. It is a math class and he will teach it in a manner befitting a religious man of logic.

Christ Church is a *constituent college* of the University of Oxford and, as such, also England's preeminent religious institution. Though Dodgson is a teacher and a deacon, he was never himself the greatest study. He's been somewhat of a lazy study, actually, for as long as he could recall, and yet one of Christ Church's greater achievers.

So where is the logic there? This has been his persistent query, ever since he was a boy. He recalls the first time of asking, when, as a boy of seven, he read Bunyan's *Pilgrim's Progress*. He's never questioned, however, his religious identity. As time has gone on, he has felt a need sometimes to broaden its scope.

Dodgson's academic standing is something of a peculiarity. His degree and accomplishments have earned him the envy of his contemporaries. He has achieved them seemingly without effort. Once he failed to attain a desired scholarship, but this was only through having refused to study *at all*. His confidence is sometimes misguided, but not often. He is said to be 'aloof' and, indeed, slighting of those he considers his inferior.

That's his reputation, anyway. He lives with it and he does not quibble. He does not think of himself as arrogant and is not interested in social climbing. He reflects upon these things in passing as he walks. He prefers though to consider the virtues of the day. His head is not always this clear. He will take advantage of his good spirits.

Ten years ago, Dodgson received first-class honors in Mathematics Moderations. Math has always been his scholastic subject of choice. His person embraces polarities: he is six feet tall and reed thin. He has been plagued by a persistent stammer since his childhood, though it is much diminished now. He is prey to chronic self-doubt, yet this is counterbalanced by a prodigious ability to solve logic puzzles. He can also *create* through writing. He received a first in math from his college and was the top of his class. He has been awarded the Christ Church Mathematics Lectureship the year before. This has given Dodgson a sense of security.

And yet, no. He drives these thoughts away. He is losing focus.

~~~

Dodgson feels himself *breaking*. He realizes he was again reflecting, on *then*. Whenever he's free of late the mind wanders, and though he's not partial to reliving his past, as he walks and tries his level best to relax the memories flood...

~~~

Next to the fore is a series of *flashes*, of a particularly unhappy period from '46-'49, when he attended Rugby School. Though Mathematics Master R.B. Mayor once praised the student—"I have not had a more promising boy at his age since I came to Rugby"—the period is marked by a sad, lonely unease, a decline even, and a good amount of time spent alone, studying in the library and in tiny, isolated spaces sometimes the size of the average broom closet.

For reason. For reason obscured by images of shadow that momentarily blind him—

Dodgson bangs into another teacher. They both drop their books, their papers, then scramble to the ground to retrieve them.

"Excuse me, sir," he says. "I'm so sorry."

"You need to stop daydreaming, Dodgson." They stand. "Were you always this clumsy?" He shakes his head before the younger teacher could answer, and paces towards the closest entrance, turning back once in consternation.

Dodgson watches him off, taking quick note of the enormity of the building...and the reflections resume.

He matriculates to Christ Church in May of 1850 but there are no rooms available. Finally, he becomes a resident in January of 1851.

Two days later, he receives a summons to return home. His mother has died. He is in tears during the entirety of the train ride and cannot hold the gaze of anyone who stares at him.

She was only forty-seven years old. "Inflammation of the brain" is listed as the official cause of death. The family is inconsolable at her funeral. His sobs ring in his ears, a memory so sharp it becomes a physical response...

Perhaps in fond remembrance of his mother, he clasps his textbooks and papers to his side, then ponders that he might be unconsciously pulling his materials closely as one may pull a drowning family member.

What is it that I'm holding on to? he asks himself. *I can't go back to yesterday because I was a different person then.*

He loses that battle, and yet he does not know why.

"HELL'S KETTLES" CROFT, LINCOLNSHIRE, JANUARY, 1844

I think I can see the bottom from here, Charles Dodgson rationalizes.

"This isn't that bad, guys," he says. "Really...Doesn't look like it's all that deep—"

"Go on, then," says Stitch, the tallest of the four and same age as the rest. "It's just a hole—"

"Darlington and Ripon had holes 'cause the houses were built on gypsum," Dodgson says. "These are not *just* holes but I think I can see the bottom, really—"

"If you can see the bottom, then jump in!" taunts Larry.

"They say the holes in Hell's Kettles are really only 22-feet deep." Dodgson says.

Larry lifts to his toes. "Nah. Still don't see anything but water. Definitely bottomless pits."

"I don't think so."

"So jump in and swim then," Brady, the most impatient, exults. "Tell 'im, Lar. Stitch. How much time we gotta waste here. Go ahead, Dodgson, why don't you? Jump in and—"

"Swim!"

He wasn't expecting the push. In reality, Larry snuck behind him and barely touched him, just a quick *tap* between the shoulder blades. But it was enough.

Once his head hit water, Dodgson could only think of one thing: *Not yet!*

Charles Dodgson will not be 12 until next week, the 27th. He's had great difficulty with friends to this point. Slight, well-mannered, but exceedingly shy and not particularly healthful, Dodgson visited The Kettles today for exactly those reasons. He swore he would be brave. He swore he would take the dare—any dare—if that's what it would take to prove himself. He will no longer allow his fears to rule his life. This is his newest philosophy.

Not yet!

How he wants to see the bottom. His eyes are open under the water; and he is not scared. For the first time in his life, he is happy. At peace.

He is at peace because he is well into the vast unknown. *Down, down, down.* It doesn't bother him that he cannot breathe. Neither does it upset him that when he looks up, he sees the other three laughing and getting *smaller,* while he becomes *curiouser and curiouser.*

Not a one of them is coming to his aid any time soon. Since he is, naturally, alone, he will continue to go *underground. Hopefully, the fall will never come to an end.* Despite his much stronger desire to continue this pursuit, however, he has to awaken sometime. That time is now.

Christ Church College, Oxford, England, Spring 1862

Not that he was sleeping. Not at all. But, like a certain fictional *Alice* who wandered into a world of *Jabberwocky,* nothing was as it appeared to be.

Where did the time go? he asks himself, as he reluctantly turns back towards his building.

Dodgson's father, also named Charles, attended Christ Church, also was mathematically accomplished. He took his Holy Orders, as had his father before him, before marrying his first cousin in 1827. The elder Dodgson dropped out of Academia to become a country parson. He would ultimately become Archdeacon of Richmond and one of the influential ecclesiastical voices of his time.

The younger Dodgson has always been a bit of a daydreamer. The first bell *chimes.* He has five minutes to return to his classroom.

What he imparted to his third child, the future Lewis Carroll—as with all of his eventual family of seven daughters and four sons—was the staid Dodgson family tradition: a dogmatic respect for the conservative tenants of the Church of England. Carroll's ancestry was northern English, primarily, some Irish, mostly conservative High Church Anglican-Catholic.

He was unwavering in his views.

The third child, and first son, was born in Daresbury, Cheshire. He was precocious early on, however, having developed the proclivity, and temerity, to ask questions.

When he read *The Pilgrim's Progress*, he became a bit too wise— "Father...why Jesus?"

The question didn't go over well, but Father was not angry. Just surprised, as if he had more work to do to convince the inquisitive boy.

"Because Jesus is the son of God."

And then, the follow-up—

"But why does Jesus have a beard if he's not human?"

"Because...son, Jesus took on human form to show us the way. He died for our sins—"

"But Father—"

"Son?"

"Then how would science explain His resurrection?"

Such was the child's overwhelming curiosity. *Logic* dictated that all fervent religious icons *must* be questioned, as anything else in life which is, after all, a matter of perspective, but his respect and love for—and occasional fear of—his father would prove the stronger agency.

And here he is today, following in his dad's footsteps.

The author of *Alice's Adventures in Wonderland* was born in Daresbury, Cheshire. His mother was the former Frances Jane Lutwidge.

"Mother...why Jesus?"

"Son?"

"Why Jesus?"

"You asked your father first, didn't you?"

"Yes," he answered shyly.

"And what did he say?"

"He said because Jesus is the son of God."

"You disagree?"

"No! That would be blasphemy!"

"What is it then, if not—"

"Is he God...or is he the son of God?"

"I love you, you know."

"I love you too, but—"

"What did your father tell you?"

~~~

Though Frances was, considerably, the more patient of his parents, she would never dare cross her husband. Not for any fear of reprisal.

Simply, a matter of respect.

When her son was eleven, her husband relocated the family to a large rectory in the village Croft-on- Tees, a civil parish in North Yorkshire.

"N-n-no. I d-don't want to l-leave h-here—"

"If you relax, you won't stammer," answered Father.

The family would stay in Croft-on-Tees for 25 years and never, not once, during his formative years—nor his adulthood—despite the chronic inquisitiveness, would the son *ever* disparage either his dad, or his Lord and Savior.

He had already reconciled his thoughts on the matter of religion versus logic *before* the move, which towards the latter stage of his life he would reiterate in a letter to his sister, Louisa:

- "I possess Free-Will, and am able to choose between right and wrong."
- "I have in some cases chosen wrong."
- "I am responsible for choosing wrong."
- "I am responsible to a person."
- "This person is perfectly good."

Dodgson weaves through a crowded corridor, evading other school folk also in the midst of transition...and enters his room.

His students already await. The door closes; the bell chimes once more. Session begins.

From this personal and professional wellspring, the seeds of *Wonderland* are planted.

Today's class was not significantly different than any other. He daydreamed a bit more than usual; that was about it. He assigned his class busy work as to allow himself to be troubled by the girl, a haunt too-long suppressed that offered him a unique and welcome comfort.

Liddell's daughter, Alice. Again.

That evening, though he would never admit to such either privately or public-wise, he pondered his next *move* in earnest. He *must* see her again. He must socially socialize with her in a socially acceptable social context.

Or something like that.

And so he meditated on the issue daily, and finally caught a solution.

Many years hence, his idea will permit the twin legends of *Lewis Carroll* and a heroine named *Alice* to fully, and finally, manifest—via an event that will permanently mark the players with far deeper resonance than any future literary myth.

This event will begin, and will end, in the summer with a perfectly-hatched plan. As for its *end*, young Alice will be regaled and the two will form an everlasting friendship that will continue to inspire his inner artist.

Damn propriety, he would consider, and more than once.

July 4, 1862

Dodgson regularly rowed the five-mile distance from Oxford to Godstow. He found the route calming and was usually accompanied by a small group of friends or colleagues.

"We will set off in Oxford," Dodgson had told her father. The dean gave his blessing. "I promise I will have them all back at a de—at a decent hour."

"Remember father's wishes," reminds Alice. "We need to be back early."

"I think I'll remember, thank you very much."

The precocious Alice nods in approval. As they prepare for their afternoon adventure, she asks, "What's our route today?"

"Our route?"

"Yeah. Our—"

"To the riverbank for tea, up the Thames, down the rabbit hole to Godstow and then—"

"The rabbit hole? What rabbit hole?"

"*What rabbit hole?* You'll see." Dodgson is charmed. "Come everyone, please."

Dodgson's friend, Reverend Robinson Duckworth, takes his seat first. As the oarsman, he is followed by the three Liddell sisters—Edith, Lorina and Alice. Dodgson enters last and they set to go. As Duckworth tosses anchor—

"So girls," Dodgson says, "Alice asked me about the rabbit hole—"

"What rabbit hole?" Alice repeats, enjoying the tease.

"Why the rabbit hole with the white rabbit, of course."

Alice shakes her head in mock frustration as her sisters laugh and the boat leaves dock.

"The white rabbit," she says. Not a question.

"Yes. You mean you never heard of the white rabbit?"

"No..."

"You sure you don't know—"

"Know what?" chimes Edith.

"Know what? Know what? Why, the white rabbit from the rabbit hole in

Wonderland..."

Alice slaps her forehead, then hides her face as she secretly laughs along with her sisters.

"Wonderland?"

"We'll save the rest for the riverbank," Dodgson says, already reveling in this utterly marvelous, sun-drenched day...

~~~

While Dodgson and Duckworth enjoyed an afternoon tea at the riverbank, the girls feasted on crumpets, sunshine, and the strange new world called *Wonderland.*

By the end of the expedition, Alice held Dodgson to a promise. She had him swear he would write the story on paper.

He would submit *Alice's Adventures Under Ground,* complete with illustrations, to a trusted mentor, George MacDonald, a Scottish Christian minister and author who himself was on the verge of becoming a key figure in fantasy literature.

"The real test," he said to Dodgson, "will be to first have my wife read it to my children."

McDonald's *test* was easily passed; his family loved the work. He encouraged his protege to lengthen the tale and submit to publishers. Both were intimidating propositions but he persevered. Dodgson would submit the incomplete work to Macmillan, who would publish the work in 1865 under a new title and authorship:

Alice's Adventures in Wonderland as written by *Lewis Carroll.*

As for George MacDonald, his encouragement would not only in part beget one mythical work, but his own fantasy efforts, such as "Phantastes" and "The Princess and the Goblin," will be publicly credited well into the next century within the personal inspirations of C.S. Lewis and, understatedly...one John Ronald Reuel Tolkien.

George McDonald, however, could never quite accept the concept of a muse.

There will be repercussions...

Scarp Publishing

Lobby. Four white cushioned couches and a receptionist's window. White walls. No art.

What's next?

A small crowd has gathered around the area's centerpiece—an eighty-five inch HD wall-mounted television. The screen is overcome with images of England's latest history-making fire, as the Bradley and Son Bibliotheque conflagration is compared by commentators to the Library of Alexandria tragedy, in terms of the nature of its losses. Lists of first-editions, original documents and other irreplaceable works opined to have been destroyed in the new fire scroll in a graphic on the left of the screen. Thomas McFee stands with Denise, his hands in his pockets. Her hand is on his shoulder, holding the remote. She turns to him but he remains stoic, pensive. Several staff members discreetly eyeball them both, checking their reactions for the purpose of after-work gossip.

Gossip, as in signs of an impending romance. Or, alternatively, the slow breakdown of a grieving Tom McFee, to be followed perhaps by a grieving Denise. Or—worse. It wouldn't be the first time for *worse.*

~~~

The term *olding* was coined by staffers a year ago in response to a leaked memo from Denise to company backers, wherein she highlighted that Scarp would thrive based on the proactive contributions of its employees. As the biggest rap against her was that she was, in truth, an employer who inhibited subordinate growth, the term was mutinously translated as *an effort to manipulate the old guard out the door.*

Talks of going public have heated of late as they had last year; when an overly-ambitious staff member then crossed Denise in front of a loyal Scarp investor. This upstart had suggested in a letter that the owner was deceitful and out of touch, that "new blood" should truthfully be considered to run the office. The boss had proceeded not only to terminate her subordinate's employment, but also had vengefully wielded her own poison pen in a guest missive to *Publisher's Weekly.* She extended permission for them to print her rant as an article.

Denise named the fired employee in the contribution she succinctly entitled, "Publishing Is Serious Business." She knew the outing would pass their legal qualifications; she forwarded a copy of the original letter. The message was clear: Don't mess with Denise Watkins.

To date, the former employee has yet to resurface. She has, effectively, been blackballed from the industry.

~~~

Denise's reputation as a bitch-goddess is something she has worked diligently to cultivate. Only Tom knows the deal. "Self-preservation," she once confided in him. "The biggest dog in the yard gets the reward."

"Ever get tired of it?"

"Of what?"

"Of the act?"

"The act?"

"You just answered my question."

Though Tom McFee is generally well-liked within the company, he is often considered enigmatic—and even austere.

Though Tom has, in effect, *made* the company, not a one of the workers could understand what he sees in her. The consensus is that if something happens to Tom, Denise will no longer be able to function.

Ding dong, the witch is dead.

Denise turns off the television. "Okay, everyone. Back to work." They slowly disperse. "Go on!" When the last of the group has left, she whispers in Tom's ear:

"Are you okay?"

He shrugs first, then nods. He is forlorn and doing a lousy job at disguising it. She is taken aback when she notices his eyes tearing. "Tom, come back with me to the office." She rubs his shoulder, as would someone who really gives a damn. "C'mon, hon. We can talk inside."

SAMANTHA AND DANIEL'S APARTMENT, CAMBRIDGE, ENGLAND

The couple opens their wedding gifts. There is no joy in their actions. Much like her father, Samantha acts on one emotion while concealing another.

Unlike him, she's much better at remaining stoic, and more consistently in control. Not perfect, but better. Because that's her natural state and she's working on it.

The gifts up to now: some money, silverware and dishes they will never use, assorted statuettes and like novelties. They sit on separate couches. Where once was clear and open floor, now there is a mess of crumpled wrapping paper and bows.

As they unwrap, Daniel asks her, "You sure you're okay?"

"I'm fine." She finds a quick conversation point and sticks it. "Ever wonder why half a wedding party shops where the couple is registered, while the other half does their own thing?" She holds up a bottle of wine.

"Not that I'm upset, or resentful or anything, I'm not. But $2.99 at the liquor store on Spring Road. Really?"

"How would you know?"

"It's where most of the office shops."

"I wouldn't know. You never tell me." They continue about their task.

Samantha becomes quiet, as if she has inadvertently disclosed a great secret.

"You sure you're okay?" Daniel asks.

"Why wouldn't I be okay"

"That's not what I asked you."

"I'm fine. Why are you pushing?"

He tosses the last of his bows onto the floor. "Because you're lying to me."

"I'm not lying..."

"Your Dad?"

"What?"

He joins her. "Move that spectacularly-toned ass, would you please?"

"Don't try to get on my good side."

"Funny."

He's getting through to her because she's allowing it. She's aware that if she speaks to anyone, it should be her husband. The intense secrecy of her job, however, has done nothing to up her game as it regards normal interpersonal communication.

Still. They have been together over six years and she is still awkward during moments of platonic intimacy.

Sexually, no problem. Strong compatibility there. Some mutual kinks, even. But emotionally? Usually she is able to act her way out of these moments but she has no bluff today. Daniel takes the small box from her hands and places it aside. He then gazes into her eyes and pulls her close.

She forces her eyes closed and grimaces like a child. *You can't see me now.*

Daniel pauses, and waits for the game to pass.

Samantha opens her eyes first, then blows a held breath in submission. "You win," she says.

Time to grow up, she thinks. "Was I right? Your Dad?"

She nods, ashamed. "You're right."

ALLIANCE

CAMBRIDGE, MASSACHUSETTS

It is the following morning, Sunday. Dawn. Still some time for the sun to rise. Daniel enters the gym, ready to go.

They made love last night. There was nothing *awkward* about it. Flesh on flesh, soul on soul. The fortune of passionate, poetic compatibility. The conversation ended with "You're right" and began again with a chaste kiss on the cheek.

"I love you," he said.

"Uh huh." She fell back asleep immediately.

Daniel was already in his sweats, car keys already in hand. Samantha will sleep in today.

He sets to spar. Daniel has been partial to the sport of boxing since viewing a *youtube* clip of Mosley—Mayweather a couple of years back at the urging of a friend. The older, well past-his-prime Sugar Shane very nearly knocked out the champ in Round Two.

Though Mayweather would ultimately win in a rout, Daniel had come away with a profound impression. This was the idea that anyone, regardless of how great or how favored, could be defeated at any given time. Henceforth this conviction would be incorporated henceforth into his personal philosophy. He thought: *I'm still young enough to attain all of my goals and nothing will stand in my way.*

Daniel adjusts his gloves and his mouthpiece. He will meet his larger foe on common ground as he does when he's *David* against much of the rest of the world—*Goliath.* Daniel has his reasons for his underdog outlook. They are specific, and shall remain privileged for just a while longer.

~~~

His sparring partner, a regular, is considerably taller and far more muscled than he. The other man is a heavyweight who outweighs Baxter by at least forty pounds. Instead of the bulk impeding his coordination, the heavyweight's conditioning is such that he's been hired to work with a number of British contenders.

Daniel asked for the best for this morning's session. He needs to be tested today, and for a reason. His wife, Samantha, does not know that tonight will be the most important of her life.

Thomas's reconciliation with Samantha figured in the equation. Daniel's marriage to Samantha figured in the equation. He waited. Now all is clear. Tonight Samantha is going to die.

Fifteen to sixteen hours. Thereabouts. This'll be the last time. Keep yourself occupied till then and we'll get the damn thing over with.

For this morning, for that purpose and in preparation, he has received exactly what he has asked for. As he watches his opponent step into the ring, Daniel recalls a phrase from his favorite film, Stanley Kubrick's *Full*

Metal Jacket. "*The crazy-brave.*"

As soon as they touch gloves for the first time, the sparring session is concluded. The *fight* begins.

Daniel loved the new girl. She would be his new focus.

He fell for her quickly. Maybe too quickly, in *hindsight. Corporal Baxter's* desperation for a normal human relationship was mindfully dismissed when fighting in Iraq. He spent four years in the army. Though this was his first war, it was no secret to anyone who knew him *back in the day* that he was quite the fighter. He had been in life-and-death circumstances before.

He was once one of the bad boys. He was spared a stint in jail—for armed robbery at a downtown Brooklyn supermarket. The beating of a cashier had nearly led to the employee's death. Daniel had agreed to register for the military.

He would make a quick one-week stop, prior to service, to speak to a much older, respected man who regularly dealt with this *type of problem.* The man would disappear soon thereafter. Daniel was hoping for some words of wisdom.

What he didn't receive, he derived on his own (and he realized soon thereafter that was likely the specific intent):

Nothing is what it appears to be...except for war, I guess.

"We're savage," he once told Samantha. "We're animals. Only in war is man true to his nature."

"And so, what is man's nature, exactly?" Samantha sarcastically queried.

"Bloodsport," he said, without hesitation. "A means to a means."

"I don't get—"

"All this ain't nuthin' but a tragic game, sweetheart, and we're the pawns."

~~~

The bell rings.

Daniel was desperate then. His father had been laid off from Wall Street. He had been a margin clerk and had held the position better part of twenty-five years. His father had received on the day of his mother's necessary "woman's surgery."

Daniel was always close with his parents. Two weeks earlier, his father said the *C-word* to him in private. He was as worried as any loving husband. The doctors said Mom should survive "because they caught it early."

When his Dad started crying, openly—the first and only time he had seen his Dad in tears—he knew the operation was a bigger deal than anyone was letting on. Further, he discovered Dad spent his savings over the years to handle other emergencies, as in paying bills and keeping his family in food and housing. They were out of money, and out of options.

There would be no gold watch to commemorate twenty-five years of his Dad's loyalty, his blood and sweat. There was not even the dignity of a retirement.

No. Not even that. Nothing

In response, though Daniel's initial inclination was to head to his dad's former office and cause all sorts of ruckus, he decided to stay with *petty theft* and find enough cash here and there to help defray his Dad's cost for surgery. By so doing he also believed he was doing something that needed to be done for his cherished mother. He was doing his part to help save her life.

~~~

There would be six robberies in those two weeks. Two coffee shops, a gas station, a liquor store, two markets, first to last. Progressively larger, equally risky. The adrenaline rush became a monster to contain; he needed more, and he needed more quickly. The crimes became less about his family and more about the acts themselves. This awareness gathered in him upon settling into his new military life. Once recognized, it caused him further frustration—and sadness.

When away, Daniel's focus was forced where it needed to be. When he returned home with four kills and a controlled (medicated) battle with PTSD, he had been able to relegate *most* of his dangerous ideation to another recess far beyond his conscious mind.

"This seat taken?"

"By you," she said.

"Thanks."

Daniel pulled in his chair, spilling his coffee in the process. He so wanted to lick the splatter off his sleeve, but how could he?

"I have napkins."

He laughed. "I knew I liked you for a reason..."

And that was that.

She asked him about his service and he gave his stock answer. Whenever he was asked about his service by well-meaning civilians, he would say, merely, "suppress and assimilate."

The rote response was deliberately enigmatic.

Thing is, his darkness could not remain suppressed, despite his best efforts, and his successful assimilation would prove only a temporary state of affairs. Time went on and he refused to accept that Samantha, as highly-educated and trained as she was, could possibly suspect a thing.

Daniel believed he was that good. Past-tense. As he outboxes his sparring partner, he contemplates his distant days. He thinks of Sam's role upon his return. He "had a future" in the Corps, as his superior officer informed him in private.

What I want with my life. To kill insurgents for a living. He was unnaturally talented and favored on the battlefield but he has been, privately, losing the battle of containment at home since the last *Abeyance.*

What I want with my life. To be a widower in my twenties.

He merely kept the demons well-hidden. They were still there. It was an issue that would bring him to the gym this morning, at an hour well before England would see its next sun. Then he would initiate the *second* phase of his breakdown.

As to the *first*: he contemplates it as he stiffs his opponent on the ropes with a furious flurry of lefts and rights.

"Brother!" The smile was wide and inviting, the pearly-whites in full sheen having taken on lives of their own. The arms were outstretched and nearly flailing, having long awaited his own return of 'normal' human contact. "Welcome back to the Heights."

X.

His sparring partner returns to his corner. The bigger man was not expecting the flurry. The speed, maybe, but he's being embarrassed.

Sixty seconds on the stool; he fully intends to knock the punk out in Round Two and get his ass out of there. Daniel has other plans.

"The Promenade hasn't changed a bit. How could you afford a place like this?"

Daniel tours Denise's brownstone in abject amazement.

"I can't, brother," says X. *"It doesn't belong to me."*

"You're being paid to watch it?"

X laughs. *"Hardly."*

"Then how—"

"I started some work."

"Yeah?"

"Yeah."

Daniel continues to look around. He scrutinizes the paintings, the bookcases. "I can't believe some people are able to live like this."

X watches him. "Come with me."

"What's that?"

"Come with me, brother. Something I need to show you."

~~~

The bell rings. Round Two.

"What is it you want to show me?"

"Not want. Need."

"Okay then." He follows X to Denise's desktop computer. *"Wanna sit?"*

"What are you doing?" X ignores him and takes the seat for himself. *"Are you out of your right mind?"* As X types, he says: *"I'm the only one in my right mind."*

"I can't do this. I'm just off the fucking bus two days ago."

"Don't worry. I got us in. I'll get us out." He presses his last key. *"Read."* Curiosity gets the best of Daniel. He bends and takes a look at the screen. *"What's all this?"*

"This is your future, brother."

Daniel reads on. *"I was right. You're out of your damn mind. What's with this 'brother' bullshit? You're Rasta now?"*

"You miss Searle?"

Daniel laughs in frustration. *"Searle's dead. Where...are you?"*

"Just curious. When you were gone I was diagnosed, you know."

"Diagnosed?"

"Let's just say, now I know how the others feel who don't belong."

"What did you do?"

"What do you mean, brother?"

374

"Again with the—" He gives up and turns back to the screen. *"What am I looking at?"*

"To answer your question: you think I'm trying too hard?"

"Too hard?"

"Trying to be social, brother."

Daniel has lost his patience. *"What is it you want to show me?"*

X turns to the screen and types. *"Remember what John Hinckley and Mark David Chapman have in common?"*

*"*Catcher in the Rye. *What's the point?"*

"You're not as stupid as you look."

"Thanks."

"Welcome." X waits for a file to load. *"Hold on."*

"I'm holding..."

Must be a large file. The download is taking much too long.

"While we're waiting, ever wonder why Salinger's work inspired so much aberration? Hinckley and Chapman weren't the only two who—"

"I think you're done." They re-engage.

The round is uneventful, a dance. The heavyweight is overly cautious though his bob-weave-clinch defense is highly-effective. He throws seven punches in the round, Daniel thirty-six but nine land. The heavyweight's strategy was to absorb the lighter man's flurries until he tired. Instead, Daniel barely threw. The bell rings. They head back to their corners.

~~~

And X reveals all.

Daniel doesn't buy it. Any of it. The Abeyance, a muse named Ara. Gods and other immortals. A tragic love story that threatens the very fabric of a universe of universes.

"I don't expect you to believe me," X says.

"Then I'm wasting my time here—why?"

"No time wasted."

"Please—" Daniel begins again to protest.

"It's about your future, brother."

Daniel is furious. *"Enough. I'm not your brother."*

"You are the only friend I have though. You go off to fight, I'm alone again and then he disappears on me too...but you came back. Broth—"

Daniel covers X's mouth with the boy's own hand, and reads. Though he is loath to listen to another word, he is interested. Fascinated really. He looks to X, then back at the computer as he continues to scroll.

"Who else has seen this? Who else is involved?" he asks. *"And by the way, before you answer, if I find out you're trying to manipulate me—"*

"No. Mark my words and then you'll question me no longer. You'll meet a girl, soon, very soon in fact. Maybe as soon as this after—"

"You speak in riddles? This is what you're saying to me"

"And she and I will work together. For a while. And then—"

"What is wrong with you? You were out of your mind before, and now—"

"I'm autistic, you know. Not capable of much better than this. That's what I meant when I said I was diagnosed."

"What?"

"The doctors said I have Aspurger's."

"What have you been smoking since I've been away?"

"Why, you want some?"

"No."

"I don't indulge anyway."

"What is wrong with you these days?"

"I overcompensate. It's a form of autism, limits my ability to be socially

interactive so I become socially inept. Know what I'm sayin' brother?"

"Make you feel better? Something to explain away your flaws."

"Yeah, it does."

"You convinced yourself of that?"

"Yeah. Works for me. Explains a lot."

"You are *sick."* He points to his head. *"Here. Nothing else."*

"You don't think so, seriously?"

"I know you too well. Nothing a good psychotropic won't cure. I got connections. You know, fuck it. Why am I engaging with this garbage? What about the girl?"

"Trust me," X replies, disappointed. *"She will become a catalyst."*

"A catalyst*? Kiss my ass."* He laughs at the ridiculousness of it all. *"A catalyst for what—"*

"You'll have your answers soon, brother..."

"That a threat?"

"No. It's the truth."

"Asshead."

"And you'll see pretty fucking quick that she will not become just your *problem."* Daniel goes back to reading. *"Yeah,"* X continues. *"And* then *you will owe me an apology."*

"You think so?"

"Goddamn right I do."

~~~

Daniel lies flat on his back twenty-two seconds into Round Three, *other plans* be damned. He did not see the punch coming. A classic uppercut, flush on the jaw. He fell to his his back straight away.

Killed by a distraction. In the service, such irresponsibility would be tantamount to genocide. If he was still breathing and the enemy was out of range, his own troops would have threatened to shoot him between the eyes for jeopardizing their mission.

That conversation with X has haunted him ever since. Because he believed X.

When he met the girl, Samantha, he was mistrustful. When he courted her, he trusted her less. Then they got married. Disingenuous though he was, he needed to see where it all was headed, as he considered X a genius. In truth, he did not receive his words lightly. He refused to buy into the drama, is all, and *X* has been dramatic for as long as they have known each other. There were reasons for that too, as also for Daniel's *arm's-length* attitude.

And then he fell in love with Samantha. After the wedding, after the reunion with Tom, he was fairly *smacked* with the realization that suddenly his life had meaning. He felt he could *begin* the long process of giving up the fight.

If Sam knew, she hid it well.

Maybe, through some miracle, they would even have a child one day. One of the trainers jumps into the ring as a ref. He raises the sparring partner's arm—no need to get him any angrier—then rushes to Daniel.

He removes Daniel's mouthpiece. "Talk to me," he says. Daniel is dazed but conscious.

"How's the other guy look?" The third man slaps him on both sides of the face. "That's for being a smart-ass and taking unnecessary chances."

The sparring partner joins him; together they help Daniel to his stool. "You're a tough little bastard," he says. "What were you trying to accomplish?"

Daniel takes a sip from his thermos, offered by the trainer. He swirls and spits the water, and responds as the trainer cuts his gloves: "Time to be taken seriously, I think."

"Was that your best?"

The gloves slip off. "It was a lucky punch. Don't kid yourself."

"What the hell are you—"

"You outweigh me by forty pounds. Was that *your* best?"

"We have a problem here?"

"Wish your wife Happy Birthday for me." Without another word, Daniel leaves the stool and exits the gym.

The heavyweight looks to the trainer, who is as confused as he is. "What the hell was that all about?" the trainer asks.

SAMANTHA AND DANIEL'S APARTMENT, CAMBRIDGE, ENGLAND

Damn him!

Samantha runs her pricked thumb under the sink so the blood can wash away. She looks around, grabs a napkin, wraps it around her injured digit and squeezes. She enters the bathroom and finds a box of bandages.

Despite her anger, and though she blames Daniel for the accident, she fully intends to have breakfast ready when he saunters through the door. Some mock indignation here, sprinkled with a hint of unreasonable pullback from any sort of affection there...In her mind's eye she accepts his apology; they eat, work on some house chores together, maybe snuggle up for an afternoon movie on television. They gorge on popcorn, skip lunch, head straight to dinner, have some dessert, get through a bit of reading, then lovemaking at night. It's a contest to better last evening's *perfect ten*, and to end the week the right way.

Certainly, though, the evening is not starting off promising. The puncture takes three napkins before the seepage is contained. She runs back into the kitchen to check the frying pan— 'Shit!" She finds that the eyes of the two over-easy eggs have stuck and burned. Now of course there's blood on the cutting board where once there were only carrots and a knife that was not quite up to task.

Can't even get breakfast right this morning. she thinks. *Did you really need to go to the gym today? It's Sunday for crying out loud. Even God rests on Sundays.*

She could never stand it when Daniel was late. It's now 10:20. He should have been back twenty minutes ago. He left when she was sleeping.

How many hours has it been?

These are the days that try her considerable patience, when her new hubby becomes a rude and inconsiderate prick. Her favorite word when she gets angry, fit for every similar occasion. Now is no different. She is overworked as usual. Bored, as he's not there to stimulate her, physically or otherwise, and take her mind off *X* and this damn end-of-the-world scenario she's gotten herself wrapped up in.

She will likely go back to work and blame him for that too.

It's Sunday! I can't downplay all this Ara bullshit for one goddamned day? Is that too much to ask? Samantha shuts the burner, tosses the frying pan in the sink and runs the cold water. She stares at the steam as it rises.

10:21.

"At least one of us tries to better themselves. I'm not exactly housewife material but at least I tried to make breakfast. What have you done this morning for me?" she says to herself.

She's reminded of that pithy little mantra they swore they would never say in the other's company—two versions, one for him and the other for her—so long as the rules were followed. So she picks up her cell from the kitchen countertop, dials, waits...and says, cattily: "It's the bitch. Go fuck yourself, you prick."

And she hangs up.

10:30.

He has not shown; he has not called. She cannot reach him.

But neither is Samantha ready to panic. For the past fifteen or so minutes she has been sitting. cross-legged, on the cheap 1960s white shag in their bedroom in front of the burning black and white tiled fireplace. She can barely stomach the rug or the design of the hearth, but she's in a destructive mode and not interested in quiet comforts.

The letter. *X's* letter to Denise. She has made no copy and considers the communication invaluable, yet she takes a perverse joy scissoring the two pages into the smallest pieces she can.

10:40.

The mass is gathered and burned, tossed into the fireplace. She watches as the paper-snow sparks, browns, bends. Blackens, becomes ash.

10:52.

Samantha is still on the floor when she hears a knock on the door. She's startled but keeps her calm.

"About damn time."

The knocking becomes louder, faster. She reaches for her e-reader.

"Can you use your key?"

She awaits a response that does not come, and gets one she does not want to hear—

"Sam, open up—"

"Christ!"

Sam stands, wipes her pants and looks around to ensure no *evidence* remains.

Good.

She unbolts the door. As she opens, a single arm—a man's arm—and a hand, the latter sheathed in a silk black glove, reaches through the crack. The hand pulls her by the shoulder and covers her mouth before the door fully opens.

The movements are cat-like swift. The interloper is either highly-practiced in the art of kidnapping, or is otherwise uniquely skilled. Samantha immediately loses consciousness. She is supported in a *fireman's carry* and *walked* outside, in the direction of a curbside-parked SUV. Its windows are darkly-tinted.

She is gently placed in the back seat, her head bowed so as not to hit the door top. The car door is closed. Samantha's abductor assumes the driver's seat and waits.

As she is taken, Daniel enters the apartment. He checks outside from the kitchen window as the vehicle's ignition is restarted. His face is utterly void of expression, his nose twitching up at the remaining stench of chloroform.

THE INFINITY PASS

Esme. Samantha's *next matter of business.*

Her image flashes in Samantha's mind like the blip of a radar.

I don't know her. Should I?

Though she sleeps, Sam is troubled as she treks the cosmos. She is stone-unconscious. She is aware of everything and nothing at once.

She *replays* her abduction. She *watches* Daniel from *above* despite his being *in* the house. She spies on him as he searches for and finds a flash drive that she had hidden in a perfectly paint-covered bedroom wall panel behind a newly-placed painting of *Blue Boy* by Gainsborough.

This mission accomplished, Daniel joins the unknown driver in the vehicle, taking the passenger seat. They drive off.

Stars? Who is "Esme?" Where am I? Unlike most others who dream, Samantha willingly approaches a precipice.

Why would he do this to me?

Her impulse is not suicidal so much as adventurous. If Daniel has indeed betrayed her, she would rather explore and take her time deciding what the hell to do with the rest of her natural life than return to the man she truly did love. *I tried. God knows I tried. What could I have done differently?*

Again, there is *Esme. "Why are you here?"*Esme says.

"Who are you?"

"I must have blacked out. Oh dear, I can't remember my name."

"Have we met before?"

"I don't think so?"

"Do I look familiar to you?"

"I can't see you."

"No?"

"Can you see me?"

"My eyes must be closed. I'm blocking out light? No...Where am I?"

"I was headed to the Pass, then. I remember nothing from there except that now I'm here."

"The Pass?"

"Voices. I heard a call. I thought I heard a call, maybe. The words, from the voices, came like an order. 'Infinity Pass.'"

"I don't understand."

"I don't think either of us is supposed to—"

"Are you my guide?"

"I don't know."

"But...I'm not dead, I don't think."

"No."

"Just visiting?"

"I think so."

"Will I see my mother?"

"I don't know."

"Who have you seen?"

Esme doesn't answer.

"Who have you seen?" Samantha repeats.

"You are the first, I think."

And on it would go. For hours? Days? Neither could see the other yet they could hear her. Somehow. Not with their ears, nor with any *earthly* cognition. It was as if the complete loss of all their sensory perceptions had given was before another, inexplicable level of awareness. Blindness and deafness merged to enhance something previously hidden and hitherto unknown. The two strangers passed in a peculiar state: one dead, and another who might as well be.

~~~

"My husband sent me here, I fear." Samantha explains. *"I'm not recalling much of what happened but that's my fear."*

"Do you love him?"

"I think I loved him. I think I loved him very much and I don't know why he's done what I think he's—"

"No children?"

"Funny. Some thoughts are so strong, others—"

"No children?"

"That's painful, I remember. I can't have children naturally—"

"Why?"

"That's what they told me."

"Your husband, he doesn't know, does he?"

"I was going to tell him."

"Your Dad?"

"No."

"Anyone?"

"A woman, a friend of my Dad's who I sometimes confide in."

"You've always wanted a child more than anything."

"Wanted to raise a little girl the right way. Always wanted to build a dollhouse for a little girl."

"You sure he doesn't know?"

"He would have no way of knowing."

"Does anyone know?"

"Yes."

"Who?"

"I thought I told you?"

"Who?"

"I don't remember her name now, but she's—"

"Who? Think."

"I told you I don't remember."

"I had hoped you would because now there's a light—"

"What light?"

"Coming for you."

"How do you know?"

"Maybe that's why you're here. Maybe because my husband sent me here because he was done with me but for you maybe there's hope. The light. You seem young. But also I believe that you are right, that you are just a visitor—"

"What do you mean?"

"I'm stuck. You...you are trailed by light. I feel shadow behind you, light shadow in this dark that races to catch up to you."

"And then what?"

"Then you must choose, I believe. That would make sense, right? If not you go forward, into the void, but you're getting a second chance, I think."

"To go back?"

"From the Infinity Pass. You must have value, which is why you are being followed this far, as far as I know.

"Is everyone who goes back followed by light?"

"Don't know but I don't think so. I sense somehow more with you but don't know why..."

"Is that where we are?"

"Where?"

"Infinity?"

"Sure. I believe."

"Now?"

"I believe so. Unless..."

"Unless what?"

"Doesn't really matter, does it?"

"Does it?"

"No. You are already trailed. You have a choice where I—"

"What kind of choice?"

"I'm speaking riddles; no matter."

"You are, why?"

"Space and time are the same. All nonsense. I forget to remember what I say and I remember to forget. Forget it."

"And what about you?"

"What about me?"

"When do you go back?"

"There is no light behind me. I go forward."

"But why—"

"I don't know. Your light is getting close. You be careful. I think you get a second chance if you follow the light but nothing comes for nothing."

"So, that's it then?"

"That's it then, honey. I think that's it then."

"I go back to the same?"

"No. You go back, I think, to what you've wanted. You would be like me if you go back to the same. I figure they have bigger plans for you."

"They?"

"I don't know."

"I can't go back to him. I can't go back to that life if he tried to hurt me."

"Or worse. Like mine. Then consider it done."

"Consider what done?"

"That."

"Who tried to hurt me?"

"Listen—"

"What?"

"The light is upon you."

"Come with me!"

"I told you I can't. I'm sorry—"

"I...I can't. I'm losing you—"

"Turn around!"

"I can't!"

"Turn around!"

"I'm trying."

"Open your eyes!"

"They burn."

"Open your eyes."

"I can't—"

"Go!"

The image Samantha *sees* before she awakens is the fiery, drooling mouth of the little dragon that has overtaken the cosmic expanse and finally caught up to her, and the quickest glimpse of the other voice, *Esme*. Esme appears to be—or has taken the form of—a mournful dwarf girl telepathically guiding the dragon ever-closer to his intended *target*.

Samantha never had a choice in the matter.

FIRE (PROVENANCE)

SAMANTHA AND DANIEL'S APARTMENT,
CAMBRIDGE, ENGLAND

Morning.

There has been an *Abeyance*, and a requisite—but this time *substantial*—correction. There was not to be another. The world was to have faced its end if there was another.

As ever, there is *reason*. Though any notion of *shift* is illusory.

"Taebal is coming," Daniel informs, over a bowl of corn pops.

"You're funny," Adriel says. "There is no such thing as dragons." She is as articulate and precise as Samantha at this early age.

"Sure there are. Ask your mother." They sit in the kitchen. A father-daughter breakfast.

"Silly." She's as precocious as Sam at that age, among other similarities.

"Read to me?"

"Read what? Now?"

"Yeah."

"But we're eating—"

"So, I like it when you read."

He sighs knowingly. "Grandpa's book."

"No, but I'm sure *he* read to Mommy when they were eating breakfast."

"*The Hobbit?*"

She shakes her head. "Uh uh."

"Umm—*Alice in Wonderland?*"

"Nope."

"What? What do you want me to read?"

"Mommy's book. There are better dragons in Mommy's book."

"Mommy's book? What book is that?"

"I know." she smiles, mischievously.

"I thought you said there is no such thing as dragons?"

"There is no such thing as make-believe dragons. *Taebal* is a real dragon."

Daniel puts down his spoon, drops elbows on table and bores into her eyes. Teasing—and yet not.

"We never read...Mommy's *book* before," he says, curiously.

"Speak for yourself."

"Speak for? What are you, two going on thirty?"

"No, silly. Still two."

Daniel grabs her cereal bowl. "Hey!"

He smells inside. "You put something in your milk today?"

"No!" She smiles, an ingratiating manipulation that no one could resist.

Daniel slides the bowl back to her. They both resume eating. "I have the bigger crunch," he says.

"I have the bigger bowl," she responds. She's right about that.

He takes the challenge. "Tell you what, you know Mommy's book isn't finished yet?"

"Yeah?"

"Between me and you?"

"Yeah?"

"Do you know how to say anything other than—nevermind. I'll tell you a secret story from her book, only she didn't write it yet. Fair?"

"Yeah."

"I'm gonna ignore you, you do that again." Adriel *zips* her lip with her thumb and index finger. She then *turns the key* and throws it away. "I won't ask who taught you that."

"M—"

"Anyway." he doesn't let her finish. "Tolkien—"

"Tolkien."

He looks at her as though she's landed from another planet. "Tolkien and his wife—"

"Edith."

"Edith. They had planned to visit America for some time, but her health wouldn't allow it. Tolkien finally flew to NYC in the fall of 1970, landing at Idlewild and thinking much about his 'muse of myth and language.' When he landed, he looked at the array of buildings and windows that seemed like so many watching eyes. But this time, his muse whispered, 'Watchers, guardians over secret gates.'"

"Scary." replies Adriel.

"Do you want me to go on?"

"Yeah."

He smiles. "You see. Well, let's pretend you're old enough to understand and not get *too* scared, okay?"

"Don't worry. I understand."

"Good. Tolkien visited New York when he was asked to review some fragments of documents containing a poem. The poem was about an ancient king who fell under the spell of a ring. These documents were written in a mysterious language, and—"

"What about Ara?"

Daniel is taken aback, but not entirely surprised. He doesn't ask but attempts to take her lead. "In this story, the documents told the story of Ara, who was the lost heroine of Middle-Earth, and—"

"It's not that different. Just wrong."

"Wrong? It's not—"

"It is."

"No, it's not."

"It is. I'm talking about Mommy's story of Ara."

"No." Daniel repeats.

"Mommy's late."

Daniel looks at the clock. "She *is* late. I thought she'd be back from the gym right now." Hasty change of subject.

"Maybe she's with *X.*"

Didn't work. "Now, how do you know about this—*X*? Hmm? Please, enlighten me."

"I know...everything." Her upper lip curls, and she breaks into a widening smirk.

"Besides, he's in New York. I think." He was joking.

"With the Professor, I think." She was not.

"Now how—"

"I want more new stor—"

The front door opens. Samantha. "I'm home!" she yells from the front entrance, before entering the kitchen.

Adriel jumps from her seat and hugs her. "Mommy!"

Samantha places her keys on the table and kisses Daniel. She's dressed in blue striped sweats—pants and jacket—with a T-shirt underneath.

"You two causing trouble today?"

Adriel glances at *Daddy*, trying her best not to laugh. He looks at her and winks. "Always," he says.

~~~

Still seated at the table, they grimace as Samantha eats her breakfast or, more accurately, *drinks* her breakfast. A protein smoothie. Peanut butter, kale, walnuts, apple and soy ice cream.

Adriel sticks her finger in her mouth for dramatic effect. "Before you do that, you should tell your Dad to start exercising and eating healthy."

"I like getting fat. My military service is over."

"Keep it up. You'll be there before you know."

As Samantha takes her last sip, Daniel stands. "Anyway," he says. "I have a surprise for you,"

"A surprise?" She turns to Adriel. "A surprise for me, huh?"

"Yep." Daniel places three envelopes on the table in front of her.

"What're these?" she asks.

"Why don't you open them?" says Adriel.

"Smartie." She opens the envelopes.

"You've been working so hard lately and you can use some time off." says Daniel.

"We're going to New York. Really?"

He kisses the top of her head, and rubs her shoulders. "I love you despite you."

Samantha is stunned. "Not that I mean to sound ungrateful; I'm not. But what are we doing in New York?"

"The tickets are actually not from me."

"They're not? Then who?"

"Denise. She wants you to surprise your Dad."

"Grandpa!" Adriel shouts.

"Really." Samantha says, undecided regarding her thoughts on the matter.

"She feels that he hasn't seen enough of you since the wedding and that, well, your Dad is becoming reclusive. He has no idea what he's been up to lately." His words trail off as he watches her reaction.

She looks down, touched and apprehensive at once.

"Well?" Adriel waits for a response. Samantha forces a smile, reaches over and kisses her hand.

"And he's going to be forty-five next week."

"That's old." says Adriel.

"And what about work?" she asks. "Someone has to tell my boss."

"Really old." Adriel repeats.

"Arranged," Daniel answers. She looks at him quizzically, and he repeats his reply. "Arranged. Your office is of the opinion that since the explosions of 2013—"

"Ka-pow," offers Adriel, clapping her hands once and spreading her arms.

"That, since then, you've hardly missed any days or taken a vacation." Samantha knows better than to press, and for now does not ask.

"Can I ask you one other question, though?"

"What's that?"

"When do we leave?"

"That's the best part," he begins.

"Tomorrow!" Adriel blurts.

Samantha turns to Daniel. "She serious?"

"Go take a shower. I'll be right there," he says. "Then I'll help you pack."

She goes to the bedroom. "Remind me to tell you about the strangest dream I had this morning."

~~~

Esme was right. Samantha does not remember a thing from the morning of her abduction. She retains some memory of her reverie. It is an allowance of sorts. Once more, there is *reason.* A terrible choice has been made...though the determination was not Samantha's.

RAY'S PIZZA, GREENWICH VILLAGE, NEW YORK

Samantha and Daniel feast on a medium *Sicilian* of cheese and mushroom. Light on the tomato sauce. Adriel's calzone has been cut into bite-sized pieces and scattered in a mess of ketchup that threatens a hostile takeover of her white paper plate.

"Good huh?" asks Samantha.

"Good huh to you," Adriel replies, stuffing two more pieces into a mouth already dribbling from overload.

"Swallowing is good," says Daniel.

Adriel opens her mouth, just another young kid showing off the contents of her meal. She laughs and chews slowly, teasingly, savoring every bite.

"Why don't you give her a call?" Daniel asks.

Samantha wipes her chin and places down her napkin. "Was planning on it," she says, before mouthing so Adriel cannot hear—

"So...fucking...good..." Daniel takes another bite in response.

Sam flips him the bird, behind Adriel's back, and steps out. The door *chimes* on her exit.

~~~

"I have a question." Adriel presses him.

"What's your question?"

"Why did Mommy do that thing with her finger?" she asks.

"Thing with her finger?"

"Yeah. There's a window there, you know. That's called a *reflection*."

Daniel is floored. "You know," she says, "one day you're gonna be dangerous."

"You said that yesterday."

He shovels food into his mouth in imitation. Adriel laughs and ups him one. Then he does. A contest in the making.

Two minutes later, the door *chimes* again. Samantha re-enters, sits and claws at her pizza.

She looks at them both. "You're such a good influence on your daughter." She paws at her slice. "Tougher to pick up the second time." She takes a bite, sloppily slurping the cheese. "She got caught up in the office. Says my father has no idea—"

"Is he there?" asks Daniel.

"No. He caught a movie at the Angelika. She rushed me off the phone so she can get here."

"So then what?"

"She's supposed to meet him there for coffee after. She'll have company."

"Ahh." Daniel says.

"Ahh..." Adriel copies, belching in the middle.

"So," adds Daniel, "that's it? That was Denise's grand plan, huh? Sabotaging your dad in one of his calm moments? "

"You all made the arrangements—"

"*She* did—"

"You know what I mean. Don't play stupid—"

"Who's playin'?" She grins. He follows.

"I'll be okay. We have reservations tonight—"

"After this?" He gestures at the carnage of the pizza.

"I know. Tonight. You'll be hungry later."

"We'll see. Gotta maintain my figure," he says.

A few moments of silence...

Daniel peeks at her as he bites. He becomes concerned when he notices his wife discreetly wiping her eye.

SCARP PUBLISHING

Denise gathers her papers and pressing files, and stuffs the ephemera into her bag. What does not fit she holds under her arm. A pen is in her mouth; Tom McFee is on speakerphone. "I told you I don't have all day." His exasperation is evident.

"I'm just 20 minutes behind. The longer you ream me on the phone the longer it'll take me to get there."

"Maybe you can take the pen out of your mouth—"

She forgot about that. She drops the pen into her purse. "Can I go now?"

"One minute later and I'm gone."

"For what? What's so important?"

He expires, as if he's been holding his breath and cannot hold it any longer. "I'm finally reading Tolkien's *Beowulf* translation and planned on spending a humble birthday in my own head."

Denise steps back, hopeful. "Finding your inspiration?"

"See you in twenty. Not a minute later." The line goes dead. "Little shit."

She rushes out her door, kicking the stopper on the way out. "Janice, lock my office please," she shouts. See you tomorrow."

Denise awaits her elevator, her arms full, her right foot furiously tapping. She has affected this nervous behavior since she was a child; when her parents finally broke her of the habit of rocking—standing and swaying back and forth no matter the situation—by working with her to replace the habit to something a bit more subtle, they thought the new tendency would quickly run its course.

Never happened. She didn't care much for them anyway so, if they were bothered, *c'est la vie.*

Ring. The elevator doors open. She will be the only passenger for now. She steps inside, almost snagging her case as the doors close.

Eight floors to go. She drops her bag and breathes a sigh of relief. Again, the tapping foot—always the tapping foot when she is in a hurry—and she looks up to the floor display.

Seven...

The display, as the elevator, is *old New York.* A floor span and an arrow. Outlaid in gold. *Big deal. It's 2015, get over yourself.* The foot taps quicker as the ride continues. Denise adjusts the work she is holding, freeing a hand which cuffs into a fist, relaxes, repeats...

Six...

Suddenly, she becomes hot, flushed, as if the air has constricted and the heaters spontaneously blasted. Beads of sweat break on her forehead, which she wipes off with the back of her hand—

Lord, I had my period last week. Not there yet. Her jaw clenches.

Four...

And then, just as abruptly, she is stricken by a throbbing pain. She drops her papers and massages her temples. Her eyes flutter and she begins to lose balance...

Three...

The doors open. She does not hear the *ring.* She manages to glimpse an incoming passenger but not his face, a *man* being her immediate and correct assumption. She does not trust her eyes but thinks he is covered in monkish brown robe and a hood. She falls and cracks her head on the flooring. She had wanted so badly to yell for help.

~~~

The last of the yellow crime scene tape is draped around the perimeter. NYPD Officer Robert Johnson reviews video with Oswald, the building's elevator monitor.

"Nothing," says Oswald. "She collapsed on the third floor."

"And no sign of entrance?" Johnson asks, though he sees for himself.

"Straight from Eight to Lobby."

"Rewind, please."

The video is rewound. "Play."

As the tape is again reviewed, they observe Denise...the tapping foot, her reacting to the *heat*...her collapse. The doors do not open on any floor until the lobby.

No evidence of any entry.

A crowd forms, pushed back by an increasing police presence. Some of Denise's co-workers are crying. Others watch quietly, smartly keeping their opinions to themselves.

"Rewind again, please."

"Tell me when—"

"Stop."

The recording shows Denise cracking her head on the ground as she hits, seeping blood just above her left ear. However, as the growing crowd continues to be ushered away, the open elevator doors punctuate a horrific contradiction. There are massive amounts of blood throughout, and a disquieting mark on the rear wall that has been seen more than once before:

"Rewind for me again, please."

ANGELIKA MOVIE THEATER, GREENWICH VILLAGE, NEW YORK

Thomas McFee sits in the cafe, sipping coffee, skimming *The Village Voice.* He looks up in response to whispering. Two servers argue who should approach, one female, one not. The server with the louder whisper has been heard. He cautiously approaches Tom with a handwritten note.

"Mr. McFee?"

"You couldn't be any more obvious?"

"Sorry." He stands there uncertainly.

"Is that for me?"

The server awkwardly hands him the paper. "I'm *very* sorry," he says. "I took the call."

Thomas McFee checks the note and immediately gets the message. He stands, knocking down his chair in the process. "Are you okay, Mr. Mc—"

"Who called you?"

Noticing his co-server intently watching, he answers: "He said he was the elevator monitor. I guess she told him that, he said, that before the accident, she called you? Then she called him and said she was going to meet you here and to call in ten minutes if she didn't come down and was still running late. He remembered, I guess, and called us because he couldn't reach your cell—"

Thomas rushes to head out the door. "Mr. McFee? Sir?"

He is about to leave when Samantha, Daniel, and Adriel enter. Sam and Adriel are holding hands, smiling. Apparently, they know nothing as it concerns Denise. Thomas McFee freezes.

"Grandpa!" Adriel breaks from Sam and hugs Thomas around his legs. He looks at the girl, then up to Daniel. He looks at his daughter.

"Happy Birthday, Daddy," she says hopefully.

Thomas McFee is about to speak. He's on the point of asking, *Who's the girl?* Instead, at a loss and overwhelmed, he shakes his head and rushes away.

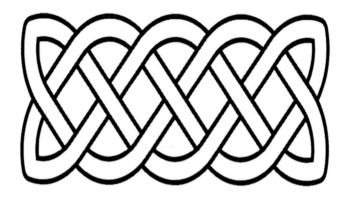

A ROAD LESS TAKEN

Taebal. Sleeping. No sense of time or place. No expectation, no journey, and no muse.

Another world, entirely. Once more the *splashing*, the *panic*. He's suffocating and looks to the sky for help. He does not know who or what he looks for. He knows only that he needs help desperately as it won't be long until he is usurped by the violent sea. He *knows* he's been here before but this time as he looks up he realizes that something is not the same.

He does not know how he arrived here, nor why. Though this time there's a difference. Until he awakens, if he awakens, the struggle to survive is all that matters.

There is no gray to the sky. This time, the sky is the color of scarlet. Crimson. And he remembers to whom he is pleading for help. The sky is the color of her hair.

As he awakens, she is the first thing is he sees. He looks around; they are atop a mountain. He gazes at her. She matches his stare. No expression, nothing to expose her intent.

And, finally, he understands. She is using him, first and foremost. He still has not determined her *reason*. Doubtless she will guide him to the raging water beneath the flaming sky and allow him to die.

SOHO ARTS DISTRICT

Matthius regards his painting of the dragon.

Something is not right.

He grabs a coffee mug from his desk and walks to his window. He looks out, and is immediately astonished at the incoming red *bleed* that appears to be overtaking the New York City clouds.

ALGONQUIN HOTEL, NEW YORK, NEW YORK

Suite 312. Daniel re-enters the main room. Has dries his hands with a washcloth, tosses it on the counter and joins Samantha on the couch.

"Well, that didn't go well," he says, rubbing his hand through his hair. "I had to tell her a story about *Alice and the Rabbit Hole* before she finally drifted off. She was Alice, of course."

"Has anything gone well since we got here?" Sam asks. "I'm sure he has his reasons but—"

Daniel reaches to put his arm around her shoulder. She flinches, and pulls away.

"Not now."

He sits back and slaps his knees. "Okay..." Silence. "At least the couch is comfortable, huh?"

"Can I ask you a question?" She begins.

"Ask away."

"What did you expect to happen when we got to New York? That we'd have good pizza and that's it?"

"The pizza was good, I agree—"

Furious, she turns to him. "I'm serious, Dan. We shouldn't have surprised him." She draws a breath. "He'll call once he gets it together."

"You think?"

"You have no idea what this is like—"

"I thought we—"

"No, I want to talk. While I can, okay?"

They talk for the next two hours and Adriel sleeps through it all. They will argue; he will rashly tell her she's acting "schizophrenic" and immediately feel guilty. She will cry in anger, he will defend himself and she will ask for him to quiet down so as not to wake the baby.

"She's no baby any more," he says. "She's three, and going on thirty."

"Save it. I heard it a thousand times this week."

This she remembers. In fact, her memory is keen up to recent events. Very keen. Before then it is *patchy* at best.

~~~

The precise mechanism of Samantha's recall is a pinwheel of complexity and contradiction. What she feels and experiences is nothing less than natural. She has little reason to furrow her brow in consideration of her own day-to-day life and lifestyle, and less reason to complain.

Whatever she does have, she accepts. Material things, hobbies, a family.

She has no idea how she got here. Her long-term memory seems *implanted*, somehow, as though the life she owns is not hers. But those long-term memories—her childhood, her *pregnancy*...are all of a piece, and all make sense as a whole.

She has no knowledge of any "book," as Adriel infrequently refers to it. She works at the Embassy, in a contained office, and maintains *Top Secret* clearance in a position that oversees and drafts confidential government records. Among them: ongoing revisions of an anti-terrorism task force effort, marking and maintaining of domestic and foreign policy bills both passed and pending, monitoring of criminal activity of non-European travelers and, upcoming, something given to her just prior to her New York trip. Something called *Project Ara*, a wordy disclosure that she will only begin to review upon her return. Try as she may, however, she cannot recall *who* had given her possession of said disclosure, only that she has received the material and is obligated to at least review it.

At random moments she'll consider: *Maybe this is the "book" Adriel refers to?*

Samantha enjoys her work. A 170 or above genius-level IQ and Mensa membership was a prerequisite to the position, and she performs admirably in respect of the lofty standards expected.

She believes that she is a contributor to the well-being of her country. And, she enjoys her rare time off.

What she cannot abide are the sporadic blackouts and *flashes* of *another* life that she privately acknowledges as remnants of a fitful dreamscape. She will sleep and then dream that she has no child and a tempestuous relationship with her dad, only to awake and feel Adriel nearby, cradled by Daniel. And...a bizarre emotional tug of war with her father that she can never quite fathom, that she refuses to speak of to either him or her husband.

Sometimes, the dreams are so vivid that she considers them to be her true world, and this, to be the dream. In her waking hours, she will sometimes flash upon something, and, just as quickly, forget it. She will passionately grasp a concept, usually in the heat of a conversation, or an argument, be eminently assured of the point she is about to make and then—forget it entirely. At work, she has the uncanny ability to bluff even her superiors. At home, she could barely fight off her frustration.

In New York, it is the last thing she wants or needs to handle.

~~~

They did not take the bedroom. They let Adriel sleep and have the bed to herself.

Sam and Daniel finally fell asleep in each other's arms, on the couch. The time was half-past seven, well too early to check out for the evening.

They started snoring at about the same time. *Knock. Knock.* They stir, lost for a moment in tired wakefulness.

Knock Knock. From the other side of the door: "Hello?"

Samantha is about to stand. Daniel presses his hand on her thigh. "I'll get it," he says, standing and walking towards the door.

"Yes?" he asks through the door.

"Mr. Baxter?" returns the other.

"Who's this?"

"Mr. Baxter, is Mrs. Baxter with you?"

"Yes?" Daniel replies.

"My name is Matthius Alexi. I'm the Operations Manager here at the hotel. I have a note for Samantha Baxter."

Daniel opens the door.

Matthius Alexi is forty-five years older than the idealistic young man for whom J.R.R. Tolkien once signed a book. He is gray yet still retains his boyish, innocent demeanor and a full head of hair. He stands in the doorway wearing a black suit.

"May I come in?" he asks.

He steps inside, note in hand. Samantha stands as he approaches. Matthius studies Sam, concerned, as she opens the note and Daniel returns to her side. Alexi glimpses only the opening sentence, including the ending ellipses: *If you want to see your father again...*

~~~

The drive is no different than surfing Mount Vesuvius during an active volcano. Through it all, Adriel sleeps, wrapped in a blanket, in the back seat.

Though the skies have darkened with the incoming night, a disquieting mass of red cloud above them, barely lightened by sun, threatens to expand and darken further. "You need to settle," Daniel said, at the wheel. "What if this is all a monster hoax?" He clearly does not believe his own words. Every muscle in his face is tightly clenched.

"My father's life is being threatened and you're giving me *what ifs?*" replies Samantha tartly.

"Not what I meant. You know that. Just looking at the possibilities."

"What would you do if he were *your* father?"

He gives in. "The same. If I still had a father."

"How much longer?"

Daniel looks at his watch. "About an hour. Maybe a little less."

"Can you step on it, for Christ's sake?" she urges him.

He glares at her, then floors the gas as she again reads the note—.

"*If you want to see your father again, proceed to a gathering tonight at Adirondack Park at 11:30 PM. Text for instructions. If you signal the authorities, the repercussions will be bleak for all. I am not bluffing. Another will join us as well.*" Samantha pauses in consideration before resuming. "*You must arrive on time and be sure to bring the girl.*" She nearly tears the paper as she reads that last. "*Your father received a similar summons. You get the point.*" Samantha stops reading, and looks over to her husband. "Professor Randolph Searle?"

"How many more times do I need to hear this?" Daniel does not take well to hearing the professor's name. "We're well on our way and you'll figure it out then."

She notices his reaction. "What is it that you're hiding from me?"

He looks at her, the veins in his neck tightening and bulging, and says nothing.

ADIRONDACK PARK, UPSTATE, NEW YORK

When they arrive, less than thirty minutes later, X is already waiting. He is alone. The note had said that another would be joining them. Daniel is stunned when he sees him.

The car is parked. They exit. Daniel reaches into the trunk and removes the gauntlet, which he has brought with them. X looks on passively, saying nothing as Daniel tucks the object under his arm and approaches.

Searle is next to arrive. Samantha does not recognize him. Samantha holds Adriel's hand, and her thoughts turn to Daniel. She has no idea what he is carrying, and her innate suspicions come to the fore: *Has he planned for this?* She clasps Adriel's hand, and walks with her as a dutiful mother guarding her child. The underground hovel, their destination, is scant yards away. Samantha will defend her child until she can no longer.

"I need for you to trust me," Daniel tells Samantha, as he grasps and lightly squeezes the elbow on her free arm. She tries to escape his grip but cannot.

"I don't know who I can trust anymore," she replies as Searle approaches. The professor is conspicuous in his evasion of X, the boy he has veritably raised as his own. Daniel follows Samantha's gaze.

"And how is my dear Adriel?" Searle asks. "Do you miss your Daddy?"

X awaits a similar question. It does not come.

The girl recognizes Searle. She tugs from Sam, who pulls her back as the professor absorbs the rest of his surroundings. Searle stoically plants his feet as Daniel, now wearing the gauntlet, aims the device towards Searle's chest.

"Daniel, please don't interfere."

X is not acknowledged. The young man has privately fretted over this gathering for days, more so due to concern over his reception from the only man he has ever looked up to than because of any end-of-the-world scenario. He glances at his one-time mentor. He looks good, Searle does. The same since his disappearance. X does not approach, however, and neither does Searle approach him. The young man wants so badly to tell the professor that he is ready to finally leave the past and help him with his work, that he is truly committed to what is left of the present. Mostly, X wants to inform the professor that he is sorry for letting him down, though he does not truly believe that he's done anything to alienate his mentor. He knows that it's all jabberwocky at this point but nonetheless...

Without forethought, he blurts, "You didn't have to leave!"

Daniel shields Samantha and Adriel by stepping between the tree and Searle. His aim does not waver.

"He's not coming," says the professor, verbalizing what they have all been thinking. "We were misguided. Now we have no choice but to work together, as I have advised from the beginning."

"Dan?" inquires Samantha. Daniel turns his head sharply towards his wife. "What's going on?"

"He's bluffing." Daniel slowly turns back to Searle. "We'll never stand with you," he adds loudly, over what seems to be incoming thunder. "What I do, I do for them."

X, meantime, rapidly loses his guard, and any semblance of control. *The beg—? Since when are—And Danny's the one who's bluffing, I know him too well. Are they working together?* He paces. It's a physical response somewhere between accosting the professor over the insulting dismissal and crying. *He betrayed me too,* he thinks. *Not him!*

"*Why,* Professor?" he screeches. Searle is about to turn, but he elects to keep his back to the boy. As X wrestles with his impulse, his fists clench, his eyes squeeze in restraint. "Why?" he repeats. "We were supposed to have more time and now *they're* here, and you're all here, because of me! If anyone survives ... including you, it's because of me!" But then X recovers his balance. *No!* he thinks, *He won't see me this way. He doesn't deserve to.*

Thomas had been expected by all. His arrival was considered a *fait accompli,* and each of the four adults, the young X included, had anticipated his aid as necessary to their chances of survival. But he and Thomas were not working together, as apparently the rest of them were. Now he understands that Thomas had likely *never* intended to show. Denise is in the hospital and has no one at her side. Daniel, a *soldier,* gave his word that he would always take care of his daughter. Samantha still has not answered the letter from X—and certainly Daniel would do a better job than Thomas. The other two do not deserve Thomas's attention.

None of which matters a whit here. Now.

"He'll be here!!" Samantha yells through the fierce, whistling wind. She cradles Adriel's head as they approach the nearest tree for a quick but vaguely-comforting illusion of shelter. "He'll be here..."

"Mommy?" Adriel is upset by the sounds, and by the increasingly-threatening dark.

"We'll stay under the tree. The branches will protect us," Samantha whispers. "Remember when we read the story?"

Adriel shakes her head in the negative. "I told you, in the books the *Ents* were scary."

"No, dear. The trees are our friends."

"I'm scared." At that, the thunder resumes and the sky momentarily *brightens*, making way for a spasmodic penetration of fire.

~~~

The *bolt* was so sudden and hit so quickly none of them quite saw it. The strike was severe, breaking the oak's top branch. Samantha had no time to escape, no warning to which to respond. The force of the thunder knocked her and Adriel to the ground.

She watched the branch helplessly as it fell but she protected the girl first, as she promised, covering the child's fragile body as best she could with her arms, chest and head. As a result, the falling branch crushed both of Samantha's legs. Adriel was not injured.

"Destiny!" said Searle, pleading with Daniel. "If we don't take action now, you can't imagine what you'll be responsible for."

The pain is near-unbearable though Samantha is not disposed to reveal her suffering. She surprises herself with her tolerance, but she knows she'll scream later.

"You want to save your wife?" Searle continues. "Then you must kill the child—NOW!"

"Daddy!" Adriel cries. She is far too young to understand his plea, but his tone implies anything but good.

Sam has dragged herself into a seated upright position so as best to maintain her hold on Adriel. Despite the calamity, she was favored by luck. She is still alive, so there is still a chance. Safety was never really an option. For her or for the others.

Searle steps closer to Daniel, who appears poised to engage the gauntlet. Though the professor believes the device is relatively useless without the blade, he remains cautious. "You need to take the child, now, while you have the chance," Searle says, attempting to appear calm. The skies are nearly completely red.

"Kill her!" The wind blisters X's face as he screams for Daniel to comply. "I'm sorry but listen to him! There's no more time!"

Daniel aims first to X, then Adriel. Then Searle. "If I take out the girl, then I take you out with her. Which is it, Professor?"

"You'll have to go through me, Daniel," Samantha swears.

"Then kill them both!" X yells.

As if in response, a burst of wind loosens the remaining, hanging portion of the branch, which falls atop Samantha's waist and pins her back to the tree's trunk. Adriel remains safe, still cradled in Samantha's arms.

Sam ducks her head as a larger branch falls, missing her face by inches.

"The tree!" X screams. "Can't you see?"

Daniel gets the reference. Again, the bellowing wind veritably *animates* the oak, causing a wild flailing and *whipping* of its thinnest branches. Tolkien's personifications, as written in his books, are nearly realized as Daniel and the others are held at bay.

Searle considers his surroundings. He eyes a cylindrical sandstorm swirling above and around the hole, within seconds entirely re-covering his hideaway.

"It's almost time!" adds X.

The professor glimpses his former protege first looking at the red above, and then checking a stopwatch from his pocket. Searle is stunned that X is referring to a timepiece, as opposed to the evidence at hand.

"It's *Wonderland*," Searle mumbles to himself in disbelief before refocusing his energies. He turns back to Daniel, referring to X. "He's right!"

Daniel snaps his head and aims the gauntlet in his direction. "If you take her down now we may still have a chance!"

The gauntlet, without warning, *vibrates*, beginning at Daniel's wrist, gradually warming and *pulsating* upwards toward his fingers, forcing his hand to open and clinch beyond his control. Daniel has dreaded as much. The instrument was far too *important* to be harmless. Though the device was never represented as such, the gauntlet was little more than an inanimate object without its attendant power. Daniel's army training, however, taught him that anything fought for is of value. Sometimes *in extremis*. He strives to remain calm as his thoughts darken in response to the device's increasing activity. He can indeed kill them all, he considers, including his wife if he so desired, and no one would be able to stop him. Or, he can kill them one by one. "Tell me why, Professor!"

"You know why—" X intervenes.

"I want to hear it from him!"

"She'll never hand over the child," Searle responds.

"She knows too much, brother," adds X.

"So do we all!" Daniel blurts.

"She's as dangerous as the child," X goes on. "Take them *both* and we can reverse this."

"The child must not survive!" Searle argues. "Samantha will do what she can to save her! Kill them both and nobody will know."

Though Searle is in accord with X, the professor still does not so much as meet his eyes.

The sky is increasingly obfuscated by the red clouds, which continue to darken in response to the quickening pulsation. Daniel notices that his *gauntlet's* pulse is wholly in sync.

A stagger of light breaks through the skies and remains visible until the clouds are swallowed by blood. The red continues to coalesce into considerably more than a simple obfuscation. In moments, there will remain no longer a patina of sun or any other physical disruption.

As the earthly troposphere becomes a near-*solid* scarlet cover, Searle cries out. "Look! Look above you! This is our destiny that only you have the power to alter!"

Shadows obscure the players. The child first, then Sam, then the others. The child does not move. The rest pause and look upwards as a disquieting *rumble* emanates from above.

"Give me the girl!" cries Daniel. "Give her to me."

"The child must die!" Searle responds.

The rumble becomes a horrific, reverberating clap of *thunder.* Or so it seems.

"I won't turn her over, Dan."

"It's happening, brother!" X is almost catatonic with panic. "Broth—"

A single bolt of fire, followed by a monstrous *roar,* escapes through a rare, as-yet-covered cloud. The bolt strikes the tree behind X, which immediately is engulfed in flames. The source is summarily smothered and the fugitive runs for safety as Daniel tracks him with the gauntlet. "I have no use for you."

Without warning *Eron,* clasping his blade, exits the gloom and steps behind Daniel. The former military man senses the new presence only when it is standing directly behind him. Searle drops his arms. This has indeed been planned all along, though Samantha's suspicions toward her husband were misplaced.

"Welcome spirit," Searle says. "What took you—"

"Dan!"

Daniel turns, but is blindsided by the over-dweller who grabs him by

415

the neck and pulls him close. So close, that Daniel should easily be able to feel the over-dweller's breath on his own face. If, that is, he were breathing.

Eron studies the terrified visage of the man who possesses what has been treasured for so long. He then slams him to the ground.

Searle approaches, through the gale winds and the beginning drizzle of blood-rain. Eron allows him his room as he kneels near Daniel. "It's quite the distance from England, Mr. Baxter, but please to appreciate that over-dwellers do not travel *conventionally.*"

He carefully removes the gauntlet from Daniel's arm. "I should have killed you when I had the chance..." Daniel murmurs.

"I have not betrayed you. I may have just *saved* you—and *him* too. Every English hunter must be attempting to collect on a bounty right about now."

X hears him, but manages to stay quiet as he instead tracks the over-dweller.

Searle stands and hands the device to its rightful owner as if in tribute.

Eron pauses for the briefest of moments, then snaps the gauntlet over his right hand and clasps the device onto his arm. He attaches the blade.

Finally, the sweord has been returned.

Eron raises the weapon overhead; the skies immediately break and lose any remaining stability. The *roar* comes again, this time louder, fiercer. Though the rain now *pours* its bloody matter, shaking the ground with all matter of mass heretofore held, the *stronger* quake that ensues represents something far more threatening.

"Taebal!" exults Adriel. She calms as she witnesses his approach, then turns to Samantha. "Mommy, he's come back." Samantha looks to the girl, who with wide-eyed innocence attempts to explain. "Just like your book said!" Samantha responds by softly kissing her *daughter's* head. "Taebal is home!" Adriel proclaims.

Taebal swoops from the crimson, taking ground and slightly stumbling as he makes his way to Eron's side. He is considerably more mature, and larger by thrice, than last they were together. He is also an over-dweller and scarred heavily. He must have seen great battle while still alive. For now, he is together again with the once-feared slayer of his ilk who eons ago had sacrificed himself to save the then-young dragon's family.

No matter of good and evil, right or wrong shall sway this dragon's loyalty. His indebtedness to Eron was once, and is now, all that matters.

The dragon stands guard as Eron approaches the child. Sam grabs her close. Eron bends down and gently takes the girl's hand. "Come," he says. His voice is hoarse, though deep, similar in intonation from a long-ago lifetime.

"No!" cries Samantha.

Adriel pulls away from Samantha, compelled to stand and accept the hand presently extended. She leaves a sobbing Sam of her own accord, allowing Eron to escort her towards Taebal.

The girl, however, stops walking upon noticing a troublesome object shifting on the ground. It is small enough for her to grasp if so inclined. The wind threatens to blow the novelty away but when it catches on a rock, its hairs still move as the rest sticks in place. Adriel looks up at Eron; he understands. Permission granted. He lets go of her hand.

Adriel bends and retrieves Samantha's rabbit's foot, which must have fallen from Sam's person upon their arrival. She is fascinated by the unusual charm but is not quite sure why; regardless, as Eron walks onward she runs to catch up to him while studying her new find.

Samantha has been watching, and suddenly realizes. She reaches into her jacket pocket then, in silent, tearful mourning, buries her head in her arms.

Searle, though curious as to Adriel's action, is impressed by the over-dweller. He addresses Eron, maintaining a safe distance:

"And so again you breathe," he calls after him. "I expected your words to return." Eron pays him scant attention. "Now once more corporeal, you reclaimed your weapon and initiated the process of again becoming whole." As Eron steps from shadow he is, truly, of the appearance of one who is rapidly healing. "The rest—whatever that may be—will take some time I'm sure, and I'd be curious to know how long. When that happens," Searle perseveres, "you will be indistinguishable from the rest of us. As once you were—"

"This," Eron replies, pointing the weapon in Searle's direction, "will be destroyed. *She* will be returned to the gods."

Adriel, very much the innocent, fumbles with her charm.

Eron's comments are not what Searle has expected. "Do you know who she is?" he asks. It's a risky question and Searle is deliberate in the asking. As before, Eron ignores him. The professor will not yet have his answer.

X intervenes, bravely turning to Eron. "And then?" he yells. Adriel stands freely, alongside the dragon. Eron neither pays X any mind. He lifts her upon Taebal's back, then himself sits behind her. "And then?" X repeats, shouting through the *rain*.

The dragon expels his fire, expiring a circle of flame wide enough in circumference to entrap the four remaining on ground. As the tree erupts in conflagration, Daniel manages to get to his feet and reach his wife. He whispers in Samantha's ear as he carries her away. "I would never have let anything happen to you." She fights nothing, having already given in to the Fates.

The tree falls. The fire spreads. Eron considers the collateral damage with indifference. Without another word, he once more raises his sweord overhead. Taebal soars, disappearing into the scarlet void as the others watch him go. Minutes later, the fire has widened substantially. The sky is a perfect red and the air below a yellow-red haze of hell.

And then...

The *bloody matter* falls harder, forming holes...for some. Crawling from the muck, making their way to their feet are *armies* of over-dwellers, landing just outside the circle. Most wear no tops; many are nude. *All* have had the X insignia, just as Searle, carved into (what remains of) their flesh—from shoulder blade to lower back.

X is slack-jawed and his mentor, stern. Daniel, on the ground, covers Samantha from the elements and all matter of the *fallen.* The nightmare continues as their *leader* approaches. He, however, is not the same as the others. He wears a robe, and his head is fully covered. He steps into the circle, in his robe, without the slightest limp. Without even the slightest injury wrought by the ever-expanding and encroaching fire.

He approaches Searle and lowers his hood. *S'n Te.* It was he who was in the elevator with Denise.

Searle regards him with horror. *X* has taken his side, but backs off as S'n Te glares. Without a word, the mystic pulls down Searle's shirt to his waist. The X scar on *his* back is in full glow, broken skin and pus illuminated by the light of the falling. Searle turns and eyeballs the unexpected visitor. S'n Te bows his head.

"Why have you come?" Searle asks.

"They are yours," S'n Te replies. "They are your army, the one you asked for." He regards the symbol. "You understand, I had to be sure..."

Daniel and Samantha are incredulous. Searle looks first to them, and then to X, who appears to not have a clue as to this development. The fallen,

S'n Te…

"Things have changed, S'n Te. My life, now—" Searle begins.

"The girl must be retrieved," warns the mystic. "She must be retrieved before they reach the Infinity Pass."

"This is why you are all here," S'n Te informs them, turning to the others. "This man, whom you know as Searle, was but a vessel. All along." X looks to his professor, who finally gazes back, and then down, to the unshaven patch of grass on which he stands. He ponders a puzzle he cannot figure and a lifetime of—*lies?* "The warning," S'n Te continues, "the cause of this gathering is mine."

When the last of the over-dwellers falls and further invasion is paused, they gather as one into rows and lines. They are in battle formation, and they bow to Searle in tribute.

He struggles to remain calm. "If what you say is true," he asks, "What if the girl is not returned?" Searle asks.

"Then *your* end of the world scenario is only the beginning."

"And *theirs?*" He cocks his head to his companions.

"Not as optimistic." replied S'n Te.

"I don't understand," protests Searle.

S'n Te considers his response. Before he answers, Searle pleads, "S'n Te I promise you, I don't understand …"

S'n Te rests his hand on Searle's shoulder. "I would submit that you do. You must confront your fear, my old friend."

The flames are almost upon them and they are about to be overtaken when another great *roar,* a fury exponentially stronger than the last, charges upon them and a *wing* breaks through the closest crimson.

"What is your decision?" S'n Te asks. "The dragons are near."

He is unable to continue. The swath of incoming flame promises to spare no prisoners as the first circle of fire is rapidly engulfed by another much larger.

KINGWAY HOSPITAL, NEW YORK, NEW YORK

Denise lies in ICU, hooked to a ventilator and heart monitor, fluids streaming through IVs that feed her and more. No medical staff is immediately present. She is monitored from a distance. Though an array of machines have stabilized her vitals, a disquieting *hum* signals a sudden drop and rise in blood pressure and ammonia levels, respectively, as she begins to shake and stir into consciousness.

"Tom," she says, breaking into a sweat, her eyes remaining closed as she tries to turn her neck. She fidgets and attempts to rouse herself but loses that battle nearly as quickly as it begins.

"As...I...lay dying..." she murmurs.

Her neck muscles betray her and Denise's head slumps as her heart rate slows precipitously.

PARK SLOPE, BROOKLYN, NEW YORK

The way things work, he thinks.

Thomas sits at his desk, facing his computer and his window. An old copy of Dante's *Inferno* rests face-down to his right.

Atmosphere. He decides. *Or else another manipulation—but who gives a damn any more?*

New *writing* appears on his monitor:

"If I had a world of my own, everything would be nonsense. Nothing would be what it is, because everything would be what it isn't. And contrary wise, what is, it wouldn't be. And what it wouldn't be, it would. You see?"

— Lewis Carroll, *Alice's Adventures in Wonderland & Through the*

Looking-Glass

The quote is followed by McFee's original words:

INTRODUCTION

The work is fiction. The characters and events are real. A contradiction to be certain.

Have you ever stared at a painting of another world, or read a book that was more visceral than what you were used to? Have you listened to a piece of music and questioned how the artist—who lived in another time and place altogether—could possibly be so detailed, so *precise*, and yet reach so far within? What is it about the artist's mind, or the artist's subconscious, that enables this otherwise-ordinary man to step out of time and place the ability and so to touch the lives of others?

Matthius Alexi believed he had the answer. He never discounted parallel universes, gods and pre-history, magic and all the rest of that *jabberwocky*. He was inspired by a *hobbit* and believed that a simple journal entry by Lewis Carroll might at once have reflected not only the author's real life as the author perceived it, but also an unexpected elucidation of what it means to be *human*.

Human. And all those beautiful and mysterious and confining and wonderful contradictions thusly implied.

In other words, nothing that we have been led to believe has ever quite been what it appears.

~~~

On the day he met Alice Liddell, Lewis Carroll wrote: *The three little girls were in the garden most of the time, and we became excellent friends: we tried to group them in the foreground of the picture, but they were not patient sitters. I mark this day with a white stone.*

Why do we blindly accept the journal of one of our most inventive men as the gospel truth? How can we be certain that this man of *nonsense* was not simply composing his own history? Throughout time lesser men have strived to compose their own history.

Or, what if Carroll was *confusing* his own history as opposed to *composing* it? Or, what if he was recording a *parallel* history, and everything did occur just as he had written, but not in the here and the now as he believed? Or...?

There is, indeed, a *Truth.*

You see, Matthius Alexi *solved* the problem by utilizing a mathematical equation. He discovered the answer to our most dangerous question: What is life?

So, who is Matthius Alexi, you may ask? Well, you may know him best by a single letter by which he has been identified: X.

X, the *real* X, is not who you think. The reality is considerably more terrible; it's just a damn shame that no one will see this. My lowest-selling book ever! But, just in case...

How do I know this, you ask? Read on.

Thomas has renovated a bit over the last while; now suffering from the occasional bout of quiet paranoia, he figures he *needs* to face the outside when he works. Because *that's* how Bradley had it in *his* basement office, facing the barred window, though he prefers to look upon the *coincidence* as *irony.* He would be loath to admit otherwise. That would be *weakness,* of some sort.

God forbid he admits to missing anyone deceased other than his wife. Or his own dad.

The radio is on, playing mostly static. In-between, words and phrases such as *emergency, effecting areas of upstate New York first and fast heading towards the boroughs, evacuation...tunnels, oceans, overseas...Armageddon* infrequently transmit with some semblance of clarity.

He doesn't care. Not now. He's come to the wrenching realization that he never did anything for himself when Elizabeth died. He refused to reorganize or follow any other of Denise's well-meaning advice...whether self-serving or not. He did not *take a trip;* he engaged in nothing common to new widowers. He thought about it, constantly. He was still, in his mind, *too young* to be *so old.* So his day-to-day went on as usual.

Work, fretting over Sam, more work and everything associated *with* work...

Most distressingly, what he didn't do for himself was *honor* his wife via his words, his writing. And now, the compulsion to do so is overwhelming.

As I wait to die. Now I smarten up. Maybe a little late, no?

As he stares out the window he recalls his wife's voice. *She* used to ask him, "Is it a need or a want?" whenever he requested anything out of the ordinary. His usual response had been, "It's whatever you need or want it to be." A non-answer. Only added to their ongoing flirtatiousness—which he knows full well has carried over, unconsciously or otherwise, to the *other woman* in his life, excluding his daughter.

The other woman. Denise. The other part of *usual.*

McFee, you really are a piece of work. When was the last time you took advantage of an honest opportunity?

Today, though he has not set to write a new book in—far too long, he finds that the old temptations have returned with a vengeance, and his chosen quote from Carroll seemed a good enough, appropriate way to begin.

At the moment.

He's wanted to write something about his wife, Elizabeth, before it was too late. He's wanted to write about Elizabeth for three disparate reasons:

to memorialize her, to convince himself that she really *is* in a *better place*, and to finally move on with his pathetic personal life.

Before it's too late. Huh. Timing being everything ...

Particularly, since it appears the world's ceiling is about to collapse and the *pulse* of that disquieting crimson sky is hastening—an identical, or continuing, sequence of events that has already occurred, or *is* occurring, somewhere upstate.

Thomas has blocked out the increasingly noisy confusion and welling frenzy of the impromptu neighborhood gathering outside. Still, neither can he help but stare at *those furious skies.* He is hypnotized by the darkening and the *roars* that are getting ever-louder by the second. And then, again, the bloody matter falls.

Before it's too late? It already is. Who are you kidding?

He doesn't move from his seat as he watches legs pass to and fro on the other side of his window, running for cover, falling, splashing blood against the glass. No. He has been through his share of New York tragedies, 9/11 among them. As then, he freezes. He *wants* to help; his feeling of *helplessness* wins that battle. But then, the rationalization that he needs to *stay put* in case someone from outside needs shelter or a phone that works and then, after that, the *despair* of lives lost...

But instead, before giving in entirely, Thomas McFee acts on a thought. He has remembered something—something that has suddenly become meaningful. He opens his desk drawer...and removes a photo that he has kept, safely, under a special rabbit's foot. On the flip side, there is a certain poem. He skims to a particular section of *Goddess Ode:*

But it is the most fanciful of man

Who is the most dangerous of man

In his blasphemous challenge

Nothing shall be as it appears

Either within the Infinity Pass

Here too-

Thomas pauses upon reading the third stanza. He grabs a pen and circles *In his blasphemous challenge*. He doesn't recall *blasphemously challenging* anybody. But he *does* recall...X. And, upon that recollection, he again gives in to helplessness.

He searches in vain, squinting his eyes as he looks through the window for a break in the *red*. He despairingly stands the photo against his computer, and then clasps his hands while patiently looking up to watch the action outside. He shakes his head at the irony:

That's it then. Over and done. All this technology—his computer, power, light. Such a waste. Nature writes the last word and we—

Tom reacts to what sounds like a car crash outside, followed by shouts for *help* not too far from his window. He regroups in seconds. *And we—we lose. The simplest of all equations, really, and we've had the nerve to challenge its solution.*

And he waits, witnessing humankind's greatest tragedy from the comfort of his desk chair. He turns, briefly, compelled to momentarily attend to a standing series of antique-framed paintings leaning against the wall near the restroom door.

The first painting, set against a stark dark linen backdrop, is of the visage of a beautiful yet formidable young woman, staring straight ahead as he had, possessed of near-inhumanly-wide, foreboding eyes and a mass of long, crimson hair. One could, correctly, assume that the other paintings are variants of this first.

Ara, Whom Alexi *saw* for the first time during the minutes of his death and haunted him ever since. And so he painted. As he ponders the form, Thomas McFee realizes he has no idea whatsoever how he came to own the works. The notebooks...*check.* The paintings...not a clue.

Doesn't matter anyway. Not now.

Thomas peers back out the window. Then at the *muse*—

She's made her decision...

...then again, the window...

In the end no creation of man was capable of making any difference whatsoever...

He steels himself, at the ready...

Prove me wr—

...when the glass suddenly *shatters* and the blood, and viscera, seep through the bars, overtaking his writer's room and threatening to introduce him to yet a lower *ring* of hell.

EPILOGUE

VIA DIODATI, LAKE GENEVA, SWITZERLAND,

SEPTEMBER, 1817

The writer wears a single black silk glove (that will one day prove historically important); the hand so-covered holds a quill pen. The pen is dipped into an inkwell.

The words that ensue will be immortalized in a fresh notebook. By the end, there will be several notebooks that cumulatively will tell this tale. Once printed, a portion of what immediately follows will read thusly:

PREFACE.

THE event on which this fiction is founded has been supposed, by Dr. Darwin, and some of the physiological writers of Germany, as being of not impossible occurrence. I shall not be supposed as according the remotest degree of serious faith to such an imagination; yet, in assuming it as the basis of a work of fancy, I have not considered myself as merely weaving a series of supernatural terrors. The event on which the interest of the story depends is exempt from the disadvantages of a mere tale of spectres or enchantment. It was recommended by the novelty of the situations which it developes; and, however impossible as a physical fact, affords a point of view to the imagination for the delineating of human passions more comprehensive and commanding than any which the ordinary relations of existing events can yield.

I have thus endeavoured to preserve the truth of the elementary principles of human nature, while I have not scrupled to innovate upon their combinations. The Iliad, the tragic poetry of Greece, Shakespeare, in The Tempest and Midsummer Night's Dream and most especially Milton, in Paradise Lost, conform to this rule; and the most humble novelist, who seeks to confer or receive amusement from his labours, may, without presumption, apply to prose fiction a license, or rather a rule, from the adoption of which so many exquisite combinations of human feeling have resulted in the highest specimens of poetry.

There will be more, but that will wait for another day. For now...The author turns to the preceding page—the title page:

FRANKENSTEIN, OR THE MODERN PROMETHEUS
In Three Volumes

The pen is placed down; the glove is removed. But the hand does not belong to Mary Shelley. This is a *man's* hand. A strong, veined man's hand.

Though Percy Bysshe Shelley, Mary's husband—sometimes (mistakenly) credited as the pseudonymous *Marlow* (a Swiss city) and widely attributed as the author of the work's original *Preface*—is considerably slighter than what is implied here, when he stands from his chair it is confirmed that his height disqualifies *that* presence. Indeed, Mary will hereinafter assume that the older Percy favored her with the words as

429

she has never before been published. And Percy? He would never deny his wife's suspicions, neither to her nor her critics. His curiosity will not remain tempered...

The true culprit stands over six-and-a-half feet tall, is thickly-muscled, and based on appearance alone *could have been* the model for Frankenstein's monster. His hair is shoulder-length and scraggly, his face scarred, lined and bearded.

One day, the world will know his purpose, and the extent of his influence on this seminal work. Nearly two hundred years from now, he will look, in all aspects, much younger.

He peeks out the window. The noon hour is pleasant enough; the sun is blazing.

The others have gone elsewhere to enjoy the afternoon.

He returns to the desk to swipe a leather medicine bag, contents unknown, and close the notebook. The desk is straightened.

Brikke leaves, quietly, closing the door on his way out...

TO BE CONTINUED

About the Authors

Joel Eisenberg has been interested in the mechanics behind artistic creation, an ongoing theme of the *Chronicles of Ara* series, since he penned the non-fiction *How to Survive a Day Job* in 2004. Interviewing 70+ professional creatives, including celebrities from several artistic industries, he credits his "mentor in a box" tome with hastening the realization of his dad's inspiring words from forty years ago. Writing a novel with similar objectives, much less a series, has been on his *bucket list* since.

Professionally, Joel has worked primarily in the movie and television industries as a writer and producer. The film he is most proud of, *April Showers*, which he executive produced, was based on the Columbine school shooting tragedy. He is a former Special Education teacher and supports school safety causes.

Joel lives with the only woman in the world who could put up with him, his wife, Lorie, and their rescue dog (repeating a not-so-subtle message there), Koko, in Los Angeles, California.

Stephen Hillard grew up in Bossier City, Louisiana, and Grand Junction, Colorado. He graduated from Colorado State University, and also earned a degree in Philosophy at Columbia University and a Juris Doctorate from the University of Colorado. Before settling into his current career as a private equity entrepreneur, Steve was a teacher at Rikers Island Prison, a welder, a carpenter, and a practicing litigation attorney. He is the founder of Council

Tree Investors, a private equity fund involved in the entertainment and telecom industries.

Steve has also been an active philanthropist, focusing primarily on higher education, as well as at-risk Latino and indigenous youth, at the Escuela Tlatelolco in Denver, Colorado. In 2011, Steve published *Mirkwood: A Novel About JRR Tolkien*, which sparked international controversy, became an Amazon Best Seller, received a national prize and was subsequently published world-wide in Spanish by Grupo Planeta.

In addition to collaborative efforts with his partner, Joel Eisenberg, on the *Chronicles of Ara*, Steve is developing other projects. These include an untitled prequel to *Mirkwood*, *Farway Canyon*, a retro-horror graphic novel about radiation, blobs, and (of course) Cold War zombies, and *KNOLL*, a novel about JFK, Carlos Marcello, Elvis, the NSA, and Edward Snowden. He resides with his wife, Sharmaine, in San Antonio, Texas.

Joel and Steve can be contacted directly through their author page, www.eisenbergandhillard.com, or their "Ara" series page, www.chroniclesofara.com.

Credits

This book is a work of art produced by TOPOS Books,
an imprint of Incorgnito Publishing Press.

Deborah Jackson
Managing Editor

Allyson Schnabel
Copy Editor

Celine Boivin
Artist

Janice Bini
Chief Reader

Michael Conant
Publihser

March 2015
Incorgnito Publishing Press

TB
TOPOS BOOKS

CPSIA information can be obtained at www.ICGtesting.com
Printed in the USA
BVOW02s0403040315

390179BV00001B/1/P

9 780986 195334